For Don,

With so much appreciation

for your gracious friendship.

Love,

The McFalands

I knew we had crossed the line a few times, but I didn't see how we could possibly be charged with this...

He was only interested in me, asked me a bunch more questions about where I was from. I was getting uncomfortable.

"You look a lot like Barbara," he finally said. "Look some like me, too."

Good grief! This guy thought I might be his son! The one Barbara Occam-Roberts never had because she wasn't really pregnant by him! He thought I was visiting my mother!

A knock sounded on the door. Shrader didn't say anything, but a woman in a deputy's uniform came in.

"Sheriff Shrader, I thought you would want to see this," she said, holding a piece of paper out to him.

He took it, looked at it, looked at it some more. He kept looking at it and said, "You'd better tell Aho and Nestorini to stand by."

She nodded and left.

He looked at me. "Well, I've got to send you over to Dickinson County. Sheriff Avanti wants to see you."

"What is this, a game of Musical Sheriffs?"

"They've got an arrest warrant out on you now, too. A real one."

"Come on. Those guys at that convenience store were the ones causing the problem. Moe's? I think that was the name there. We just roughed them up a little. We were protecting everybody else. Ask anyone who was there, especially that woman in the Obama tee-shirt. Sagola? What the hell is that? We'd never even heard of Sagola before."

He looked at me blankly. "I don't know what you're talking about," he said. "Sheriff Avanti says you murdered a doctor at the VA hospital in Iron Mountain."

Joe Kirk lost a leg. Lonnie Blifield lost his eyes. Victoria Roundtree lost her skin. "Zan" Zander lost his mind. Four homeless and hopeless Iraqistan Vets who accidentally end up living together on an old school bus. With nowhere to go, and nothing else to do, they lurch from one VAMC to another, getting no help because, like the thousands of other Iraqistan Vets who are homeless, unemployed, and suicidal, they do not trust the system and refuse to "come inside." After another fruitless stop, at the VAMC in Iron Mountain, Michigan, a doctor is found dead, and the Vets are accused of his murder. Distrustful, strangers to America, to each other, and even to themselves, they must become a unit to learn who really murdered the doctor, so that they can stay free. In doing so, they uncover far more, about themselves and about their country, than they dared even to imagine…

KUDOS for *Vets*

In *Vets* by John Robert McFarland, Joe, Zan, Lonnie, and Victoria are four homeless and disabled Middle-East war vets, riding around in Zan's old school bus. They may not have a permanent address, but trouble seems to have no problem finding them just the same. They get attacked by Indians, refused medical assistance by doctors at the VMAC hospitals, and finally accused of murder. A murder they didn't commit. And until they can prove their innocence, they can't continue on their way in the school bus, but how can they prove it with no money and no way to get any? But while they may be disabled, they aren't stupid and it doesn't take them long to figure out they are being used as scapegoats. This is a great book. It's sad, funny, poignant, and heart-warming—sometimes all on the same page. It's a story anyone who's ever been a vet or known a vet will definitely relate to. ~ *Taylor Jones, Reviewer*

Vets by John Robert McFarland is probably the best book I've read in quite some time. I absolutely loved it. I can't remember the last time I laughed—and cried—so hard. *Vets* is the story of four disabled and homeless Iraqistan vets. Zan has PTSD—well, they all do, but his is extreme. Lonnie is blind. Victoria is disfigured. And Joe has a prosthetic leg—in which he hides a Beretta. Did I mention they all have PTSD? They ride around in an old school bus belonging to Zan. None of them are sure exactly how they all got together, but they make the best of it. Sort of. When they get into Upper Pennsylvania, things go from bad to worse, including their luck, and they end up accused of murdering a doctor at the last VA Medical Center they went to in Iron Mountain. Since they are innocent of the murder, they have to, somehow, pool their meager skills and resources and prove it. Not an easy task, especially when they often break minor laws just to survive, such as breaking and entering, accidentally kidnapping babies, escaping from custody, resisting arrest—just to name a few. *Vets* is extremely well written. McFarland has a way with words that makes reading the book a joy. It's the funniest, saddest, most heart-breaking and heart-warming book I've read in ages. This is one you will want to keep around to read over and over again, just for the sheer pleasure of it. Bravo, McFarland. Well done. ~ *Regan Murphy, Reviewer*

ACKNOWLEDGEMENTS

I want to thank all the folks at Black Opal Books for their friendly competence in bringing this book to fruition, so thank you, Lauri and Mike and Jack, and Faith, here's an ellipsis just for you…

VETS

John Robert McFarland

A Black Opal Books Publication

GENRE: MYSTERY/SUSPENSE/WAR-MILITARY

This is a work of fiction. Names, places, characters and incidents are either the product of the author's imagination or are used fictitiously, and any resemblance to any actual persons, living or dead, businesses, organizations, events or locales is entirely coincidental. All trademarks, service marks, registered trademarks, and registered service marks are the property of their respective owners and are used herein for identification purposes only. The publisher does not have any control over or assume any responsibility for author or third-party websites or their contents.

VETS
Copyright © 2015 by John Robert McFarland
Cover Design by Jackson's Cover Designs
All cover art copyright © 2015
All Rights Reserved
Print ISBN: 978-1-626943-13-1

First Publication: AUGUST 2015

All rights reserved under the International and Pan-American Copyright Conventions. No part of this book may be reproduced or transmitted in any form or by any means, electronic or mechanical, including photocopying, recording, or by any information storage and retrieval system, without permission in writing from the publisher.

WARNING: The unauthorized reproduction or distribution of this copyrighted work is illegal. Criminal copyright infringement, including infringement without monetary gain, is investigated by the FBI and is punishable by up to 5 years in federal prison and a fine of $250,000.

ABOUT THE PRINT VERSION: If you purchased a print version of this book without a cover, you should be aware that the book is stolen property. It was reported as "unsold and destroyed" to the publisher, and neither the author nor the publisher has received any payment for this "stripped book."

IF YOU FIND AN EBOOK OR PRINT VERSION OF THIS BOOK BEING SOLD OR SHARED ILLEGALLY, PLEASE REPORT IT TO: lpn@blackopalbooks.com

Published by Black Opal Books **http://www.blackopalbooks.com**

DEDICATION

*This book is dedicated to all military veterans,
especially to those of the wars in Iraq and Afghanistan.*

CHAPTER 1

Joe

"Victoria has to pee."
Zan kept his eyes on the road, holding at a steady forty-three miles per hour, the maximum the bus would do before it began to shake.

"Zan, Victoria has to pee."

Zan's eyes swept from side to side. I knew those eyes. They were scanning for roadside bombs. In the middle of Michigan's Upper Peninsula.

"Zan, there are no IEDs here."

Zan's eyes kept on scanning. "I know that," he said.

"I can see your eyes, Zan."

He slowed more than he needed to for a gentle right curve. "You never know what those Canadians might have snuck down and…"

Good. He was returning to the UP, returning from his slide back into Iraq. Otherwise I was going to have to drive. Not easy with one leg and a cantankerous clutch.

"Victoria," I reminded my best friend. "She has to pee."

"Victoria always has to pee."

I felt my neck muscles tightening. I didn't want this again, the constant struggle between Zan and Victoria.

Zan never wanted to stop the bus, even though there was no need to keep moving. We had no place to go. We drove just because we had no place to stay, either. But Zan felt safe from enemy fire in the old school bus when it was on the move. Or what passed for *on the move* at forty-three miles per hour.

Victoria did not feel safe in the bus, or inside of anything else. She had been trapped in a burning Humvee. She was claustrophobic and wanted to get out of the bus as often as possible. She used the need to pee as an excuse. Why she ever got into the bus in the first place was one of life's great mysteries.

I was caught in the no-man's land between my best friend and a woman I hardly knew. It was definitely not a demilitarized zone.

"Shoulders aren't wide enough to pull off," Zan said.

"Victoria doesn't like to go behind a tree anyway," I reminded him.

I glanced over my shoulder. Victoria flashed me the sign language *P* symbol again. I didn't like to sigh. The one time I tried it at home, my father knocked my block off. I could feel one coming on, though. I should have thrown Victoria off the first time she got on the bus. Now I couldn't get rid of her, because of Lonnie.

Then I saw salvation, just ahead on the right. It was one story, with a drunken roof line, mostly tar paper on the sides, with some crooked furring strips and beer signs to hold it on, and two gas pumps out front. It also had a chipped concrete statue that looked like a giant pig with antlers. A faded wooden sign followed the roofline and proclaimed, *Eat at Moe's and Get Gas.* Another sign said that Moe featured *Pasties and Smoked Fish Fudge.* I hoped that smoked fish was not the flavor of the fudge, but I couldn't tell from the sign.

"Look, Zan, a convenience store. We can stop there for Victoria to pee."

I had put up with Victoria and her frequent "need" to pee because she made dealing with Lonnie a lot easier. As long as we had Lonnie, I needed Victoria, and I didn't know how to get rid of Lonnie.

Zan wasn't slowing down, so I repeated: "Look, Zan, a convenience store. We can stop there for Victoria to pee."

Zan didn't slow down. "It doesn't look that convenient."

"Probably our last chance for beer before we get into the next county. It's dry."

I didn't think Michigan had any dry counties, but Zan wouldn't know that.

He took his foot off the accelerator. "We got any money?"

"Enough."

We didn't have enough money for beer, not if we wanted food and gas, but what the hell?

Then it occurred to me that if we got beer, Victoria would have to pee again that much sooner, for real, so we really should go on, but Zan was already slowing to pull in.

I grabbed my leg and strapped it on, then zipped the lower part of the pants leg onto the shorts part.

"Which side is the gas fill on, Joe?"

If I could just zip Zan's memory on as easily as that pants leg…"The other one."

Zan had already pulled in beside the gas pumps. "Oh. I guess we can turn it around to get gas after we get the beer," he said.

After we get beer we won't have money for gas. I thought it, but I didn't say it. Albert Zander was my best friend, but Zan sometimes forgot that, too.

"Maybe they'll have Leinies. They ought to have Leinies. This UP thing is part of Michigan, but it ought to be part of Wisconsin, for God's sake. Didn't they look at a map when they started parceling out the states? You shouldn't ever give a state a name with *sin* in it, because the people will take that as an invitation and drink light beer. Ought to have Leinies in a place that ought to be Wisconsin…"

With that, Zan was out of the bus and heading for the door of the store.

I got out and hobbled a bit as I got worked onto the leg. I tried to make it look like I was just cramped up from riding. It bothered me that I was that vain. Hell's bells, there wasn't even anybody in sight, and I was acting like Miss America might see me and be turned off by my leg, instead of everything else about me that turned women off, like quoting my grandma and saying stuff like *hells bells*.

Lonnie was getting off the bus. Victoria was behind him, his controls hidden in her hand. I hoped she would leave Lonnie outside. I hoped she would stay outside with him. There were several cars in front. That meant customers inside. I didn't know how Yoopers would react to a semi-black woman with no hair and lots of pink splotches. Or how they would react if their women went ga-ga over Lonnie.

It was the kind of place that would have a lunch counter and some tables, maybe even a pool table. I didn't want to deal with the stares of people inside. I definitely did not want to deal with Lonnie if anybody made a smart remark about Victoria's looks.

"The bathrooms are probably around back, Victoria. Probably have to get a key inside first, though. No point walking around there first. I can get the key. You and Lonnie can hang around out here—"

"No need for that, Joe," Lonnie said, too loudly, in his best man-about-town voice. "You know how I love to look at the wares. Let us enter yon establishment, my controlling woman."

He laughed, a beautiful sound, except I was getting fed up with…people. And I was fed up with myself for caring about people and what they might think.

"There's nobody out here, Lonnie. You don't have to make anybody think you can see—"

Oh, hell, what was I doing? I didn't care what the hell Lonnie did, or what happened to him. Or Victoria, either. Let him walk into a wall. I had no business playing nursemaid. That was one of the nicknames the guys in my unit had for me, *Nursy*. That was until they found out I had spent a year in theology school before I joined up. Not a whole year, but enough that they called me *Preacher*. I didn't like nicknames. There were too many of them that went with the name *Joe* already.

Zan was no place in sight, which meant he was already inside, either grabbing Leinenkugel beer and telling them I would pay, or complaining that they didn't have Leinies. Lonnie and Victoria were headed inside. I stopped at a wooden map board just outside the door.

Hell, we weren't even on the right road. We were supposed to be on US 2 going east toward the Mackinac Bridge, so we could go down to the lower peninsula, the ones Michigan people called "the mitten." Instead we had gone west on 2, and Zan had made a turn up Michigan 95, and I hadn't even noticed. I followed Lonnie and Victoria into the store. The story of my life—always on the wrong road, but I just keep going along.

When I stepped through the door, the place was pretty much

as I figured it would be. I'd been in redneck hangouts in Indiana and South Carolina and Texas. They were all the same. They came out of a catalog—the same tattoos and Harley shirts and pool tables and beer signs and antlers and smells and beef jerky sticks. And the same women.

This one also had the promised pastries and smoked fish and fudge, and rows of low, dirty grocery shelves with cans of beans and sacks of snacks and everything from WD-40 to fan belts, plus a Blue Bunny ice cream freezer beside the cash register at the end of the lunch counter.

It didn't have the sounds, though. It had no sounds at all. There were plenty of people—some pool players, some folks sitting at tables, a couple on stools at the counter, a big-bosomed woman behind the counter. But they were frozen in place, like they were in Edward Hopper's *Nighthawks* painting.

Zan was at the back, peering carefully into the oversized refrigerated drink cases. He didn't seem to be aware of anything except his search for beer. Lonnie was started down the aisle between the potato chips and anti-freeze, Victoria close behind him, but they had stopped still. Lonnie was looking straight ahead, toward the back of the store, if you could say that a blind man was "looking," but I could tell that he had tuned into the silence and was waiting for something. Victoria was edging up close to him, trying not to be noticed.

I was a little bit embarrassed that the one thing in that whole tableau that I noticed most was the bosom of the woman behind the counter. It was *really* noticeable, though, at least in part because there was a portrait of the forty-fourth president of the USA on it, with a smile wider than the mouth of the Mississippi River.

"I told you to get that thing off!"

That from a guy standing beside the Blue Bunny case, wearing a floppy Aussie hat, one side tabbed up. His voice wasn't real loud, but it didn't need to be. I had heard voices like that before, often enough from my father, just before he began pounding on my mother.

There were two other guys who were obviously with him, because they were all dressed alike, and they didn't look like anybody else in that place. They were outsiders, not Yoopers.

The three of them were outfitted like dude hunters, all new stuff, all expensive. Guys from the city out for a week of "roughing it" with ten thousand bucks' worth of gear.

Except these weren't city dudes. These guys had that special soldier look. Not just any soldier. Mercenary. The hard type. I'd seen plenty of that type in Iraq. They weren't soldiers anymore, though. They were the civilian contractors. Civilian, but there was nothing civil about them. They sneered at those of us in uniform, because we were taking all the chances, and they were making all the money.

The one doing the talking didn't need to worry about his back. The two others had stationed themselves at strategic points so that they had control of the room. It was an automatic squad configuration.

That was when I noticed the TV suspended above the counter, up above the rows of cigarettes. Or what was left of the TV. The front was smashed in, and there was a can of Havoline oil sitting in the middle of the shards. Probably 5W-30, considering that 5W would be about as heavy as a motor could take most of the year in the UP. There was a pyramid of oil cans beside where the talker was standing, without the top can.

I finally looked at the *face* of the woman in the Obama tee. Maybe forty. Probably real pretty once. Eyes as big as her headlights and getting bigger. Full lips without lipstick, beginning to tremble. Shards of smoky glass in her midlife-red hair.

"Easy everybody. Nothing going on here. Go back to your pasties. Let's get going, Jay. Profile down."

It was the guy at the other end of the counter, beside the pool table. He sounded to me like the number two guy, trying to placate the leader of the bunch. I didn't see a weapon on him, but I was pretty sure all three of them were armed. And I was pretty sure "Jay" wasn't the guy's real name.

"I told her to get that nigger traitor off her boobs and she's going to do it! That's the profile here that's coming down."

The woman just stood there, her eyes blinking. The man called Jay took a step toward her. She made a little whimpering sound and reached down and grabbed the bottom of her shirt and began to pull it up.

Everybody was watching the woman. I reached down and

began to unzip my pants leg. I glanced left. Zan had disappeared. Lonnie had squeezed by Victoria in the narrow aisle and was sliding his way back toward the front of the store.

I knew what Lonnie had in mind. I don't know how, but I knew.

Victoria didn't know what Lonnie was going to try. But I could tell she recognized the mercenary. She didn't know the man, but she knew the type. She was desperately working Lonnie's control pad, trying to get him away from the guy, back down the aisle, into the chips or dips or something.

The woman's shirt was coming up, and so was Lonnie, behind the guy called Jay.

"Behind," the number two guy said softly.

Jay whirled, saw Lonnie's lifeless eyes, frowned, a moment of confusion on his face. He wasn't the kind who would mind slugging a blind man, though. He turned full toward Lonnie.

Guns appeared in the hands of the other two guys. I had gotten up against the end of a counter and gotten Judas unclipped and had the Beretta out. I needed to stop this now. I put a bullet through the can of Havoline in the TV, hoping the noise and the flying oil would get attention. It didn't. The number two guy pointed his gun right at me. He was left-handed, so I put one into his left shoulder, then shot off his left earlobe just to show off.

I didn't think, just did what came naturally to me. I didn't exactly aim a gun, short or long. Gun barrels and triggers and bullets just sort of followed my eyes. I thought about knees, but these were hard types. If they still had guns in their hands, they would use them, regardless of knees. I took out the number three guy's right shoulder with the same sweep of my eyes.

Their guns clattered to the floor. There was some moaning and cursing, but these guys were pros, and the pain hadn't really hit yet.

It was all the distraction Lonnie needed, and when Jay yelled "What the fuck?" that was all the locating he needed. His hands were just a blur as he clapped them full onto Jay's ears. Jay let out a cry of pain that I suspect he couldn't even hear. The force of Lonnie's blow probably blew out his eardrums. Victoria grabbed his gun arm, wrenched it around behind him, and pulled it out of his hand, dislocating his shoulder in the process.

Victoria waved the gun in the air and went into full combat command mode.

"Cleanup," she called. "Lonnie, stay where you are."

She turned to the woman behind the counter, who had her shirt about half-way up.

"What are these guys driving?"

The woman just looked back at her, still too petrified to talk.

"I saw 'em pull up in a black four-by-four. Parked out back."

It was an old man, raggedy gray beard, greasy Stormy Kromer cap, looked sort of like a rutabaga. He was sitting at a chrome-edged table with a woman who looked quite a bit like him.

A sixteen. It figured that they would be in a sixteen. It also figured they would leave the keys in it. They were the type to be ready for a quick getaway, any place, any time. Victoria must have figured it the same way.

"Go get it and bring it around front," Victoria said to the old man.

He didn't hesitate, just got up and went out through a back door.

"Help me get these guys out front," Victoria said.

I was busy putting the Beretta and Judas together so that I could walk. I kept the Beretta out, though. Zan was back at the beer case, like nothing had happened. Where the hell had he been? No time to think about that.

A couple of pool players stepped up, grabbed Jay by his good arm, and dragged him through the front door. The number two guy was bent over and moaning, but he was able to give me a hard stare. He grabbed the last guy by his good arm and led him outside.

I followed them.

The old man had their black sixteen out front. It was a Lincoln MKS. At least they had a Michigan car in Michigan. Well, Ford was Michigan, and Ford owned Lincoln, but no telling where the thing was built, probably Timbuktu or Kentucky.

Another older guy, with a gray ponytail, had followed us

out. He had a tattoo on his arm that spelled out MOE in little anchors.

"Shouldn't we call an ambulance, or the sheriff, or something?" he asked.

"I don't think they want that," I said. "Too much paper work."

I didn't know who these guys were, or why they were there, but I knew how they operated. They wouldn't want the law involved any more than we did.

I nodded at the pool players, and they rammed Jay into the back seat. He had recovered enough to try a glare at me as I pushed number two into the suicide seat. I didn't bother with trying to put a seatbelt on him. The first guy I'd shot still had his right arm so we pushed him in behind the wheel. He drove off with one hand, heading north up Michigan 95.

Victoria emerged from the store with a gun in either hand and another under her arm, 9 mm Glocks, the merc's best friend.

Lonnie stumbled out the door behind her, looking more like a blind man than I had ever seen him. "That was good, Victoria," he said. "Did you hear what she said to that woman, Joe?"

I could tell he was upset that Victoria had forgotten about him and was trying to cover it up.

"No, I don't think I heard her. Kind of loud in there."

"She told that woman to keep her shirt on. That's what my grandpa used to say when somebody would get too excited."

He kept chuckling. I liked him for remembering his grandpa.

CHAPTER 2

Lonnie Blifield was a nuisance. Hell, he was a whole burlap bag full of nuisance. He was blind, but he refused to act like a blind man. He refused even to admit that he was blind. Blind and unwilling to admit it. The worst kind. At least, that's what my ex-wife, Claudia, had always said.

Actually, she was just a girl in my Child Development class. We were teamed up as a pair to "raise" a couple of bags of flour through Erikson's first five stages of psycho-social adjustment. We didn't have to get them through the sixth stage, Intimacy v Isolation, because, as college students, we were in that one ourselves. I decided if I had to be married to Claudia one more semester I would opt for isolation.

"A man should know better than to marry a woman named Claudia, because she's named after her father, and a father-in-law named Claude will always make trouble, because when he was a kid, the other kids called him Clod, and it left him permanently…uh…troubled."

That's what Zan had told me when he learned I was coupled up with Claudia. He would have said "permanently fucked up," but Zan honored my commitment to Grandma. I had promised her I wouldn't cuss and, most of the time, I was able to keep that promise. When my friends and teammates learned of my commitment, they honored it too, by not cussing in front of me themselves, which is pretty impressive for college students. I never cussed even in the army, even in Iraqistan. Then came the goddamned VA.

Zan and I picked Lonnie up as he was walking away from the goddamned VA hospital in Iowa City. The goddamned VA wanted you to call it a VAMC, VA Medical Center, to differentiate it from the non-medical ways the goddamned VA used to screw you. Everybody just said VA, though, or GDVA.

We were pulling away in the bus when we noticed this tall blond young guy. He was handsome in a World War II sort of way, like Nile Kinnick, for whom the football stadium over the hill had been named.

Zan and I had played football in that stadium. We had seen the pictures of Kinnick, the All-American, Heisman Trophy winner even, the World War II hero. He was a pilot who had been killed on a training flight.

"Some hero," I said to Zan back then, when we came to play. "Never even saw the enemy."

I winced as I remembered that, a wince that went from my scalp to my toenails. If you died in the uniform, it didn't matter how or when it happened. I knew that now.

Lonnie had marched resolutely down the VA driveway and then down the middle of the street, cars zigzagging around him. For a while Zan just followed behind him in the bus, even though we were taking our half out of the middle, so that the constant stream of mini-vans and SUVs and pickups and sixteens wouldn't run over him.

Zan always referred to four-by-fours as sixteens, and he never failed to cackle at it. Zan was a genius at some things, but humor wasn't one of them.

"We'd better get him out of the street," I'd said.

"Why? This is fun," Zan had said.

"There's something wrong with him, Zan. He doesn't act like he knows where he is."

"Of course, there's something wrong with him, Joe. He just left the VA. If there wasn't something wrong with him when he went in, there's something wrong with him now."

A Jaguar swerved hard to miss him. The driver honked his horn, stuck his head out the window, and yelled something at Lonnie. Lonnie said nothing in reply, but he did stick up one finger in the Hawaiian good luck sign, and he kept marching.

"I think he's blind, Zan."

Zan snorted and pushed on the horn and made a sound with his mouth like a sick goose. He knew the horn didn't work, but he liked to push on it anyway, just so he could make the goose noise.

"If he's blind, how come he doesn't have a dog, or one of those white canes with the barber pole stripes on it?"

"Because the VA wouldn't pay for a dog? Or a cane?"

The quickest way to get Albert Zander on my side was to criticize the VA.

"Yeah, you can bet on that, pardner," Zan said.

Still, though, he just herded the bus along behind Lonnie, until finally Lonnie was off the pavement, onto the little hill, and headed straight for the river.

"This is great," exulted Zan. "It's just like the old slogan: *Hire the handicapped. They're fun to watch.*"

I did not remember any such slogan, and the thought of losing my home or my butt to a smash with a garbage truck or a black and gold bus with a picture of a big scary chicken on it was not my idea of fun. The locals called the big scary chicken a Hawkeye, but I knew it for what it was.

"He's going to drown, Zan."

"Naw, it's not a big river."

I waited.

"I bet he knows how to swim."

I waited.

"It would be fun to see him make a big splash."

I wasn't sure we could wait any longer. Thankfully, Zan relented and pulled to the curb—in the oncoming traffic lane, of course.

I still had Judas on from being at the VA. Judas was what I called my artificial leg. I used the swivel handle to get the door open, hopped out on my real leg, steadying myself with the unsteady door, and yelled at the handsome young man marching toward the river.

"Hey, soldier. You got time to join a couple of buddies in a beer?"

Lonnie came to a halt and did a parade ground about-face.

"What brand?" he shouted back.

Hell, didn't this guy know about *Beggars can't be choosers*? That's what my grandma always said. I wasn't sure she was very reliable on the subject, though. She'd never turned a beggar away in her life, especially not her grandson. If she were still alive, maybe I wouldn't be living in a school bus.

"My buddy here is partial to Leinenkugels," I said.

"Okay, cool, awesome," Lonnie replied, like it was dialog he had memorized for a high school play.

It was then that I realized Lonnie wasn't really that particular about his brand of beer. He just needed to hear me talk some more so he could get a fix on my voice. As soon as he had it, he marched straight for us.

"Hope you don't mind riding in this old school bus," I said as he approached. "And I've got a leg off, so I'll have to get in first, if you don't mind."

I kept talking to let Lonnie hone in on my voice and to give him information that he needed without making it look like I was talking to a blind man. I swung back into the bus but kept up the chatter as I did so.

"Yep, damn steps, hard to climb with only one real leg."

I figured Lonnie could hear my voice going up the bus steps and be able to follow it, catch on to how many steps. I was right. The blind man got on without a hitch.

"Where do you want me to ride?"

"Right there behind the driver is okay. I have to stay on this side to stick my false leg out into the aisle."

This guy obviously did not want anyone to realize he was blind. I hoped my example, talking about Judas, would make the new guy realize it was okay, that he could admit he could not see. I didn't believe in talking about your feelings or the past. Most vets didn't. That was only for VA social workers. I did believe in facing the facts of right now, though. If you didn't stand fast in the right now, you slid back into the past, or into the future, which might be worse.

"Driver here is Albert Zander. I call him Zan. I'm Joe Kirk. We were in Iraqistan. I lost a leg. Zan went crazy. The usual stuff."

"Yeah. Me, too," Lonnie had said.

I didn't know whether he meant he had been in Iraq and Afghanistan or if he meant that he had gone crazy. Of course, they usually went together, regardless.

Zan and I had gone to the Iowa City VA to get medicine for

Zan. We had not been able to get Zan any medicine, but we got Lonnie.

We were in Iowa City because I had sold Zan on the idea of making a tour of all the cities where we had played football, a thousand years ago, when we were teammates and roommates at IU, Indiana University. It was really to visit VA hospitals to try to get help for Zan's brain, some sort of help that he would actually accept.

We went to Madison before Iowa City. We had gotten smeared at Camp Randall Stadium a couple of times. Our success rate at the VA hospital there turned out to be a little less even than we'd had at Camp Randall. We went back to Iowa City to go down to Champaign Memorial Stadium, site of another series of defeats.

Now, with Lonnie along, we headed east out of Iowa City but only got as far as West Liberty before the sun went down. We camped at an old fairground where they hadn't cleaned up yet from a rodeo. Lonnie never said anything the whole way, just ate what I cooked up for supper. When I said it was time for bed, and told him there was no place to sleep except the aisle of the bus, he got in, lay down, and went to sleep.

The next day, at what passed for breakfast, I said, "Look, I understand about not wanting to talk about stuff. Zan and me, we don't talk about stuff much. But we need something to call you besides *Soldier*."

"*Soldier* is okay."

"That's that, then," I said.

We got on board and got the bus lumbering off. About ten miles farther on, he spoke into the air between me and Zan. "Lonnie Blifield."

That was all he had said about himself. He never explained why he had been at the VA or where he was from, never questioned where we were going. Whenever Zan and I talked, though, he cocked his head and listened closely.

Now we had Victoria, and she had mastered the controls that Zan had worked into Lonnie's red and black lumberjack vest.

When Zan's brain was working, he was a technological genius. He had been a football major at university, so he must have learned the tech stuff in the army. Zan's brain was very much an on-and-off affair, however. He had some sort of brain injury, and migraines, and PTSD, no doubt. In an "on" period after we pulled Lonnie off of the street and into the bus, Zan had placed remote-controlled nodes into the vest.

We had been traveling east from Iowa City, because I liked to keep the sun in Zan's eyes in the morning. It made him squint and kept him from scanning the shoulders of US 6 for IEDs.

"I think I know what to do," Zan had muttered at the morning sun.

I didn't think much about it. Zan often mumbled, and he always thought he knew what to do.

When we got to Davenport, US 6 took us right by a big mall.

"This is the place," Zan said as he pulled into the parking lot.

I didn't question what place it was, or why Zan thought it was *the* place. One place was as good as any other to me. I took Lonnie into the Barnes & Noble for coffee, using my lead-by-chattering method. Zan headed off by himself.

I got Lonnie settled at a little table across from the pastry display case.

"They don't have table service here, Lonnie. I'll go order at the counter. What do you want?"

"Dark roast."

Well, at least we had the same taste in coffee.

When I returned to the table, walking carefully to keep my leg straight so I wouldn't spill the coffee, Lonnie was leaning over the rail beside our table.

The café area of the store was built on two levels. There was a row of tables a couple of feet below the rail. Two girls, maybe twenty, probably shop girls from one of the kinky clothing stores in the mall, were sitting at a table below, looking up at Lonnie like they had just seen God, or maybe Johnny Depp.

"A blonde should wear a warmer color on her lips," Lonnie was saying. "Otherwise she seems too remote. Now you," he said, his head turning toward the girl to his left, "a brunette is already more available, especially if she is cuddly like you, so you need a lighter shade. Not much. You're beautiful already, but why not reach for perfection?"

The chubby brunette giggled and smoothed back her hair.

"What about me? Don't you think I'm perfect already?"

It was the other one, a blonde. Standing up above them, I could see dark roots.

"Of course you are perfect," Lonnie said, "but as a slender blonde, your aura must be elegant. Remember that elegance is beauty plus organization. So you must do something about those earrings. They are not organized."

I began to hum *Golden Earrings*. I quit after a few bars, though. It was one of my grandmother's songs. Lonnie and the shop girls would never recognize it, never "get" how clever I was. I made a point of scraping my chair on the floor so Lonnie would know I was back.

"Dark roast, Lonnie."

I leaned over the table, spoke the words just above where I put the coffee down. Lonnie wouldn't like it if I said something like "Dark roast at twelve o'clock," the way you should for a blind person. Lonnie didn't like it anyway. His voice cooled as he turned toward me.

"A bagel would be nice," he said.

He obviously wanted to be alone with the girls.

I thought about it. I remembered the joke Zan told every time a bug hit the windshield.

"You know what's the last thing that goes through a bug's mind when it gets smashed on the windshield, Joe? Its ass!"

I thought about getting Lonnie a bagel for as long as it takes for a bug's ass to go through its mind when it hit the windshield.

"Get your own damn bagel," I said. "I'll be in self-help section, if I can find it."

I picked up my coffee. The girls gave me dirty looks. Lonnie Blifield, however, looked very satisfied. He would have the girls all to himself, with no one to suggest he could not see them.

"Not a damn one of those three is going to get the joke about *if I can find it*, either," I muttered as I limped off to the History section.

I like to read about World War II. I hoped the books about Iraqistan would be in Current Events instead of History, because I did not like to read about that desert, about those mountains. For me, those wars would never be history.

I picked up Jon Meacham's book about Churchill and Roosevelt, tried to remember what page I had been on the last time I was in a bookstore. I couldn't afford to buy books, and I was never in one place long enough to borrow from a library, so bookstores became my library. Yalta, that was where they were.

Then I turned back toward the café. Lonnie was still jabbering. The girls were still giggling and looking up at him the way my grandmother used to look at me before—

That damn Lonnie wasn't blind! The blonde *was* slender, and she *did* have awful earrings and her lipstick *was* pale. The brunette *was* cuddly, if you considered *cuddly* to be a synonym for chubby, and her lipstick *was* so bright they might as well be in Alabama. Lonnie could *see* them.

But I knew he couldn't *see* them, not with his eyes. He was seeing them some other way.

How does he do that? And what does he learn about me when he listens so carefully to Zan and me talk?

That was when Zan arrived. I saw him approaching through the big windows in the front and went to the doors to meet him. He was carrying a Goodwill bag and one from Radio Shack.

"If you want coffee, I'd better get it, and then we can sit over in the easy chairs there. Lonnie doesn't want anybody around right now."

Zan looked over toward the café.

"Hell, no, man. I'm going over there. He's got *dames*!"

No one had ever suggested that Albert Zander might be gay.

"Hell, no, man, that's not right—"

I turned to look. The girls were pushing up from their table, obviously getting ready to leave. Each held one of Lonnie's hands and they were pulling him down over the rail to kiss him. Lonnie was smirking like Captain Jack Sparrow.

"You women remember me when you go to bed tonight," we heard him say, sounding more like Rick in *Casablanca* than like Captain Jack.

I began to hum again.

"You must remember this, a kiss is just a kiss…"

Zan sighed.

"I'm just like poor Herman Hupfeld," he said. "He wrote the words and music both for that song, but did he ever get any broads because of it? No. Sinatra and Bogart, they got the skirts from that song. Of course, it doesn't help any, getting women, if your name is Herman Hupfeld."

I stared hard at my friend.

"How do you know these things? I've known you since college, and you've never said a thing about any Herman Humpfield. And how do you know he never got any?"

Zan laughed, a bitter dry sound. It was nothing like the laugh from when we had started out as freshman roommates.

"Hupfeld, moron, not Humpfield. Of course, maybe if his name had really been Humpfield, he might have gotten some, humped the whole field, but I know he didn't, because his name was Herman, which meant when he was a kid, the other kids called him Her-man, and pointed to the ugliest girl in the class when they did it, and it left him permanently damaged."

Zan sighed. "Get me a mocha. I'll gather up lover boy and get started."

He held up the Goodwill and Radio Shack bags.

"What you got in there?"

Zan held the sacks open so I could look inside.

In the Goodwill bag was a red and black lumberjack vest. It looked like a Filson. I reached in and pulled the neck back to check. Yes, Filson. It hadn't been worn much.

In the Radio Shack bag was a collection of wires and gadgets that meant nothing to me.

"What you going to do?"

"I'm going to wire up Lonnie so you can control him like a puppet. Give him an impulse on the right side of the vest, he'll turn right. Impulse on the left, turn left. Two impulses, stop. I've got it all worked out. I'll need to remodel the vest some, but it'll still look the same. We've still got that sewing kit, don't we?"

"Yes."

I didn't like this plan. I didn't want Zan using Grandma's sewing kit. It was all I had left of her.

"Zan, I know you can do the electronics, but we can't control Lonnie like a puppet. He won't even admit he's blind—"

"No sweat. That's what this is all about. This is how he keeps on acting like he's not blind. If he runs into stuff, people will know. If we tell him stuff out loud, people will know. This way, it looks like he knows. Go get my mocha."

I didn't like this part of the plan, either. Caffeine and chocolate and Albert Zander's brain wiring were not likely to be a good combination. But—

I shrugged. It would keep Zan busy, and what else did we have to do?

"Okay, but how are you going to get Lonnie to go along with this? He already thinks nobody knows he's blind."

"Oh, hell, Joe, I was a psych major. I'll be sensitive. I know how to do stuff like this."

He started off toward where Lonnie Blifield still stood, seemingly watching the shop girls as they left the store and went out into the mall.

"No, Zan, I was the psych major. You—"

But Zan was already gone. I walked back to get into the coffee line again. I caught the eye of a pretty woman at a little table. She quickly looked away. I tried to lock my back so that both legs moved in the same way. It didn't work. What the hell? What would I do with a pretty woman even if I could pick her up? Better not to think about pretty women, or anything else, better just to—

That was when I heard Zan.

"Look, Lonnie, man, you're blind as a bat. You can't hide that. But with this vest I'm going to make you, everybody will think you see better than anybody."

Great. So much for being sensitive. Now Lonnie would probably walk off in front of a garbage truck. So what? What responsibility did I have for Lonnie Blifield? Except we were both vets, and that—

"Will I look good in the vest?"

"Hell, man, it's a Filson. Everybody looks good in a Filson."

"I prefer Carhartt."

"Did I say Filson? I meant Carhartt. Everybody looks good in—"

"Sir? I said, What can I get you? This is the third time you've been here this morning. You must really like coffee."

Her voice sparkled. So did her curls. She had dark blonde hair, and she was staring at me from behind the order counter.

"Oh, sorry. I was sort of off...not thinking...I need a mocha for my friend."

She looked toward the doors, where Zan was leading Lonnie out.

"Not the good-looking one. He's not the mocha type. I guess I'd better get him a bagel, though."

I didn't know why I was jabbering away at her. I hadn't talked to anyone but Zan for so long. It was just—

"Oh, he's good-looking enough, that's true, but *you* are the good-looking one."

My God, was she flirting with me? She seemed so sincere about it. I remembered a line from something I had read, a long time ago, back in college. *Make ready with bells and with drums for the pure-hearted girl.* A Chinese proverb, I think it was. I needed bells and drums.

Our hands touched as she gave me the mocha and the sack with the bagel. A special smile made her face light up like more metaphors or similes or something than I could...what, shake a stick at, that's what Grandma would say.

I made a point of limping as I passed the pretty woman at the little table. I'd show her. I wouldn't think about her ever again. I would spend my life thinking about the pure-hearted coffee girl. At least until I met someone who replaced her in my dreams.

I am so pathetic!

I had to grin at myself. And somewhere Grandma was LOL.

CHAPTER 3

I had to drive. Zan was too busy with Grandma's sewing kit and his bag of electronic stuff. We could have just gone to a park, maybe some place along the Mississippi, and sat there while Zan did his thing and Lonnie munched his bagel. It would have been easier on my leg, and Zan's fingers.

It would have been pretty, too. Davenport displayed plenty of gold and red trees in autumn. Maples, mostly, I thought, were the ones that turn. Oaks were later. I was never much good at tree identification, except apple trees, certain times of the year. It bothered my father a lot, that his son did not know one tree from another. Moline, on the Illinois side of the river, had pretty trees, too. Then there was the river itself. When you had spent four tours on a desert, water always looked nice, any kind of water.

But Zan was into a focused spell, as long as he'd had since we had reconnected. He always felt better if we were on the move. I wanted that spell to last as long as possible. Also, I wanted to try the VA in Danville, a hundred miles south of Chicago, fifty on beyond Champaign, so I made my false leg work the pedals and headed us east.

"Just keep the old bus rocking, Joe, but don't get into an eighteen to twenty-two. Anything below, anything above, that's okay."

That's what Zan had said the first time I drove.

"What in hell are you talking about?"

"Eighteen to twenty-two. That's the rhythm that makes people sea-sick. And car-sick. And bus-sick."

"Eighteen to twenty-two whats? And per what?"

Zan, though, had seen something along the road that sent him into IED lookout mode, so I had never gotten an answer.

As I drove now, I could only hope that I wasn't causing eighteen to twenty-two whatevers. Most of the time, Zan couldn't remember where he was born or what he'd had for lunch, but he could remember some obscure thing he had learned in *Health for Jocks: Staying Eligible for Football* class about what caused seasickness.

I shook my head and herded the bus across the river and through Moline and East Moline and Silvis. I managed to find old US Highway 150. I figured we could take it all the way down to Danville, without having to get onto I-74, its parallel. The bus couldn't do interstate speeds.

I knew that 150 crossed the Illinois River at Peoria. I thought we might find a place along the riverfront where we could camp.

We were going through a town called Orion when Zan got one of his headaches. Maybe it was all the close work he was doing on Lonnie's vest. Maybe it was something else. Whatever the reason, he fell into the aisle between the seats, crawled to the back, held fast to the legs of the back seats, and thrashed around on the floor.

At least the floor was clean. That was my doing, although it wasn't my bus. It was Zan's bus, except he didn't seem to know that most of the time. It was filthy when I first got on, so I decided it had to be cleaned. I got the junk and dirt in the aisle swept out. After that, I sort of lost interest. I didn't stay interested in anything for very long anymore.

Zan and I had been assigned as roommates our freshman year in the football dorm at IU, Indiana University.

I was a quarterback from Princeton. We won the state championship my senior year. My arm was weak, but accurate. My feet were quick, so I could scramble, but I was slow, so I never got very far if I was forced out of the pocket. I was undersized for a quarterback by Division I standards. They didn't call it Division I anymore, though. Now it was The Football Factory Division, or something like that. I was six-two, and there were successful QBs who were shorter, but, as one coach put it, "You *look* small." But the IU coaches signed me to a scholarship because, "He knows how to win." That's what they put in the press release when they couldn't get anybody better.

Unfortunately, those coaches were gone after our freshman year. The new coaches didn't like my size or my speed or my attitude. So I spent my time running the scout team, learning a new offense every week so that the defensive starters could practice against the offense that *Whatever State* would run against them.

Zan was an undersized linebacker from Gary, "The only white football player in the whole damn city," as he put it. He started every IU game for four years, from "true" freshman on. The team won very few of those games, though, and Zan assigned the blame to himself, the guy who had always won before, but couldn't get his teammates, and sometimes even his coaches, to buy into his gung-ho overachieving drive to success.

After the last game of our senior season, as always, a regular-season loss to hated rival Purdue and not a bowl game, he had packed up and driven away without a word to anyone, including his roommate.

I had not seen him or heard from him for five years, and then there we both were, at the VA in Indianapolis, both getting the run-around. I had a prosthetic leg that didn't work, and Zan had migraines, an overachieving drive to insanity, a dozen conspiracy theories, and an old school bus. With no place else to go and nothing better to do, with some mismanaged memory of how much fun it had been to room with him, when actually it had been chaos most of the time, I got on the bus with him, and we drove away.

A doctor at the Naptown VA told me there were only two kinds of wounded Iraqistan vets, the insiders and the outsiders. The insiders were fighters, he said, the heroes. They took their injuries as a challenge to overcome. The outsiders were, well, Zan and Lonnie and Victoria and me, the paranoids who didn't trust anybody. The doctor said we would be lost until we came inside. What he didn't understand was that even paranoids had real enemies. And they were on the inside.

Zan had to focus. Lonnie had to see. Victoria had to run. I had to forget. We couldn't do any of those on the inside. Sometimes being lost was better than being inside. That was how vets felt. Sometimes it was better to be outside, on an old bus to nowhere.

I had no idea where or why Zan had gotten the bus in the first place, or how long he had been living in it. It looked like he had been trashing it for years, but our dorm room had looked like that by the second day.

He had done nothing to change it. It still smelled of first grade fear, fourth grade puke, and eighth grade yearning. It still had the original seats, with the original gum stuck underneath. Well, he had made one change. He said it was against the law to drive a yellow bus if it were no longer a school bus, so he had covered it with some sort of gray stuff that I guessed was paint, except it never seemed to set up. I tried to keep away from the sides because the paint remained tacky and would glom on to you if it got a chance. At least it didn't run in the rain.

Zan kept a sleeping bag and camping equipment on and under the seats, along with an assortment of junk that he had managed to acquire along the way. He just slept in the aisle between the rear seats, with the back door open.

I couldn't do that, for a lot of reasons, including whatever besides Zan was crawling on the floor, so I got a board and put it across the aisle, between the second-row seats, and slept on that. It was hard as hell, but I'd slept on worse, and there wasn't any sand blowing in.

I sure got more than I had bargained for when I got on that bus.

Zan was out of his head most of the time. There were occasional periods when he was his old self, though, and he would act like he didn't even know about his crazy periods. Then we had good times, remembering Saturday afternoon games and late night boorass sessions.

There was a counselor at the VA who had tried to convince us we should talk about the crap that happened to us, and that would be some sort of step toward "normalcy" or "fitting back in" or some bunch of bullshit. Zan and me, we couldn't take that. We were like a lot of other vets, too afraid of the future to want to fit into it, too haunted by the past to open the door to it.

We had to live right now, only right now, just hang on hard to the moment. Zan and I, we never talked about the army, why we joined, what happened while we were soldiers, what happened after we came back, why we both felt most at home and at ease on an old school bus running a route to nowhere.

Most of the time, though, Zan was in such pain, both in his brain and in his body, that I decided I just had to do something about it. Old habits died hard. I had tried to keep him on some kind of level when we were roommates in college, and it felt like I should keep doing it.

I guessed I was about two tires short of a Humvee myself. I had the crazy idea that somewhere there would be a VA where there would be some new Indian doctor who wasn't yet aware that the VA was supposed to save the government money instead of treating vets.

So we started our odyssey.

Just saying *odyssey* made me remember reading Homer back in Lit class at IU, and that made me cry. I didn't cry at the bad stuff. I cried at the good stuff, because it was so rare. Lit class was good stuff, mostly because of Becky Garlits. After Lit class, though, Becky turned out to be real bad stuff.

"You'd better do something. He sounds pretty bad."

It was the first thing Lonnie had said since we left the mall in Davenport. We were almost to Galesburg by then.

"Nothing to do. Just have to wait it out. He always comes out of it."

I wasn't sure that was true. He'd had these fits before, it was true, and he had come out of them, it was true, but I was no doctor. I never knew what would happen. I figured I could get some street drugs that would calm him down, but they might make things worse. Brains were funny things that way.

I was in a funk. Either he'd come out of it or he wouldn't. Either we'd find a new Patel who could do something for him or we wouldn't. What difference did it make, either way?

I didn't much like thinking that way, and I didn't like Zan being in so much pain, but I just plain didn't know what else to do or any other way to think. Sometimes there wasn't much in that moment we hung onto so hard, except waiting for another moment.

I was hoping Lonnie would say something else so I could jump down his throat. I figured I could take out my helplessness on him, since he was even more helpless. He didn't say anything more, though.

Zan kept thrashing around, but his moaning got down to Halloween ghost levels. I began to feel lonely. I had avoided talking to anyone since I got back, except for Zan when he was in a normal period. Zan and I had been on the bus together for only about a week, and the normal periods were not many. Now I wanted to hear a normal voice. Lonnie had a good voice, a nice baritone.

"Back there at the mall, Lonnie. You got those girls pegged exactly, the hair, the lipstick, the earrings, everything. How do you do that?"

He didn't say anything for a long time. I began to think he was in a trance. Maybe he was going back to denying his blindness again. Finally, where there was a sign claiming some place called Dahinda was off the highway to the north, he spoke.

"They weren't girls. They are called women now, regardless of what age they are."

"Right. That makes it real nice for the molesters. *I know she was only nine, your honor, but everyone was calling her a woman, so I thought she was.*"

"Those women at the mall were not nine. One was nineteen and the other was twenty."

"You know that the same way you know about the lipstick?"

"No, they told me."

He sounded so smug, I had to laugh out loud. That got Lonnie to laughing, too. It was like some damn dam was released. We laughed so hard I almost ran off the road. After we calmed down, I realized Zan had stopped his thrashing and moaning and was just lying there between the seats.

Either Lonnie and I were calmed by Zan's silence, or he just didn't want to answer my original question about how he knew so much about those girls, or women, or whatever. Either way, we both accepted the new silence and drove on.

CHAPTER 4

We had gone on a while when I saw a sign for the town of Kickapoo.

"That's what we did to Purdue that year, remember? We kicked the poo out of them."

The voice came from about three rows back. Zan had gotten up and was just sitting there, looking out the windows.

"We won by one point, Zan. Not exactly kicking the poo out of them."

"Yeah, but it was Purdue, man. Any time we beat them, it was kicking poo."

"*Anytime* was only one time, Zan. We put only one *I* on that chain on the Old Oaken Bucket."

He didn't respond to my downer comment, but instead said, rather cheerily, "Speaking of poo, I'm hungry."

I did not want to pursue the ways his brain might be connecting poo and food. "There's a sign for a state park," I said. "Jubilee College State Park. We could stop there and fix some lunch."

Neither Zan nor Lonnie said anything, so I drove us to the park, got out the hibachi, and fixed us some lunch. My leg was giving me fits, so I was thinking it would be nice just to stay where we were. Zan packed up the lunch stuff, though, and got behind the wheel, so we took off again. I was never very good at simply saying what I thought would be best, or saying what I needed.

I was glad he was driving when we got to the Illinois River. We went across the river and took the highway north, up toward Spring Bay, just poking around, looking for a way to get to the river bank some place where nobody would throw us off for trespassing. That meant a lot of dead-ends and backing and filling, which is not easy in an old school bus with a balky clutch, even for a guy with two good legs.

By the time we found a spot, it was close to dark. We got out, opened up the back door to the bus, and got out the cooking gear.

"This place has bad vibes," Lonnie said. "Bad smells."

I sniffed, and so did Zan, but I didn't smell anything out of the ordinary. Just the usual river odors. The place was weedy and gulched and it looked like it had been used pretty hard in the past. Ashes from several old campfires, cigarette butts, fuzzy condoms, fast food cups, and plastic bags. The trash was all pretty old, though, like nobody had been around for a while. All the smells had been washed out of it, at least for my nose. It looked like it had been a teen-age party spot, but the parties had come to an abrupt halt for some reason. My guess was the cops.

"I don't smell anything, Lonnie," I said. "Just the river."

He didn't say anything, just kept standing there, his head cocked to one side. Lonnie was a few inches shorter than I, making him an inch or two below six feet. He had light blue eyes, the eyes of an athlete. People with light eyes were better athletes. They had better eye-hand coordination. They could hit a baseball, make a basket. His build was more like a gymnast, though, and while his eyes were light, they didn't have any light in them.

He had blond hair that had been cut short but was growing out into a head of curls like Art Garfunkle. With his head cocked like that, he reminded me of a cocker spaniel, except in his white tee-shirt and blue jeans, he was hard and lean, more like a German shepherd.

"We'll just have to make our own bad smells," I said. "We're having beans tonight."

Neither Lonnie nor Zan said anything back to that, either. Zan was in a sort of trance, moving around okay, not looking for hostiles, but not exactly with us, either. That was an improvement over headaches, so I didn't disturb him, just started trying to concoct a meal by myself. I usually had to do that, anyway.

I had the cans opened and rinsed them, with the skillet heating over the charcoal in the hibachi, when the pickup rumbled in.

It was black and long, one of those extended cab things. My father worked in the factory that made Toyota Tundras. I wondered if maybe he'd helped build this one. It was almost dark by then, though, and I couldn't make out what brand it was. Pickups all looked alike anymore. You had to be able to see the logo or icon, what my grandma always called a hood ornament.

Being reminded of my father put me into a foul mood. He was why I joined the army.

Against my advice, Zan had backed the bus in, so the tail was toward the river. I had been worried that we wouldn't be able to get it to climb back up the incline. Reverse was the strongest gear on a bus, so I thought we should have it ready for the climb back up. It wasn't much of a hill, but the bus didn't want to go up hills of any sort without a running start. The ground was fairly hard, though, and it was nice to be able to watch the river and listen to it while I was cooking, so I had decided I'd worry about getting out in the morning.

The pickup slewed to a stop beside the bus. The driver cut the motor but left the radio and lights on. The lights weren't pointed directly at us, but they spread a wide glow, especially since he had his high beams on. The radio, or maybe it was a CD player, was spewing out some sort of heavy metal-rap-seagull-in-pain stuff. It sounded like an initiation ritual for the Indian Thugees, or maybe it was just for thugs in general. I could hear voices above or behind the "music." It sounded like they were arguing.

My head began to hurt, so I knew it had to be getting into Zan's torture chamber of a brain. I looked over at him. His eyes were wide, and sweat was running down his face. He had taken a step toward the truck when somebody cut the radio. In the aftermath, the silence was unnerving. Even the birds, mosquitoes, and frogs had shut up.

All the doors of the truck opened up and people sort of spilled out.

I was closest to the driver's side. I could see the driver get out and another guy from the seat behind him. I wasn't sure about the other side, just that there were some others over there.

The driver was about my height, but built bigger. Not all of it was muscle, though. I could tell that by the way the tattoos on his upper arms sort of danced around as he moved. His forehead was in the blueprint stage of baldness, and a short ponytail was dangling down his neck. He was wearing a checked shirt with the sleeves ripped out, apparently trying to look like Larry the Cable Guy.

He didn't sound like Larry, though.

"You motherfuckers—what the fuck you doing—this is our fucking place—get the fuck out of here."

Well, it did sound a little bit like Larry, except this guy was dead serious about what he was saying.

And he was way overwrought, so worked up he couldn't even form a simple fucking sentence. It didn't make sense. We were just some vagabonds in a school bus. All he had to do was politely tell us to move along. We wouldn't have done it, of course, but he didn't know that. Not yet.

Then the people on the side away from me moved up in front of the headlight on that side of the truck. There were two men and a woman. They were back-lighted, so I couldn't see their faces well, but I could see enough to know that this woman was a girl, regardless of what Lonnie might say. She looked fifteen to me, maybe sixteen. Her shirt and bra were pulled up, and the guys on either side of her were holding her arms down and pawing at her breasts.

Here was that *girl-woman* dilemma in spades. She was definitely built like a woman. There was something about her, just the way she stood, that said she had been a woman for a long time and was weary with it. But she was just a girl.

The pony-tailed driver marched over to the front of the truck's grill. That was when I remembered that I should have looked at the hood ornament to see what make of truck it was. Now I couldn't see it because he was standing in the way. That made me think of my father again, and that made me mad. Maybe that's why Ponytail himself was so mad, I thought. Maybe his father was a school-bus driver.

I was mad enough to take my leg off. I started edging toward the end of the bus so I'd have something to lean against.

Ponytail continued to spew fucking words around. *Inchoate* was the word that came to my mind, and I was proud of myself for thinking of it. It was a word we used a lot in Child Development courses. The development of language in children was inchoate. My father was so pleased with my choice of a college major: *First fucking person in the family to go to college and he studies Home Ec.* It wasn't Home Ec, of course. They didn't even have Home Ec anymore. Couldn't call it that. Everything had to be a fucking science...

I felt myself getting madder and madder as I looked at that fucking ponytail, and those fucking girl molesters. I was mad enough to take off my leg when Lonnie spoke into one of Ponytail's inchoate gaps.

"Let the woman go."

How in the *hell* did he do that? She hadn't said a thing. How did he know she was there? He seemed to have some sort of "blindar" for girls.

"This is no woman. This is a cunt. And she's mine, all mine. Ain't she pretty?"

That from the guy on her left, a smaller version of Ponytail, except without the ponytail, and he could form a sentence. He flopped her breast up and down a couple of times as he said *mine, all mine.*

"Yeah, mine all mine."

That from the one on her right, who did the same breast flop. He was taller than the one on her left, and skinny, and it sounded like he had something wrong with his throat.

"Let her go."

Lonnie was taking short gliding steps, but not toward the girl. He was moving toward Ponytail. I didn't like the look of that. Ponytail might be inchoate, but he didn't look impotent. He was a stick of dynamite with a lit fuse. It was sputtering, but it was going to flare up any second. If Lonnie got too close, Ponytail would deck him. Lonnie wasn't moving like a blind man, and it wouldn't have made any difference to Ponytail, anyway. He was the type who would knock down a blind man or a pregnant woman or anyone else who got in his way.

"No problemo, guys. We'll just keep things cool. I'm sure these boys here are getting ready to leave."

That was the guy who had gotten out of the seat behind Ponytail. He looked sort of like George Costanza, from the *Seinfeld* TV show, without the glasses. He was wearing a denim pants and jacket outfit that was almost clean.

"Shut up, George."

Ponytail spat it over his shoulder. *George.* That figured.

I didn't want to take my eyes off Ponytail and Lonnie, so I reached out for the corner of the bus, feeling for it.

"Hey, that dickhead's going for something, Chug," the guy called George said.

So Ponytail was called *Chug* by his friends. One look at his belly and you could see why. I was sort of disappointed, though. I had gotten used to him as Ponytail.

Lonnie stopped moving. That was good. I figured I could talk us out of this, but not if Lonnie got into Chug's face. Then Chug made a mistake. He spoke again.

"Hold it right there, dickhead," he said to me.

Lonnie started his glide again, slightly longer steps this time. Then I remembered how he navigated. He was gliding instead of stepping to feel his way in unfamiliar terrain. He had stopped his glide because Chug was no longer giving him a homing signal. It was like blind bats. They use echo location to avoid flying into walls. Calling me *dickhead* meant Chug was sending out a signal again. Lonnie was homing in on it, and I was going to have to get that damn Judas off in a hurry.

CHAPTER 5

The guy called George apparently thought he was the voice of reason, as far as that bunch went. "Hey, why don't you dickheads just clear out? We're going to have a little party is all. Not enough room for you, too."

He shot a glance at the girl as he said that bit about *not enough room for you, too*. I didn't like that. I didn't like to be called a *dickhead*, either. He must have picked up on how I felt.

"No reason to get worked up," he said. "Tootie here is a volunteer, right Tootie?"

He switched his gaze from the girl to Lonnie while he talked. He had to crane his head around Chug to do it.

I had gotten my shoulder up against the bus and was letting my arm hang down beside it. At least, that's how I hoped it looked. I was actually unzipping the leg of my pants. I always wore those pants where you could zip off the bottom and you've got shorts left. It made getting at my leg a lot easier.

Volunteer? That sounded too much like army talk. I had known guys like this in the army, and I didn't like them. They weren't soldiers, just thugs in uniform. And *volunteer* in army talk meant the exact opposite.

My eyes were adjusting to the natural dark and the unnatural truck lights. I could see the girl better now. I gave her a closer look. She was neither resisting nor resigned. She was there, and she wasn't there.

She had figured me for the lead dog on my team and was looking back at me, sizing me up, trying to see who I really was, what she could expect, the same way I was looking at her.

It wasn't a hopeful look. I had seen that look before, in the eyes of women in Iraq. They didn't think we were there to help them. They thought we were just waiting our turn to hurt them.

Every day children starved and women were raped, and I didn't do anything about them. I didn't usually even think about them. They were all over the world, and there was nothing I could do to help them. Sometimes, though, one of them was right in front of you, and you had to make a decision.

Or not. Not if Lonnie made it for you.

He was almost up to Chug, but he couldn't go any farther without an echo ping from that pony-tailed asshole.

I had gotten the zipper on my pants leg undone and had reached inside and gotten hold of the quick-release lever on my leg. I was ready. So I said it.

"What do you think, Chug? Your dick's probably too short to get inside of Tootie anyway, so what the hell difference does it make?"

It was sort of funny. All the way through high school and college locker rooms, all the way through four tours of Iraqistan, hotbeds of filthy language, ordinary and imaginative, I honored my commitment to Grandma. I never said a cuss word, never said a dirty word of any kind. My grandma always said that cussing was the refuge of those who couldn't think straight. She always told me that I was a straight thinker. Then came dealing with the damned VA, and I didn't think straight anymore.

Chug gave me a baleful look and started sputtering. That was all the sound Lonnie needed. He stepped up in front of Chug.

"Look at me, short dick," he said.

Chug glared. His eyes flamed. He wound up for an uppercut. I didn't know whether he was going to go for Lonnie's chin or his groin. I unlevered my leg and pulled out the PX4 Storm, the little Beretta. I figured one shot into the air would freeze the bunch and then I'd point the Storm at Chug, tell him to take his bunch and go, and that would be the end of it.

Oh, and I'd ask Tootie if she wanted to go or stay, and she would say that she would go with Chug and the gang, because she really was a volunteer, which wouldn't be true, but she was afraid of them, and would have to deal with them again sometime, and she knew she wouldn't get any lasting help from me, because all I had was this crappy bus, and I would be gone in the morning.

None of that took account of Lonnie.

Chug took a deep wheezing breath as he got his big fist with tattoos on the knuckles back into full throttle position. I guessed Lonnie had been waiting for him to get his mouth wide open. Or maybe closed. Either way, Lonnie read the wheeze. Then his hands were a blur. Palms open, they came at Chug's head so fast I really didn't see them. They smacked his ears like a couple of mule kicks.

I was pretty sure they blew his ear-drums out, because the last time I saw him, the George Costanza guy was shoving him into the back end of the pickup. I don't mean the back seat, but into the bed. Chug was howling like a banshee and holding his head. Costanza was going to have to drive and I didn't think he wanted to have to hear Chug howling in the seat behind him while he did it.

Costanza was the only one left to drive because the guys who had been pawing Tootie were out of action, too. They were barely able to crawl. While everybody was looking at Lonnie, Zan had moved around behind them. When Lonnie made his move, Zan made his, and crashed the heads of the Paws Brothers together with a move that would have made the linebackers coach yell *Why didn't you do that in the Ohio State game*? Actually, I think Zan *did* do it in the Ohio State game, but those guys were wearing helmets.

The Paws Brothers managed to get into the truck. Costanza put it into reverse, gunned it up the incline, and spun dirt in low gear while Chug continued to howl.

The light had changed. A big orange harvest moon had come up during that little bit of time that Chug and his bunch were there. In its glow, we looked like a little tableau of terra cotta soldiers in a cave.

We were all still, frozen exactly as we had been. Lonnie stood on the balls of his feet, with his legs spread just far enough for action balance, his arms down at his sides now. Zan was behind Tootie, in a linebacker stance. Tootie stood exactly as she had been, her arms at her side, her breasts sticking out like a couple of melons in the moonlight. I was standing there like a flamingo, on one leg, but leaning against the bus, an unused Beretta in my hand.

It seemed like we stood there a long time. I stuck the Beretta back into my leg, hooked it on, zipped my pants leg back on, hoping nobody would notice. Even Zan didn't know I carried heat in my leg. I could hear Lonnie breathing hard.

"You'd better put your boobs back in your shirt, miss."

It was Zan. I didn't know he could sound so polite.

Slowly, Tootie reached up behind her, unfastened her bra, got it down over her breasts, refastened, pulled her shirt down.

"What is your real name?"

It was Lonnie's rich baritone this time. The contrast made Zan's tenor sound higher than it really was.

"You can call me what you want."

She sounded even younger than I figured she was, but her voice was narrow, hard, flat.

"Let's call her Esther, like in the Bible," Zan said.

"You don't know anything about the Bible," I said.

It was irrelevant, and I didn't know why I said it, but this was Zan, and I was the one who was supposed to know something about the Bible.

"A lot of stuff has happened since we roomed together, Joe."

"Her name is *not* Esther," Lonnie said.

He turned in a little half-circle, hands out, palms up. I made a mental note to stay away from those palms. He made another half-circle. At first, I thought he was having trouble seeing in the dark. *Well, duh, he has trouble seeing in the light, too.* Then I realized he was appealing to Esther, a request for her real name.

"Are you blind?"

Her voice was a little fuller this time, but more like a little girl, too.

"No."

"Yes, he is. Blind as a bat," Zan said, sounding like he thought it was at least half-funny.

"He's not blind *as* a bat," I said. "He's blind *like* a bat. Sees things other people can't. It's just a different way of seeing."

I didn't want Lonnie getting mad again and popping Zan's ears.

"Actually, Esther is a nice name," I said, "but Lonnie would like to know your real name. That is, what you would like to be called."

Damn. I was sounding like that damned George, trying to placate everybody.

It had only been a little while since I had gotten away from PSAS, what the VA called *Prosthetic and Sensory Aids Service*, where they gave me the damn no-good artificial leg, vowing never to talk to anybody again. But I didn't have any place to go, so I went home.

It wasn't my home. It was my mother's home. It had never been my home, and it sure as hell wasn't now. I had stayed there just long enough to be reminded of why I had left in the first place. I hobbled out of there doubling my vow never to talk to anybody again.

Now here I was playing peace-maker again, trying to make everybody happy, just like I had in my family and on the football teams and even as a soldier. It had never worked. It was never going to work. But I kept doing it. It was some kind of perverse emotional addiction. I hated myself for it. For a bunch of other stuff, too.

I didn't give a damn about Lonnie. Or the girl. Or even Zan. I called him my best friend, but that was just because he was the only person in the world who might be a friend of any kind. And he was right: a whole lot had happened since we'd been roommates.

I didn't know what had happened to him, and he didn't know what had happened to me. All we had in common was in another time, another world. So why should I care?

"Rachel," she said.

"Rachel is a nice name," Lonnie said.

"Biblical, too. How come they called you *Tootie*?"

I wished Zan would leave well enough alone.

"I'll do anything with anybody for a toot."

She said it flat, like she didn't care, but she was just like me. She hated herself for it. And for a bunch of other stuff, too.

"If you've got food, though—it would be nice to eat before

we do it—I'm pretty hungry—can't pull a train on an empty stomach."

She tried to giggle when she said it, make it sound like she wasn't really asking for anything, just a bite to eat before she put out for everybody, nothing unusual, didn't want anybody beating on her because she was asking for too much.

I only cried at the good stuff—at whatever was just, whatever was pure, whatever was lovely—but I felt like crying then.

Lonnie did. He just sat down and bawled. Here was a guy with deadly hands, quite willing to injure a man permanently, bowing his head down and bawling, those deadly hands hanging at his sides.

"Aw, man," Zan said. He looked up at the moon. "Haven't you got supper ready yet, Joe?"

"Hey, I got interrupted."

"I didn't mean to—"

Zan and Rachel and I were all talking at once while Lonnie cried.

Zan went over, took Lonnie's hand, and started leading him over toward the hibachi.

"When I get that vest done, man, it'll be like you aren't even a bat. Little impulse here, little impulse there, you'll know exactly where to go, what to do."

Like that was what Lonnie was crying about. I knew enough psych to know that Rachel had triggered the tears, but that he was crying about a hell of a lot of stuff beyond her, even beyond his own blindness.

Hey, tears from blind eyes. Zan noticed them, too.

"At least his eyes work good for crying," he said to me.

Zan turned to look toward Rachel. She was standing where she had been, but I could see tears on her cheeks, too. Men usually cringed when women cried, but I figured that was a good sign.

"Hey, Rachel, come over here and give Lonnie a hand," Zan called to her. "I've got to get stuff out of the bus."

She was slow getting started, but then she began to trot and was almost running the last two or three steps.

"Here, hold old Lonnie in place," Zan said, passing Lonnie's hand over to her.

She stood beside him, holding his hand, both of them crying. Zan got into the back of the bus and got a camp lantern, our lawn chair, and little campstool. I got busy whipping up the hibachi coals and sorting out our strange assortment of plates and silverware.

"Joe's got to use the lawn chair," Zan said as he set things up, "because of his leg, and I have to sit on the campstool, because I'm crazy, so you two will have to sit on the ground."

That was interesting. It was the first time I'd heard Zan acknowledge that there was anything wrong with him. Normally, in his good spells, he acted like he didn't even know he had bad periods.

Besides, why should he get the stool just because he was crazy? It was sort of like Elijah in his contest with the priests of Baal. *You go first, because you are many.* There wasn't any reason they should go first just because they were *many*. Old Elijah was just setting them up for his big dramatic finish. I had studied all that once, and I tried to remember where it was. *The Book of Kings*, maybe? I wondered if Zan was setting us up for some big crazy showdown. That would be hard, sitting on a campstool.

Rachel accepted it, though. She sat down on the ground, pulled Lonnie down beside her. I got the food and the plates organized. Zan passed everything out. Lonnie had trouble getting the food to his mouth. I thought maybe he was still choked up. Then I realized he was eating with his left hand, so that he could keep his arm in touch with Rachel's while she ate with her right hand.

I felt good. Rachel was beginning to understand that we were different. We weren't going to gangbang her. We were going to help her. Then reality finally found its way into my brain.

Hell, we weren't going to help her. If we stuck her on that bus and took her with us, some state cop someplace would stop us and arrest us for transporting an underage girl across state lines for immoral purposes.

My best hope was that it would be in Illinois and they'd put us in the governors' wing at Joliet, or wherever it was they jailed all their ex-governors.

But I'd been in the army. That was jail enough for one lifetime.

Besides, what help would we be? She needed things we'd never be able to give her, like sanity, and a home, and an education, and years of post-molestation psychiatry.

As I watched her sit there, though, cross-legged, her arm brushing Lonnie's, I knew we weren't different, anyway, not in her mind. We were just more guys. She didn't recognize some great goodness in us. For one thing, of course, we weren't that much different from other men. The main thing, though, was that she wasn't different, either, just because she was with us.

She did whatever the men she was with required of her. If they wanted sex, she gave it. If they wanted comfort, she gave it. She would go down to the river and wash the dishes if I asked her to. She had no self.

That was the way I felt after Becky Garlits dumped me. My self was all in her. Becky—

Damn. I didn't want to think about her, but...

I sat there, spooning lukewarm beans into my mouth, and looked at our pathetic little tableau in the light of that big harvest moon. Zan was content. Banging the heads of those guys together seemed to have cleared his. Lonnie and Rachel were content, just sitting together, listening to each other crunch corn chips.

I listened to the water in the river, going someplace, not caring where, just flowing. That was me. I didn't have a self anyway.

So we ate supper. Then we all looked at one another and, without a word, we packed up, and somehow the bus climbed the hill, and Rachel directed us to a house along the highway, where she got out. She didn't say it was home. It was just where she got out of the bus. I watched her go into the house. Zan put the bus into gear.

What happened there, at the river, with Rachel, it was just another battle in a war as long as history. In war, you fought a battle and forgot it and went on, waiting for the next fight. Forgot it? Yeah, maybe your brain did, but your heart didn't.

CHAPTER 6

We didn't get any help at the Danville VA. Instead, we got Victoria. And her perennially full bladder.

This sort-of-black woman just got on the bus and sat down beside Lonnie.

I'd seen worse-looking woman, but I couldn't remember when. No hair. Skin that was pink in places, and at least two shades of brown in other spots. Also, I was sure I had seen better figures, but I couldn't remember those, either. The stuff that was covered up with jeans and a long-sleeved shirt just took my breath away. So did her face and head and hands, the parts that weren't covered, but for a different reason.

"This isn't a public bus, ma'am," I told her.

"I know," she said.

She just kept sitting there. She was coiled tight, but not uptight. She looked like she was used to fighting and surviving.

"We don't know where we're going," I said.

"I know," she said.

"We don't have any…facilities…for a woman."

"I know."

Zan would probably have thrown her off, but he was down with a migraine, rolling around on the floor in the back of the bus, holding his head.

She just sat there beside Lonnie and held his hand. Lonnie was beaming, the way he always did around women. What if he could really see her, I mean with his eyes?

Well, what was it to me? With Zan down, I had to worry about driving the bus. I just shrugged my shoulders, got behind the wheel, and started up Illinois 1 past a sign that said Rossville and Hoopeston were places up ahead where people had memories and hopes—places for us to pass on through.

My hesitation about Victoria wasn't because she was mostly black. I had nothing against black people, even though I grew up in Indiana's deep south "pocket," what I called "The Mississippi of the North." If you'd played football or been a soldier, all you cared about was the color of the uniform, not the color of the skin.

I liked to think of myself as a man who liked everyone, regardless of race—except for terrorists, and politicians, and bankers, and motorcycle riders, and lobbyists, and hunters, and gun nuts, and preachers, and casino operators, and cops, and radio talk show hosts, and brewers of light beer, and child abusers, and school bus manufacturers, and Pentagon politicians, and civilian contractors, and the GDVA, and doctors, and lawyers, and relatives—except grandmas—and anyone on TV, except for the beautiful semi-black women who keep popping up on the news channels.

Victoria, however, wasn't one of those beautiful semi-black women, like you see on TV. She might have been once, but the fire when she was trapped in that Humvee had done her a lot of damage.

If she'd been in a Rhino Runner, like Haliburton built for Rumsfeld to ride around in when he came to tell us how we were winning the war by being so lean and mean that we were going backward every day, she might have been okay. In a regular Humvee, no way.

All I knew when she got on the bus was that she had no hair, and she had brown skin some places, with lots of garish pink splotches, but she had a figure that yelled *Woman*!

Lonnie couldn't see her, though, He just grinned when she sat down beside him and took his hand. That Lonnie was the only guy I ever knew who was literally a chick magnet. I mean, he was the North Pole for women. He had been grinning ever since Victoria got on the bus.

Zan had finished up the controls in Lonnie's vest as we drove down 150 to Danville. Now, before we even got to Hoopeston, Lonnie had told Victoria all about his remote-controlled buffalo-plaid vest like he had thought it up.

She started carrying the controller all the time. Whenever we got out of the bus, she practiced with it, sending Lonnie up to within an inch of a tree or a rock and then veering him off just in time. Lonnie acted like it was the greatest game ever.

Zan had gone through one of his headaches. It had wiped out the memory of what he had created. Now he thought that Lonnie was some sort of shaman, able to see without eyes. I reminded him of what he had done with the vest, but he just looked at me like we were in some sort of science fiction comic book and I was the alien.

Lonnie and Victoria together were damned good at making it look like Lonnie could see, and he didn't have to use echolocation, but it worried me. I didn't expect Victoria to stick around. I didn't know anything about her, but I never expected a woman to stick around. Lonnie had done pretty well just relying on blind man's bluff, that ESP ability he had. If he got to relying on a woman who was bound to leave, well, his "last state would be worse than his first,"

Our first state had been Indiana, which was bad enough. Now we were in Michigan's Upper Peninsula, the UP, which was about as bad a state as you could be in, so I was hoping it wouldn't be our last.

Okay, apologies to Jesus for changing the context of that statement about "states," but *out of context* is about the only way Jesus was ever quoted. It was a good thing I didn't believe in Jesus anymore, or I'd have to be apologizing to him all the time.

Now here we were in the UP, heading back down for East Lansing, maybe, where Michigan State had whupped up on us once or twice upon a time, driving away from yet another VA hospital, the one in Iron Mountain. We had angled up through Illinois to Rockford, then angled back east through Wisconsin to Green Bay, and on up to Iron Mountain.

We hadn't scored any medicine at the VA in Iron Mountain, either. The doc had been sympathetic. He wasn't a Patel, but he was new enough to think the purpose of a VA hospital was to help vets. He was also new enough that he didn't want to buck the system. Or else he was scared of something. We'd had a strange sort of conversation.

At least no one new got on the bus this time. *Thank goodness*, as my grandma always said. "Methodists don't say *Thank God*. We say *thank goodness*." That's exactly what Grandma used to say.

I did believe in Grandma, so I still had to apologize a lot.

I guessed I should apologize to the UP, too, even though the people called themselves Yoopers. It was a beautiful place, even in the winter, which was fourteen months long every year. It was just that, after being too hot for too long, I had no desire to replace "too hot" with "too cold."

I should have apologized to Victoria, too, for lusting after her, but I was sure I wasn't the first guy to do so. She really did have a figure. I couldn't even remember when Victoria told us her name. Some place between Hoopeston, Illinois, and Crivitz, Wisconsin, I thought.

As soon as Zan found out her last name was Roundtree, he smirked to me, "A woman should never have a name that includes *round*, because some juvenile wit will call her Roundass, which is what we should call Victoria. That broad's built like a brick shithouse."

"That's impolite," I said. "The proper term is *outhouse*, and *built like one* originally referred to an ungainly girl, not a voluptuous one."

"I apologize," Zan said. "It is your brain that is built like a brick shithouse."

That was sort of fun, sort of like being back in our room in Bloomington, back in the locker room. It definitely was juvenile, but what could I say? What could you expect out of deformed ex-jocks? Neither one of us said anything like that in front of Victoria or Lonnie, of course.

CHAPTER 7

I now used the concrete pig or bear or whatever it was at Moe's Eat and Get Gas as a weathervane and made sure I got Zan started the right way this time. He was so busy popping a Leinie and enjoying drinking and driving that he didn't notice we were going back from Moe's convenience store the same way we had come. I wanted to be sure we didn't encounter the Lincoln. I didn't want to run into those uglies again. They would need medical attention, but they would have had their own ways of getting it. Those guys were the type to have more guns in their SUV and wounded they might be even more lethal.

I had seen a road back a few miles, with a sign for a place called Felch. I figured we could go east there and eventually cut a highway that would take us south to US 2 on a different road from anything the Lincoln would use. Hell, if we had gone the right way out of Iron Mountain in the first place, we would never have had to deal with them. I had shot two men and Lonnie and Victoria had disabled another one just because we were on the wrong road. That had happened too often in Iraqistan, killing people just because they were on the wrong road. I didn't feel as bad this time as I had back then, though.

We got down to the sign to Felch, made the turn, and started through even more trees than we had been in.

"I never got to pee," Victoria said.

I glanced at Zan. The Leinie was no longer in evidence. He had gone into full paranoia mode, driving hunched over, scanning the roadside, looking for IEDs.

"Do it out the back door," I said to Victoria.

"I'm no man," she said, her voice flat.

"I've noticed," Lonnie giggled.

Oh, shit, I've got a pisser and a giggler and a psychotic.

But Victoria went to the back of the bus. I didn't look back. I was worried about Zan driving in paranoid mode with a can of beer and a load of adrenaline in him. Or did he have adrenaline worked up? He had been MIA back there when the action started.

I heard Victoria open the door. It stayed that way for a long time, so I guess she accomplished whatever she needed to.

She came back to her seat with Lonnie. Zan kept driving. I just sat there, looking at pines and birches, wishing I was looking at the maples around the stadium in Bloomington on a Saturday afternoon.

I didn't know how much time had passed when Lonnie said, "I've heard that voice before. The guy who told the woman to take her shirt off at Moe's."

So what? My adrenaline was long gone, and I didn't care to hear about Lonnie's super powers. He was just trying to make up for being left out of the action.

"Yeah, great," I said.

So what? Lonnie heard voices. It was what blind people did.

"Back at the VA hospital in Iron Mountain. That's where I heard it."

CHAPTER 8

Zan began to swerve from side to side, all the way from one shoulder to the other. I wasn't too worried, because we hadn't seen a car for five minutes, but that was the thing about roads like that: everybody assumed there was nobody else on the road so they could drive any way they wanted.

"What's wrong?" I asked.

"Just taking evasive action," he muttered.

"You think this will impress the deer?"

He didn't answer, just kept swerving and looking for IEDs.

"Maybe I should drive, so you can concentrate on the Leinies," I said.

"Good idea," he said.

Beer always seemed to temper Zan's paranoia.

I was hoping he would wait for one of those little roadside parks, where you pull clear off the highway onto a little side road that puts you behind a stand of trees, where they have a drinking fountain and a couple of outhouses. That way I could have plenty of time to adjust my leg. But he swerved onto the shoulder, or what passed for a shoulder, as though it were an emergency. He jumped up and got into the second seat with the Leininkugels.

"Anybody want another?" he asked. "No point in letting it get hot."

One thing about Zan, he was always generous with his beer.

Victoria, though, was already out the back door and headed into the woods. She had been antsy the whole time we had been on the road since Moe's Eat and Get Gas place.

"Do you think she's okay?" Lonnie said.

"Doesn't like being cooped up in here," I said. "Those guys back there brought up bad memories for her."

It didn't occur to me that she might actually have to pee. I figured the stop at Moe's was a ruse just so she could get out of the bus. And what had she done out the back of the bus? Probably just hung her head out so she wouldn't feel like she was in an old school bus. Or in a burning Hummer.

After all, if she had really needed to pee when we encountered the mercenary goons at Moe's, she would have done it in her pants when the shooting started. Or maybe not. She was a vet, after all. We never got scared. Hell, no. Not in the present, anyway, only in the past and the future.

Zan was only on his second Leinie of this stop when Victoria reappeared from the woods, pulling up her jeans. I guess maybe she really did have to pee. She hung around outside until I had my leg adjusted and actually had the motor going before she hopped back on, though.

The sun was throwing dappled patterns onto the pavement through the birches. Dark would be coming on pretty soon. I didn't know where those mercenaries were headed. Just because they went north originally didn't mean they wanted to. That might have been a feint. They were the kind of guys who wouldn't take kindly to what happened to them, especially in front of witnesses. Wounded, they would be even more dangerous. We couldn't outrun them, but we could hide.

Also, it was pretty sure the people at Moe's convenience store would call the sheriff, despite what I said. He would get the state smokies onto it. Someone would mention a school bus and the misfits on it who did some shooting. They would put out an APB or BOLO or whatever they called it now on both the sixteen and the bus. It was probably easier for UP cops to find an old school bus than a black SUV. Hell, every second vehicle in the UP was a black SUV.

I saw a sign that said *Sliver Lake*. It was not a regular Michigan DOT sign. It was old and beat-up, but had a sort of rustic wooden fading charm. A lake would be a good place to camp, a good place to set up a defense. Nobody was paying any attention, so I took the turn.

We hadn't gone very far when the road began to narrow.

Then it became dirt. Soon the weeds were high and brushing the sides of the bus. There wasn't any place to turn around. I sure as hell couldn't back the monster all the way back to the highway. I just had to keep on keeping on. The woods and the dusk closed in on us.

I heard a clunk. I looked into the rearview mirror. Zan had fallen into the aisle and was rolling around, clutching his head.

"Shoot me," he wailed. "Somebody just shoot me."

Victoria pulled out a Glock. Hell, I had forgotten she still had the guns of the uglies.

"Victoria, no!" I shouted at the rearview mirror.

She grabbed the barrel and gave Zan a firm whack on the head with the butt. It had the desired effect. Zan shut up.

I breathed a sigh of relief, almost. What had I gotten into? I didn't know a thing about Victoria except that she had been caught in a burning Humvee, knew some hand-to-hand combat and how to give orders to clean up a mess, and that she had to pee a lot. What if she had actually shot Zan?

The road began to widen again then, though, and I saw some buildings up ahead in the gathering dark. I wasn't sure that was a good thing. I just wanted a camping spot, not people. People meant telephones, and contact with the cops, and...

It was a ghost town. Abandoned. No people, no cars, but a real town. A main street, with commercial buildings, and a couple of side streets with houses, and a big barny building at the end of the main street. I didn't see any utility poles, though. Some buildings weren't exactly in bad shape, but there were drooping shutters, and it looked like only two or three of them had ever had paint. There were weeds in the streets, and saplings were peeking into the back windows of the buildings on the outside streets.

There was light in a window of a building on the main street. A fading sign had once said the building was a hotel.

I pulled up in front of it and stopped, mostly because there wasn't any place else to go, and I was tired, and...who cared?

Victoria jumped up, goose-stepped over the wheezing form of Zan, pulled him down the aisle toward the back end, pushed the back door open, and jumped down.

"Give me a hand back here," she yelled.

I heaved myself out of the driver's seat, picked up my leg, almost fell off the bus, got mad at my leg and threw it aside, leaned against the bus, and hopped down its length to the end.

Lonnie got off, got disoriented some way, started wandering off toward the other end of the street.

"Back here," I yelled at him.

He started back toward us, like a blind man would. It was the first time I had seen him that way. He had been so sure of himself back there at Moe's, knowing just what to do and when to do it, even without his sight, maybe because he was blind. But now he was wearing his vest, and he had assumed Victoria would direct him, but she was busy trying to slap Zan awake.

"I shouldn't have hit him so hard," she said. "I didn't mean to. He was in a lot of pain. We might give him a pill, if you've got anything, an aspirin or something, but that's probably counter-indicated after the head whack. Hell, I hope I didn't give him a concussion."

With me it would have been babbling, but with Victoria, it was thinking out loud in a rational way. I thought about what she had done back at that convenience store, and I looked at Victoria in a new way. She wasn't just a great figure inside of burned skin. She had a brain and knew how to use it.

Only Zan's head was outside the bus.

"Let's get him all the way outside," she said.

She started tugging. I leaned up against the bus and tried to help her get Zan out without falling down myself. Lonnie came up from behind and bumped into me. I lurched forward, tried to use Zan for support, which was stupid, since he was suspended in midair. Victoria was on Zan's other side, and my lurch knocked her down onto her butt. She was still trying to hold Zan up, though. That didn't keep me from falling on him and forcing him on down onto her. I felt a weight on my back and knew that Lonnie had come up and fallen on us, too.

"My God, the circus has come to town, but all they brought were the clowns."

I managed a sideways peek from above Zan and Victoria and under Lonnie.

There stood a petite woman with an old-fashioned kerosene

lantern, held high. I was surprised at the lantern, then realized it was pretty damned dark down in among the tall pines, with the sun already down below their top line.

The woman was blonde, maybe fifty, not much more than five feet, a pageboy haircut, a blue chambray shirt, blue jeans, snowy white running shoes, and glasses on a woven leather lanyard hanging around her neck.

"Ma'am," I said, "Could you help us get un-piled, please? One of us has a head injury, but I'm not sure anymore who it is."

Lonnie used me as a pushup board and went up so fast the little blonde woman jumped back.

"Lonnie Blifield at your service," he said, looking where her voice had been, but where she wasn't anymore.

"Mr. Blifield," she said, "the next one down has only one leg. Can we get him up?"

"Oh, yeah. He's better on one leg than most men on two. But wait a minute...where's your leg, Joe?"

"Back beside the bus. I'd be obliged, ma'am, if you could get it for me..."

Then I remembered that I had put the Beretta back into Judas.

"No, Lonnie, you get my leg. I'd better explain us to..."

"Barbara," the woman said. "Barbara Occam-Roberts."

Lonnie didn't want to leave the women but he didn't want to admit he couldn't find my leg on his own, either, so he started off.

"Barbara Occam-Roberts? The novelist?"

In the lantern light, Victoria's eyes lit up like fireflies down home. I looked around, as best I could in my position on top of the body pile. I didn't see any lightning bugs, but it would be too late in the year for them. I was pretty sure we were too far north for them, though, even in the good old summer time.

"Guilty as charged," the blonde woman said.

"Oh, Ms. Occam-Roberts, your novels got me through some tough times."

"Barbara, please. Occam-Roberts is too much of a mouthful. And it looks like you're still in tough times, down there at the bottom of the pile."

She set the lantern down, got hold of my arm, and began to pull. I braced my one knee on Zan's back and together we got me up to where I could lean against the bus.

Victoria's face did something I had never seen before. It went into a smile, a big one, showing surprisingly nice, even white teeth.

I had not realized that she barely opened her mouth, even to talk. The smile went out quickly, though, and she looked away in a way that was almost girlish in its shyness.

"Oh, Ms. Occam—I mean, Barbara, you can't believe what an honor it is to meet you."

Victoria's voice was taking on some quality I had not heard before. I had heard the name of Occam-Roberts, but I had never read any of her stuff. Victoria, though, was obviously a fan.

"Oh, for heaven's sake," Barbara said. "It's an *honor* to meet Michele Obama or Oprah. All I do is write novels. It's only a *pleasure* to meet me, and sometimes even that is in doubt."

Victoria smiled again. "Oh, you talk just like you write. That's the voice I heard when I read *Fishing On the Moon*."

"I can hear fishy voices really close by."

It was Zan's groaning voice from under me. Good. He was coming around, and he sounded rational.

Lonnie reappeared with Judas. I leaned against the bus and got it on, keeping the gun out of sight. Barbara and Lonnie managed to get Zan off of Victoria, who scrambled up like a wrestler.

"If you need something to eat, come on in. I can rustle something up."

"Begging your pardon, ma'am," Zan said, "but that's dangerous, inviting strangers in. We might be a band of outlaws."

Barbara Occam-Roberts looked us over, all five feet of her.

"Oh, I could beat the crap out of all of you," she said. "Besides, it will be more interesting if you're outlaws. *Are* you outlaws?" she said.

"Only if you count shooting people as unlawful, and only Joe does that."

Zan was back into rational mode with a vengeance, and now I wasn't sure that was good. I didn't want anybody talking to a stranger about shooting. I needed to get us into something else in a hurry.

"Ma'am, please pay no attention to Albert Zander. We call him Zan. I think you've been introduced officially only to Lonnie. Your fan here is Victoria Roundtree, and I'm Joe Kirk. We actually *are* a bunch of outlaws, but we never do harm to someone who feeds us."

"That's good enough for me," she said, turning back toward the hotel building. "I hope you like breakfast for supper. What I've got is bread for toast, and bacon, and I can scramble eggs."

We followed the bobbing kerosene lantern like a bunch of puppies. The idea of eating real food inside a real building, maybe even at a real table, had us all in a jolly mood. She flipped some switches.

"There's a generator out back, so I have electricity in here. There's none outside, though, so I use the lantern there."

The old hotel wasn't exactly a hotel anymore. The first floor had been turned into a huge one-room apartment. One front corner was obviously Barbara's writing area—three file cabinets, two desks, a big table with papers all over it, two computers, a printer. The other front corner was her reading area—two recliners, a floor lamp, book cases clear to the ceiling, stacks of books and magazines on the floor. One back corner had a big double bed, and the other back corner was a modern kitchen with a drop-leaf table.

"You guys make that table out bigger and set it. Leaves are underneath. Plates and silverware are in that sideboard. Victoria and I will rustle up the grub."

She elbowed Victoria and said, "Men like it when you talk about grub."

Barbara smiled. She didn't even seem to notice Victoria's odd appearance and, in the older woman's presence, Victoria seemed to be totally unaware of it, too.

The two of them worked in the kitchen, jabbering like old friends. I was real happy for Victoria. I felt a little bit lonely myself. I didn't think toast and bacon sandwiches, with scrambled eggs, ever tasted so good. We scarfed up everything before us with gusto and gladness. Then we just sat, satisfied to be there, at a real table, indeed. Then I asked the question that had to be asked. "That sign out on the highway, that says Sliver Lake. That's supposed to be Silver Lake, right?"

"Oh, no. There are Silver Lakes all over the place. There is just a little sliver of lake here, so my father thought the name should fit the place. I think when it was a logging camp, before he bought it, it was just Forest Camp Number 9, or some such."

"Your father bought the whole town?" Victoria asked.

"Yes, but it's not as grand as it sounds. I was just a girl, so I don't know the details. It was abandoned. He thought he could turn it into a tourist attraction, and lost the family fortune, which wasn't much to begin with, in the process. I inherited it, but I can't sell it, so I come up here to write. I always think the remote location will give me the isolation and inspiration I need to write, and it does, but it gets sort of lonely some times."

She did something with her hands that I didn't understand. Victoria did some sort of hand signal back at her.

"What the hell is that all about?" I said.

"Girl talk," Barbara said. "We found out while we were cooking that we both know sign language."

"I thought you only knew the symbol for *P*," I said to Victoria.

"I can do all of American sign language," Victoria said. "I can read lips, too. My little brother is deaf. And don't curse in front of Ms. Oc—I mean, Barbara."

"Hey, she's the one who said *crap,* when she threatened to beat it out of us. All I said was *hell*."

It was so surreal, vets arguing about which words are more profane. Surreal or not, it felt good, just people sitting around with full stomachs, taking it easy.

"You said you come *up* here, to write," I said, "which means you are usually some place that's *down*."

"Every place is *down* compared to the UP. I live in Indianapolis most of the time. My husband just couldn't take the winters up here."

"Indiana," Zan mused. "Joe is from Indiana. Played football at IU."

Barbara's mouth literally dropped. "I knew there was something wrong with you," she said. "I was a cheerleader at Purdue."

I usually shoot anyone when I hear they are from Purdue, but it would be hard to get my Beretta out, sitting at the table. Also, there was the sadness around her eyes. She worked hard at being upbeat. I got the impression that *upbeat* was her default setting, but there was something else, too, forlorn little lambs looking up and out from the corners of her blue eyes.

Besides, I was too busy trying to figure out Zan to waste a bullet on a Purdue girl. Had he actually forgotten that he was from Indiana, too, that he had played at IU, too, that he had started every game while I rode the bench? Was his brain getting worse? Did that whack from Victoria do some new damage? Did I really need to take him to a VA hospital and leave him, *require* somebody to do something about him? I didn't think I could do that. Better to die fast outside the system than to die slow inside it.

I watched him out the corner of my eye. Everything seemed okay, or at least okay by Zan standards.

"Sliver Lake is such a beautiful name," Victoria sighed. "I wish we could stay here forever."

I was thinking the same thing myself, until dawn, when the Indians attacked.

CHAPTER 9

Sort of a late dawn.
After supper, everybody was tired. Somehow Zan and Victoria ended up in the kitchen together, doing the dishes, which was an interesting combination to watch. Zan washed and Victoria dried. Zan whistled while he worked and tried to wash fast enough so that Victoria could not keep up. Victoria glared at him but otherwise didn't acknowledge his presence. Once again I wished I had never let Victoria stay on the bus. She and Zan were never going to get along.

Soldiers needed a unit. In battle it was the only thing that mattered. Vets didn't have that unit anymore. We'd lost it one way or another and, most often, it was a bad way. We wanted a new unit, needed it bad, but were afraid of it, for fear we'd lose it again. So we found something wrong with the others, so we would not get too close to them. That was what was working on Zan and Victoria. Or maybe not. Hell, what did I know?

I knew I liked Barbara's coffee. Lonnie and I chatted with Barbara at the table and finished up the exceptionally good coffee she had brewed. I felt bad about draining the pot into my cup without offering to share with Lonnie. I felt good drinking the coffee, though.

Lonnie turned on his charm, the way he always did in the presence of women. Part of charming a woman was to get her to talk about herself. Lonnie did that, of course, in his usual way, which was to tell Barbara all about herself even though he had never met her. She fell for it for a little while, because it was a damn good parlor trick, but then her writer gears clicked in. She wanted our story.

"Never associate with writers," Grandma used to say. "The ink-stained wretches always want to find out your secrets so they can put them down on paper. Then everybody knows them."

Grandma obviously did not live in the present age, when writers had swipe-finger instead of ink stains, and the secrets were on screens instead of paper, and they were not secret from the spies that lurked in the ether out there.

"But Grandma," I would protest, "you read all the time."

"It's good to know other people's secrets," Grandma would say. "Just don't let them know yours."

"Ms. Occam-Roberts," I said, "you have been exceptionally hospitable, and you deserve answers to your questions, but I'm so beat from driving that bus with one leg, and Zan had one of his headaches today, and…"

I went on so long about what a rough day we all had, without saying anything about the incident at Moe's, that Zan and Victoria were able to finish the dishes, and Barbara was looking like she knew I was giving her the run-around.

"However," I went on, "tomorrow morning it will be our turn to treat you to breakfast, and we'll be rested…"

"And you'll have had time to think up some stuff to tell me and confer with each other to be sure your stories are straight," Barbara finished. "Well, that's okay. You're wrong about owing me answers. Hospitality doesn't create debtors, just friends. But seeing as how you're all so worn out, we'd better figure out where you can spend the night."

"Oh, that's no problem, ma'am," Zan put in. "We've got sleeping quarters all fixed up in our bus."

I had never thought of the floor of the aisle between the seats or my board as "quarters," but Barbara looked relieved, like she hadn't really known what to do with us, and nobody else protested, so we said goodnight and trooped out to the bus.

"If you think I'm going to spend the night on this contraption when there are a whole lot of nice empty buildings around here, you've got another think coming," Victoria muttered when we got to the bus.

"Me, too," Lonnie said.

So that's why they had not protested sleeping in the bus.

They weren't going to anyway. They were going to spend the night together. When had they thought that up?

Well, hell, why not? Why shouldn't they spend the night together, and why should I care what they did? Except it made me feel even more alone. And I felt guilty when I said to myself that it was good that Lonnie was blind or else he would never have taken off with a woman who looked like Victoria. And since he was so tuned into what other women looked like even when he couldn't see them, how come he didn't see what she really looked like? Probably because he'd used some braille on her and after that nothing else mattered.

Lonnie and Victoria headed off down the main street. Zan just got into his sleeping bag and started snoring. I was left sitting in the first seat, thinking. I got cold and rummaged around until I found an old IU sweatshirt that Becky Garlits had bought me because she didn't know that only fans, not athletes, wore that sort of stuff. It made me feel warmer and colder at the same time.

The light in the writing corner of Barbara Occam-Roberts' hotel-cum-hideaway was still on when I finally got my sleeping bag and took it to the other side of the street, on the porch of what looked like it had been a general store. I took my leg off and crawled into the bag. It was cold, and I didn't think I could get to sleep, but that was the last thing I remembered thinking before I woke up with an odd feeling, like I was still in a dream story.

The story must have involved birds. I could still hear them, calls far enough away that they seemed like memories. I didn't recognize them, which didn't surprise me. I wasn't a bird guy. Get beyond crows, geese, and doves and I had no clue.

Gray morning light was beginning to slide into a paler shade, like a woman in plumber's overalls trying on a wedding dress. Through my grogginess I remembered that last night I had promised Barbara we would treat her to breakfast. I was thinking about which beans to open to go with the Spam when I noticed that the light was on in the kitchen area of her place. Last night she had fixed real coffee in one of those dripolator things. I wondered if maybe she was there in her kitchen even now, fixing real coffee. I got my leg on so that I could go see.

I was just stepping up onto the boardwalk at her front door when it opened. Barbara looked exactly like she had the night before, except she was wearing a Purdue sweatshirt.

"Eeek," she shrieked.

Women often do that when they see me, but they are not usually carrying a cup of coffee, which flies up into the air when they shriek and arches toward me. I tried to bat it away. That did a lot of good. Most of the coffee got through my defenses, but I did manage to catch the cup.

Barbara recovered fast. "Oh, I'm so sorry, but you scared the liver out of me."

"No problem," I said. "I was hoping to get coffee from you."

"Well, you got it. I was just on my way to find you. I thought you might be caffeine-ready this morning. At least you've got cream with your crimson."

She laughed a little, looking at the fading cream-colored block Indiana across the front of the crimson shirt. That's one of the Purdue songs they use to taunt IU people, singing the IU fight song as "We shall fight for our cream and coffee," instead of the proper "We shall fight for the cream and crimson." Of course, we sing "Moo, Moo, Purdue," so it evens out.

"Come on in and I'll fill that up for you again."

I limped in after her. I wondered just why I was the one she had come looking for. The others liked coffee, too. I looked at the cup. It said, "Writers are better at describing how to be better lovers."

She filled the cup up. "You took it black last night, so I guess…"

"Black is beautiful," I said.

"Speaking of that, I'm embarrassed to ask, and Victoria is such a nice woman…"

"Not to mention your number one fan," I said.

"That does give her extra credence, but…"

"Humvee explosion," I said. "And fire following. That's about all I know. Zan and I were roommates in college, but we hadn't seen each other for five years when we teamed up again a couple of weeks ago, by accident. That's how we got Lonnie and Victoria, too, by accident. We're all vets, that's all I know for sure, and that's about all we have in common. Now let me ask you something."

She waited, the corners of her mouth turning up ever so slightly.

"Why did you really take us in last night, and give us supper? The first thing you did was invite us in. You didn't even blink. Victoria looks like…well, you know, and the rest of us aren't much better. A woman here alone, you really should be more careful. Except you seemed to know…"

She looked into some distant place. I could see the sad places in the corners of her eyes, even sadder in the weak dawn light. She shivered, wrapped her arms around herself, stepped back through the door. I followed her and closed the door against the chill.

"I know who you are," she said. "As soon as I saw you. Just…"

I thought she was going to cry, but she straightened her shoulders and went on.

"I had two sons. Harlan I still have. Michael was a pharmacist and proud to be a member of the National Guard. He was going to get married when he got back from Iraq. Instead he came back home in a body bag, and Bush and Cheney wouldn't even give him the honor of showing his flag-draped coffin when he finally got home." Her voice trailed off as she turned her face back toward me. "I know who you are. I knew as soon as I saw you…"

I waited, but she didn't say any more.

"You're very generous to us," I said, "considering how you must hate us."

"Yes, I do, and I hate myself for hating you, and I hate the war and the government. But maybe Michael is the lucky one. Poor Victoria—And Lonnie, so gallant, and so blind. Zan is so crazy—and you're…"

I really wanted to know what she was going to say about me, but she didn't get to finish. The door opened quickly. Lonnie came through in more of a rush that he intended. Victoria was pushing him.

"There's something funny going on out there," she said.

"Bird calls," Lonnie said. "But they aren't birds."

Barbara Occam-Roberts opened her mouth to say something, but she didn't even get started that time, because that was when the Indians attacked.

It started with the face at the window.

It was Victoria who let out the *eeek* this time. She was looking toward Barbara's writing corner. There at the window, in the semi-light of dawn, was a hawk-beaked face covered with war paint.

Then all hell broke loose. There was shrieking and yelling and drumming and the beating of hooves. Something thudded into the front of the building, followed by another.

"That was an arrow," Lonnie said.

I pushed Barbara down behind the counter that separated the kitchen from the rest of the room.

"Don't—" she started, but that was as far as she got.

I think it must have been my leg that stopped her. She was right down at knee level, and I was getting pretty good at zipping my pants leg off, so all of a sudden there it was, right in her eyes, my artificial leg, which is really just a bunch of metal rods. And that ugly stump. Barbara had seen Judas but not my stump. It's a shock to see a stump. I suspect it's an even bigger shock to see a Beretta with it.

"Those sound more like snares than war drums," Lonnie said.

Victoria was looking out the front window.

"Come here, Joe," she yelled.

I grabbed the Beretta and took the time to snap my leg back into place and trotted up to the window. I could move pretty fast on Judas if I ignored the pain and the way I looked. I peered out the glass over Victoria's head.

They were Indians all right, in war paint and feathers that looked authentic. Also sweatshirts, blue jeans, and running shoes that didn't exactly look like original Ojibwa garb. Lonnie was right. The guy with the drum had a sparkly blue snare that looked like it was right out of a high school marching band. It was slung around his shoulder. A couple of them were riding horses up and down the street on either side of the bus and shrieking. They weren't riding Indian style, though. They were atop Western saddles. Most of them were just milling around and yelling, but one was down on his knee with a bow and arrow and taking aim on Barbara's place.

"That asshole!"

Not a very nice thing for a pretty writer to say.

Barbara was up from where I had pushed her down in the kitchen and out the front door, yelling at the guy with the bow and arrow.

"Outhouse, you turd. I'd have your balls on my mantle for this, if you still had any."

She shook her fist at him. He took aim with his bow. She beat a hasty retreat back inside.

"That's Ernest Althaus. He couldn't hit where he aims with that contraption, but he's got Parkinson's, so he might hit me by accident. Calls himself some sort of chief, White Knife, or something like that. Ought to be Yellow Streak, or Yellow Stream. He thinks they can scare me off, that—"

Her words were getting faster, and her voice was getting louder, but I lost the rest of what she said in the general noise from the street. I was sure, though, it was not complimentary.

"The natives are restless," Lonnie observed, smiling, very pleased with himself.

Several of those natives began to pull stuff out of backpacks and canvas bags. They threw the stuff on the street between us and the bus.

I'd always had exceptional eyesight. It was one of the things that made me a good high-school quarterback. Would have made me a good college quarterback, too, if it hadn't been for stupid coaches and Quint Rosten, who beat me out for the position, and beat my time with Becky Garlits. Even in the dim light, I could read the names on the bags—Bay College, Super 1, Snowbound Books. I could also see that the stuff on the pile was paperback books, but I couldn't read the titles on them. The pile was getting pretty big.

One of the Indians had a torch. Not the electric kind, the way the Brits say, but a burning firebrand thing, like the peasants carry when they're storming the castle.

Somebody had a red can of something. He poured it over the pile. Barbara's eyes were even better than mine. She could read the words on the things they were throwing onto the pile. Or else she knew from past experience. "They're burning my books, the Philistine turds," she yelled.

The guy with the torch touched it to the pile and jumped back. Barbara's books exploded and started to burn.

That was too much for Victoria. She was through the front door faster than…something that was real fast.

"How dare you savages burn the books of one of the great writers of our times?" she screamed.

It sounded so droll, so old-fashioned, calling them savages, especially from Victoria, who looked pretty savage herself.

It definitely had an effect on the Indians, though. I suspected it was Victoria's looks more than her words that made them start backing up.

The torch guy stepped back along with everyone else, right up against the bus, and suddenly the bus was a huge pyre of fire.

That's when Victoria really went bonkers.

"Zan's trapped in the bus," she screamed.

She took off for the front door of the bus, realized the fire and the crowd were in the way, reversed direction like a running back cutting away from the tacklers, headed for the rear door of the bus, was confronted by a half dozen especially hard-looking young guys in their twenties wearing identical black leather fingertip coats with a small broken arrow stenciled above the pocket. They looked like James Dean impersonators, pretending to be tough gay guys. They didn't part, and she didn't stop. She hit them hard, like a fullback going into the defensive line.

I knew what she was feeling. She was back in that burning Humvee, trapped again, this time in Zan's body.

Somebody had jumped on my back and had two small arms wrapped around my neck and was pushing my right arm up into the air and yelling the same word over and over.

Don't…don't…don't…

"Don't hurt them!" Barbara kept yelling. "Don't hurt them!"

I grabbed Barbara's hand and pried it off and shot two rounds into the air as I started running to the bus, following Victoria, Barbara hanging onto my back like an old cheerleader who fell off the top of the pyramid and was clinging to whatever she could grab on the way down. That must have been a real sight for the Indians in the tricky light of dawn and the fire, a man with mismatched legs running and shooting with a blond monkey on his back.

Except Zan wasn't in the bus anymore; he was leaping off the top of it, right out of the flames, onto one of the horse riders, kicking him off of the horse and taking his place, all in one remarkably awkward motion. Jumping on was all he knew how to do, though, from the looks of it. The horse took off down the street with Joe holding onto the saddle horn with both hands.

Victoria couldn't see him, though. She was still fighting her way through the throng of tough guys, screaming "Zan! Zan!"

Frankly, I wasn't worried for Victoria. She was smaller than any of the tough guys, but I had seen her in action. If I'd had money to bet, and the willingness to lay it down, I'd have put it on her.

Lonnie didn't know how well she was doing, though. He was suddenly past me and into the fray, following the sounds of Victoria's screams, delivering karate kicks by sound, most of them whistling through air, but a few actually connecting with shins and ribs and defensive arms. The guy was blind, but he had obviously been a Tae Kwan Do student at one time, probably a black belt.

Barbara had slipped off my back along the way and worked her way back to the older guy with the bow and arrow. He was lying on the ground in a loose heap of limbs and feathers. She was standing over him, breaking his bow on her knee, yelling stuff at him, and calling him Chief Outhouse.

Then there was Zan again. He had gotten hold of the horse's reins and was riding back down the street at full gallop, twirling a lariat over his head, screaming out defensive signals from his days as a middle linebacker at IU. "*Aztec Four*! *Crimson wide*! *Dog free*! *Lorelei*! *Lorelei*!"

He was hurtling pell-mell at the swirling crowd of Indians. They began to scatter, dashing for the fronts of the buildings along the street and then disappearing between them. The guy with the snare drum wasn't fast enough, and Zan roped the drum right out of his hands as he rode by, dragging him for a few feet before the shoulder sling that held the drum gave way.

A young woman with a long black braid ran up to Barbara, gave her a shove, dropped to her knees beside Chief Outhouse, and began to feel his legs and arms for breaks. I expected Barbara to jump on her back, but apparently she saved that treatment for one-legged men. She just stood there with her hands on her hips and looked disgusted.

It was over as soon as it began. Everybody else had disappeared.

The black leather coat guys limped off, giving everybody the finger as they did and yelling guttural stuff that I couldn't understand.

Zan slipped off his horse, which promptly ran away. Where in hell did a Gary, Indiana, boy learn to ride a horse like that?

Lonnie and Victoria stood there, holding each other, adrenaline running down. They began to walk over to us without letting go of each other. It looked like they were in a sack race.

"My God, Victoria," Barbara said, "you really laid into those guys in the leather jackets." She turned to Ernest Althaus. "Who were those turds anyway? I've not seen them before."

"That's Razer Kawbagam." It was the long braid woman who answered. "He's just a thug. And those guys with him, they're just as bad as he is, fooling around all day, never working, think they're big. Call themselves the Broken Arrows. We didn't want them to come."

She looked away. I got the feeling that she was lying, but I didn't know why.

"You're all thugs as far as I'm concerned, Melva," Barbara said. She said in an almost affectionate way, though. "Get out of here, you morons," she said to Ernest and the woman she called Melva. "It's not going to work."

"You're going to let them go? But they burned up my bus!" Zan said.

"That's a good point," Barbara said, turning to Ernest and Melva again. "What are you people doing, burning up buses? Where's Sleeping-in-the-Shithouse, anyway?"

"He had to work at the casino this morning," the guy with the broken bow said.

Melva jumped up and stood with arms akimbo, mimicking Barbara. "That's disrespectful, white woman. You know what his real name is, but you choose to call us all by dishonorable names that you make up."

"Well, who just called me White Woman?" Barbara replied, but without much force.

Melva ignored her. "You stay here, Father," she said to Ernest Althaus. "I'll get the car."

She turned and started jogging down the street toward the entrance.

Barbara shouted after her. "You tell Sleeping-in-the-Shithouse to come himself next time and not to send a bunch of amateurs."

She looked rather satisfied with herself.

"Who's this Sleeping-in-the-Shithouse, anyway?" Zan asked.

"An old boyfriend," Barbara said. "From when I was a teenager and this place was supposed to be a tourist trap."

"Are they Chipahoys?" Zan asked.

Nobody knew if he were serious, so Barbara just said, "Ojibwa, mostly. But Chipawa is another name for them. Let's go up on the porch. We'd better wait outside until Melva gets back with the car. Don't want anything to happen to old Ernest."

We stood in little clumps on her porch, which was also the boardwalk, Lonnie and Victoria in a clutch, Barbara and me in the middle, Zan off by himself.

I looked at the bus and realized it was just that tacky paint that had caught fire, not the bus itself, which was why the fire was over so quickly.

"What in hell did you paint that bus with, Zan?"

He shrugged. "Some stuff I found at the back of the lot."

"The lot? What lot? What are you talking about?"

"The movie lot, down in Flint."

"Flint, *Michigan*? You've got to be kidding. They film movies in Hollywood," Lonnie said.

"No, not anymore," Barbara said. "I don't mean—they still film in Hollywood, of course, but Michigan is the up and coming place. They've got all those big empty auto factories they can turn into movie lots, and the state has given them tax breaks up to Armageddon, and maybe then, too, if they can film it."

"Yeah," Zan said. "I worked down there. They were paying me like, nothing, so when I got the bus, I figured they owed me at least some paint."

"Oh, my," Barbara said. "That's a special paint, but I don't think they call it paint even. It's for movie fires. They can coat something with it and set it on fire and it makes a really great picture for the camera, but it doesn't destroy whatever is supposedly burning. They can burn it over and over again."

"You know a lot about the movie business, Barbara," I said.

"Anyone who wants to get her books made into movies stays up with what the back-stabbing morons are into now," she said.

Then something else occurred to me. "Zan, did you *act* in the movies?"

"Naw. I did a little bit of everything, but mostly stunts."

"Like jumping onto horses?"

He laughed. "Yeah, that's how I got the job. They were making a western. Can you believe it, a horse opera in an old car factory? Anyway, I told them I could do horse stunts."

"Had you *ever* ridden a horse before?"

His face darkened. "Didn't make any diff. It was just mostly falling off anyway."

He shrugged and then shivered a little. It was cold, and he was just wearing a tee-shirt and jeans. A tee-shirt was enough in a zipped-up sleeping bag, but out here in the street on an autumn morning in the UP, it was like wearing nothing. Still, I didn't think his shivers were from the cold. I had ridden horses growing up in southern Indiana, so they had me riding them in the 'Stan, too, going after Taliban in places vehicles couldn't go. I suspected that Zan had done his stunt training that way, too.

Barbara noticed the shivering. "Come on inside, you idiots. It's too cold out here. Melva can't be far off now. They always park their cars where I can't see them but where they don't have far to walk to get to them. You promised to fix breakfast, Joe, and I'm holding you to it, but you can do it with whatever is left over in my larder."

CHAPTER 10

Larder. I hadn't heard that word since Grandma…
We got inside. Zan snuck up behind Victoria and tickled her in the ribs. She slapped his hands away.

"Be careful," I said. "She's lethal."

"I know that," he chortled. "Wow, what a one-woman wrecking crew. I just didn't know she was so in love with me. *Zan! Zan!*"

He did a passable imitation of Victoria shouting his name when she thought he was trapped in the burning bus.

She turned around and pushed a brown and pink finger into his chest. "Don't ever touch me," she said. Her big brown eyes bored into him. It was a damned awkward moment. "And don't ever scare me like that again," she said and flounced away like the Easter Bunny going off to fling eggs at unsuspecting children.

I started laughing. I couldn't help it. Barbara did, too. Zan looked like he didn't know what was happening. Lonnie started laughing. Victoria chuckled. Then we all lost it, even Zan, whooping and giggling and finally falling onto the floor and rolling around until we were exhausted.

Barbara crawled to a table and used it to pull herself back up.

"Oh, God," she whispered. "I haven't laughed like that since—"

She started giggling again, wiped at her forehead, pushed her hair back. It didn't really need it. I had never met a woman like her. She was grieving the loss of a son and always would, she had been up all night writing, gone through the equivalent of a bar fight, plus a falling-down laugh fit, and she still looked like she had just been sipping tea with church ladies all morning. On top of that, she could call people *turds* and *assholes* and give them names like *Sleeps-in-the-Shithouse* and make it sound like Katie Couric giving the news.

It was nicely warm inside, and the laughing had warmed us up, too. We finally lapsed into a sort of normalcy. Victoria and Lonnie sat down at the table. Zan wandered in circles. Barbara and I went to the kitchen. Barbara poured coffee and passed it all around. I started looking for stuff to eat.

The room was big, but it was easy to carry on a conversation with everybody from anywhere.

"How did you get on top of the bus, Zan?" I asked. "We thought you were still sleeping inside when the flames went up."

"Naw, I got to thinking it would be fun to watch the stars last night. No city lights out here. You can really see them. So I took my sleeping bag up top and watched the stars until I fell asleep."

"Barbara, you said *they always park down where I can't see them.* This has happened before?"

"Any time I'm here, but usually not quite as organized as this. They must be getting serious about driving me out. It's usually just a nuisance. They want Sliver Lake, but they don't want to pay for it. They claim it's theirs by heritage, or something. That's why I can't sell it. They've got the place tied up in the courts. They figure if they can keep me from having any peace to write, I'll give up and sell it to them for a song, or just give it to them. Some of them, like Ernest, are actually old friends, from when I was up here as a high school and college girl. I hope you didn't hurt anyone too badly. I usually just ignore them. They've never had to fight before."

"Well, *I* hope we hurt them," Victoria said. "They have no right to bother you."

Barbara laughed. "Well, if you didn't hurt them, it wasn't for lack of trying. Good grief. You people are the seven-legged, six-eyed, three-brained equivalent of Jack Reacher."

"It would *take* that many legs and brains to equal Jack Reacher," Victoria said, a heavy sigh holding up her words.

Victoria apparently ranged widely in her reading tastes.

"Who the hell's Jack Reacher?" Lonnie said. "Haven't you people noticed that I can't watch movies?"

Now that was interesting, Lonnie not only admitting he was blind but using it as a bid for sympathy. I realized Lonnie was jealous. He didn't like Victoria talking that soulful and wistful way about another man. I suspected that Lonnie was jealous of any woman being interested in any man but him.

"He's not an actor—" I started, but Victoria interrupted.

"I love books," Victoria said. "People can look any way you want them to in a book."

"I'm a little bit offended," Barbara said, although she didn't sound it. "I always thought I described people so well that everyone saw them just as I do."

"Oh, that's true," Victoria said. "You are wonderful with descriptions, but in a book, there's still room—"

"Who the hell is Jack Reacher?" Lonnie fairly yelled it.

"He's a made-up hero," I said. "In books. He was an MP—"

"He was an MP and he's a *hero?*" Now it was Zan's turn to yell in dismay.

My guess was that he had more than a few run-ins with the Military Police along the way, so I thought it might be good to change the subject.

"Time to eat," I said. "Get to the table."

I had put a continental breakfast together—toast and bagels with juice and coffee, and thimbleberry jam.

When we had finished, Barbara swept her arm over us in a single arc, as though we belonged together some way, instead of being a misfit clutch of strangers who just happened to fall into the same pit together.

"We need to wash those clothes you're in," she said, "There's a washer and dryer in the room behind the kitchen. You do have something to change into, don't you?"

She wrinkled up her nose as she looked us over, and I didn't blame her.

"Uh, Zan and I have some things in the bus, and some of them might fit Lonnie, but Victoria got on the bus without even—"

"Female supplies?" Victoria said, her eyes boring into me

like I was a pile of something misogynistic she had just stepped in.

"—a purse," I finished up. "And women always have purses, so I figured she was one step in front of the law, and we were the getaway bus, so what could I do?"

That wasn't what I had thought at all, but it sounded like—I don't know, maybe John Wayne in *Rio Veterans Affairs*?

"Oh, Lord, what *have* I gotten myself into?" Barbara emitted a bleating sigh like a sheep, but it was a sheep in wolf's clothing, or in a mother's better memories.

"I'll get our clothes from the bus," I said. "Anything in there will need to be washed, after that paint burning."

I didn't want to say that Zan and I had worn all our stuff without washing for as long as I could remember and they badly needed washing anyway.

When I got to the bus, I got to thinking about our situation. Sliver Lake might be just a sliver, but it wasn't as remote as I had thought. If the cops or the guys from Moe's asked in McFarland or Trombly or some other little town, someone might well mention Sliver Lake and the cute hermit writer woman, and they might figure it was worth a look. On top of that, what if one of the Indians was really hurt and went to the hospital and somebody made a report?

The inside of the bus was amazingly untouched by the fire. Those movie people really knew how to do a "smart" fire, a lot better than the military knew how to do a so-called "smart" bomb. I gathered up our clothes and piled them onto Barbara's porch. It was a pitifully small pile.

I drove the bus down to the big building at the end of the street. It had high double doors that swung out reluctantly on rusty hinges.

Inside was a bunch of antique machinery I didn't recognize, except for an old Case tractor. I managed to push some stuff around enough to get the bus inside. I walked back down to Barbara's, limping on Judas. Then it occurred to me that once the fight in the street started, I hadn't even noticed my artificial leg, even with Barbara on my back. I had just done what had to be done.

When I got back, the pile of clothes was gone. Inside, Victoria and Lonnie were sitting in the recliners in robes, with blankets on their laps.

"Zan's in the laundry room, doing the washing," Barbara said. "I only have two robes, so he's naked, I think."

She made it sound like a warning. She didn't know that I had seen Zan naked a thousand times. I wondered, though, if I saw his body naked in Barbara's laundry room now, if it would have changed as much as mine had from our days in our dorm room and the football locker room. Neither of us was the man we had been back in college, and none of the changes seemed to be for the better.

Barbara was much smaller than Victoria, but she rummaged around and found some sweatshirts and a coat, and even a purse for her.

"You're so much more than just a great writer, Barbara," Victoria said, sniffing a little. "You're a wonderful friend to people you don't even know."

Barbara gave a little embarrassed shrug. Lonnie turned his head, as though he were looking out the window. I wasn't very comfortable with this whole scene. I preferred the tightly wound Victoria, not this almost-maudlin one. Time to change the subject.

"What do you do when you're not writing, Barbara?" I asked.

"I used to edit a newspaper, but now when I run out of ideas for novels, I write pieces for Christian women's magazines."

Just then Zan appeared in the laundry room door. Thankfully his clothes had gotten dried, or close to it, and he was dressed.

"You?" Zan screeched. "Potty-mouth Barbara, calling everybody *turds* and *assholes* writing for Christian women? Christian broads must be a whole lot different these days."

Zan meant it to be funny. Victoria didn't take it that way. "Don't talk to her like that or I won't save you next time."

She didn't put a lot of energy into it. She was comfortable there in the recliner and the blanket.

"*Next time*? You didn't save me *this* time!"

They continued sparring, but it was more like a debating team, not caring about the subject so much as just wanting to carry the day. I stopped listening. My leg started hurting—the stump that was still there and the part that was gone, too, so I took Judas off and just sat there, thinking.

Next time…that was a strange thought. Would there be a next time? Why was there even a *this* time? Why was I here, with this bunch? Zan and I had been friends once, but I had known a linebacker who could figure out in a nanosecond what the opposing quarterback was going to do with the ball. I didn't know this movie stunt man whose brain played tricks on him all the time. Most importantly, I didn't owe him anything. I didn't owe anybody anything. It was time for me to move on. Alone. I didn't know where, but—

That was when we heard a car drive up.

Barbara ran to the window. "It's the sheriff. Where's the bus?"

"I put it into that big building at the end of the street," I said.

"Okay. You're not here then. Get into the laundry room."

It wasn't hard for Zan. He was right there. It took Victoria and Lonnie a little longer, but they got the blankets thrown off and got out of the recliners. Victoria's robe came open for just a moment.

I got the idea that her figure was even better than it looked like with clothes on, but the rest of her skin didn't look a lot better than what showed most of the time, and I looked away in embarrassment. She left Lonnie on his own, and he ran into a chair as he followed the sounds to the laundry room and muttered something.

I was farthest from the back of the room. The sheriff was already pounding on the door. With my leg off, I knew I would never make it to the laundry room.

"Hold your horses. I'll be right there," Barbara yelled at the door, giving me time to grab my leg and half-hop, half-dive behind the kitchen counter. She made sure I was out of sight, waited another moment for the hell of it, and just as the pounding started again, she threw the door open and said, "Why, Sheriff Shrader. You haven't come calling in such a very long time."

"Hey, Barbara. I need to talk to you about what happened out here this morning."

His voice was cultured, pleasant, but all business, and a little embarrassed.

"Well, good, Del. I hope you're going to throw that whole lot into jail for a long time. They keep coming over here and trying to hassle me into giving them this whole place for nothing—"

She was sounding very offended. He wasn't having any of that, either. He had an agenda, and he was sticking to it.

"The people who are here with you? They beat up on the Indians. Are you hiring bodyguards or something? You know violence isn't part of the deal."

"And just what deal is that? They get to come over here and harass me and you don't do anything about it and I'm not allowed to either? I don't know of any *deeeal*!"

I felt a little sorry for Sheriff Del Shrader.

"Besides, there's nobody here anymore. They were just old friends traveling through. Naturally they came to my defense when Chief Outhouse and those Broken Arrow thugs assaulted me. But they are gone now."

"From what Melva tells me, these didn't sound like friends of yours."

"You were my friend once, and look how *you* turned out!"

There was a strained silence.

"May I come in?"

"You certainly may not. We have nothing to talk about."

"I'd like to look around, make sure you're okay."

"That's very thoughtful of you. I've been up here off and on for ten years, and you've always been very nice to look out for me and make sure I'm okay. Oh, wait, this is the first time, isn't it?"

There was a rather long silence, and then the sheriff spoke again. "I know I should have come before, Barb, when…you know…your son…but I didn't know what…I knew you didn't want to see me, and I figure that would make it worse. I wouldn't have come now, but I've got to do my job. The sheriff over in Dickinson County asked me to be on the lookout for a bunch traveling in a school bus. Seems there was a brawl up Sagola way, and they were in it. Hurt some people pretty bad."

"Well, you can tell the sheriff over there that you have done your duty, which is more than you did by me when you got me pregnant, you rapist. Yes, that's right, rape. I was only seventeen. How would the people of this county like it if they knew their sheriff was a rapist?"

I hoped nobody could hear my chin hit the floor, and I *really* hoped Victoria would not come charging out of the laundry room and beat the hell out of the sheriff for having violated her heroine about...oh, forty years or so ago.

"Barbara...I never...pregnant? Why didn't you tell me?"

That pleasant professional voice at the door had gone totally unfocused.

"Get out of here, Delbert Shrader, and don't ever come back, unless you're willing to compensate my husband for raising *your* child."

"But I never even—"

Then the door slammed, hard.

There was a long silence. I waited. Everybody else waited. The silence sounded like the whole world was waiting. Finally I heard a car start up and drive away. I poked my head up from behind the counter, afraid of what I would see. I wasn't very good at comforting distraught women.

Barbara stood there with her hands on her hips and a big smile on her face. "I nailed that bastard good. I've been wanting to do that for so long!"

The laundry room door opened. Victoria was just a pink and brown streak as she dashed toward Barbara. Then she stopped short, four feet away from her. "Oh, Barbara, Barbara—"

Barbara waved a small hand toward the door in a dismissive flutter.

"But that awful man, what he did to you—"

Awful man? Did Victoria think she was in an English country novel now? Barbara brought out a softer side of Victoria than any I'd seen before.

Zan and Lonnie had emerged from the laundry room. Lonnie was dressed now, too, apparently without help, since he was wearing my shirt instead of his. They didn't try to advance into the room, just stood barely inside the door, which I thought showed more wisdom than I had expected from either one of them.

"No wonder you're such a good writer. You've suffered so much."

There was hurt in Victoria's eyes, and she didn't even know about Barbara's son. I wondered if she had a Del Shrader in her past. Well, what woman doesn't? Except for Becky Garlits, of course.

"Oh, Vicky, for God's sake, she's a big girl now—"

So Zan wasn't being wise after all, just slow to get into the room. I winced. He really didn't know about Barbara's National Guard son. Victoria whirled around to face him.

"My name is Vic-*tor*-ia!"

I started trying to get Judas on, so I could get between them, but Barbara saved the situation.

"Oh, Victoria, you're right, I've suffered, but it's not because of Del Shrader. It's true that he deflowered me, but I didn't get pregnant until I was married, years later. I just said that because it was the quickest way to get rid of him. I figure whatever that other sheriff wants you for, I'm on your side. And also because after he got bragging rights to me he dumped me for Susie Yomo, who had boobs even bigger than yours. You tit queens have such big advantages in getting the guys."

"Barbara! Have you *looked* at me?" Victoria was truly shocked.

"Yes, I have, Vic-*tor*-ia, and I see a beautiful woman of great character who will come to the aid of a friend when he's in need even if he is a stupid man who calls you Vicky."

She gave Zan a scornful glare, but it didn't last long, because Victoria was suddenly in her arms, and the two women were hugging and crying like they had just discovered what happens when you put chocolate on peanut butter.

Lonnie looked self-satisfied, like he had known how this would turn out, but, despite his ability to read women, I was sure he was faking it. I mean, no man could figure out how this stuff happened or what it meant or what you should do in the meantime.

Zan looked like he was going to have a headache. I suspected I looked like a man who knew he had to get a hell of a long way away from these people.

CHAPTER 11

The Hermits

"I told you Hove was going to go off the tracks."

"Zeke is the best we've got. He's always delivered."

"I thought we were talking about Hove. Who the fuck is Zeke?"

"The one we call J."

"Figures"

"But he's been getting crazy, dammit. Any fool could see it."

"Who do we have that's any better? Come on. You want a dirty job done, you've got to get a dirty guy."

"Besides, he's crazy enough that he provides his own deniability. Who will believe it if he talks?"

"Yeah, so why did we send Hank Keel and MacArthur with him? They're not crazy enough to have deniability. Gordon Liddy's crazy, but everybody believes him."

"The damned idiots were supposed to look like they were just up there on a fishing trip. Then Hove has to go and get worked up over a tee-shirt—"

"It wasn't just the shirt. It was that picture of enemy number one on it."

ತಲಿ

The *Hermits* all talked at once, because each one thought he was in charge, the only voice that counted. They were meeting in an undisclosed location. The locations of the Hermits were never disclosed. No one even knew that there were locations, for no one knew the Hermits existed, not even the board of Algonquin Associates, the chief civilian contractor for all things military.

The Hermits liked to think of Algonquin Associates as the atom that kept exploding in order to power the US empire, and of themselves as the nucleus of the atom. They called themselves the Hermits after Peter the Hermit, who was, erroneously, credited with starting the Crusades.

They were the new crusaders, charged with keeping the peace of the world through the might of the US military empire, because it was clear that the US President and his namby-pamby congress were too busy with keeping themselves in political power to wield the real power toward the necessary end. The Republicans and Democrats were all the same. They didn't want to govern. They didn't want to protect America. They just wanted to get elected and get free jaunts to Caribbean islands to visit their off-shore accounts.

Mao had been right about one thing: power came out of the barrel of a gun. The Hermits were the only force in America willing to admit that and act on it. That was one thing they agreed on.

ϾϾϾ

"So what do we do now? Have Hove and his *Shoguns* outlived their usefulness? Are we going to have to *outplace* them?"

"Can they be useful at all anymore? I mean, they all got their shooting shoulders shot up. We ought to hire the guy who did that."

"Do we even know where they are?"

"Of course. Erskine has them tracked electronically a dozen different ways. The Shoguns don't know it, of course. I don't know how Erskine manages all that stuff, but I'm glad he works for us."

"How do we know he does? He's the electronics genius. None of us has the smarts to monitor him. Maybe he's a mole for somebody else."

"Don't get paranoid. Who else would pay him what we do?"

"Paranoia is what keeps us in business."

"That and the ability of our TV and radio outlets to keep the public scared to death."

"Don't forget our special friend and his no-bid contracts."

"Yeah, yeah. We owe everybody. What are we going to do about the Shoguns?"

"We've got to outplace them—"

"We still need them. I think we can rein Hove in, and Keel and MacArthur are still okay, once their shoulders heal. The people at that convenience store are scared to death. A little fear and a few dollars and we've got nothing to worry about with them. Wouldn't it make more sense to outplace that school bus bunch?"

CHAPTER 12

Joe

There was something I had to know. "Barbara, you said that telling that sheriff, Del Shrader, that he got you pregnant all those years ago was the quickest way to get rid of him. But you're smart. You're a famous writer, which means you're all over the internet. You know he'll Google you and find out you didn't have a child until you were married. He'll wonder what happened to *his* kid. Did Barbara have an abortion? Did she put it out for adoption? And he knows about…Michael…"

I didn't know how much I should say about the son who got killed in front of the others, so I just let it trail, and she didn't say anything.

"He'll be back," I said, "the sheriff, wanting answers, and you'll have to come up with something. You don't owe us anything. You don't even know us. Not really."

"It's no secret, Joe." She turned to the others. "I had a son, Michael, who was killed in Iraq."

Victoria gasped. "The one the sheriff—"

"No, Michael was my younger son. I have an older son, Harlan. But I do owe you, Joe, all of you. If Michael came back like…disabled…I would want…"

"I'm sorry I said anything, Barbara. I just thought…I don't want you to get into trouble because of us."

"She told the sheriff what she did because she *had* to," Victoria blurted out.

"Oh, Victoria, I wish all my reviews were written by you,

but I didn't have to lie to Del. I wanted to, in order to hurt him. I'm so angry all the time, and the people I want to lash out at, I can't get at them, and there was Del, right there, and I really was mad at him for dumping me, even though it was forever ago, so..."

Barbara and the others went on talking, but I wasn't listening, just watching. It was such a strange and comfortable tableau, almost like a family. Barbara was a genius at providing hospitality. I was sure that she didn't do it just because she thought she should, just because we reminded her, somehow, of her lost son, but because it came naturally to her. Most of what we claimed were demands of God or commands of the Devil were really just what was natural for us.

What came naturally to me was aloneness. I wasn't a part of this little impromptu family in Barbara's remodeled hotel. I had never been a part of any family.

I was the odd man out, the loner, even with the people around me right then. Barbara had her husband and her other son and her writing and her faith. Lonnie and Victoria had each other, strange and tenuous as their relationship was. Even Zan seemed to fit in, having a role to play, teasing Victoria and Barbara, the funny brother.

For a soldier, the unit was everything, especially in action. Units, however, were not always harmonious. There were personality conflicts and differences of opinion, like Zan and Victoria. We weren't going to form a unit, though, I could see that, because we had all been wounded too badly, emotionally as well as physically. We were mourning the loss of our former units, too. We were all searching for a new unit. Especially for vets, it was "any unit in a storm," as long as it was one we choose instead of one that was forced on us. Maybe there was hope for the others, to be a unit, or to find one. I knew it would never happen for me, though.

I tuned back in while Barbara was talking.

"...I don't think it's safe for you to leave until we know we're not being watched. Those Broken Arrows are the type to want revenge, but not the type to be up front about it. Del will tell Melva Althaus that you're gone, though, and she'll beat the tom-toms. So those Broken Arrow guys will figure they lost their chance. But Del was always the suspicious type. He might station one of his deputies out where the Sliver Lake road meets the highway to see if you're still here."

"Gee, I wonder why the sheriff would ever think you'd tell him a lie," Zan said, a look of total innocence on his face.

Victoria looked like she was going to tear him an extra one, but neither one of them seemed to be into the game anymore.

"But what if the Broken Arrows decide to take some revenge on you, knowing we're gone?" Victoria said.

"That's another advantage of having the sheriff think he owes me. He'll also tell Melva that I'm untouchable. I won't even have to worry about the Indians being a nuisance anymore. Del will tell Melva to call them off. I can get back to my writing. In the meantime, I need to go to town to get more food. Doing that, I'll be able to check on surveillance before you try to take the bus out of here."

"Yeah, and I need to check on the bus to be sure the hoses or the brake lines or something didn't get burned up," Zan said.

That sobered everybody up. Barbara went out the back and drove away in a light blue PT Cruiser. Victoria told Lonnie to sit at the kitchen table so they could talk while she cleaned the place up. Zan and I went to check on the bus.

The bus looked like it had been to hell and back, which was pretty accurate. It took an hour to check everything over, but it was as good as it had been before, which meant not very. We opened the doors and the few windows that weren't stuck, to air it out. When we got back to Barbara's, I had the impression that Lonnie and Victoria may have been doing more than talking, but what the hell? Except it made me feel even more alone.

Barbara returned with groceries and the news that there was indeed a sheriff's car parked out on the main road. We ate lunch without much enthusiasm. I figured I could return a bit of Barbara's hospitality by getting everybody out of her hair so she could write, so I told everybody to leave by the back door and keep out of sight in case the sheriff's deputy decided to take a closer look.

Zan disappeared into the woods. Victoria and Lonnie went to wherever they went. I made an attempt at cleaning out the bus but got distracted by the logging tools and machinery in the big barn building. It must have been a museum of some sort when Barbara's father was trying to make Sliver Lake into a tourist attraction.

We gathered again at supper time. I got there first so Barbara wouldn't have to cook.

"Keep on writing," I told her. "I'll fix up something for supper."

"Okay," she said, but after a while, curiosity got the best of her. "You don't owe any explanations, Joe, but—beyond being vets—who the hell are you people, and where do you come from, and why are you together? I mean, I know you said it was all accidental, being together...and...oh, forget I asked. It's just that—"

"Barbara, if I knew the answers to any of those questions, I would be glad to tell you. The truth is, one by one, we just got on the bus..."

I could have told her more, that we were all escapees from the VA, but I didn't have a right to tell about anyone but myself, and I didn't want to talk about me. I didn't have to think about it anymore, though, because the back door opened and the others came in.

It was a restless evening. Even in a family, especially in a family, when you come down from a high time, there's a vacuum. That's when things get tense. That was when I would go to Grandma's house. So I went to the woods. I told the others I was going to watch to see when the sheriff's car was gone.

I walked down the Sliver Lake road until I was about even with where Barbara said the deputy's car was parked. Then I worked my way through the pines, hemlocks, and birches until I found it. I cleared a place where I could sit down and still see the car.

I couldn't sit cross-legged, so I stretched Judas out straight and crossed my good leg over it. A long time ago, I would sit totally still for hours at a time, praying and meditating, waiting for God to speak to me, the way Grandma said happened to her. Then, in the army, in Iraqistan, I would sit totally still for hours at a time, watching, waiting for a chance to kill someone. Now I sat totally still, watching the deputy's car, waiting for him to leave, so that I could, too.

When I was a kid, my father would try to get me to sit still in the woods while we waited for a deer or a rabbit or a squirrel to show. I didn't want to shoot the animals, though. The animals were my friends. So I would make just enough noise to scare them off, just enough that he would think I did it because I was an awkward klutz. He didn't know I could sit silently for an hour in Grandma's living room while we meditated. Grandma called it praying, but we never said anything. When it came time to kill men, it was those sessions in Grandma's living room that earned me the name of *Reverend Death* from the other guys in the 'Stan, because it was there that I learned to hear even the slightest sound as I shut out all the other distractions.

In my Iraq tour, it was mostly just *The Reverend* or *Preacher* that the guys called me, after they learned that I had gone to theological school for a little while before I joined up. When the brass found out my special skill with *a long gun*, like they called them in John Wayne movies, it was off to the 'Stan.

I thought that was why I joined the army at the age of twenty-three, my love of guns. I didn't know why I loved guns so much. Becky Garlits claimed that she had gone off to be with the starting quarterback instead of the backup because the backup was bad in bed. If Becky was right about how bad I was in bed, maybe it was true that guys who loved guns were making up for physical deficiencies.

Maybe it was just because shooting a gun gave me a sense of satisfaction. When my father took me hunting, I found out that I had a natural knack for shooting. He would point out a squirrel that hadn't been scared off by my noisiness and tell me to shoot it out of the tree. That squirrel hadn't done anything to me. We didn't need to kill it to have something to eat. So I would aim for a twig on the tree branch, right beside the squirrel, or at a knot on the trunk, just above it. The twig would fly off, or the knot would become a hole, and the squirrel would duck for cover. My father didn't know where I was aiming, so he despaired of me ever becoming a marksman. He finally gave up on my shooting, at least I thought he did, the same way he had given up on everything else about me. But I knew I could hit where I aimed every time, and that made me feel good.

It wasn't just the love of guns that led me to the army,

though. It was the absence of any other kind of love. Grandma died in my senior year at IU. The last time I saw her was after a game, another game I didn't get to play in.

When *my* coach, the one who recruited me because of that *ability to win*, despite my physical shortcomings, was fired after my freshman year, they hired a guy who thought he was the emperor of football. Or the pharaoh, judging from the weird Egyptian-looking uniforms his wife designed for us. Unfortunately for me, he was "a pharaoh who knew not Joseph."

I ran the spread offense in high school, lots of short precision passes. I was good at it. The same eye-hand coordination that gave me accuracy with a rifle gave me accuracy with a football. I had rifle accuracy, but not rifle range. The new IU coach was an advocate of the big play. He wanted a quarterback who could throw the ball seventy yards. Quint Rosten could do that. Of course, none of our receivers were ever in the area where he threw it, but it was dramatic. The coach claimed we had to have drama to put fans in the stands, and once we got the fans, we could recruit better players, and then we would win more, and then...

He lasted three years. Turned out the fans didn't want drama, they wanted winning football. Unfortunately for me, his years were my years, years when we faced teams running the spread offense. As the scout team quarterback, I picked our defense apart every week with my precision passes, mimicking the offense they would face that week. It never got through to the coach that if I could do that to *our* defense, I could do it to our opponents' defense.

I never got into a single game, not even the one Grandma came to, the last time I saw her. My parents never came to my games, even in high school. Grandma went to every one, even those on the road. She drove to every one by herself. She could have gotten a friend to go with her, but I don't think she wanted to share that experience with anyone else. For her, there was one woman in the stands and one player on the field.

She had her first stroke just after I went off to college. Nobody told me about it until she explained why she couldn't drive up to Bloomington to see my games there. I was happy she never came, since I never got into a game.

In my senior year, though, she came to the Iowa game. Drove up by herself. How she managed that, or how she got home alive, I don't know. But there she was after the game, waiting for me outside the stadium, sitting on a little folding stool, Becky Garlits at her side.

It was clear that Becky didn't want to be there. She resented Grandma even more than she resented Zan, as a rival for my affections. With good reason. But Grandma had called Becky and asked her to meet her and take her to the stadium. In her mind, Becky had already given up on me and gone over to Quint Rosten, but neither Grandma or I knew it. Grandma looked real bad, but it was her last hurrah. She wanted to see her grandson in that cream and crimson uniform.

It was a measure of how much Grandma wanted that October Saturday that she was willing to share it with Becky. She had met Becky only once, when I took her down to Princeton. We were there only long enough to see Grandma, not anyone else. Grandma told me after, though, that Becky was not the right girl for me. "I like her. She's got ambition. She's a nice girl, Joe. You could do a lot worse. But…it's that ambition. When she gets a better offer…"

I assumed she said it because she was as jealous of Becky as Becky was of her, but it was because she loved me a lot more than Becky did. What college guy takes romantic advice from his grandma, though?

Becky left as soon as I arrived.

"I'm sorry you came all this way and didn't get to see me play," I said to Grandma.

"I got to see *you*. That's what counts."

I offered to take her someplace to get something to eat. She wanted to get home before dark, though, and I wanted to get into bed with Becky, so I told her how to find Highway 45 and let her go.

When Grandma died, I didn't know how much she meant to me. I had Becky. I thought she was all I would ever need. Then Becky left me for Quint Rosten. Zan left after the Purdue game. I had nothing—no letter jacket, no girlfriend, no roommate, no grandma. I sleep-walked through the rest of the year, going to classes and writing papers just because they were there.

The army recruiter almost got me then, at the spring job fair. His pitch sounded good. I was a college grad, or soon would be. I could be an officer. Serve my country. "An army of one."

Most of all, I could show my father, the Gulf War vet, the son of a Vietnam vet, who thought that any true patriot would do his time in *the service*, as though the military was the only way to *serve* your country, and that his son was a namby-pamby because he played quarterback because he wasn't tough enough to play *in the trenches*.

The army recruiter wasn't the only one on campus that day, though. Way off in a corner was a table that said Garrett-Evangelical Theological Seminary. At the table sat the most beautiful woman I had ever seen. She was tall and sat even taller, perfect posture, feet firmly on the floor, hands folded neatly on the table, only her head turning, so that her light gray eyes could take in the whole scene. I followed the beam of those eyes right up to her table, like a jet follows a homing beam to land safely. "You're a good athlete, aren't you?" I said to her.

As a pickup line, it was about par with my other abilities with women.

"Don't let the light eyes fool you," she said. "I'm just a runner."

So she was smart, too. She knew that light eyes meant quick reflexes.

"Where do you run?"

"Chicago. That's where Garrett is, in Evanston."

She pointed at her sign.

"What do you do there? I mean, besides run."

"I'm in the admissions office."

"What happens to people you admit?"

I was willing to say anything to keep the conversation going.

"They lose their faith. Then they become ministers. Do you have any faith? We're a liberal seminary, so we can't admit you unless you have faith we can make you lose."

She sounded like I was actually trying to get into seminary, when all I really wanted to do was get into her...

But wait a minute. Recruiters didn't say things like that unless...

"You're trying to keep me out," I said.

"Not at all," she said. "We don't get many students right out of college. They're mostly second and third career anymore. We'd love to have you. But you need to know what you're getting into. Most college guys who are interested in theological school have gone to a para-church group in college. They think seminary will be all prayer groups and praise songs. Garrett is academic. It's tough. It's like medical school for soul doctors. You have to work hard, all the time. You have to think hard, find out what you really believe, not what some praise song writer believes. Jesus said to love God with your mind as well as heart and soul and strength. Can you think?"

She was making theological school sound worse than the army. Or better.

The hard-thinking part appealed to me. I used to consider myself a thoughtful guy. Other people did, too. Grandma did. My high school coach and teachers did.

But all the major decisions I had made were—if you could say I actually made them—just a snap moment, done on intuition, not *thoughtful* intuition, like the people who claimed that they trusted their intuition. I had never even known I had intuition. My major decisions hadn't even been gut decisions. They'd been more feet decisions. My brain got tired of thinking so my feet got up on their own and went some place, and the rest of me, including my brain, just went along. But she was still talking...

"It's a United Methodist seminary, but we have students from many denominations, and none."

"My grandma was a Methodist..." I was sort of one, too, since Grandma had taken me to church with her until I thought I was too old for that. "I'm Joe Kirk."

She stuck out her hand. It was long and elegant. Each finger was long and elegant, too, and ended in a perfectly sculpted and polished nail, except for the ring finger. It ended in an ugly stump at the first knuckle. I took her hand and tried to shake it but she squeezed rather than shaking.

She looked at me with those light gray eyes and said, "I'm Anna Williams. With a name like Kirk, you ought to be in seminary."

I had no idea what she meant by that, but I didn't care, because I was in love. I wanted to take that stumpy finger and kiss it and make it well. I wanted to let it beckon me inside of her so I could see if she had some other missing part, a vacuum that I could fill with my own damaged soul. It sounded so corny, or worse, but it was what I was feeling right then.

She was older, like maybe twenty-five, or even thirty, but who cared? I knew that I was going to go to theological school.

It was a miserable time. I didn't fit in, and I didn't last the whole year. I was just there to try to capture Anna Williams, body and soul. But she was gone almost all the time, out recruiting other saps like me. Then she left to get married.

I didn't want to be a preacher. Almost all the students were older, like Anna had said, second and third career people. The people my age were all flaming liberals who laughed, or worse, when I said that God had made America great so we could save the world and that George W. Bush was one of the few Christians with enough vision to see that.

One day there was a guest preacher in chapel. Usually the chapel preacher was one of our own professors, or sometimes a senior student. If they had a guest in, it was a bishop passing through or some famous theologian from Europe or Asia. I heard some other students saying they weren't going to chapel that day because this guy was just an old alum who had never done anything except be a pastor in churches. Naturally, I decided to go just because they weren't.

The guy's name was Wilkey. He was old, but he had a strong voice. He preached about repentance. Then he pulled a guitar out of the pulpit, walked out front, and sang a song he had written. The chorus was "Just turn around and go the other way, that's repenting."

I remembered once we had been at Grandma's for Sunday dinner. Grandma said something about how she almost had not gone to church that day because a guest preacher was going to be there.

He was a seminary student and he had been there before. "He's just so shallow," Grandma said. "He thinks all it takes to be a Christian is to wave your hands in the air and say *Praise the Lord*. He's just plain stupid."

"Well, who with any brains would go into the ministry?" my father said.

Grandma didn't say anything about church or preachers after that, not if my father were present. Grandma didn't like my father, anyway, and was just as happy not to have to talk to him at all.

I thought that as I sat there, wilting under Dr. Wilkey's gaze, the last guitar chord dying away. *Repentance means turning around and going the other way.* Hell, it was time for me to repent. I got up and walked out and went another way. I went down to the army recruitment office.

In Iraq, in the 'Stan, there wasn't a day I didn't repent again, repent of what I had said to those students at Garrett. It was time for me to repent once more.

I sort of felt responsibility for Zan and his addled brain, because we had been roommates once, but there was nothing I could do for him. He needed professionals.

I had everything I needed in the pockets of my zip-off cargo pants and my photographer's vest.

Then I got to thinking about what Barbara had said about hospitality being a Christian virtue and responsibility.

"Thank goodness I don't believe that Christian crap anymore," I said out loud.

The purplish dawn light started slanting through the pines. I walked out of the woods, through the ditch, and up onto the shoulder. Just in case those mercenaries from the convenience store or some Broken Arrows came along, I unzipped my pants leg, got the Beretta out of Judas, put it into the pocket of my vest, hooked Judas back up.

I didn't know it then. The sheriff's deputy was gone, but I had company. Someone had been watching me the whole night.

There wasn't much traffic on the road. Nobody stopped. I had nothing else to do, so I began to walk. It wasn't long before Judas lived up to its name. I was limping badly when I heard it behind me. I stopped. It pulled up beside me. The door opened. I sighed. My foot made the decision. I got on the damned bus.

CHAPTER 13

Nobody said anything, but I knew they would never trust me again. You don't just walk out on your unit.

We drove to nowhere. A sign confirmed it, Michigan Highway 28, a slow road to nowhere.

Barbara had put some groceries onto the bus. We came to a little roadside park with a picnic table. I fixed sandwiches for lunch. We sat there for a while.

Finally, Zan said, "The birds are too loud. Let's get moving."

We got back on the bus and started driving again. I got to thinking about Zan feeling better on the move. But sometimes the headaches hit him while we were in the bus, too. He had been so close to normal at Barbara's. That was confusing. Maybe he just needed a home, some place like Barbara's.

We spent the night at another roadside park. I did the best I could with cans of stuff in a skillet. It tasted pretty bad after eating at Barbara's. The next morning, I looked through my pockets.

"We're out of money," I said.

"I've got an ATM card," Lonnie said.

"Hell's bells—" I started. I was going to say *Hells' bells, why didn't you tell us before now*? But *Hell's bells* was a Grandma phrase. I was beginning to sound like Grandma. I didn't want to. It made me think of her. That was too painful. I had so many good memories of her, but all I could see was the big empty hole in my life where she used to stand to hold off the demons.

"Well, let's use that damn ATM card for beer," Zan said.

He was downright enthusiastic.

"Yeah, let's find another convenience store like that last one," Victoria said, her voice dripping with sarcasm. "That turned out well."

"It was because you always have to pee…"

Zan was off, and the three of them argued like they were little kids. I didn't listen. I just got onto the bus and sat there and waited. Finally they all got on, too, with Zan behind the wheel, and we started off again. I spent most of the time looking for signs of a grocery or service station that might have an ATM. A long time went by without anything at all like that.

"Sometimes I feel like a motherless child…"

At first I thought it must be Victoria, the voice was so high.

"Sometimes I feel like a motherless child…"

I looked around. Victoria was staring out the window. It was Lonnie singing.

"Sometimes I feel like a motherless child…"

What a voice range. His normal baritone was up at least to lead tenor, almost to high tenor.

"…a long way from home."

Another voice joined in, Victoria singing harmony, a full contralto, rich and shadowy, like a cup of dark roast with a shot of espresso in it, what they called a Redeye at the IU Union building.

"…a long way from home."

When they were done with "Motherless Child," Victoria went into "Lonesome Traveler." Lonnie switched to harmony. It was clear that these two had sung in choirs.

Then I got a surprise. When they had finished "Lonesome Traveler," Zan started on "Amazing Grace."

I had never heard Zan sing, except for the occasional raucous team rendering of "Indiana, Our Indiana" after one of our infrequent victories. He had a decent baritone, though. I thought, *What the hell? I know the bass part for this.* Suddenly we were a quartet. We weren't going to cut any CDs any time soon, but it felt damned good. They might not trust me ever again, but at least they let me sing with them.

I forgot about looking for an ATM.

We could see the little entrance booth to the Mackinac

bridge, the only link between Michigan's upper and lower peninsulas, when the unmarked brown car pulled around us and slowed down. Flasher lights started up in its back window. A siren sounded. There was a brown sheriff's car beside us and a white van with a light bar behind us. Behind the van with the light bar was a satellite van with a big 6 on the side. A voice from a bullhorn told us to pull over.

It was way overkill. *Three* cars? A guy on foot could have trotted up beside us and pulled us over.

"I don't think we're in Kansas anymore, Toto," Zan said.

"What's going on?" Lonnie asked.

"Police are pulling us over," Victoria whispered to him.

Lonnie laughed in that nice baritone. "What? We're speeding?"

"That Sheriff Shrader said they're looking for us because of that business at the convenience store," I reminded him. "It's just going to be a formality, though, them following up on some talk from that Moe or somebody. I don't think the law can do anything about it, unless those guys I shot file a complaint, and I really don't think they're in the picture anymore."

We pulled over. Uniforms piled out of the cop cars like a circus act. They surrounded us, 38s drawn and pointed at us. A bullhorn told us to get out of the bus.

"Don't you do anything," Victoria whispered urgently to Lonnie. "They've got guns out,"

"Don't you say anything, either," I said to Zan.

That would be bad, if they found out about the Beretta in my leg, because cops don't like people with secret guns. I wasn't really worried about Zan saying anything about the Beretta, though. It was his smart mouth that worried me.

Cops *really* hated smartasses. A gun wasn't as bad as a smartass because a gun gave them an excuse to shoot you. If you were a smartass, all they could do is threaten you. Unless you were in LA. Then they could beat the crap out of you. Oh, and any place else they thought no one was looking.

Then I remembered the Glocks Victoria had taken off the jerk at that convenience store.

"Victoria, where are those guns that you—"

She didn't let me finish.

"I forgot them. I left them at Barbara's. In that old house where I slept last night."

Well, that was one less thing to worry about.

Zan pulled the handle for the door. I got out, trying not to limp. Zan followed, his hands up in the air in a sarcastic show of compliance. Lonnie came next, his head cocked, listening as I hummed a little tune to tell him where we were standing. I probably should not have chosen "Born to Run" as his location song.

As each of us got out, the cops drew in a little closer, intent, their guns in two-handed stances. A couple of them had to get down into the ditch to get behind us. I was beginning to worry about this show of force. Way too much. I assumed it was just for the TV cameras. I didn't like it, though, that the TV people had arrived with the cops, as a part of their entourage.

A girl who didn't look much older than high school, a girl Lonnie would say I should call a woman, was holding a microphone and trying to climb up the ditch slope to get a camera angle over the scene. A fat guy with a big 6 on his tee-shirt and a camera on his shoulder was trying to follow her. They weren't making much progress. I couldn't tell if it was because of her high heels or his big gut.

Then Victoria got off. Every last one of those cops took a step back. I had gotten used to Victoria, but it was the first time they had seen her. I tried to look at her as a first-timer and had to admit that she was remarkably scary.

One of the cops in the ditch stumbled as he tried to back up. He fell on his ass and his damned gun went off. The idiots actually had the safeties off and their fingers on the triggers! Fortunately, the fall backward had him pointing the 38 straight up. The TV girl screeched and ran into a stand of birches. Her camera man slipped on the slope and lost the camera as he slid back down into the ditch.

The rest of the cops were on us like Wal-Mart shoppers at a Christmas sale. The first I knew of it I was on my face in the grass of the roadside shoulder, my arms wrenched back and my wrists in cuffs. Lonnie and Zan were in the same position, Lonnie spitting grit out of his mouth because he hadn't gotten as far as the grass. There was a black shoe on his neck.

"You spit on my shoe, boy, and your ass is grass, and I'm the lawnmower."

It sounded like the same voice that had been on the bullhorn. Lonnie tried to twist around to spit on the shoe, but the shoe pressed down and Lonnie gagged. I wondered if the cop had checked first to be sure the TV camera wasn't rolling.

Then things went quiet. I heard another car drive up, fast, slam on the brakes. A door slammed.

"Sheriff's here, Clint," someone said, not much above a whisper.

"I can see that, asshole."

The shoe came off Lonnie's neck.

Gravel crunched near my face, someone else approaching

"Clint, what the hell is going on here?"

"We're apprehending fugitives from Delta County, Sheriff. The call came in while you were at lunch."

The way the guy called Clint said *lunch*, I got the impression the one he called sheriff was taking a long siesta to screw Clint's wife.

The uniforms who were slow to jump Zan and Lonnie and me got stuck with Victoria. There were two of them, and either they hadn't noticed the arrival of the sheriff or didn't care. They were still advancing on her, but slowly. One had cuffs in his hand. Her back was up against the bus, and she was glaring at the two guys.

"You touch me and you will never have children."

There was no emotion in it, nothing like I had seen when she thought Zan was trapped in the burning bus. It was cold and measured and just loud enough to carry. Gone was the rich contralto.

The cops froze.

"She won't let you cuff her. You'll have to shoot her," I said to the black cop shoe by my face, trying to be loud enough for the guy in the shoe to hear but not Victoria. "Won't look good to shoot a Medal of Honor winner."

"What the hell did you say?"

"I said you'll have to shoot her. She's claustrophobic. Got caught in a burning Humvee."

"Back off, men. You, get up."

Somebody kicked my leg. It clanged, and he said *Shit*. Sounded like Clint.

"What in hell's wrong with you?"

The sheriff's voice. I didn't know if he meant me or the cops.

I rolled around, trying to get up. At first, I thought I was just acting, trying to show them they had over-reacted. Then I found out that with only one working leg and my hands cuffed behind, I really couldn't get up.

"Somebody help him get up."

The sheriff's voice was really disgusted, but I still couldn't tell if he meant me or the cops.

Some hands got me by the arms, pulled me up. I staggered, started to fall again, but they held me in place.

I was face to face with an Ernest Borgnine impersonator in a brown sheriff's uniform.

"You got a prosthetic leg?"

"No, I just work out a lot."

So much for worrying about *Zan* mouthing off.

Borgnine looked more interested than annoyed, though.

"What's this crap about a Medal of Honor?"

"That's Victoria Roundtree," I said. "Everybody knows about her and what she did in Iraq."

I was hoping hard that there was at least one UP sheriff who didn't know about her at all. But what the hell? She deserved that medal as much as anybody else, so why not give it to her?

"You all vets?"

"Iraq and the 'Stan," I said.

I refused to say *Operation Freedom* and that sort of bullshit.

Borgnine hitched at his belt. "This is ridiculous," he muttered. He walked around in a little circle, came back to face me. "What the hell are you doing up here?"

"We live here," I said, putting as much indignation into my voice as I could.

"Where?"

"In that bus."

He was mulling that over when Zan decided to get into the act.

"Hell, we're not vets," he said. "We're Canadian terrorists.

Except we were on vacation down here, getting some pasties. Can't get 'em with rutabaga up north. Leinies, too. You boys don't have any Leinies on you, do you?"

"Don't get smart, boy," Borgnine said.

This was escalating into something that wasn't going to do us any good.

"Sheriff, we're sorry. I apologize for my friend here. But I don't know why you stopped us. I'm sure we weren't speeding in our home there."

I nodded toward the bus.

The sheriff pushed his hat back. "You some of those homeless vets? That it?"

"That's about it," I said.

"Shit. I hate that. I'm a vet, too. Desert Storm."

Then Clint got into the act. I looked around. Sure enough, the TV people were back in business.

"There's a warrant out for them from Delta County, Sheriff. Armed and dangerous. Four people in a black bus. Beat up some Indians."

The sheriff held up a meaty hand. "Like who cares?" Then he paced around some more in his little circle. He looked up, noticed the TV people. He lowered his voice, talked directly to me. "I'd normally take vets into the Legion hall and give you a beer—" He looked over at Zan. "—even though we're not fancy enough to drink Leinies. We make do with Bud."

He turned back to me. "But if there's a warrant out for you, and even Clint Denoo isn't stupid enough to get that wrong, I've got to send you back to Delta." He made a shooing motion at his chief deputy and a beckoning motion to a couple of other uniforms. "Take the cuffs off 'em," he said.

The uniforms leaned down and un-cuffed Zan and Lonnie. Zan took his time about getting up, but Lonnie jumped up like Tigger and started wiping the grit off his face.

The sheriff leaned in closer to me. "He blind?"

"Yeah. He's the one beat up the Indians."

The sheriff snorted. "Figures," he said. "That messed-up looking girl? She really a Medal of Honor winner?"

"All the way," I said.

"Shit. Well, nothing I can do about it. I've got to put you in that van and send you to Sheriff Shrader. One of my deputies will drive your bus back so it'll be in Escanaba when you need it. Wait a minute. They said you're armed. You got any weapons?"

"Just my leg," I said.

He chuckled.

"Yeah. I'll bet Clint's toe is still stinging from where he kicked you."

I chuckled, too, but for a different reason.

They loaded us into the white van. Two deputies got into the front. We sat on benches in the back. Victoria began to pick stuff off Lonnie's face.

"Shithead cops," she said, loud enough for the deputies to hear through the grill.

"What did you say to them?" she whispered to me. "I know you said something about me."

"I told them you are a former Miss Congeniality winner." She glared at me. "You're also a Medal of Honor winner," I whispered.

"Damn! That's impressive," she said.

"I thought so."

"Is the bus close," Lonnie whispered.

"Not much," I said. "It can't keep up with this van."

"They're probably stealing our stuff," Zan said.

That made Lonnie laugh. "I can get us out of this," he whispered in my direction. "I can pick locks. Once we get to the jail, if the bus is there—"

"Lonnie, how far will we get?" I asked. "Even if we get out of the jail, how far will the bus get before they catch up with us? Let's just wait and see what's going to happen. There's something fishy about this. Besides, we'll get some of that good jail cooking."

"Yeah, that will be an improvement over yours," Zan said.

"What do you mean, something fishy?" Victoria asked. She looked more worried than I thought the situation warranted.

"Shut up back there," the deputy riding shotgun yelled.

Zan gave him the finger, but he got the desired result. We sat back there, together, but each alone with our own thoughts.

I tucked away the fact that Lonnie could pick locks. I figured it might come in handy some other time. I did wonder, though, just how and when he'd learned this skill.

I hadn't answered Victoria's question. *Something fishy*? Why did I think that? That chief deputy way over-reacted to whatever threat we might be. Beyond that—oh, who gave a damn? Not me.

Sheriff Del Shrader met us personally when we arrived at the Delta County jail. We filed by him in silence. He acted more like he was our host than our jailer.

"You hungry?" he asked.

None of us said anything.

"You got ID?"

"ID about what?" Zan said, in an Alabama accent he may have learned in Gary, Indiana.

"Very funny," Shrader said. "I kicked the slats out of my crib the first time I heard that one."

"Have you arrested us because our jokes are stale?" I said.

"I haven't arrested you. But I have to question you because Ernest Althaus made a complaint against you."

"That's bullshit and you know it," Zan said. "Those Indians attacked us. They even burned up our bus. We were protecting our property and ourselves."

"And Barbara Occam-Roberts," Victoria added.

That brought a dark look to the sheriff's face.

"I asked if you have ID."

I pulled out my billfold and shoved it toward him. He threw up his hands.

"Take it out," he said.

"Ah, they caught him stealing stuff out of billfolds and now he has to be careful," Zan said.

Shrader pointed his finger at Zan. "You don't have anything worth stealing," he said.

"Except our dignity," Lonnie said, staring over the sheriff's head, emphasizing that he couldn't see him, and didn't want to.

"Look, I'm sorry if we've inconvenienced you," Shrader said, "but there are some questions that need to be answered, and you're the only one who can answer them."

I wondered why he said *one* instead of *ones*.

Sheriff Shrader turned around.

"Follow me," he said over his shoulder. "I've got some food for you."

I wasn't eager for jail chow, but I was hungry. I shrugged and followed. The others fell in behind me. Shrader went into a conference room. There were fast food sacks on the table, and a plate of brownies that looked homemade, and a stack of paper Halloween napkins.

"Help yourselves," Shrader said.

"We always say grace before we eat," Zan said.

What the hell was he up to now?

Lonnie immediately broke into song. "The Lord is good to me, and so I thank the Lord, for giving me the things I need, the sun and the rain and the apple seed. The lord is good to me. Amen."

"I hope you closed your eyes," he said.

"Apple seed?" Zan said. "Are these sacks full of apple seed?"

I didn't realize I was crying until Victoria handed me a napkin. That was the grace Grandma and I used to sing together when I ate at her house. She called it "The Johnny Appleseed song." I talked about Grandma too much. I couldn't help it. She was my still point in the turning world. So sue me.

Had I ever told Zan about Grandma and me singing that? But he wouldn't have known Lonnie would sing it. Where did Lonnie learn it? Too much thinking, not enough eating. I reached for a sack, sat down, and started eating. The others did, too.

After a minute, Shrader tapped me on the shoulder.

"Bring your food and come with me," he said. "We need to talk."

"Don't go, Joe," Zan said. "He's taking you to the third degree room."

Zan was already into a second burger and didn't sound like he was all that concerned.

I took my sack, picked up a brownie, and followed the sheriff. Whatever was going on, I could probably sort it out better without the others.

Shrader motioned for me to sit at a little table in his office. There was a coffee pot on a side board. He poured us each a cup and sat down. "Sheriff Ivaco from Chipawa County called me while you were on your way down here. He apologized for the way you were treated. His chief deputy is running against him in the election and he wanted to make a big splash for the TV cameras, apprehending dangerous fugitives. We don't have dangerous fugitives around here much, so I guess he figured he'd better take advantage of the opportunity. I just needed you back here for questioning."

"How come you told them in the warrant we were armed and dangerous?"

He snorted. "I said nothing of the sort. There isn't even a warrant. I just sent out a BOLO and told them to send you back here."

"Just because that old Indian told you a bunch of stuff you know isn't the truth?"

"Well, it's a bit more complicated than that. Actually, it was his granddaughter, Melva, who made the complaint. We have to take her seriously. She's the *de facto* leader on the rez. Got an engineering degree from Michigan Tech and a master's from MSU. Now she's sort of a general advocate for her people. She and Barbara don't get along. You know how it is, women…"

He kept talking. I was listening with only half an ear, remembering how nice it had been at Sliver Lake, at least when we weren't fighting Indians. Then I realized Shrader was asking something.

"Why were you visiting Barbara?"

I had finished up my sack of burgers and fries and was into brownies and coffee.

"We weren't visiting her. We're just traveling. We saw the sign to Sliver Lake and thought it might be interesting to see. Didn't know there was a little town back there."

He sighed. "I guess I'd better see your ID after all."

I pulled out my billfold, got out my driver's license, and handed it to him.

He looked at it, looked back at me to check the picture, turned it over. "This is expired."

"Sorry. I was kind of busy getting my leg blown off the month I was supposed to get it renewed."

"It's from Indiana."

"Yeah. Travelers sometimes come from other states. Tourist bureaus like that."

"Barbara's from Indiana. Indianapolis. Just comes up here to write."

"Yeah, Victoria thinks she's the world's best author."

That should have set him off to inquiring about Victoria, why she looks like she does, and Lonnie, why he's blind, and Zan…

But it didn't. He was only interested in me, asked me a bunch more questions about where I was from. I was getting uncomfortable.

"You look a lot like Barbara," he finally said. "Look some like me, too."

Good grief! This guy thought I might be his son! The one Barbara Occam-Roberts never had because she wasn't really pregnant by him! He thought I was visiting my mother!

A knock sounded on the door. Shrader didn't say anything, but a woman in a deputy's uniform came in.

"Sheriff Shrader, I thought you would want to see this," she said, holding a piece of paper out to him.

He took it, looked at it, looked at it some more. He kept looking at it and said, "You'd better tell Aho and Nestorini to stand by."

She nodded and left.

He looked at me. "Well, I've got to send you over to Dickinson County. Sheriff Avanti wants to see you."

"What is this, a game of Musical Sheriffs?"

"They've got an arrest warrant out on you now, too. A real one."

"Come on. Those guys at that convenience store were the ones causing the problem. Moe's? I think that was the name there. We just roughed them up a little. We were protecting everybody else. Ask anyone who was there, especially that woman in the Obama tee-shirt. Sagola? What the hell is that? We'd never even heard of Sagola before."

He looked at me blankly. "I don't know what you're talking about," he said. "Sheriff Avanti says you murdered a doctor at the VA hospital in Iron Mountain."

CHAPTER 14

"Now I don't know what *you* are talking about! How could we have murdered somebody there? We were at the VA in Iron Mountain just long enough to get thrown out."

I knew after I said it that *thrown out* would give the wrong impression. Too late to do anything about it.

Shrader looked at the paper again. "Did you see a Dr. Alan Judson there? Was he the one who threw you out?"

I had to take time to think back, which probably looked to Shrader like I was stalling. But a lot had happened since we were at the VA in Iron Mountain, and not much had happened while we were there, so what did you remember most in a deal like that? "Look, Sheriff, I barely remember being there. We were trying to get some medicine for Zan. He gets migraines. We got the usual run-around." I didn't tell him the rest of us had problems we didn't get any help with either. That would just complicate things. "Yeah, I think Judson was the doc's name. He was a decent guy. Tried to help out but the bureaucrats wouldn't let him. I don't think he had been there very long. When he told us there wasn't anything he could do, we left. End of story. No big deal."

Shrader shrugged. "Well, it's out of my hands. All I can do is send you characters back there. You can tell your story over there, but…"

Hey, what happened to 'Maybe you're my long-lost son'? That ought to count for something…

I thought about the Beretta.

"Sheriff, there's no need to disrupt everybody else's life.

I'm the one they want on this stupid murder rap, and I'm the one you wanted to talk to, so if Sheriff Ivaco's guys have gotten our bus over here yet, no reason the others can't continue on vacation."

That sounded stupid. We weren't on vacation. But I hadn't been searched yet. Shrader wasn't going to. He had wanted me just to see if I were his son.

When they threw me in the clink in Iron Mountain, though, they would do a search. People were usually squeamish about my leg, and the Beretta wasn't out in plain sight, but it was still not good to have cops finding unregistered guns on you, any place.

I wasn't too worried about what would happen if they found the gun in my leg. I knew it hadn't been used to shoot any doctor. It wouldn't look good, though. And there were other things they could nail me on: unregistered, concealed without a permit, borrowed from a general who didn't know what happened to it…

I needed to slip the gun to Zan and keep it away from the law.

"So you're the one they want, eh? The warrant says *four* suspicious suspects traveling in an old school bus. What made you think that *you* are the one they're after?"

He was in full sheriff suspicious mode.

"Because *you* said so," I said, trying to match his tone.

He shrugged again, went over to his desk, pushed a button on the intercom. "Margaret, tell Aho and Nestorini to gather up the people in the conference room and put them in the van." He released the button and looked up at me. "I'm supposed to cuff you now that you're suspects, but you're veterans. I don't want to do that. Do we need to use the cuffs, or are you going to cooperate?"

I didn't know what to do to get out of this, but I knew cuffs wouldn't help the plan, whatever it was. "We'll cooperate, but you'd better let me tell them about it."

He pushed a button again. "Margaret, tell Aho and Nestorini just to wait in the van. I'll bring the prisoners out."

Prisoners? I didn't like the sound of that. We weren't guilty of anything. Well, that wasn't true, but we hadn't murdered any

VA doctor—just thought about it, and the ones we thought about murdering weren't in Iron Mountain.

There was a whole bunch of stuff I wanted to say, but I knew none of it would be helpful, so I just got up and went back to the conference room. Shrader jumped up to follow me.

"Give me a minute alone with them," I said. "It won't be to plot any getaway. We've got nothing to worry about."

Actually, I knew we had a hell of a lot to worry about, and I was sure I didn't have any idea yet just how much.

I went in and told them to finish up the brownies while we talked. I told them what Sheriff Shrader had said about why we were wanted back in Iron Mountain. One and all, they proclaimed that it was stupid and that we were being singled out just because it was easy and because the cops were lazy. It got loud and profane. I didn't try to dampen it down. They needed to vent, for a lot of reasons. I knew Shrader wouldn't wait forever, though, so I finally put up my hand for silence. Victoria hadn't been saying a whole lot anyway. Zan saw my hand and cut off in mid-sentence. Lonnie went on for a few words and then got the idea.

"Look," I said, "we've got two choices. If we cooperate, we get to ride in the van without cuffs. We'll explain over there, and they'll let us go, and we'll be back on our way."

Our way to where? It didn't make any difference. Any place was as good as any other.

"Or we can fight it out, get beat up, get real charges against us for resisting arrest and escape. And, if we do escape, how far will we get? We're in a strange town with a hundred miles of wilderness and water on every side."

I waited. Nobody said anything.

"Okay. Let's get this done." I opened the door. Shrader was standing there. "Lead the way, Sheriff," I said.

He did. We followed. We went out the door marked *Prisoners Only* to the parking area. Another van was waiting, two deputies in the front seat. Shrader opened the back doors and we climbed in.

"We'll be taking your bus over to Iron Mountain," he said. "They want it for forensics."

I nodded.

"You want me to say anything to Barbara?"

He looked right at me. I tried to look misty. "Yeah. Tell her I miss her home cooking."

That ought to mess with his mind, and it was even the truth.

He gave me a funny look and closed the door. It made a sound like an echo.

We rode in silence from one jail to another. It was getting to be a habit. As they got us out of the van, the deputies talked about how it hadn't taken any time at all to transport prisoners, since they had gone from the Eastern Time Zone to Central, somewhere between Escanaba and Iron Mountain, but it would take two hours to get back to their families. That sounded to me like a good summary of what life was like for any person in a uniform, twice as long to get back to reality.

One of them got in front of us, the one with Aho on his name tag, and tried to line us up. We just stared at him, even though I was sure three of us wanted to say something rude about his name, even though the UP was full of Finns, and it was a common Finnish name. I figured Lonnie would, too, if he could see the tag. Being blind can get you into a lot of trouble, but it can keep you out of some, too.

We just shuffled around, and Aho gave up on the line idea. He led the way in, and Nestorini brought up the rear.

It was a nice new red brick building on the back of a big old red stone court house. We filed through the *Prisoners Only* door into a bare reception area. A big man in a brown uniform was arguing with a young woman about my age. He reminded me a little of Tom Selleck, the actor, without the moustache, and twenty years younger, but just as mean and shifty in the eyes.

"Look, Reverend Linden, stop following me around. You're not supposed to be over here. There's nothing I can do about it anyway."

Reverend? She didn't look like...

But how are girl preachers supposed to look? This one was in jeans and running shoes and a blue chambray shirt. She looked like a younger version of Jill Taylor, the mom in that *Home Improvement* sitcom that was popular when I was a kid. I used to watch it with Grandma. Grandma would laugh and then say, "If grunts made the man, Tim the Tool Man and your father would be president and vice-president." That was the best thing Grandma ever said about my father.

I vowed to watch more current TV. The only celebrities I could compare real people to were has-beens. Yeah, like we were going to get cable on the bus.

The reverend was dangling an open backpack from the end of one arm. It was one of those real little ones, the kind ergonomic women use as purses, so little it didn't even reach the floor, the way a real backpack should when you let it hang at the end of your arm. She was talking with her other hand, as well as her mouth.

"Sheriff, the woman's at risk. She's going to get beat up again—"

The sheriff broke in, waving his arms right back at her. "But she won't press charges, dammit, pardon my French, and there's nothing I can do if she won't. You know she's at risk. I know that guy she lives with is a total—well, you know, but she's free, white, and twenty-one—"

"Sheriff Avanti, that's offensive, and you know it—"

She kept on talking. The sheriff looked around for a way to escape. He saw us and the Delta County deputies. "Thank God," he almost shouted.

The reverend turned to see what he was thanking God for. She didn't look like she thought we were God's best gift-giving work. That was also when I got an idea.

"Reverend Linden!" I exclaimed. "How long has it been? My goodness, it's wonderful to see you again."

I was walking toward her with my arms out-stretched, exaggerating my limp. She looked alarmed, which was what I wanted.

"Oh, I'm sorry. About the limp. You don't know about my leg." I reached down and unzipped the pants leg. I was getting good at that. I let it drop just as I got to her. Her eyes got wide and she looked away, as people always do when they see Judas. That's what I wanted. With her eyes examining the pop machine to avoid my leg, and my back shielding me from the sheriff, I popped the Beretta out of my leg and into her open backpack. "Oh, darn, I'm sorry," I said, in my best country boy style. "That pants leg keeps coming off. Wal-Mart stuff, you know—"

Just then a big hand grabbed me by the shoulder and spun me around. I staggered and tried to hold Judas in place.

"What the hell are you doing?"

It was the sheriff. Aho and Nestorini were right behind him, looking a little embarrassed. They hadn't kept a very tight hold on their *prisoner*.

"Uh, Sheriff Shrader said not to cuff 'em or anything…" Aho was trying to explain.

"Do I know you?"

Reverend Linden stepped in, making it difficult for Avanti or Aho to get at me. She was making a point of looking at the leg now, her cheeks red, chagrined that she had looked away from a deformation. Professional Christians weren't supposed to do that.

"Joe Kirk," I said. "You visited me in the hospital, after my leg was blown off. I was in pretty bad shape…"

She wrinkled up her face in one of those trying-to-remember looks when a person knows damned well there's nothing to remember. "Oh, yes, the hospital—"

"You two can reminisce later. These are murder suspects. Dr. Judson. Remember him, Reverend?"

"Don't be supercilious, Sheriff. It does not become you."

I liked that. She was going to out-word him.

Then we heard the moan, like the ghost of Christmas-never. We all turned toward the sound. It was coming from Victoria, who was curled up in a little ball in the corner. Lonnie and Reverend Linden started for her at the same time.

"Jesus, Mary, and Joseph. What the fuck is that? Looks like somebody rode her hard and put her away wet."

Sheriff Avanti was not a subtle man.

"You prick," Reverend Linden muttered as she ran toward Victoria.

She wasn't being real subtle, either.

Deputy Nestorini got hold of Lonnie's arm to try to hold him back. Lonnie shrugged it off and kept going toward Victoria. Nestorini tried again, and Lonnie reversed the whole thing, got hold of the deputy's arm, flipped him in a cartwheel. Nestorini ended up sliding down a concrete wall. Aho grabbed his nightstick and went for Lonnie. Zan put him into a chokehold and the nightstick clattered on the floor.

This wasn't going well.

"She's a veteran, Sheriff," I yelled at Avanti. "Post-Traumatic. She was trapped in a burning tank. Claustrophobic. She can't be in small places like this."

One of my rules was that I didn't tell anyone I was a vet. I didn't ask for sympathy because of my leg. I didn't take any favors, either. I wasn't a hero just because I was in uniform. That wasn't my rule for any other vet, though. Telling the exact truth wasn't a rule, either.

Lonnie had gotten to Victoria. He stumbled over Reverend Linden, pushed her out of the way, and was down beside Victoria, holding her.

I heard a gurgling sound.

"Zan, let the deputy go," I said.

"Oh, hell, I'm not hurting him. We're just playing around, ain't we Ahole?"

"He was a linebacker," I explained to Sheriff Avanti.

Zan let Deputy Aho go and he slid to the floor, holding his throat.

"You people are in a shitload of trouble now." Avanti glared at me. "And that goddam Shrader is, too, for not transporting you according to regulations."

"Cut Dad some slack," I said. "He was just taking it easy on us because I told him it would be okay. I didn't expect these deputies to attack us."

"*Dad*? What the hell are you talking—You said your name is Kirk."

"It's a long story. Right now, though, Captain Roundtree needs some attention at the VA hospital. She's going into shock. I've seen her do this before."

I figured Victoria would last better at the VA, even though she was trying to get away from them, than she would in a jail cell. I thought she might get more attention as an officer. Hell, for all I knew, she *was* a captain.

"You could put a guard outside her room," I said. "She's not going any place, though. She's too debilitated. Almost catatonic most of the time. Weak as a kitten. That's the catatonic part. Besides, she didn't kill any doctor. She can't even defend herself. Look at her."

Victoria was still moaning. Lonnie was rocking her like a baby. Reverend Linden was still beside them, on her knees. It looked like she was fingering a rosary, which didn't make any sense. Catholics didn't have female reverends. Her open backpack was dragging on the floor, and I could see my Beretta in it. I needed Miss America. If she walked in, all the men would look at her. I settled for Miss Direction. "I'm really sorry, Deputy Nestorini, about Lieutenant Blifield pushing you up against the wall that way, but as you can see, he's blind, so he doesn't see where people are."

Nestorini was trying to push himself up from the floor and not doing a very competent job of it. "He didn't *push* me. He *threw* me. He assaulted an officer—"

"He's got PTSD, too, Sheriff, along with the blindness. Got blinded trying to save his men from a sneak attack. Did it, too. All of them escaped without a scratch. He was the only one hurt. The worst thing was the eye operations afterward. Had to stick a needle right in the eyeball. Might as well have been at Gitmo. All that pain, and still didn't do any good. Not right, not right at all."

I was laying it on pretty thick, but Avanti seemed to be buying it. I was running out of bullshit, though. I had never been very good at that, anyway. I needed some more to explain Zan and his chokehold on Deputy Aho. Reverend Linden became a distraction, though.

Big tears were running down the pastor's face. "I'll be responsible for her," she said, dipping her head toward Victoria. "I can stay with her at the hospital."

"She's a damn murder suspect, pardon my French, of a doc at that very same hospital, dammit. How do you think they're going to react over there if I tell them they've got to take care of somebody who murdered their brand new doc and the only protection they've got from her is a goddam preacher, pardon my French?

"Well, you could do both, Sheriff," I said. "Send Reverend Linden to the hospital with Captain Roundtree, and post a guard on her room, too. Otherwise, do you have facilities here to accommodate a female American hero without sending her into claustrophobic hysterics? The Commander in Chief won't look very favorably on that. You know how his wife is about taking care of military families."

"Right. Like the C in C is going to pay attention to every soldier who comes through the Upper Peninsula."

"He'll hear about it when word gets out that you've got a Medal of Honor winner locked up here on false charges."

Sheriff Avanti screwed his face up into a grimace that was more like Don Rickles than Tom Selleck. I decided to use that Medal of Honor gambit more often; it worked every time.

"I've got to let go of custody if I send her over there," he said. "The VA has their own police."

I knew that, of course—as many VA facilities as I'd been in—but I didn't see as how that would be a problem. The VA didn't have its own justice system.

"Well, hell's bells, they'll give her back," I said. "They're just there for—" Dagnabit, I was channeling Grandma again. *Hell's bells*. That was her phrase. *Dagnabit*, too, for that matter.

Sheriff Avanti interrupted without even putting his hand up. "I don't know what the hell this new bunch of VA cops is there for," he said. "Whole new bunch, when that new administrator came in. Don't look like your usual VA cops. More like Special Forces."

"Doesn't matter who the particular guys are," I said. "If you want her for a civil crime, they can't keep her away from you."

I didn't know if that was true, but I had my ego involved now in getting Victoria into the VA. When my ego got involved, bad things usually happened.

"I ought to go over there myself, make sure," he muttered, "but I can't be in two places at once, and I've got to deal with the rest of you and these Delta County deputies…"

He glared at the deputies and blustered some more, but he finally agreed to call the VA hospital to make arrangements to send Victoria there, escorted by a deputy. He not only agreed to let Reverend Linden go along, but he personally cuffed Victoria's right wrist to the pastor's left.

I cringed when Linden slung her open backpack over her

right shoulder, but nothing came flying out of it. The Delta County deputies whined some more, but Avanti blamed them for not having us under control when they brought us in, regardless of the orders they had from their own sheriff. He sent them back with a verbal message for Del Shrader which included a lot of French, without his usual apologies for it. I figured the annual picnic of the Upper Peninsula sheriffs could get interesting.

It could get interesting over there in general if Aho and Nestorini had been paying enough attention to hear me call their sheriff "Dad" when I was talking to Sheriff Avanti, too.

Zan, Lonnie, and I ended up in the cells, without much chance at getting out on bond, since we had no money, no place to go if we got out, and no vehicle to go in. Probably no bond for murder suspects, anyway, especially without a lawyer. We might have gotten a phone call, but Avanti was still threatening to charge us with assault on police officers as well as suspicion of murder, and none of us knew anybody to call. Not just in Iron Mountain, but anywhere.

It also turned out that the Medal of Honor gambit worked only until somebody checked on it. *Damn Google and the ATV it rode in on.*

CHAPTER 15

Rickie

Rickie Linden wanted to keep her arm around Victoria on the way to the hospital, but she couldn't, cuffed to the strangely colored woman the way she was. Damn that sheriff, anyway. He had taken special delight in putting a cuff on her. She just knew it. It was bad enough for a SoCal girl to be facing a second winter in the Upper Peninsula without having to deal with cretin sheriffs, too.

She made do with reaching across and holding the other woman's rough, mottled hand. The deputy kept looking at them in the rearview mirror and sneering, like he thought they were lesbians or something. Or maybe he always sneered at everything, the way everybody in the UP said "Eh?" after everything. *Eh*? What the hell was that? She might as well be in goddam Canada, pardoning the French. Goddam, now she was sounding like that goddam sheriff. She took a deep breath—and immediately regretted it. The woman beside her smelled of sweat and body odors she didn't want to identify. Rickie vowed she would not cry.

It wasn't the first time she'd been handcuffed. A fraternity guy at USC had put the cuffs on her once. *'Come on. It'll be fun.'* Most of the world's troubles started when a man said that to a woman. It had *not* been fun, and she vowed she would never let anyone put her into bondage of any kind again. But Sheriff Avanti had cuffed her to this strange woman before she really understood what was happening. Hell, she wasn't sure of anything that had happened once that Joe Kirk and his friends had walked into the Dickinson County jail. But she really felt for this Victoria. From all that Joe Kirk had said about her…the agonies she must have been through…and the way she looked now…how could Rickie not try to keep her out of a jail cell that would drive her as crazy as a "cask of amontillado" in Edgar Allan Poe's scary story. And who was Joe Kirk? She had never visited someone like him, had she?

Victoria moaned and groaned all the way to the hospital, and continued to smell. The deputy continued to sneer. The mile down Stephenson Avenue seemed like it was a state long.

The sheriff had called ahead. The VA was ready, but not happy. The deputy pulled his car into the circular drive in front. He had to park behind an empty VA police car that was blocking the main part of the sidewalk, including the wheelchair ramp. A VA cop who looked like he spent most of his time pumping iron met them at the front door. He brusquely took charge of "the prisoner" and told the county deputy to leave.

"Don't you want the key to the cuffs," the deputy said.

"*We* know how to deal with cuffs, whether we have a key or not," the weight lifter said, his voice dripping with arrogance.

But he stuck his hand out. It made Rickie think of a cat that got scared by a shadow and then sat down and licked its butt like that was what it intended all along. She wanted to giggle at the image and stuck her free hand over her mouth to make sure she didn't.

The deputy looked at the women, shrugged his shoulders, tossed the key up where the VA cop could grab it out of the air. The VA cop watched him all the way out the door. Then he turned abruptly and walked to the elevators. Rickie had a wild urge to flee out the door after the deputy, and she suspected Victoria did, too, but they had no choice but to follow.

The elevator was slow. They waited in silence. When the doors finally opened, the officer went in first. Rickie started to squeeze in behind him but Victoria held back. "I can't," she moaned.

"Claustrophobia," Rickie said. "We'll use the stairs."

She pushed the "close" button and stepped out. The weight-lifter grabbed the closing doors and pushed them back open.

"The hell you will," he snarled.

He grabbed the women and tried to stuff them back into the elevator. The doors closed on them, Rickie and the man inside, Victoria outside. He got the doors open again and tried to pull Victoria in.

"What in the *hell* is going on here?"

It was a nurse. Tall and capped. You never saw a nurse in one of those white caps anymore. Rickie knew her, though. This nurse was one of her parishioners.

"None of your business," the VA cop said, trying to keep the snarl out of his voice and not succeeding.

"Claustrophobia," Rickie shouted out. "We can use the stairs. Thank God, Flo—"

The nurse ducked down and shook her head so violently at Rickie that her cap almost flew off. Then she took hold of Victoria and began pulling. "If this is one of our veterans, then it *is* my business," she said, loudly. "Is this the veteran we were told to expect?"

"Yes," Rickie grunted. She knew from her previous visits there that patients in a VA hospital were always referred to as veterans, not patients. But why would Florence act like she didn't know her?

The cop threw up his hands in disgust.

"I'll walk them up," the nurse said, and she did.

The cop clumped up the stairs behind them. The VA had apparently faced this kind of thing before. They had a special room for Victoria. It wasn't all that much better than a jail cell, except there were windows, without bars. No need to worry about someone getting out the window on the fourth floor. The regular rooms were clean and spacious, the way the whole hospital was. Rickie knew because she had called on veterans in the regular rooms.

The cop took the cuffs off the women, pushed them into the room, and pushed the one comfortable-looking chair into the hall to use for his vigil. Victoria sat on the bed. Rickie perched on a straight chair.

"This isn't my floor," the nurse said. "I'll let the people at this station know you're here."

The nurse left. Victoria stopped moaning. She looked downright composed, like she was dealing with the whole mess now better than Rickie was. Rickie sat and wondered why her own parishioner acted like she didn't know her. The silence got long. Rickie hit upon a neutral subject.

"Who *is* Joe Kirk, anyway, Victoria? May I call you Victoria? I know Joe said *Captain* Roundtree—"

"*Victoria* is okay."

She had a nice voice when she wasn't moaning.

"Well, then. Good. Oh, Joe Kirk. He acted like he knew me, and he said I had visited him in the hospital. I did CPE, but I don't recall anybody like him—"

"What's CPE?"

"Oh. Clinical Pastoral Education. It's a hospital internship for ministers. I was at the University of Iowa hospitals for a year as part of my seminary education. We had a lot of different kinds of patients, but I don't remember—Besides, wouldn't he have been at a VA hospital? They've got a big VAMC in Iowa City, but I never did any work over there."

"He's sort of good-looking," Victoria said, "if you can get by the limp and clothes and haircut. I think a woman like you would remember a man like Joe."

The pastor felt a flush coming up from somewhere into her cheeks. "What do you mean, a woman like me?"

"Free, white, and twenty-one," Victoria said.

Rickie couldn't help but laugh at that one. "Oh, that sheriff, isn't he a Neanderthal? He says things like that all the time. I'm not sure if he's serious or just playing a role. I've only been here a year and a half, and I don't know him very well. I'm involved with domestic violence victims, though, so I have to deal with him every once in a while—almost always without any results."

Rickie felt Victoria's big brown eyes boring into her as though they were lasers.

She seemed such a different woman than she had been in the jail. She looked the same, though. You couldn't change those looks.

Rickie was almost surprised that the woman's appearance didn't bother her. Not as much as those eyes.

"Is that why you're doing this? Sort of an extension of being a domestic violence social worker?"

Rickie flushed again. "Oh, I just do this as part of my ministry. I'm not a social worker."

Victoria and her eyes kept boring in. "Why are you doing this, Rev. Linden? Taking care of me? Why do you care? I'm nothing to you. Why should I trust you?"

Rickie was getting the idea that Victoria was beating around the bush, changing the subject every time it got close to her own situation.

It was a good question, though. Why should this military veteran trust a woman like her, who had never suffered in her life, unless you counted living in the UP in winter? And being an orphan with parents—

She wasn't sure any number of words could result in trust, but she was a woman, and she knew that any trust from one woman to another at least begins with words. "I'm not really sure, Victoria. It's a matter of hospitality. You're either a host in the world or a guest, somebody who expects everyone else to treat them like a guest. Christians are the hosts of the world. Of course, these days that's the last thing anybody thinks when they hear the word *Christian*, The Christians you see on TV act like guests. Everybody is supposed to cater to them, do what they want."

Victoria was nodding acceptance, but Rickie couldn't tell if it was because she agreed or just wanted to keep her talking so she wouldn't have to say anything about herself. It sounded like bullshit to Rickie. Did she really believe this, or was it just stuff she was repeating from seminary?

"You don't always get to choose where and how God calls you to be a host," she continued. "I wanted to be a hospital chaplain. That's why I did that CPE at Iowa. I wanted to work with George Paterson, the chaplain there, learn from the best in the business. But I couldn't get a hospital job when I graduated, so here I am, a priest in the Godforsaken UP. That includes taking care of anyone God puts here, even if it's in Sheriff Neanderthal's jail."

Victoria nodded again. "I didn't think women could be priests," she said.

"Oh. Yes, that's right, with the Roman Catholics. But I'm the rector—uh, that is, the pastor, or priest—at the Episcopal

Church here. It's sort of the Anglican Church in the US."

She looked down at herself—shirt, jeans, running shoes. She usually tried to look like the part of a pastor when she was out in public, to remind herself more than anyone else of who she was, but the trip to the sheriff's office had been an emergency.

"Reverend Linden—"

"Please. Call me Rickie. Reverend Linden is just something I use when I have to deal with officials like the sheriff. I'm so young, and I'm a woman, and nobody takes me seriously, so I use the title then. Like the Roman Church, Episcopalians call priests *Father*, but obviously they can't call me that. Some of my congregation tried calling me *Mother Linden*, but I'm the youngest person in the congregation…"

She trailed off. She was babbling. This was way too much information. Victoria didn't really look uninterested, though, more like she was waiting for something.

"I don't think I've ever known a woman named Rickie."

Rickie took a long breath.

"It's not even my name. I'm officially Richard Michelle Linden. My parents wanted a boy." It was more than that. They had not wanted just any boy. They had wanted a boy to replace the one who was murdered. Ten years old. They even gave her his name. He had been Richard Michael. She had grown up with old parents who constantly grieved the death of their first Richard and could not accept their second one because she wanted to play with dolls. "You've never met a Rickie, but I've never met a Medal of Honor winner before."

"Yeah, about that…" Victoria sniffed and looked around the room. "You'd think they'd have snot paper in a hospital room," she said.

"I've got some," Rickie said. She reached into her backpack and felt something hard.

What was going on? She pulled the backpack up high so that she could see into it but Victoria couldn't. A gun! Rickie didn't know anything about guns, but she knew this one wasn't for deer hunting. She was into the sheriff's office off and on, enough that everyone there recognized her, but they still gave her bag a look whenever she arrived. That meant the gun had gotten into her backpack while she was in the jail or now that she was at the VA. *Gotten into*? What was she saying? It had not gotten into her backpack by itself. Someone had put it there.

Was she being set up? The sheriff was a jerk, and that deputy who drove them over was a smirk, but she couldn't really believe either one of them had slipped a gun into her bag. To what end?

Wait a minute. Dr. Judson had been murdered right here at the VA. Had he been shot? She couldn't remember now what the newspaper had said, or even if it said how he was murdered. Could someone here, someone who had shot the doctor, have slipped the gun into the bag after she and Victoria arrived? But how?

Victoria sniffled. Oh, right, she was supposed to be getting Victoria a tissue. '*Snot paper*' she'd called it. *Yeewh*. Rickie rummaged around, found a little pack of white tissues, acted like she had been looking for them but just couldn't find them, held the bag shut, walked the tissues over to the bed, went back to her chair, pulled the bag up high again.

The damned gun was still there.

Okay, she had to think this through. The gun wasn't necessarily the one that had shot Dr. Judson, *if* he had been shot. Of course, shooting was the usual way people got dead in the UP. Guns and snowmobiles. Put guns, snowmobiles, and booze together and you had the city crest of Iron Mountain. Guns were the religion here, and The Second Amendment, or at least its last half, was the paper pope. *Ex cathedra. Ex alive.*

Okay, she was stalling. This wasn't getting her anyplace. Her mother had ranted at her, morosely, but it was still a rant, from first grade on, about keeping her backpack closed. That was why she had always left it open, hoping something important would drop out and make her mother mad. Even after she left home to go to USC and then to Seabury-Western Theological Seminary, she had never zipped up the damned backpack. It had not occurred to her that the bigger problem would be someone putting something in, like a damned gun.

Got to stop saying damn so much. Those other words, too, especially the F *Word. Going to do it in a sermon some time if I don't watch it. Then they'll decide that even though they can't get anybody else to come up here and pastor this little church,* nobody *is better than a girl from California. Okay, think about it.* The gun wasn't in her bag when she went to the jail. They had searched her when she went in. Could the deputy who searched her—No. She watched him as he looked in the bag. Then the sheriff. Why would he—

She thought back through the whole time in the jail, when the group from Escanaba came in, and that strangely attractive guy claimed he knew her—Oh.

Unconsciously she began to hum a song her mother had sung when she got teary about the first Richard Linden and thought the second one wasn't listening. '*It had to be you...*'

It had to be Joe Kirk who put the gun into her backpack.

CHAPTER 16

Victoria

Victoria eyed the priest woman. She thought she could trust her. Rickie was a Joe Kirk type. White liberals were so easy to con. But what could Rickie Linden do for her? Victoria would have to think that through, but she couldn't be too slow about it. When they came looking for her, and they found out she had been alone with Dr. Judson…

The claustrophobia came and went now. She had found, though, that she could use it to her advantage. She knew what would happen if they got her into a jail cell and started running her info. She had a better chance of making it out of a VA. She had done that before.

So she had curled up into a ball in the corner and moaned. Joe fell for it. She knew he would. He thought he was a tough guy, a hard case, no illusions, but he had that savior complex. He couldn't say *no* to somebody in need.

That's why he had let her on the bus in the first place. That's why he had picked up Lonnie off the street. That's why he kept looking for help for Zan. Yes, she could con Joe and let him do the rest of the conning.

It had worked perfectly. Except now she was back in a room at a VA hospital, with a guard outside the door, just like before, in Danville.

She had been lucky, in a way. The VA in Chicago had one of the best skin graft doctors in the whole VA system. She got to go home for her treatments. Except it wasn't home anymore. And once the people in her neighborhood and in her church took a look at her, they stopped being happy she was there.

At first everybody had been real big on what a hero she was. The Chicago newspapers played it up. One of the TV stations did a special on her. The first sweet little blond bitch they sent out to interview her threw up when she walked into the room and saw what the fire and the doctors had done to Victoria. They had to send another one the next day, a middle-aged Latina with hard eyes. She thought the best approach was to talk about how bad Victoria looked.

Victoria had thrown her out. They ended up with a one minute bit on the no-o'clock news, using her official army photo from when she first made PFC.

Then her doctor was gone. One day he just wasn't there. "Left to pursue other opportunities," they told her. "Don't worry; we've got other doctors just as good."

They weren't. They weren't Dr. Allison, either. Victoria and Dr. Allison were a team. Together they could stand the pain, stand inflicting it, and stand taking it. She couldn't take it without him. She tried, though. Nobody could say she didn't try. Her mother said it, anyway, but her mother usually said things about her only daughter that nobody could say.

Then the "just as good" doctors were gone, too. "Consolidating services in another location," they said. "You'll need to go to Danville."

She did. She had to ride a bus. She hated buses. She had buried her head in a Barbara Occam-Roberts novel, *The Raven's Other Quote*. It got her through the bus ride.

She had stumbled onto the novels of Barbara Occam-Roberts by accident, but she'd loved them from the start. The women in her novels were smart, learning against all obstacles, thinking great thoughts. That's the kind of woman Victoria wanted to be. She would never be beautiful, not now, but she could be smarter than any man.

They didn't have any skin doctors at the Danville VA. Someone in Chicago had given her the run-around. The people in Danville didn't seem surprised she was there, though. They said they would sort it out.

They put her into a funny room. It was a double. Not double beds, but a room behind a room. They took her into the second room and told her to make herself comfortable. She got another Barbara Occam-Roberts novel out and began to read.

She got restless, went out into the hallway. The top administrator came running and told her to wait. A special doctor would be in to see her. They took her back to the interior room and closed the door as they left.

She didn't like the second room. She didn't like closed doors. She went out into the first room. She cracked the door open. She heard them talking in the hallway. It wasn't a doctor who was going to come to see her. It was the MPs. Detective investigators. She heard the VA people coming back toward her. She hurried back to the room behind. She pulled back the drapes on the window. It had bars.

So they had finally learned about what led up to the inferno. She should have known it would happen, but she had gotten used to denying reality...

Her squad was where it wasn't supposed to be, doing something they weren't supposed to do, in a Humvee that wasn't theirs. She hadn't even known. She thought it was all legitimate, just executing another dumb order. She found out later that the guys hadn't wanted to take her, but it would have looked funny if they'd left her behind. She knew how the army worked, though. Once something got out, somebody had to be blamed, somebody on the lowest scale of the ranks.

They had settled themselves into the anteroom, two of them, regular VA cops, not MPs yet, playing cards. She opened the door to the room, walked through the anteroom to the hallway. They watched her, but she didn't take any of her stuff, even her purse. Just walked down the hallway to the women's rest room. One of them came out into the hallway and watched. They were satisfied. They knew a woman wouldn't go any place without her purse. She stood inside the door, counted to ten, stuck her head out. The watcher was gone, back to his card game in the anteroom. She went the other way.

Then she saw the white guys. One of them had eyes that wouldn't move. One of them had wild eyes that moved too much. One of them limped, the kind of limp that came from an ill-fitting prosthesis.

She recognized those kinds of eyes, that kind of limp. She

had seen plenty of those eyes, those limps, since…since the thing she would not name.

No. She wasn't going to do that anymore. *The inferno.* That's what it was. She would name it. She might not go much farther, not yet, but she could go that far.

The white guys were dirty and scraggly. Rebels. Hard cases. Bad boys. She liked bad boys. Her brothers were bad boys, the ones still alive.

It was the one with the eyes that weren't eyes that drew her. He was handsome as a movie star, and muscular, in a wiry way. He moved like a panther, but a panther who had been set down in a jungle he couldn't recognize. If she had met him on the street, back before the inferno, he wouldn't even have looked at her. If he could see her now, he would react like everyone else. But all he could *see* was her voice. '*Your voice can charm the savage beast, Victoria.*' That's what Reverend Wright had told her whenever he wanted her to sing a solo.

These guys were white, but skin color didn't mean a damn thing to her anymore. If it did to them, too bad. She followed them outside. They walked toward a decrepit bus. She didn't like buses. She almost turned around. Then she remembered what was there and what wasn't there.

Wild-eyes and the limper stopped to talk. They didn't seem to be arguing, but it was a serious discussion. The panther boy went on ahead, cocking his head, tacking left and right, finally heading straight for the bus.

She'd walked on past the other two, following the panther, and climbed onto the bus.

CHAPTER 17

Alan

Three weeks earlier:

Doctor Alan Judson needed a smoke. He hadn't had a cigarette since the baby came. Zoe wouldn't stand for it. That was fine. That was the way it should be. When a man became a father, he had to grow up. Zoe had laid down the law—no more hunting, no more snowmobiles, no more motorcycles, no more cigarettes. She wasn't going to raise this baby by herself. That's what she said, and she was right. When a man became a father, he had to put his child first, and Alan Judson was ready.

That was why he had switched over from the group practice out by the county hospital to the VA. He was making less money, but he had regular hours. He could go home, play with the baby, have supper with his family like a civilized man. No more *on call*, no more midnight trips to the hospital. Once he was home, he was home, and he was glad to stay there.

Charlene had kidded him, said he called it *growing up*, but it was really just getting old. Charlene had been his nurse at the group practice for at least a dozen years. She was one of those second-career nurses, started working for him when she was fifty, like he was now, almost. She was the only one who had been honest with him when he married Zoe. '*You old goat, she's young enough to be your daughter. What's wrong with you?*'

Charlene was the only thing he missed from the old practice.

But she had been wrong, and she admitted it. Zoe was the best thing that ever happened to him. Until Kirk came along.

That was one reason he had been drawn to Joe Kirk, the name. Kirk certainly wasn't his choice for his son's name. It was Zoe's father's name. Zoe's father wasn't much older than her husband, and he had been opposed to her marrying *that old man*. Zoe wanted to name their son after her father. It had always been her dream, she said. When you're an older husband to a beautiful young woman you know damned well could have done better, you don't argue much. You just feel lucky.

Of course, holding his son, saying his name, he hadn't even thought of his father-in-law. This little *Kirk* was entirely his own person. The name belonged to him alone.

When Joe Kirk had come into his office, though, he had gotten that strange feeling, that foreboding, that premonition that he was looking at his own son thirty years into the future. It wasn't a pretty picture.

Not that Joe was bad-looking. He was over six feet. His dark blond hair probably would have been okay, except it was a crew-cut on its way to becoming a golden retriever, after retrieving. Looked like he might have been a hockey player, a defenseman. But there was the leg that wasn't there, and the limp that was. He wasn't exactly dirty, but he was shop-worn. The blue eyes were haunted by something Alan Judson couldn't fathom. Those eyes were out of nowhere and going steadily toward nothing. Alan Judson didn't want that for his son.

Joe Kirk had those other vets with him. They were a doctor's worst nightmare. They wanted help, as long as they didn't have to jump through the hoops. Didn't they know that life was nothing but hoop jumping? What could you do for people like that?

They didn't ask for much, really. Medicine for the wild one's headaches. He wouldn't sit still for an exam, of course. The blind one—there was nothing to do for him. And the woman—my God! What had they done to her? He was no skin specialist, but, some of the work on her was first-rate, but they needed to finish the job, and...

He could tell, though. They weren't asking—but they were hoping—for miracles. Not for someone to make them whole.

They were past that. They wanted the miracle of someone taking them seriously, respecting them, not giving them a handout, but giving them what they had earned, respect.

Alan wasn't in the social work end of veterans affairs. He couldn't do anything about the VA bureaucracy that left vets without a job or a home or an income or respect. He was just a doctor.

That was what Simmons said. God, what a harridan! Florence Kneightly had been his first nurse at the VA. She was still on staff. He wished he could have her back. She was a brand new nursing school grad, just an LPN, wore that outdated white cap, but she was in her forties. She understood the world and people. They worked well together. Then along came Simmons.

What a piece of work! She was the opposite of Charlene and Florence. He almost had the idea that she had been assigned to take Florence's place to be sure he did *not* help anyone. She took one look at Joe Kirk and his friends and announced that there was nothing he could do for them.

"Get them out of here. They aren't ours. They've got to wait their turn. Some of these veterans—They think they can jump the system. Well, without the system, there's chaos. They're military. They should know that. You take orders and do your duty. They've got to stay within the system. You can't do anything for them if they won't cooperate. You're not a social worker. You're *just a doctor*."

He wasn't getting any help from the VA bureaucrats even at doctoring, though. Everything he tried to do...there wasn't any money. It was almost like they had no idea that they were supposed to be taking care of these people, these damaged people. Dammit, if you sent people off to war, you had an obligation to take care of them when they came back! He had felt good about going to work for the VA, because he could be a part of that.

But he'd had to turn Joe Kirk down, tell him he couldn't do anything about his ill-fitting leg, that he couldn't even give him any meds for his friend's headaches, couldn't even write a scrip.

Was this the last straw? At first, he thought it was just incompetence, this failure to help the very people you were supposed to help. That was an element of faith in the Upper Peninsula—anything the government tried to do was done incompetently. Private enterprise always worked better. *Unless private enterprise was run by humans, too*, he thought.

There was something rotten at the heart of the whole damn system, though. It wasn't just incompetence. He almost had it figured out. He had gathered the evidence. If he was right…

Damn, it was so preposterous, so extreme. Was he reading it right? How could something like that be going on?

He didn't want to blow any whistles. That was nothing but trouble. He was the newest doctor in the whole place. If he bucked the system, there would be hell to pay. But when you're a father, you've got to put your baby first, and he didn't want his little Kirk to grow up and be like Joe Kirk.

To salve his conscience, he had stuck a twenty into an envelope and put it into one of the many pockets in Joe Kirk's photographer's vest while Joe was getting dressed. The twenty was his coffee money for the week. Well, Zoe would let him have more when he told her what he had done with it.

It was too much to think through without a cigarette, though. So here he was, out behind the maintenance building, smoking a cigarette he had liberated from the pack he knew was always on the table in the grounds crew's lunchroom.

Alan was the type of doctor who preferred to take his breaks with the grounds crew. Zoe wouldn't let him hunt anymore, but it was less than a month until deer season. The guys of the grounds crew would be talking about their camps and their guns and their exploits of last year. He enjoyed that. They were all out working on fallen leaves, though, so he walked out through the back door to take in the dry smoke from distant burning leaves and the hot smoke of the cigarette.

He heard a funny motor sound and walked down to the end of the building. There at the far edge of the parking area was a strange-looking old school bus with an unjustified motor. That's what his father always said about a motor that was out of whack—it needed to be *justified*. Joe Kirk was just swinging up through the door. As soon as he was in, the bus lurched off.

That's when he saw the big black SUV bearing down on him. It was accelerating fast. He jumped back behind the building and felt a whoosh of hot fumes rake at him. He started backing up. So did the SUV. It whined and came at him hard. *Reverse is always the strongest gear*, he thought, *for people as well as cars*. He jumped aside. The SUV slammed into the metal side of the building and rattled it. He started running for the back door of the building. He heard the SUV shifting gears. It accelerated hard again and came after him. There were short concrete pillars sunk into the concrete around the back door to keep trucks from backing all the way into the door. He jumped behind the first one. He was almost to the door. The SUV was beside him.

He heard somebody yell, "Just go ahead and shoot the bastard," and he knew that Zoe would have to raise their little Kirk alone.

Just don't let him grow up to be like Joe Kir…

CHAPTER 18

Joe

They put Zan and Lonnie and me into three different cells. No surprise there. Didn't want us coordinating our stories. Except we didn't have any story to coordinate. What worried me was that, if we told the truth, they wouldn't believe it. Not just the truth about not murdering that doctor. Four vets who didn't even know one another just happened to be touring the sites where a couple of them used to play football and on the way stop at VA hospitals and—

Oh, yeah, this was going to go over real well.

I demanded to see the sheriff to ask him what the hell was going on. The deputy said the sheriff didn't want to see me. That took care of that.

Then the preacher came back. That's what we always called them in *The Mississippi of the North*, that southern "pocket" of Indiana. Not pastors or reverends or ministers, but preachers. That year that I was in theology school, I got into trouble for that, especially with the women. I had the feeling I might get into trouble for that with this one, too, but I was glad to see her. I was surprised at how much.

Especially since we didn't have to talk through that glass with the little microphones. She was claiming priestly privilege to see me in person. I had the impression that the sheriff either liked her or was afraid of her and so gave her more consideration than he would otherwise.

I guessed when I was watching *Home Improvement* with Grandma, Jill Taylor was just another mom. In her guise as

Reverend Linden, she was really sexy. I had not noticed how good-looking the preacher was when she had been in jeans and running shoes. She must have been about thirty but had a figure like she was twenty. Today she was dressed in a form-fitting navy blue suit with matching pumps. The heels weren't too high, as if she was trying to look like a sedate preacher instead of one foxy lady.

She was wearing a clergy collar with a shirt in a subdued black and blue tartan plaid. She had a discreet silver cross around her neck. The shirt bulged the silver out very nicely.

She also had that little backpack dangling on her shoulder. It was open.

Having been in the army, I had long ago lost any special cachet for a woman in uniform, if *cachet* could be used as a synonym for lust, but this was a uniform I hadn't really seen before, not like this, anyway, and I liked it a whole lot.

She saw that I was examining the plaid shirt.

"It's not a clan tartan. It's the clergy tartan," she said. "I wear it when I go to jails and hospitals."

Right. As if I was just wondering which tartan it was. "Oh, yeah, I'm sure the cops recognize a clergy tartan right off. Wouldn't know you were a preacher otherwise."

Then I remembered that she had a gun with my fingerprints on it in her backpack. I couldn't afford to piss her off. If she were half as smart as she looked, she would have figured out by now just where that gun came from. Well, she didn't have the gun in her backpack, of course. Even though she was a preacher, and known to them, they would have at least run her through a metal detector, or eyeballed the backpack. But she had it somewhere.

"I'm sorry, Reverend Linden. I don't mean to be a jerk. It just comes naturally."

"Somehow, I suspect that is a learned response, being a jerk," she said. She gave me a shy little smile. "You can dispense with the *Reverend* stuff. Call me Rickie."

This was going really well.

"I found something in my backpack. When I was over at the VA with Victoria. I—"

Whoops. It wasn't going nearly as well as I had thought. But the mention of Victoria gave me a chance to change the subject. "How is Victoria?" I asked.

"I'll get to that. Don't change the subject." Women always seemed to think I was trying to change the subject. "I want to know about—" she continued.

I definitely did not want her saying *gun* where the eavesdroppers could hear, and I had no doubt somebody was listening. A deputy was standing where he could watch us to be sure she didn't slip me a hacksaw, but he was supposed to be far enough away he couldn't hear. When you were in jail or in the army, though, you had to assume that they had the place bugged. Come to think of it, now that the Patriot Act had declared that everybody in the country was unpatriotic, you had to assume you were bugged just because you were in America.

"I know. You're wondering why I didn't take you to the prom. I know now that was a mistake. Lucille Bottoms wouldn't put out."

She gave me a valley girl eye-roll, but she took the bait, or got the message. "Like you could make better time with me than with someone named Lucille Bottoms, or like they would even let you into Adolfo Camarillo High School," she snorted.

Oh, this was good after all. I had her now. So she was from Camarillo. That valley-girl stuff was for real. Or maybe not. I wasn't sure Camarillo was in the right valley to produce valley girls, or any valley at all. I had never been there, but I just happened to know that the high school in Camarillo was named for old Adolfo.

"If they let Tony Lindquist in, they'd let anybody in," I said.

Tony was our place kicker at IU, and he went to *Adolfo High*, as he called it. I gathered *High* had a double meaning. Tony was the only California guy on the squad. He hadn't gotten any scholarship offers out west because he was a soccer guy who had started kicking footballs only in his senior year. It's a good thing he had to come to IU. His kicking accounted for most of our scoring.

It was very satisfying to see that little silver cross jump when she gasped. "My God, how do you know about Tony?"

"I have my ways," I said, trying to sound mysterious. "However, you mentioned your backpack…"

"Is lighter than it was. I had to clean it out. Victoria needed tissues—and women's things."

She rolled her eyes toward the deputy. Talking about *women's things* was a good way to get a man to stop listening.

"Well, that's good," I said. "Got to keep things organized. I try to, with my photographer's vest, even though I don't have a camera, except they took the vest away from me, of course."

"I'd like to know why I should continue to keep things organized," she said. "Sometimes organization can lead to trouble…"

She trailed off. So she had the gun, she knew where it came from, and she wanted to know what to do about it. She was giving me a chance to explain things before she turned the gun over to the sheriff. That was great, except I didn't know what to tell her that would help get me out of jail. I wondered why I even cared. Jail wasn't so bad. They had showers, once in a while. They had food and TV. I could probably get a book or two to read. I didn't have any place to go or anything to do. Jail would be hard on Zan and Lonnie and Victoria, but I didn't have any responsibility for them. There were people in jail unjustly all over the world, and I didn't do anything about them. Neither did anyone else.

I didn't know what I would have told her, but I didn't get the chance. Sheriff Sam Avanti himself was coming in with a booming call of "Time's up." He really did have a thing about this woman preacher and, looking at her again simply as a woman, I could see why.

She glanced up at the quickly advancing sheriff then turned her big liquid brown eyes back at me. "Do you have a lawyer?" she asked softly.

"I guess they'll assign one," I said.

"Time's up," the sheriff yelled again, almost on us now. "That's enough time for confession even for a mass murderer."

"I'll get you a lawyer," she said.

"Stay organized," I replied.

She was a conspirator. We had a "little secret." It concerned a gun. I couldn't think of many people who would agree to hang onto a secret like that for a stranger. Was it just because she was a preacher and used to keeping secrets? Was it her nature, in her genes, to be a secret keeper? Might she want me?

Men always thought that. *She wants me.* That was the reason women did anything, according to us. Well, if it were true with Reverend Rickie, she was going to be disappointed if she got what she wanted.

What the hell did the sheriff mean by "enough confession even for a *mass* murderer?"

We were accused of only one murder that I knew of. Not even "accused." Just "suspected," or something like that.

I watched her walk down the little hall from my cell to the door. Her backpack swung back and forth on her shoulder. Her hips swung in rhythm with it inside the tight blue skirt. Her heels tapped out a code message on the hard floor.

Then I wrenched my eyes away from the preacher and on to the sheriff. I didn't want him to see me watching her. I just didn't like to have people see what I was watching anytime. It gave them too much knowledge about my soul. But I didn't need to bother. He was the one who was embarrassed when he realized I was watching him watching her. I figured I'd better not get into a pissing match with him about the preacher.

"She's young enough to be your daughter, you know?" I said.

So much for no pissing match.

He sighed. "Yeah, but I always had a thing for…"

He let it hang, and I figured it was a good chance for me to jump us onto tracks I wanted to run on.

"How are Zan and Lonnie doing?"

"If you think being sullen and uncooperative are good things, they're doing fine. I think the blind one is on a hunger strike, or maybe he just doesn't like the food. Hard to believe. He won't say anything except *Ask Joe*, which is the same as the crazy one, except he's got a bigger cuss word vocabulary."

The sheriff was being downright civil. That made me uneasy. It also made me think I could press a little bit. "Sheriff, I don't understand why we're here. You can't keep us in jail unless you arrest us. You also have to offer us a phone call and a lawyer and read us our rights…"

He beckoned to the deputy by the door. He came squeaking down the hallway to us on thick-soles. He was an old guy, fifty or more, with a big belly. Probably was a road deputy before he got too fat to fit behind the wheel, so now he was relegated to jail duty.

"Unlock it," the sheriff said.

The deputy didn't look interested one way or another. He just unlocked the door.

"Come with me," the sheriff said.

I pushed the door open and limped after him. He led down a couple of halls to his office. It was decent-sized, with a lot of wood, especially a big wooden desk. He went behind it, sat down in his swivel chair, stuck his feet up on the desk. He was wearing cowboy boots, of course.

There were two wooden captain's chairs in front of his desk. I sat down in the one nearest the door and stuck my leg out.

"Thing is," he said, "you're guests. You've got no place to live, since we're running your bus through forensics. Don't have a lot of forensics people up here, so it takes a while. I've looked at the stuff we took from you when we stuck you in here. About two dollars in change, plus a twenty, and an ATM card. The card is legitimate, issued to an Alonzo Blifield. I assume that's the blind guy we took it off of, except it's been canceled. Anyway, you're not going to be eating out or getting a motel, unless we find a secret cache of gold bars in that ugly bus. You with me so far?"

I nodded.

"You could arrest us for vagrancy, but you haven't—"

"Right. I could arrest you for assault on those dumb Delta County deputies, too, but that's really not in anybody's interest. We don't need the publicity, arresting four vets for vagrancy, when the number of homeless vets is a big enough scandal the way it is."

"You sound like a vet yourself, Sheriff."

"Yeah, but not like you guys. I was in the Guard but got out before 9/11. Wasn't trying to get out of my duty. It was just time to do other stuff, and I sure as hell didn't know 9/11 was coming, or maybe I would have stayed in, who knows? Anyway, my time in the service wasn't like yours."

"Sounds like you've been researching us."

"Oh, yeah. Albert Zander, Joseph Kirk, Alonzo Blifield. They all exist in the records."

Those formal names for Zan and Lonnie made me realize the sheriff now knew more about them than I did.

"Would be nice, of course, if you had some sort of ID on you, so we'd know you're who you say you are."

"You've seen my driver's license, Lonnie's ATM card..."

He must have taken something off Zan that had his name on it. I couldn't recall that any of us had called him anything but Zan, and Zan himself probably wouldn't have cooperated by telling his real name. Probably told them he was Napoleon or Johnny Depp or some other make-believe swashbuckler.

"Yeah, yeah. I believe you're the three musketeers, or the three amigos, or something. There's this thing with your Medal of Honor winner, though, like she isn't. In fact, there's no record of a Victoria Roundtree in the military at all."

CHAPTER 19

Victoria

Victoria sat on the edge of her bed and stared at the bare floor, trying to pull some meaning from it, or at least some information. A plan, that would be better. *Give me a plan, floor.*

She had to get out. If they had traced her to Danville, they would be able to find her here. She should have just stayed with Barbara Occam-Roberts. She could have been a maid or something. Of course, Barbara had not asked her, and she couldn't leave Lonnie.

Oh, God, Lonnie. I can't leave this damned Iron Mountain without Lonnie. What are they doing to him over there in the jail? How will he get along without me to guide him?

Well, he had gotten along without her before she had climbed onto the bus. He didn't even have his control vest before. Zan had just created it, but neither Zan nor Joe knew how to use it. It was she, Victoria, who had mastered that.

How had Lonnie gotten along before the vest, before her? In the times they were alone together, they didn't talk about the past. She knew nothing about Lonnie, except that she could not go without him. But go she must, because they would track her down again.

How in the name of all that was evil had they traced her to Danville? Oh, that was *why* they had sent her there, why nobody there knew anything about treating burn victims. Danville was a setup, get her away from her friends, where nobody knew her, grab her, and...

What? What did they want? Why couldn't she think? She hadn't been thinking clearly since Iraq. She had tried not to think about Iraq at all, about any of it. Whenever it tried to get into her head, she would go to her happy place, just like her little brother used to signal her to do when they had to escape and there was no place to go. Now, though, she was going to have to be like a woman in a Barbara Occam-Roberts's novel. She was going to have to put on her big-girl panties and do what had to be done.

She smiled as she remembered Barbara and Sliver Lake. She smiled even as she thought of Zan, the ludicrous sight of him on horseback, and the way they had laughed. Even in the midst of the chaos of the awkward Indian attack and the bus catching on fire, everything had seemed so right. And then Joe deserted. And they were on the bus. But Barbara...

Barbara was so different from what Victoria had imagined. Victoria had read *The Unauthorized Biography of Tulips* first. She thought it was by a black woman. It read like Alice Walker or Toni Morrison. She had read everything she could find by her new author. Then by total chance, there she was, right in front of her, the author herself, so totally well put-together, so trim, so crisp around the edges, not big and earth-toned, but little and blonde. And almost brittle, she was holding on so hard. Victoria understood at least a little of why Barbara had to be so keen, so honed. She hoped that Barbara understood at least a little of why Victoria had to hold on so hard, too.

Damn, this wasn't getting her anywhere. She had to stop thinking about what might have been and concentrate on what she had to do now. If she could just figure out—why now?

They knew *who* she was in Chicago. They knew *where* she was. Why hadn't they come for her then? Because they didn't know yet? About Sarge and Wong and—maybe. Oh, no, they wanted to get her to Danville because...

It was too confusing. Her head began to feel like Zan's. Maybe *Algonquin's man in Washington* told them to send her to Danville. And who the hell was *the man in Washington*? High up there somewhere, able to pull all sorts of strings, make things happen. Whenever one of them came around to talk to Sarge, and Sarge had some complaint or question, they always said they would take it up with *Algonquin's man in Washington*.

Sarge didn't really mind Victoria. Whatever she did, whatever she said, he would say the same thing: '*Just like a woman.*' She could say she loved puppy dogs or liked to shoot ragheads, and he would say, '*Just like a woman.*' It wasn't mean. He wasn't really trying to put her down. It was his way of acknowledging she existed but didn't matter.

She understood. She really was the least important of them all. She was just along to do the search if they had to deal with women. She didn't like that duty, but it had gotten to the point where women were as likely as men to have explosives strapped on them. Somebody had to do it.

Wong was the important one. He was the interpreter. He looked like he was Chinese, but he spoke better English than anybody else. He had graduated from some fancy college, Yale or Harvard or one of those, and he had learned to speak Arabic there. He could carry on with Arabs the way her father did with his buds on a street corner in Chicago.

She and Wong were the outsiders. The others were owned by the contractors. The damn contractors. They owned everything and everybody. It wasn't the army's war. It certainly wasn't the nation's war. The folks back home thought if they sent you some canned peaches and toilet paper and called you a *hero*, that was the end of it. And there were few enough who did even that. *We support our troops.* Right up to the point "we" had to do something more than slap a sticker on the back bumper.

It was the contractors' war. They did everything, from providing "security" for diplomats and visitors to building the biggest damn military base in the world,

The contractors owned the soldiers, too. No more than they needed. They didn't want to share the wealth. If they really needed a particular soldier, one with the skills and without the conscience, they'd buy him outright. Go to *the man in Washington* and get him out of the army and into their own ranks, pay him ten times what he was making as a soldier. Ten times, hell. A lot more than that. Everybody made more than the soldiers. Truck drivers making a hundred thousand a year. If they made that much, she could only imagine what they paid the ones they called *the skilled workers.*

There were the *mow-rons,* of course. That's what the contractors called soldiers they wanted, who wouldn't give up the uniform, who thought this war was about *serving their country,* somehow. Oh, how the contractors laughed at that. *It's about money, mow-rons. Money and oil. Oil is money. Money is oil. You mow-rons...*

They never tried to recruit Victoria, of course. She didn't have the necessary *skills.* They wanted Wong, though, and his Arabic. Wong was the biggest *mow-ron* of all, though. He bled red, white, and blue. This was all about keeping America safe and bringing democracy to the world, as far as he was concerned. Hell, the guy was a Republican. The longer the war went on, there were fewer and fewer of those *in the sand,* but Wong stayed the course.

Wong was gay. He had to keep it quiet, even used Victoria as a *beard.* She didn't mind. He was a good guy. She went along with it. She didn't approve of gays and lesbians. Reverend Wright said they were against Jesus. But she liked Wong. She knew they needed him, too. The strange thing was that the contractors didn't care that he was gay, but the army did. She used to tell him he was a mow-ron, like the contractors said, because he kept on being the big-time patriot when the army and all the folks back home thought he was a second-class citizen at best.

She and Wong both knew that their unit worked for the contractors. Most everybody did. But little stuff didn't amount to much. Mostly just to keep them on the stick, dangling the carrot, in case they needed something special in a hurry and nobody else was available. Or so there would be some low-level grunts to blame in case something went wrong.

She and Wong didn't know, though, that day, that last day, that they weren't on one of their routine patrols. *Routine* was never routine, anyway, so, nothing out of the ordinary.

The farther they went, though, the stranger Sarge started acting. Then even Victoria began to realize that they were where they had never been before, a place where they definitely were not supposed to be. Wong began to ask questions.

"Shut up, you faggot."

Sarge had never said anything like that before. Sarge and the others all knew, or at least suspected, but nobody said anything. They needed Wong too much. Liked him, too, for that matter. In the sand, it was all about your unit. Even Wong, with all his patriotic-nationalism bullshit, believed that. When it came right down to it, the only thing you fought for was the guys in the foxhole with you, or the guys in the Humvee.

"That's not right, Sarge," Victoria said.

"Just like a woman," Sarge said. Then he started yelling, but not at her or Wong. "Those bastards. That's not ragheads. That's Algonquins…"

Then everything went to hell. Reverend Wright had been right. Hell was a fiery furnace.

CHAPTER 20

Joe

The next morning, a new deputy came and got me and took me to "the library." It was a room the size of a closet, with a metal table, two metal chairs, and an old *Reader's Digest*. I figured the sheriff wanted to grill me without having my dirty carcass in his office. I slumped down in a chair and stuck out my leg, hoping the sheriff would come in fast enough to trip over it before he saw it.

Instead of the sheriff, though, the door opened and a short old man in a rumpled gray suit and a tie-less white shirt came in like a Cooper Mini on steroids. I had to get my leg out of the way in record time, and my stump protested. I must have made a face.

"No, no, don't get up," he said, advancing on me with a pudgy hand stuck out. "I'm Tom Carroll. I'm a lawyer. Reverend Linden sent me."

So Rickie was true to her word. That was nice.

The lawyer's hand was dry and stronger than I expected. He dropped down heavily into the chair on the other side of the table, and I could see that he had a comb-over that was pretty decent, as comb-overs went. He had reader's bags under his eyes and a lot of wrinkles.

"Reverend Linden said you and your confederates, three I think, are suspected of murdering a doctor here at the VA hospital."

"I suspect we're all four guilty of plenty of murders."

He jumped up. He threw his chair aside against the concrete

block wall. He grabbed the *Reader's Digest* off the rack, threw it on the floor, and stomped on it. He took off his suit coat and threw it on top of the overturned chair. He leaned over the table as far as he could, got into my face as close as he could, and yelled, "Goddammit, I don't have time for this. This is serious business. You're in a shit-load of trouble. I'm your lawyer. I can't have you lying to me or beating around the bush. I've got to know the truth, the whole truth, and nothing but the truth if I'm going to defend you. I'm on your side, even if you murdered the whole VA, but I've got to have the truth."

His voice wasn't really loud, but intense. His breath smelled like burnt toast.

A deputy's face looked in the little window in the metal door. Apparently he didn't care if the library got trashed, because the face disappeared.

The lawyer reminded me of my football coach at IU. He would rant and rave, get up into your face, call you scum and worse, threaten you with anything he could think of. At first, it was intimidating. Then I got used to it. It was just an act. The more he did it, the less we paid attention. That was what this was—an act. As acts went, it was sort of like his comb-over, not all that bad.

I stared back, not to get a staring match going, but just because it seemed like the polite thing to do. Also, because I wanted to outstare him. I still liked the little competitions. It was the big ones I could do without.

"I murdered a whole lot of people in Iraq and Afghanistan," I said. "And they tried to murder me back. I've been yelled at by West Point grads who are seven feet tall and were as willing to murder me as much as anybody else. I don't worry about what people in suit coats think, even if they're not in their suit coats."

His face broke into a lopsided grin. "Oh, sorry about that. It works with everybody in Indianapolis." He pulled his chair back into position and slumped back into it. The suit coat slid off it onto the floor. He didn't bother to pick it up. He stuck his hand over his heart and counted. "I'm too old for this," he said. "Got to get a different way to cut through the crap. Everybody in jail lies. The suspects, the cops, the lawyers. I've got to get my clients to tell me the truth or I can't figure out how to deal with the lies the cops and the other lawyers tell. You're too smart for me."

Another act, but I was too smart for it. Or maybe not.

"Indianapolis? Is that where you're from?"

He seemed satisfied with his heart rate. "Yes. I'm just up here on vacation."

Now that we weren't doing the stare competition, he looked at everything but me.

I wondered if that was part of the act. "But will they let your practice law up here?"

"Oh, yes. I went to University of Michigan Law School. Took the bar exam. Keep up my membership here. Illinois, too. I have a pretty wide practice. Or did. I'm close to retired now."

"So why are you willing to take us on while you're on vacation?"

"Reverend Linden. We met one morning down at the Moose Jackson Café. I take a break for coffee mid-morning, wherever I am, even if I don't have anything to break from. Saw her there, all by herself, reading a book by William Sloane Coffin. Bill was an old friend of mine, from civil rights cases. I commented on it, and we got to talking. I see her down there most mornings when I'm up here. We talk about what we're reading. Do you read, Mr. Kirk?"

"Just books by Barbara Occam-Roberts," I said.

"Barbara Occam-Roberts? Hmm, I don't think I know her work. I'm mostly into classics, nothing since Balzac."

I shouldn't have said that. He was being civil. But *read*? What did he expect of a guy with no money and no library card? Besides, Barbara was from Indianapolis, too. You ought to support your hometown author. Obviously, they ran, and read, in different circles.

"I appreciate you coming," I said, "but we don't have any money."

Didn't even have a good ATM card anymore.

"Reverend Linden retained me. My usual. Ten thousand dollars a day, plus expenses."

Does a preacher have that kind of money?

He saw the look on my face and laughed out loud. "She

gave me a dollar, Mr. Kirk. That's all it takes to make it legal, and all I need. My practice now consists of doing favors for friends and tilting at windmills. Let me assure you, though, that I am still tarp as a shack." He laughed again, looked at me sideways to see if I got it. "You said you *murdered* people in Iraq?"

I didn't think about it. I just started talking. Some part of his act to get people to tell him the truth must have been working. "I went over there thinking I was defending my country—and freedom in general—that if I killed people, it was because it was war, and there was no choice. Turns out there was some truth in that, but I learned that anytime you kill somebody, it's murder. If we don't call it what it is, we'll keep on doing it and saying it's okay. It's not okay. I wouldn't mind seeing the whole VA dropped down a hole, but I'm not going to murder some doctor, even if he is VA."

"Any chance one of your friends could have done it?

"No. We were together the whole time, except when Victoria went to the restroom, and I'm sure the doctor wasn't in there. Look, Mr. Carroll, we were just in the VA there for maybe…I don't know, thirty minutes, maybe forty."

"You were there because…"

"Trying to get some medicine for Zan."

"Which one is he?"

"The one who's not blind or female."

I guess his act had worked. I told him what he wanted—the truth, the whole truth, and nothing but the truth. I took him through the whole thing, how Zan and I had been roommates, how we ended up in the bus together, how we got Lonnie and Victoria, how I didn't know anything about any of them. I didn't bother with the incidents at *Moe's Eat and Get Gas* or at Sliver Lake. They didn't have anything to do with the murder of this Doctor Judson, and…well, we didn't look all that good in those incidents.

He sat there, looking at the walls, listening.

"Uh, do you need to take notes, or something?"

"No, it's all in my head now."

"But since you're on vacation—"

"Oh, it's not really me who's on vacation. My wife loves to

shoot animals. It's better than shooting me, which she seems to think is her only alternative. She has a deer camp, the whole schmeer. But I refuse to be up here during deer-hunting season. I don't mind if she kills a bear every year. My father was from Alabama. He never went to college, but if you live in Alabama, you're required to choose either the Auburn Tigers or Plainsmen or War Eagles. Good grief, that team has a lot of nicknames. I can never remember which one they're using now. Anyway, you have to choose Auburn or the Alabama Crimson Tide as your team. It's the law. My father grew up on a farm, so he chose Auburn. Alabama was our big rival. Bear Bryant beat us every year, so, yeah, shooting bears is okay, but Bambi's mother? That's not right. So I come up with her for a couple of weeks before deer-hunting season. Then I go home."

"Well, that's what I was going to ask about. You go home. How will you see us through if there's a trial?"

"Oh, there won't be any trial. By the time I get through with these Nimrods, they'll buy us a private plane just to get us out of here."

I appreciated his confidence, but I didn't share it.

CHAPTER 21

Maybe Tom Carroll wasn't as powerful as he thought. Or maybe his act didn't work on Sheriff Sam Avanti. Anyway, we were still in the jail the next morning. I was still in my own cell for breakfast, as I had been for everything else since we became "guests" of the county. The coffee was cold, the eggs were bad, the oats were worse, the toast was burned. They were better than I would have fixed behind the bus, though, and almost as good as we ate when the contractors were feeding us in Iraq, so I ate them. I figured Zan probably did the same. Lonnie, though…

It wasn't hard to figure why the sheriff thought he was on a hunger strike. I didn't know anything about Lonnie's past, but he had the attitude of somebody used to having a chef do the cooking.

When I heard footsteps, I assumed it was the fat deputy coming to get my tray. It was, but he had the sheriff with him. The deputy unlocked the door, the sheriff beckoned to me, and I limped along behind him like a hurt-paw puppy dog.

"Sheriff, as much as I appreciate your hospitality—"

He held up a hand and kept on walking. "We'll talk later," he said. "That hotshot lawyer from Chicago is tearing me a new one. I don't like it."

"I thought he was from Indianapolis."

"Same thing. Down there some place where they grow corn and stuff."

"I don't think Chicago has room to grow corn."

I was going to say more, about how Indianapolis had advanced to the place where corn wasn't growing in the streets there anymore, either, but he was moving fast, and I huffed and puffed to keep up. I figured we were going to his office so I could sign some papers, or whatever you do when your lawyer has gotten you out. Instead we went to the conference room.

He pointed at the door. "I'm not worried about you escaping, or plotting to, so go ahead, but don't take all day."

He waited. I pushed the door open. There sat Becky Garlits. Or Becky Rosten, as she was now.

She looked up at me and started talking like she always had, blaming me for stuff I didn't even know I was involved with.

"Damn. It's a long way up here," she complained. "Almost five hundred miles. It doesn't look that far on the map. Got backed up for a long time at Osh Kosh with an accident on the road. Almost hit a deer. Almost got run over by a log truck. This is the end of the world. You should fit right in, Joe."

"Thanks for coming to comfort me."

I hoped it was as sarcastic as I wanted it to be.

She didn't seem to notice.

"I assume you didn't drive all the way up here this morning."

"No. I got tired and spent the night in a place in Wisconsin called…Crivitz…I think. Anyway, I've got to get started back soon so I can make it all the way home today."

All the way home. I got a flash show of Grandma's house, and the locker room at IU, and that last mountain in the 'Stan, and wondered how far I'd have to go to get all the way home.

I spread out my arms, looked around. "How in hell did you know about…"

"You probably don't remember Yvonne Williams. She was a DG, too."

DG? Oh, yeah, Delta Gamma, Becky's sorority.

"Later we did our MSWs together at Illinois."

Good grief, on top of everything else, she was a Whining Illini. That's what we called the U of Illinois football people, instead of The Fighting Illini. Not the team so much, as the fans and their sports writers. If they lost, especially to us, it was only because somebody screwed them, not because they weren't as good.

"Anyway, Yvonne works in Detroit. Plenty of social work

there. I guess the Michigan papers cover stuff that happens even up here, since it's technically part of Michigan, even though it looks on the map like it's part of Wisconsin."

Getting an MSW had not made Becky less pedantic. She always acted like she had to instruct me in everything, including—

"Anyway, she recognized your name. I guess I used to talk about you a lot, God forgive me. She emailed me, so I looked it up on the web—"

She looked out the window. It wasn't a sunny day, but it looked good to me out there, even with winter coming on. *Out* would be a good place to be.

"You're a bad penny, Joe. I hadn't thought about you in years, and then Yvonne called me about you. Emailed, actually. I don't know why. She was always nice enough before. Anyway…"

Becky Garlits was sort of like Iraq. I hated what she had done to me, and I didn't want to think about it, but she was part of my world.

She was shorter than I remembered. I was sure she was the same five feet and three inches of curvy brunette she had always been, but when we were together in college, she was always taller than I was because she was in charge. She had a clear sense of how things ought to be. When she wanted to explain to me the way things ought to be—and the way they were thus going to be—she made me sit down while she stood. She seemed pretty damn tall.

Back then I was just so glad to be with her that I went along with anything she wanted. *Pussy-whipped*, Zan had called me. I didn't care.

Now she was just a short, beautiful, curvy, tired-looking, short-haired woman in a dark blue suit and matching low-heeled pumps, carrying a big blue purse that looked more like a briefcase. Surely, she hadn't driven all that way dressed like that. Who was she trying to impress?

Hell, why should I care what she wore or what she looked like or why she did her act? I got over her a long time ago. *Right*.

She pulled a handful of printouts from the big purse and

waved them like a queen dismissing the peasants. "I see from the articles that you've hooked up with Zan again, too. No wonder you're in trouble. He was always just a dumb jock, and that's all he'll ever be."

That cleared up how Becky felt about Zan, except that had never really been in doubt. Becky had always had a possessive streak. When we were a couple, she had not wanted to share me with anybody else, especially Zan. She sensed that Zan was more of a threat to her exclusive hold on me than any girl would be.

"I don't suppose you've kept up with me, either, so I should tell you that I am the head of the social work department at St. Francis Hospital in Springfield, Illinois, and my husband is the medical director, as well as being chief of surgery. He's the youngest ever to hold either of those jobs."

I was really nonplussed now. She sounded so smug. Did she really think she had to brag about something like that to me? What did I care? And *my husband*? Like we hadn't played on the same team for four years, and she hadn't dumped me for him as soon as he became the starter, and I didn't know his name?

"You mean the quarterback we called *Butterfingers* is a surgeon?"

Becky squared her shoulders. "I did not come all this way to hear you belittle Quint. I came because…when I saw about your current troubles, I couldn't help but feel a little guilty. I know it must have hurt you badly to lose me. So—you'd better sit down."

"I'm okay," I said.

"All right then, you were always stubborn. But here's the truth. I never really loved you, Joe. I thought I did, but I didn't. That didn't make any difference, though. You were a good man then, and I loved the idea of being in love with a good man. That kept us together longer than it should have. You weren't that good in bed. That should have been a sign to me. Sex was more important to me than it was to you. If I had broken it off earlier, maybe it wouldn't have hurt so much. I'm sorry, but you needed to hear that."

If she had broken *what* off earlier, my dick? I thought that would have hurt just as bad, any time. She was breaking it off now, and it sure as hell hurt. How in hell could she think sex wasn't important to me, the horniest of all horndogs?

And why in hell did she think I needed to hear that? People always excused themselves for saying the wrong thing by blaming it on the person they were saying it to. *She* needed to say it, or thought she did, so she was claiming I needed to hear it.

"You kind of look like you're not so sex-crazed now, Becky, what with the business suit, and being head of a department, and all," I said.

What kind of lame statement was that? What was I talking about?

She took a deep breath. I knew better than to interrupt Becky when she drew a deep breath, or any breath.

"You were always able to focus on the irrelevant, Joe, but that wasn't the main thing you need to hear. I don't know why Helen told me all this, and I didn't want to hear it, so I wasn't listening all that well, but…"

Helen? Who the hell was she talking about? Grandma? Her name was Helen. Helen Cone. She didn't have a middle name, so if she needed a middle initial she used *N*, for Newsome, her maiden name. But I didn't want to hear Grandma's name on the tongue of Becky Garlits. I knew where that tongue had been.

"…it was that time she came to the game, your senior year. She thought we were still together. I guess we were, technically. Like I say, I guess she thought someone should know, in case she died before she could tell you, or something. Anyway, she chose me. I wish she hadn't." She looked out the window. She seemed to be thinking that *out* would be a good place to be. I know that's what I was thinking. "Anyway, your mother had an affair with their preacher. I think she said his name, but I can't remember—"

"Franklin Prashwell," I said.

I barely had enough breath to get it out. It didn't even sound like my voice. Grandma had told me, more than once, about the big tornado that had come through Princeton when she was just a girl. "It wasn't like they say, Joey, not at first, about sounding like a train, and all that." At first, I could see it, that big black swirling cloud. I thought it would be swirling air at me, but it wasn't. It was taking it away from me. It reached right down into my lungs and grabbed all the air. That's what a tornado is like, greedy. It wants everything, even your air. After it takes your air, then you hear the train, and you feel the force, like a big hand pressing on you, like it doesn't care what happens to you, but first it takes away your air. You can't say anything. You can't even breathe."

That's the way it was now. The tornado named Becky Garlits had taken away my air. Now I could hear the train roaring in my ears. The tornado didn't seem to notice, though. Just like Grandma said, that big hand pressing on you didn't care. Becky was going right on.

"...anyway, Helen felt bad about it, you not knowing. But she said she didn't know how to tell you. Then too much time went by. You should have been told right when it happened."

Right when it *happened.* I knew what *it* was. *It* was that day in the woods.

CHAPTER 22

My father had been taking me hunting since I was ten. I thought he'd figured out that I missed the animals on purpose, but he was impressed with my marksmanship, used to brag about it to his buddies. It was the only thing I could ever remember that he said about me that was positive, and I knew about it only because I overheard a couple of his friends.

We didn't have a bad relationship then, just a distant one. It was about standard for fathers and their sons in southern Indiana. In most places, I suspected. Especially fathers who had been off in the Gulf War and missed seeing their kids when they were babies and little. Especially fathers who worked long shifts at the Toyota plant for foreign wages and foreign bosses and came home tired and just wanted a beer and wrestling on the TV.

Dad especially hated working for *the gooks*. His own father had been killed in Vietnam when he was little, and Dad was always sorry that he had not been able to fight in that war. "It was the politicians who lost that war for us, not the soldiers like my father," he used to say. "That was the real war against the real enemy."

He never said exactly who *the real enemy* was, but he called any oriental a *gook*, like the Japanese and the Koreans were as responsible for the death of his father as the Vietnamese.

He and I didn't hug or talk about stuff. He didn't help with my homework or read stories to me.

He wasn't an athlete. We never played catch or tossed the football around.

We did other things together sometimes, though, man stuff—like raking the leaves and, especially, hunting.

Everything changed at the start of the seventh grade, though. I went out for football. I not only made the middle school varsity, I became the starting quarterback, ahead of the eighth-grader who had started the year before. The coach said he had never seen a kid passer with the kind of accuracy that I had.

I figured my father would be pleased, brag to his buddies about my marksmanship with a football, the way he did about what I could do with a rifle. But things in our house suddenly got very tense. My mother and father began to fight about everything.

I wondered, the way kids did, if it had something to do with me playing football. That was the only change I could see in our routine. I thought maybe I should quit, return things to normal. How did you figure something like that out when you were twelve? I was afraid even to go to Grandma.

Once I came home after a game and Mom had a black eye. Dad didn't come home until late that night. He stumbled around in the dark, cussed, and fell onto the sofa, instead of going to their bedroom. I knew something was bad wrong. He was a beer-at-home guy, not a tavern drinker. I sat on the edge of my bed and wondered what to do. I didn't know how long I had sat there like that when I heard him crying. Then I heard my mother crying in their bedroom. I thought one of them would get up and go to where the other one was, but they didn't. I slumped down onto the floor and laid there until I fell asleep, but I didn't cry.

They never said anything about it. They didn't say much at all after that, to each other, or to me. Dad just sort of ignored both of us. He started taking his supper into the living room on a tray and eating in front of the TV. Mother and I ate alone in the kitchen. She didn't talk to me, either. I lived in my room, and in the locker room.

Sports was my salvation. Football in the fall, basketball in the winter, track in the spring, baseball in the summer. I could not only throw a football where I wanted, but I could do the same with a baseball and basketball. I couldn't hit a baseball much, though, and I was slow on the basketball floor. I was a starter in those sports all through high school, and I ran the five thousand meters in track, the slow guys' race, but it was obvious that football was my sport.

My room, the locker room, and Grandma's house.

After my mother's black-eye incident, I finally told Grandma about what was going on. She looked like she saw that tornado from her girlhood days coming back. She took both my hands in hers and looked me straight in the eye. "Joey, things happen in a marriage. Eva is my daughter, and I love her, but she made a bunch of bad choices. She shouldn't have married Norman in the first place. They weren't suited to each other. She shouldn't have converted over to that so-called Bible church of his, with that charlatan preacher, Franklin Prashwell. Your parents are having problems in their marriage now. It happens in all marriages. Some people work it through okay, and some don't. I don't know how Eva and Norman will come out of this."

I thought she was through, that she was going to let go of my hands, but she loosened her grip, then it came back all the tighter.

"Joey, your mother made bad decisions, but I can't find it in my heart to condemn her, because she gave me you. I don't know if she'll make good decisions now. I do know, though, that you mustn't blame yourself. Children do that when their parents have troubles. You're not to blame."

I was able to exhale then. I was old enough to know I hadn't done anything to cause problems for my parents, but I was young enough to still have that guilt she was talking about. I wanted to be sure. I could be a little kid with Grandma. "You mean it's nothing to do with me, Grandma?"

She let go of my hands and stared at the big picture on her wall. It showed Jesus carrying a sheep, with some other sheep trailing along, like they were jealous of the sheep in his arms and wanted to be carried, too.

"You're not to blame," she said.

It was during football season in eighth grade when the *it* happened. By that time, Dad was no longer a beer-at-home drinker. He spent most evenings and weekends at the Legion hall.

One Saturday morning, early, he shook me awake. "Get dressed," he said. "We're going hunting."

I was dead tired. We'd had a game the night before, the warm-up game before the varsity played. But I wasn't about to say no.

Dad drove a Toyota Tundra. It must have bothered him, driving a *gook* truck, but it was what they made where he worked. They probably would have fired him if he drove a Ford. We got into it and took off for the woods west of town, out beyond the old Negro settlement, almost to the Wabash River. He pushed the truck down a little road that was more like a deer path. When we couldn't go any farther, he pulled up and turned the motor off.

We got out. He got into the long tool chest in the Tundra's box and pulled out our rifles. I didn't have a rifle, but when we had been hunting regularly, he had designated one of his, the older one, as mine.

He handed it to me. "Come on," he said.

He knew where he was going as he tramped through the floor of fallen leaves. I struggled along behind him, half asleep. We got to a long clearing on a ridge. He sat down on a stump that was mostly hidden behind some secondary growth. We could still see the clearing, though, and if any deer wandered into it, they wouldn't be able to see us. The stump was big enough I could have perched on it, too, but I sat down on some leaves.

I didn't know how long we sat there. I must have dozed off. I came out of it when I felt him shaking my shoulder. I looked up, expecting to see a deer in the long clearing. Instead, there were three hunters, working their way slowly along the other side.

He handed his rifle to me. "Look through the scope. See that guy at the end?"

I looked through the scope. I recognized the man. I didn't go to his church, but everyone knew him. It was the preacher at the Bible church.

"You see him?"

"Yes."

"Shoot him."

"Shoot him?"

"You deef, boy? Or are you just an echo? It won't hurt him. It's a paint pellet. Won't even sting. It's a joke."

I had to figure this out, and I needed time, so I did what I usually do, I stalled. "But how did you know he was going to be here?"

"Those men he's with, heard them talking at the Legion last night, about going out this way today. They cooked this up as a joke. He's so proud of that stupid vest with all the pockets. Dresses to hunt like some city dude. They thought it would be funny to get paint all over it."

I'd heard of paint pellets, but I thought they took special guns instead of regular rifles. "It's not a very nice joke—"

"Goddam it, it's just paint. Washable even. It'll come right out. It's just a joke."

It sounded like he was making it up as he went along.

"It's your joke. You should do it."

"Goddam it, boy, you're so goddam proud of that goddam eye-hand coordination shit. You think I don't know you always shoot twigs off branches instead of hitting squirrels between the eyes, the way you could if you wanted to, but you're too goddam chicken to shoot a goddam animal? Shit, who even says stuff like *eye-hand coordination*? The goddam gooks at the plant, that's who. You talk like a gook. Well, use that goddam eye-hand coordination you inherited. Get that rifle on your shoulder and shoot that goddam son-of-a-bitch!"

This sounded like more than a prank. I was a kid. I didn't know what to do. I did as he said, put the rifle to my shoulder, more to stall for time than anything else. But he had reminded me of something, shooting twigs.

The preacher was wearing one of those caps with fleece earflaps that you tie under your chin, except when they're up, you tie them together on top of the hat. I sighted on the strings on top of the hat. When I couldn't stall any longer, I pulled the trigger.

The preacher dropped to his knees, then went down on his face. The other men turned around and ran back to him. My father jumped up and began to run across the clearing.

I looked at the rifle, held it sideways. The scope wasn't even with the barrel. It tilted downward. The rifle had fired low.

I got up and ran after my father, but not very fast. I knew before I got to the other side that there had been no paint pellet in that gun.

My father and the other men were standing over the preacher when I got there. His cap was still on his head, like the bullet had pressed it into his skull, with a bullet groove down the middle and a lot of blood.

"Is he dead?" my father asked.

One of the men dropped to his knees beside the preacher, grabbed his wrist. Then he looked up. "Good God, Norm. What the hell?" he sputtered.

Dad jerked his thumb at me.

"He's not as perfect a shot as he thinks he is."

He seemed pleased. I didn't know if it was because the preacher was dead or because he had proved I wasn't as good as I thought I was.

I looked down at the rifle in my hands, the one I had just used to shoot the preacher. Why would my father hate someone so much that he wanted to kill him? Worse, why would he use me to do it? I couldn't believe he was setting me up to take the fall. But I was the one holding the rifle that had killed a man, and his Legion buddies saw that.

The man holding the preacher's wrist sighed. "He's alive. Strong pulse." He looked closer at the wound. "I think it just grazed him. Lots of blood because it's a scalp wound. It knocked him out, but he's okay." He looked up at his hunting partner. "Get me something to put on this wound to stop the bleeding. We've got to carry him out and get him to the hospital."

The other man grabbed a big bandana out of his pocket and handed it to him. He pressed it on the wound.

"I can help carry," I said.

He didn't look up. "No, boy, you get the hell away from here. And take that son-of-a-bitch with you."

"Shit," my father muttered. He took the rifle out of my hand and began to trudge back across the clearing.

That was the end of it. My father never said a thing about it again. Neither did anyone else. Reverend Prashwell never reported it to the police, and neither did the guys with him. They put out the story that it was just a hunting accident. Those happened all the time, so nobody gave it a thought after that.

It was like it had never happened. Sometimes I even wondered if it had, if maybe I had dreamed it, or thought it all up because…hell, who could know why? But I knew it was real. I knew it had happened. I just didn't know why.

The one thing that changed was my father. He had been ignoring me. Now he became downright hostile, like he was mad at me because I had failed to murder a man he was mad at for some reason.

Then I stopped thinking about it. I never told anybody about it, not even Grandma. I pretended it had never happened. I slept at home but I didn't live there. I hardly ever saw either of my parents. I stopped eating with my mother in the kitchen. I left the house every morning and didn't come home until bedtime. I went to school and played sports and worked a job and went to Grandma's house. I went to college and seminary and the army without ever thinking about it, without ever dealing with the total betrayal by my father. We were Abraham and Isaac without the happy ending. Now it was back. I was going to have to do something about it, and all because of the tornado named Becky.

Some people became teachers because they hated kids, some nurses because they hated sick people, some cops because they hated everybody, some soldiers because they hated themselves. Some become social workers because they hate poor people. Not just poor in the pocketbook, but poor in any way, bedraggled, down in the dumps. They became the one-eyed king in the land of the blind. Or, in the case of Becky Garlits, the no-eyed queen. I hated her, because I was so weak I couldn't even hate myself. Still, I felt I had to justify it somehow, explain to her what Grandma had told her, and why.

"When I was in eighth grade—"

Becky gave me that look like she was talking to a retarded kid again. "No, Joe. It wasn't when you were in eighth grade when your mother had the affair with that preacher, Prashwell, or whatever his name is. It was when your father was in the Gulf, in Desert Storm. The preacher is your real father."

CHAPTER 23

Florence

Florence Kneightly shook her head. She felt the cap move. She was the only nurse in the whole place who wore a cap. Kenny had sent it to her from Iraq, as a graduation present. Well, not really from Iraq. He got it on eBay and had it sent to her directly. Must have seen old movies and thought that was the way nurses still showed they were grads. She felt silly in it, the only cap in the whole damned place, but it had come from Kenny, dammit, and she was going to wear it.

She wasn't just the nurse in the funny cap. She was also new. That was why she had been assigned to Dr. Judson. He was new, too. Apparently Simmons felt Florence had broken him in so Simmons could put somebody else in Florence's place. She continued to look over Florence's scrub cloth shoulder, though, and it made her nervous.

Florence shook her head again. She did it whenever she couldn't understand the way people acted. She shook her head a lot. Even as a girl. Her father used to laugh and say she was going to shake her brains out. Maybe she had.

She couldn't understand, though, why there had been so little mourning over Dr. Judson. Maybe it was shock. Hard to mourn for real when you're in shock. Or because he was new. Not many of the staff knew him that well.

Mostly, though, it was fear. Ira Gasaway, the new administrator, and that nurse he brought with him, Simmons, had said all the right things, done all the proper things, but it didn't seem real. More like something they had read out of a manual. Now they acted like it was over and everyone was supposed to get back to business, which meant cutting costs. Only on patient care, though, not on supplies. Trucks arrived all the time, with supplies that weren't really necessary, so many they couldn't use them up in a century. Gasaway had even taken a couple of veterans' rooms for storage and was drawing up plans to add a whole storage building onto the maintenance building.

The thought of the maintenance building made her shudder. Not shake her head, but her whole body. She didn't need to shake her head. She knew all too well what had happened there, behind it, where she had found Dr. Judson's body.

Gasaway and Simmons said it must have been those vets in that school bus, the ones Dr. Judson had sent away. Gasaway said that's probably why they did it, but that Dr. Judson was just following standard protocol.

She knew that wasn't true, though. Dr. Judson wasn't much on protocol. That's why he hadn't gotten along with Gasaway and Simmons. He had come on board just before they arrived. He had told her once he was sorry that he had done it, sorry that he had left the group practice out by the county hospital. He must have really meant it because, normally, he kept his own counsel, and he never spoke nastily about anybody.

That was why she didn't think those school bus vets would have killed him because he turned them away. He seemed to like them. She hadn't been in the whole time he was talking to them, but there had been no hostility in the air. It was more like disappointment, for Dr. Judson and those vets both. In fact, it was more on Dr. Judson's part. The vets seemed to take it for granted. Dr. Judson was the one who was shaking his head about how he couldn't help them.

Damn, she was sorry she had ever become a nurse. She hadn't wanted to. She was a good student. Nobody in her family had ever gone to college. She was going to be the first. She had wanted to be a literary person. She loved words and stories. Maybe she would actually write stories herself someday. In the meantime, though, she could be a magazine writer or a teacher. Then she got pregnant, and all that was out the window.

Marv wasn't real smart, but he wasn't a bad boy. In fact, he was a nice guy. He had been so damned insistent, though, and she wanted a boyfriend, someone to take her to the prom. She got a whole lot more than a prom date out of it.

He'd turned out to be a fairly decent man. Worked hard. Didn't complain much. Didn't cat around, at least not that she knew about. He spent most of his time at the lake or in the woods with his buddies, hunting and fishing, but all the men did that, even her father.

He kept being insistent in bed, though. After their fifth child was born, she was the one who became insistent. Either he got snipped or she was going to cut the whole thing off. He wasn't the sharpest pencil in the box, but he was smart enough to choose right on that one.

Then when the last two were in high school, Florence had figured it was her time. But there was just the community college. She could get her degree there in English or History, but a two-year degree wouldn't get her a job in teaching, or anything else. If she wanted a job, she could be an accountant or a welder or a nurse. She needed a job if any of the kids ever got beyond community college, and Jimmy might make it. He was a lot like she had been at his age.

So there she was, back in school, with a whole bunch of girls the age of her daughters. They called her Grandma, and worse, Florence Kneightlygale. She hated that.

She hadn't hated Dr. Judson, though. He was a really good man. She liked working with him. He didn't think her cap was funny. He had a son, too, and he understood. She liked dealing with the veterans more than she thought she would, too.

She had thought it would be hard, because she would be thinking about Kenny all the time. Her oldest boy was back in Iraq, on his third tour. What if Kenneth came home from Iraq like these boys and girls they treated every day? What if he came home burned beyond recognition, like that Victoria? Florence couldn't stand it. But she would want someone to take care of him, like she was taking care of these other boys. She'd want the best care possible for her boy. So she gave the best care she could.

So did everybody else in the hospital. Sure, their equipment wasn't the latest, but they did the very best they could with what they had. Until Gasaway and Simmons came and treated the veterans like they were roadblocks on the way to…what?

Nobody knew. Where were they supposed to be going if it wasn't to better patient care? That's what Dr. Judson had said, and he was right. He was also dead.

CHAPTER 24

Joe

Tornado Becky left, again, just walked out. Why had the bitch driven all this way to tell me? But I didn't have any energy for being mad at Becky anymore.

A new tornado was here now, taking away my air, making me think of Grandma, making me remember when I went to her and asked her why my parents were acting like they were.

I remembered that now as though it had just happened in this room, with Grandma across the table instead of Becky Garlits. When I asked Grandma if it had something to do with me, she had worded it so carefully, and I hadn't even noticed. Grandma hadn't said that it had nothing to do with me, just that I wasn't to blame. It had *everything* to do with me. And Grandma knew it.

Grandma knew! She had to. But why didn't she tell me? Why didn't she explain why my father treated me so bad and my mother didn't defend me?

My father. I was still calling Norman Kirk my father, but I was really Joe Prashwell. Oh, God, No! Norman Kirk was my father, except he hadn't been much of one. In fact, he'd been a terrible father. He'd even tried to get me to kill my real father. But my real father deserved to be killed, the son-of-a-bitch. No, I was the son of the bitch, and the son of a goddam hypocrite preacher. I had no real father. Maybe that was why I went to seminary, looking for the Father in heaven. Hell, no. I didn't go looking for a father in heaven, because there was no such thing. I went to seminary because I had been betrayed by Becky Garlits and I was desperate to get into the pants of Anna Williams. The oldest of motives: *cherchez la femme.*

But my father—no, not my father, Norman Kirk. He had treated me okay until—oh, that's when he found out, just after I started playing football, and I was bragging about my great eye-hand coordination, and he found out that I got it not from him but from the preacher of his own church, who had nailed his wife while he was off defending his country.

How had he found out then? And why had it taken him so long? It was a small town, after all, and—

Oh, hell. My head was beginning to envy Zan.

Then a funny thing happened. I began to feel sorry for them, all of them—my mother, and Norman Kirk, and Grandma, and Prashwell, and even Becky. They had all betrayed me, one way or another, and I was the one feeling sorry for them. That didn't make sense.

I didn't have time to think about it anymore right then, though.

Sheriff Sam Avanti came into the room. "Today's your lucky day," he said.

I didn't have enough ambition to get up and slug him. I didn't even stick my leg out. "You don't know the half of it."

"I thought seeing an old girlfriend would cheer you up. She must have the hots for you, coming all that way from Kentucky, or wherever."

I was beginning to get the idea that people in the Upper Peninsula of Michigan were like New Yorkers in one way. They didn't have much of an idea of the geography of the rest of the country.

"I don't think I want to be your guest anymore, Sheriff. I've got some things to do."

I didn't know what they were, but you didn't just find out that you were the bastard son of two bastard fathers without doing something stupid, like join the army. Whoops. Already did that. Didn't work out that well. Maybe the circus. A one-legged trapeze artist ought to be a draw. I was sure as hell in some sort of high-wire act without a net. Being suspected of murder didn't seem all that important anymore.

"That's okay," the sheriff said. "Can't afford to feed you at public expense any more anyway. Tom Carroll, your hotshot attorney, or at least he thinks he is, has agreed you'll stay here in Iron Mountain until we get this cleared up. We've run the forensics on your bus, and it's clean, so we'll release it to you so you'll have a place to live. We'll even give you a pass to the county park. There's camping there. We can keep an eye on you, in case you need anything."

He didn't have to say that he wasn't worried about us taking off. How far could a blind man, a one-legged man, a crazy man, and a three-toned woman go in a dilapidated school bus?

Then Tom Carroll came swimming in. That's the way he walked, like he was swimming in deep water. He had a hell of a dog-paddle. "Sorry to be late," he huffed. "Met a young woman in the parking lot getting into a car with an Illinois license plate."

"You make a habit of stalking pretty young women with out-of-state license plates?" Sam Avanti's voice was dipped in sweet and sour sauce, without the sweet, like he figured Carroll for a dirty old man.

Then I thought of the way the sheriff looked at Reverend Linden and said, *Takes one to know one*. But I didn't say it out loud.

Carroll didn't seem put off by the sheriff, just as if it was another step in the constant awkward competition of *Dancing With the Stars*. In this case, the stars were tin.

"As a matter of fact, I do, especially if the sheriff has let them visit my client without my consent." Carroll turned to me, in his bob and weave style. "The young lady, Mrs. Rosen, I think she said her name was, seems to think she brought you bad news—"

"That was no lady. That was a tornado," I said.

I didn't want to talk with anybody about what Becky had told me until I had figured it out. Then I wouldn't want to talk with anyone about it, either.

The sheriff turned to Tom Carroll. "Look, I know a lot of the folks who work at the VA. They're good people. Dedicated. Hard working. They have a reputation for taking good care of their patients. I don't want you poking around over there and bothering them."

"It's okay," I said. "We'll just go out to that park and get on with doing nothing."

I needed time to think. I didn't want to *talk about* it, the way Becky always wanted to talk about stuff. God, the woman still didn't know that there was a good time not to talk, like when you were telling somebody their whole life was based on a lie, and they almost killed their father, because their father told them to.

Think, time to think. Okay, I couldn't think it through on my own. I needed someone to help me sort things out, even if we didn't talk about it. Zan? Lonnie? Victoria? Tom Carroll? Reverend Linden?

No. I needed Barbara Occam-Roberts. She had been a jilted lover, and she was a mother who lost her son, and somehow, this was about jilted lovers and mothers home alone, and men off at war, and the goddam preacher taking advantage.

I remembered that other preacher, Wilkey, in chapel just before I walked out of Garrett Theological Seminary to join the army. He had said that sin was always love gone bad.

If a novelist-lover-mother couldn't make sense of love gone bad, who could? And I remembered how we had all laughed there in her big room, how that made me feel whole for the first time in…maybe forever. I wanted that feeling again. I needed it. Sure, the sheriff said I was supposed to stay in Iron Mountain, but I went all over the mountains of Af-Pak without the US Army or the Taliban, either one, knowing where I was. I could make it to Sliver Lake and back without anyone ever knowing I was gone, even on one leg.

"Just give me the keys to the bus, and Lonnie and Zan," I said to the sheriff. "We'll pick up Victoria and—"

"You'll have to get along without your *Medal of Honor* winner," Avanti broke in, with a sneer in his voice. "Seems she's wanted by the MPs about something else."

I opened my mouth, and he held up his hand.

"Yeah, yeah, I buy the part about her being claustrophobic because she was trapped in the burning Humvee and all that. They say there's no record of her because of national security, but they say that part about the burning is real, even if the rest of what you told me was a bunch of shit. We won't bring her to a cell over here. We'll keep her over at the VA until the MPs get here. Then it's up to them."

I didn't like the sound of that, but there wasn't anything I could do about it. Besides, I didn't owe Victoria anything. I didn't even know her. I didn't owe anybody anything. I didn't even know anybody, most especially myself.

The sheriff turned to Tom Carroll again. "Remember what I said about not bothering people at the VA. Those are good people, but Dr. Judson's murder combined with that new administrator has them spooked. If your clients get arrested and charged, then the folks over there will be fair game for your questions. In the meantime, leave them alone. That goes for you, too," he said to me. "You just stay in that bus."

"Where else would I go?" I said.

CHAPTER 25

They brought Lonnie and Zan out. Lonnie was in one of his *Don't-touch-me* moods, so nobody did. Zan lifted his eyebrows. That was the extent of our greeting. Sam Avanti gave us the curious eye, but Tom Carroll didn't seem to think it was strange. I introduced him to Zan and Lonnie as the lawyer who had gotten us out. That caused the sheriff to switch from curious eyes to rolling ones.

I thought about hitting him. I wanted to hit somebody pretty bad. Sam Avanti didn't look enough like either of my fathers, though, to make it worthwhile. I made do with humming "I Shot the Sheriff."

I explained to Zan and Lonnie about how we were going to stick around Iron Mountain for a while "to give the sheriff a hand." They knew what I was saying. We were out of jail but not free to go anyplace.

I told Lonnie that Victoria wouldn't join us for a while since they were working on her at the VA and she couldn't have visitors. The sheriff kept a straight face while I lied. It wouldn't make any difference to Lonnie. He couldn't see the sheriff's face. Knowing the MPs were after her would make a difference to Lonnie, though, and to Zan, too. Lonnie liked Victoria, and Zan didn't like MPs. I didn't want to have to deal with their likes and dislikes. I had enough of my own.

The deputy gave us our stuff back. Wasn't much. With my vest, though, there was an envelope. Those photog vests had a lot of pockets, and I sometimes forgot where my Swiss Army Knife or my Chap Stick was, but I didn't remember having an envelope like this anyplace in that vest. I started to tell the deputy it wasn't mine, but then I noticed a funny little mark up in the corner, a little ballerina, like on a music box, with the words, *Pennies From Heaven*. I remembered there had been a whole stack of those on Dr. Judson's desk. I looked inside. A twenty dollar bill. So Judson had assuaged his conscience by giving me secret money. I hadn't even known it was there.

I handed Lonnie his remote-control vest. He didn't put it on.

"No use without Victoria," he said.

"I could use the remote control," I said. "I could at least keep you from running into stuff."

He just shook his head.

I envied him. He was sad that a woman was no longer in his life. I was glad that all the women in my life were gone.

Tom Carroll went out to the parking lot with us. He examined the bus as if he had seen too many Jurassic Park movies and was afraid this dinosaur would come to life.

"The sheriff wasn't entirely candid with you," he said.

"Big whoop," I said. "Why doesn't that surprise me?"

Zan and Lonnie and Tom Carroll all looked at me like they were a little bit afraid. That was when I realized we were a group and I was the leader. Group members didn't like to have the leader acting like all he knew how to do was sneer. Big whoop. I didn't ask to be anybody's leader. By God—

But the lawyer was going on. "There is a good bit of tension between the sheriff and the cops over at the VA. Our good sheriff Avanti continues to act like he is in charge and this is his investigation, but he is not getting much, if any, cooperation from the VA police. I used that to our advantage. That's why you're out."

He seemed quite pleased with himself. He puffed up so much his wrinkles disappeared, at least some of them.

"If there's so goddam much tension or whatever between the cops, how come we can't just leave this effing hell hole? It's like the effing black hole of Calcutta here." Zan had said almost nothing about his Iraqistan days, but he must have spent some time with British troops there. He had never said *effing* back in our football days.

"You're very knowledgeable, Mr. Zander," Carroll said. "Actually this place is very pleasant until the snow comes, but

I'm impressed that you know about the black hole of Calcutta."

I felt a little twinge of nostalgia. I was the one who had forced some history onto Zan back at IU. He had a preference for any event with a bizarre name.

"I *live* in the black hole of Calcutta," Lonnie said.

I got the idea he was trying to be funny, but it was so morose that we all sobered up and just stood there.

Finally Zan said, "We need to get some food. I miss Joe's cooking."

He sounded like he meant it. It was nice to be missed by someone, for something.

I pulled my pants pockets inside out. I kept all my stuff in the vest pockets. It was easier having the stuff on my shoulders than bopping around on my leg.

"We need some money," I said.

I had Judson's twenty, but I wanted to hang onto that.

"I've got money," Lonnie said. "And I could sure use some real food, after this jail crap. It was even worse than what the contractors fed us in the desert."

"Uh, Lonnie, I'm sorry, but the sheriff checked that out. Your ATM card is no longer good."

"Goddammit, he cut off my card. That was all I had left."

"No problem. I can give you some money for food," Tom Carroll said.

Lonnie was no longer listening, though.

CHAPTER 26

Lonnie

That ATM card was all I had left of her. Goddamn him. Goddamn his eyes. I hate him. If I could see him, I would kill him with my stare. I would split him in two. I wouldn't need my hand, just my stare…

⁂

Hogarth Blifield was not just a Virginia state senator, he was *the* Virginia state senator. Some said he was the Virginia Senate itself, the Ted Stevens or Robert Byrd or Jesse Helms of Virginia, as powerful and as mean as those US senators, but on the state level. One yellow journalist had dubbed him "Virginia's Prime Senator." He hadn't meant it nicely, but Hogarth Blifield took it as a mantle, wrapped himself in it, subtly encouraged others to introduce him that way. Governors came and went, but the Prime Senator really ran the country, which was the state of Virginia.

The state of Virginia was the nation, as far as Hogarth Blifield was concerned. Who needed anything else? Sure, he'd had plenty of opportunities to go to Washington, but what would he be there? Just another cog in the wheel of the Washington machine. In Virginia, though, he was the wheel itself. He was the one who gave with one hand and took with the other. No bill, no contract, no candidacy succeeded without the approval of the Prime Senator. Governors came and went. Regardless of political party, they were there simply to carry out his orders.

Lonnie had never understood that. He did not understand power and its use, its necessary use by those who, by birth and merit, were given the task of using the power to keep the rabble from pillaging and sacking all that the real people had done to build up the culture.

Lonnie was a mama's boy. If it were not so unthinkable, he might think the boy was gay. How in hell did the Cheneys stand it, anyway? But it was different with a girl, of course. Girls who liked girls didn't do the disgusting things that boys who liked boys did to each other.

Lonnie was such a namby-pamby. He was afraid to bait a hook. He was afraid to shoot a duck. Hogarth had given up on him when he was ten. It was Emily's fault, of course.

"Hogarth, not everybody has to be like you. Let him be himself. Leave him alone."

Hell, yes, not everybody had to be like Hogarth Jefferson Blifield. Not everybody *could* be like him. Hell, *nobody* could be like him. But his own son needed to make the effort at least. Except Emily seemed to think Lonnie was her son, not his. Hell, she wanted him to be like *her*.

He didn't play real sports, like football, or baseball, or even basketball. He played a lot of other sports. Hogarth had to admit that. Sometimes people would tell him how good Lonnie was at some sissy-boy sport. Those were people who didn't get any face time with Virginia's Prime Senator after that. They didn't get their bills passed or their contracts approved, either.

Lacrosse? Whoever had even heard of Lacrosse? A Redskin sport.

Tai Kwan Do? Gook slight-of-hand. A lot of bowing and board-breaking. Bowing was for Democrats and board-breaking was for carpenters.

Gymnastics? A bunch of sissies. He might as well have danced ballet or skated on ice in sparkly tights with a titless little Jap girl. Hell, those fancy skating boys were always grabbing those little Jap girls in the right places, acting like it was part of the skating routine, but what was the use? There wasn't anything to grab.

Some people said that Lonnie was a musician. Hell, singing wasn't being a musician. Anybody could sing. It wasn't like you had to practice. Did they have any tenors in the marching band at football games? If a kid was in the band, at least he *went* to the football games, even if he didn't play in them, except at halftime. Lonnie sang sissy-boy music. Some people even said he could have sung opera, and meant it as a compliment. Lonnie was so backward, though, he couldn't sing by himself. He was in something called a "chorale."

He even sang in the choir at Emily's Episcopal Church. That was okay in its own way. A man needed to keep on the right side of the church. Preachers could get goddamn feisty if you didn't keep them in line, especially the dark-skinned ones, and some of those Episcopal types were almost as bad. If you knew any history, you knew you had to keep the preachers quiet.

Hogarth knew history. He had been a History major at the University in Charlottesville. He knew even then that one day he would be the Prime Senator of Virginia, although he didn't know that name for it yet. A lot of would-be *leaders* majored in business or finance or some made-up thing like *Political Science*. Hell, there wasn't any science to politics. Politics was football without the helmets. You put a bunch of big mean people out in front of you and then you grabbed the power and rammed it down the throats of anybody who got in the way. That was what you learned from history.

Lonnie followed him to the University. Even majored in History. He didn't learn anything from it, though. Didn't even learn about the right way of being in *The Service*.

After UVA, Lonnie went to *The Service*, the way all Blifield men did. Blifield men, though, worked their way up through the ranks. Better to start as a junior officer and work up, but some had started as enlisted men and ended up as officers, and that was okay. They did it in a branch that took some brains, or political connections, like the navy or air force. Certainly not the army. Certainly not the infantry. Sometimes you couldn't work your way up.

Hogarth understood that. There wasn't enough war sometimes. Then, however, you were smart enough to go through ROTC or use political connections. Not the flyboy academy in Colorado, or Annapolis.

Hogarths were not professional soldiers. They were citizen

soldiers. They wore the uniform long enough to hone their credentials for real leadership in politics.

Finally Hogarth had just given up. It wasn't the first time. He gave up on Lonnie when he was ten, and when he was in high school, and when he was in college. It was hard to stay given-up on your only son. Every once in a while he would go back and try to beat some brains into the boy, but Lonnie was as thickheaded as his mother was flexible. Emily could bend and bend and still not break, still keep control of the boy. When Lonnie joined the army—a Phi Beta Kappa graduate of the university as a goddamned private—he even had a Rhodes Scholarship and didn't use it. Good God, how stupid could a smart kid be? It had to be his mother's goddamn influence.

⁂

After the University of Virginia, Lonnie went into the army. The reasons were simple. Military service was part of his tradition, on both sides of his family, and he honored that. He really wanted to "join the navy and see the world." His mother's family was full of naval officers. But his father had been a "martini officer" in the navy. No way could he be part of that. Besides, he knew it would drive his father crazy if he ignored the Rhodes and joined the army, as a private. So he did.

His mother understood. She didn't like it, but she understood. She was okay with the army, with being an enlisted man, with Lonnie sticking his thumb in his father's eye. It was the Iraq war she could not abide. Like any mother, though, her main concern was for her son's safety.

As far as she was concerned, a country wasn't worth serving if it wasted its young men on a war that wasn't only useless but counter-productive. Sacrifice for your country in a noble cause, like freeing the slaves or defeating the Nazis or preventing another Holocaust? Yes. Sacrifice for your country, and the world, by going after al-Qaeda and the Taliban? Yes. Sacrifice for the obscene profits of Hogarth's oil company buddies or for the cheerful and incompetent megalomania of people Hogarth helped put in office? No way.

It was the one time Lonnie and his mother ever had a heated

discussion. She was usually so classic, so calm, so much above the fray. The idiocy of this war, though, was a passion with her, all the more so because she could not say a word about her opposition to it to anyone but Lonnie. She had to continue to play the dutiful wife to Hogarth Blifield, supporting the party line.

Take the Rhodes, she begged Lonnie. It will make you a better soldier. At least wait until there is a new administration in Washington, one that has enough sense to wage the right war in the right place.

Lonnie, though, had come under the influence of the charismatic young history professor, Yavelle Williams. Williams was bright and black. He had been a basketball star at William and Mary. As the joke went, he had been the William on a team of Marys. Then he had given up a Rhodes scholarship at the start of the first Iraq war, under the first George Bush, to join the army. His story had inspired the Middle-East scholars at the New Patriots Institute to take him under their wing, shepherd him through a PhD at Yale after his army stint—surprisingly short and combat-free—was over, and get him onto the faculty of the University of Virginia. He was the poster boy for the bright new "progressive conservatism" championed by New Patriots.

His story and his philosophy inspired Lonnie. "Progressive conservatism" would extend the best of American values and blessings around the world.

"The same old crap in a different pot," his mother had said. "Because the pot is black and beautiful, you don't notice the color of the crap, but it's there."

The greatest regret of Lonnie's life was not his blindness. He deserved that. He had been blind to reality, now he was blind to everything. No, his greatest regret was that he could not apologize to his mother, not tell her that she had been right.

It was while he was in Iraq that his father dumped his mother for a girl. Not a woman. That was what she was—a girl—so call her that. Younger than Lonnie himself. Hadn't even married her, just moved out and shacked up. Everybody in the state knew about it, but nobody said anything about it. Technically Hogarth and Emily Blifield were still married.

Then his mother killed herself. Nobody told him about it.

Hogarth Blifield pulled one of the many strings he held. He didn't want Lonnie coming back for the funeral. He knew what would happen. He had Lonnie's letters and emails censored. Lonnie hadn't even known it. So he didn't learn about his mother's death until the email from an insurance agent.

Mattie Loveland was his mother's cook and confidante. Hogarth had told Mattie that Lonnie was on a secret mission and couldn't be reached so he couldn't come home for his mother's funeral. Of course, Mattie Loveland wouldn't trust Hogarth Blifield with a wooden nickel. In truth, though, that was another string Hogarth had pulled. Lonnie actually was sent on a secret mission to keep him incommunicado.

When Lonnie did not reply to any of her letters or emails, Mattie went through her son. Mattie's son wasn't a Loveland, one of the censored names. He was Herschel Williams, an insurance salesman. He emailed Lonnie and asked him to make contact about an insurance matter. Lonnie recognized the name as Mattie's son. They had never played together as children, but they had met a time or two in teen years, when Herschel would pick up his mother after work. Lonnie replied to the email.

It was an insurance salesman he barely knew who told him that his mother had put Hogarth Blifield's shotgun into her mouth and pulled the trigger.

Emily was an old-fashioned woman, a southern belle in the best sense of that phrase, a woman of culture and kindness, without a hint of racial animosity. Indeed, her household servants were her best friends. Because she was a belle, however, it had never occurred to her to question the Blifield family finances. Hogarth gave her a generous allowance for personal and household expenses. Nothing, however, was in her name. She had no will. She left nothing to her son. Except that ATM card she had given him.

Lonnie had thought his father knew he was using his mother's ATM card. Well, it wasn't actually hers. She had given it to Lonnie. But it was in her name.

But his father had to know. Somebody had been paying the bill. Oh, the lawyer. There would have been some kind of legal stuff to go through. The lawyer would have been paying the bills until it was settled. When the bills started coming to his father, Hogarth Blifield had cancelled the card. It neither increased nor diminished his hate for the man who had killed his mother, killed her spirit and killed her will to live, but it gave him a strange sense of freedom. He had been taking money from the man he hated. He had told himself it was really his mother's money, that she had earned it just by being married to the Hog, but…

Being blind was a different kind of freedom, too. Crazy incident. Three of his buddies were killed, but he was hardly marked. His good looks were still there, the nurses assured him. He would never see again, though, the doctors informed him. At first, he had been in a cave with no one around. Then he began to listen. What he heard were the sounds of his mother.

Emily Blifield had taught her son to listen, to listen to sighs, to double meanings, to rustlings, to footsteps, to voice differences. It had not been intentional teaching, but she was his buoy in the ocean of loss, the loss of his father, which had seemed so overwhelming when he was a boy and seemed so necessary now. He had listened for the buoy, listened to the buoy, and he had learned what little sounds meant, especially the little sounds of women. Now, in his blindness, he could listen to anything and hear the levels of meaning below the surface. Especially, though, he could listen to women, read them, persuade them, just because he could tell them more about them than they knew for themselves. That was the legacy from his mother, and it was why he would be able to use Victoria to do what he could not see to do, to kill his father.

What was it Janis Joplin had sung? *Freedom's just another word for nothing left to lose.* Lonnie had nothing left to lose. When you've got nothing left to lose, you might as well go out in a blaze of glory. Now he just had to get Victoria and get to Virginia.

CHAPTER 27

Joe

Tom Carroll said he didn't think we would have any more trouble. That was a hoot, but I tried not to let out an actual hoot. Trouble followed us around like the little black cloud followed Joe Bftsplk in my mother's old *Little Abner* comic books that Grandma kept in a box in the basement.

The lawyer told us that he had explained to the prosecutor that her only evidence was that we were suspicious-looking characters but we were really just homeless veterans. She was sympathetic because her father was a vet. It seemed that being a vet was a helpful thing with everybody except the people who were supposed to help us, the Veterans Administration. Anyway, the prosecutor told the sheriff to let us go unless he came up with more evidence.

We stopped by a grocery store called Super 1. Lonnie wouldn't go in. Zan and I cruised the aisles, getting only a few stares. We were dirty and needed haircuts, but we didn't look that much different from everybody else in the UP. I filled up my cart with fresh produce and canned goods. Zan filled his with Leinenkugels. We paid with Tom Carroll's cash and had plenty left over.

"Either lawyers are overpaid or being one makes you a soft touch," Zan said as we pushed our carts back to the bus.

He didn't know the real reason Tom Carroll was on our side, because the girl preacher, Rickie Linden, had persuaded him to take care of us, just because she had the hots for me. Yeah, right. Sure, she was nice to me, but that's just what preachers were required to do, be nice to dirty, homeless, legless, penniless, gun-loving father-murderers. A beautiful SoCal girl could do a whole lot better than me, and if she didn't know it, she was too stupid for me.

This was great. I could push her away either because she was too pretty or too stupid. I didn't tell Zan any of that, though. I didn't tell him about Becky Garlits's visit, either. We got to the bus and began to unload our carts through its back door.

"If I ever have a kid—Leinenkugel—that's the name," Zan said.

"What if it's a girl?" I said.

"That's the girl's name," he said. "A boy, I'd name him Joe." The next thing I knew, Zan was shaking my shoulder. "Hey, Joe, hey. I didn't mean anything, like to upset you, or whatever. I just thought…Gee, man, I'm sorry."

I was sitting on the blacktop, beside the grocery cart. I had no idea how I got there or how long I had been there. I was crying like a baby. No, babies couldn't cry that hard. I was sobbing, shaking all over. I looked down, and I had two legs, two *good* ones. My old leg was back! Goddamn! Two good legs. I wasn't making any noise, just shaking. Then the legs began to wobble, like heat mirages at the end of a long corn field during detassling season, and my old cargo pants were back, and my stump hurt, a dull, aching throb, like it had been there for a thousand years and would be there a thousand more.

Fortunately, we had parked at the far side of the lot, beyond the yellow lines that the pickups, vans and SUVs were too big to fit in so that everybody was always mad because they kept opening their doors into each other. We were far enough away from that door-banging action that nobody was watching me. Except Lonnie. He had gotten out of the bus and was standing there, his eyes back in the direction of the store.

"The woman brought him bad news," he said.

"What woman?" Zan asked.

"I don't know."

Zan looked at me. "Was it that preacher?"

I shook my head. I hoped he could tell it was different from the shaking I was doing in general.

He squatted down beside me.

"Joe—"

I shook my head again, reached over, and took his hand. "Help me get up."

Lonnie reached his hand down on the other side. I took it and let them pull me up.

"I'll tell you later," I said. I didn't mean it.

We followed the directions the sheriff had given us to get to the county park. When I saw it up ahead, I looked over at Zan. "Zan, I need to say this now. What you said back there, it was the nicest thing anybody has ever said to me."

He made the turn for the park. "Yeah, I could tell by your reaction."

I had to laugh. It was so droll, the way he said it. We were still laughing when we opened the door to show Sheriff Sam Avanti's pass to the caretaker. He didn't think anything was funny.

"Damn stupid sheriff," he said. "Too late for camping. We close up first of November."

I knew I had lost track of time, but…

"Is it November already?" I said.

"Hell, no," he muttered. "Damn stupid campers. Don't even know what month it is. Park it where you want. No competition. Everybody else is too smart to be out here this time of year."

He handed the pass back and stalked off. Before I could get the door closed, he threw over his shoulder, "You're gonna git damned cold, regardless."

I knew he was right. The feel of winter was in the air and in the light, with the way the light italicized everything beside the lake. We weren't prepared for winter in any way.

Then I forgot about winter. Even forgot about the way I had blubbered when Zan said he would name a son after me. Forgot about Becky Garlits and the pain in my leg and being king of the bastard orphans, or whatever status my two fathers had given me.

Rickie Linden was driving up.

Toyota Prius, of course. Not many of them in the Upper Peninsula. Mostly huge pickups and SUVs and vans. But Rickie Linden wasn't an Upper Peninsula girl. She was a SoCal girl. As she got out of her car, I began to hum it, "I wish they could all be…"

She was wearing jeans, white running shoes, and a short-sleeved yellow tee-shirt. I sort of missed the preacher uniform, but she looked awful good this way, too.

"Don't you know it's gonna git damn cold?" I called as she started toward us.

I hated that. I didn't sound like the caretaker, and she wouldn't know what I was referring to. I just sounded stupid. What a dumbass thing to say.

"She's wearing that for you, dumbass," Lonnie said out of the side of his mouth.

"Lonnie, how in the hell do you do that? You don't know what she's wearing. Besides, you don't even know who it is."

"It's Mother Linden," he said. "And whatever it is she's wearing, it's for you."

"Dumbass," Zan added.

I decided that, the first chance I got, I would shoot them both. Right now, though, I couldn't get at the gun in my leg because I had to bend over the other direction so that the bulge in my pants wouldn't show. Oh, and also because the gun wasn't in my leg anymore. The preacher had my gun. Did she ever.

She grinned as she came toward us. It looked to me like her white running shoes weren't even touching the ground, she heeled and toed so lightly.

"You were imitating Oscar," she said. "Pretty good, too. Pay him no mind. Everyone calls him *Oscar the Grouch*, with good reason. Hi, Lonnie. Hi, Zan."

"Good afternoon, Mother Linden," Lonnie said, with a trace of southern gentility I'd never noticed before.

What was this *Mother* business? Was he insulting her? Or did he know something I didn't.

Her eyes got big and she flashed him a little half-smile. "Lonnie, you must be Episcopal."

"My mother was."

He sounded sort of sad.

Rickie must have seen my confused look, which is actually my default look. "Episcopalians call their priests *Father*," she said, "the way Catholics do. They call us women priests, *Mother*."

"It says in the Bible, *Call no man on earth Father*," Zan said. "I guess it doesn't say anything about *Mother*. Come on, Lonnie. We've got Leinies to sort out."

Zan turned abruptly and headed for the back end of the bus. Lonnie gave a little bow and followed the sounds of his steps. They weren't loud. We were camping on old grass. Lonnie had no trouble staying in Zan's wake, though.

Rickie looked a little confused herself, or maybe bewildered.

"I've never heard Zan quote the Bible before," I said. "I don't know where he gets that stuff."

"I don't think he likes me," Rickie said.

"No. He's just taking it out on you. It's another woman he doesn't like."

"The one who came to see you this morning?"

"You know a lot."

"Tom Carroll told me."

"Thanks for getting him to go to bat for us."

"It's just lucky I happened to meet him at the coffee shop. I Googled him. He's real famous down in Indiana." That seemed to exhaust that subject. She was looking at my leg and trying not to. "Maybe we should sit down," she said.

We walked over to a picnic table. I tried not to limp. We sat in the sun. It felt good.

"I noticed in the jail, that first time, when we had that fracas, with the deputies, that you had a rosary."

She laughed. I remembered how Grandma used to say that the first time a baby laughed, it broke into pieces, and that was how we got fairies. Rickie didn't laugh like a baby, but there was a fairy-like lilt to it.

"I'm what they call High-Church Episcopalian. Anglican. Church of England, only in America we don't want to say that, so we're just Episcopalian. But we're like Catholics without the pope."

"I didn't know Catholics had *Mothers* as well as *Fathers* for priests."

She laughed that fairy laugh again. "I guess I'm part of the liberal wing of the High-Church Episcopalians, if you can call anything Anglican liberal. So, I guess that means we're Catholic except for the pope *and* women priests."

I wanted to keep her talking, just to hear her voice. Usually the best way to get anyone to talk is to ask them to talk about themselves, so I did. "It's kind of unusual, women priests. How did that happen?"

That was a stupid way to ask it. "How did that *happen*?"

She took the bait, though. I had the feeling that she was biting intentionally. "I went to USC for undergrad," she said. "One of the girls in my dorm was Episcopalian, and one Sunday she wanted to go to church. She looked in the phone book. The nearest Episcopal Church was St. Stephen's. It was in a sort of run-down neighborhood. She didn't want to go there by herself, so she asked me to go with her. I didn't have anything else to do, so I went. It was like a cathedral. That's a technical term for us but, back then, to me a cathedral was just a big church that looked like something out of Europe. I'd never been to an Episcopal Church or a cathedral before, or any church much. My friend didn't like it, said it was too liberal for her, so she didn't go back. But I felt something there, something I hadn't ever felt before. I started walking over there by myself. I got really involved. Spent more time there than I did at college. One thing led to another."

"So you decided to be a priest?"

"Not exactly. I was getting ready to graduate. I didn't have any plans, anything I really wanted to do. I knew the idea of me being a priest was stupid, for a lot of reasons, but the priest at St. Stephen's got me a scholarship at his old theological school, said it would give me some time to figure things out. So I went to seminary, and one year led to another, and then…"

"What seminary did you go to?" I asked.

She looked at me like she thought it was a strange question, at least coming from me. "Seabury-Western, the Episcopal Theological School in Chicago."

"Evanston, actually," I said. "West Jesus Tech."

She squealed and slapped her hand on the rough gray board top of the picnic table. I flinched just a little, in case she whomped down on a pile of bird poop.

"West Jesus Tech? Where in the world did you hear its technical name?"

I took a deep breath. I knew this was going to lead me down a winding primrose path. I didn't know where it led, but I was pretty sure I didn't want to go there. I let the breath out. "I went to East Jesus Tech," I said.

That was what the students at Northwestern's tech school, which was just north of Garrett, called the seminaries. Garrett and Seabury-Western were across Sheridan Avenue from each other.

"No!"

She blew out the *No* like a foghorn. I looked around to see if the sulky caretaker or somebody else might think I was molesting her.

"You think I'm too dumb to go to seminary?"

"I think you're too *smart* to go to seminary!"

I had to laugh at that one. It was nice to laugh, to feel the happy rumble in my own throat. "Well, there was a time when I wasn't this smart."

She distractedly reached up to her neck, fingered a silver thread so thin I hadn't even noticed it before, pulled a discreet little silver cross out of her tee-shirt, fingered it as she looked at me.

I guessed that little silver cross sort of mesmerized me. Or maybe it was where it came from that fascinated me. Anyway, I went down that primrose path. I understood then why she had taken the bait so readily when I asked her to tell me about herself. I owed her my story now.

I told her about Grandma and playing football in high school and IU. I told her about Becky Garlits and going to Garrett seminary. I told her about joining the army. I told her about losing my leg and meeting up with Zan again at the VA in Indianapolis. I told her about how we got Lonnie and Victoria.

I didn't tell her about what I did in the army. I didn't tell her just how I lost my leg. I didn't tell her about my two fathers.

She was a good listener. And a good questioner, without really questioning. "You've packed more into a third of a lifetime than most people could in two lifetimes," she said. "Football, son, grandson, seminary, army. It must have been hard at times to know which of those was the real you."

"I guess up until the army, the real me was the one called *not-good-enough*. My parents—they treated me like I wasn't good enough to be their son. My football coach at IU said I wasn't good enough to play. Becky Garlits said I wasn't good enough in bed. At seminary, I was as out of place as a hippo in the ballet. All the other students were there to be chaplains or professors. Some of them, even preachers. I was just there to get into the recruiter's pants."

"Were you successful?"

"Are you kidding? First, she was out recruiting all the time, and then the football season wasn't even over when she went off to Oklahoma or someplace to get married. I think it was Oklahoma, maybe Kansas. I know it was some place in the Big Twelve."

She took my hand. I didn't much like to be touched. This time, though, I didn't mind. She pulled each of my fingers out to its full length, each in turn, very gently. "You're very good at going to your third receiver if the first two are covered," she said, very softly.

"Wow. You really know football," I said.

"My grandfather was a coach," she said. "And now your third receiver is covered and you're scrambling for the sidelines."

"You ought to talk to Zan. You think like a middle linebacker."

"We're not talking about football. We're talking about you not being good enough. Why weren't you good enough in seminary?"

She was pulling more out of my fingers than I wanted to let go of. But I didn't want her to let go of my hand. "Everybody there was into social justice and gay rights and against the war. I had grown up where you believed everything the president said just because he was the president, and you joined the army and served your country just because it was the patriotic thing to do."

"Were you good enough in the army?"

"Oh, hell, yes. Better than good. I was the best. I loved guns. I'd been to college. I knew how to lead a team. I knew how to improvise when the game plan broke down. Pretty soon, our officers were asking me what to do and how to do it. I was right where I belonged."

"So you found the real you?"

"In the army, it was all so damned clear. I never had a moment's doubt. Dr. Weiser, the counseling prof at Garrett, said that you can't run away from your problems, but I did. He said wherever you go, your problems go with you, because they're in you, but they weren't with me in Iraqistan."

"Iraqistan?"

"What we call it if we've fought in Iraq and the 'Stan both. Iraq and the Af-Pak border are a lot different, geographically, but they're the same if you're a soldier."

"Did you leave your problems, the ones that made you leave Garrett and go into the army, did you leave them in Iraqistan?"

"Yeah. I left them there, along with my leg. Problem is, when I got back, there was a whole pack of new ones waiting for me."

"Or maybe the old ones in different uniforms?"

We had talked a long time, or at least I had. The sun was only a rack of orange spears through the tall pines around the lake. Rickie had her arms around herself. Her satin arm-skin had become burlap with goose bumps.

"Gosh, Rickie, I'm sorry. I talked too long. You're cold."

"Not long enough, scrambler. You're not going to get out of bounds this time, and you're definitely not going to use concern for my temperature to avoid the hit. Becky came to see you today. She had to drive a long way. Even though she's married, it's obvious she still cares about you, to come all that way when she found out you were in jail."

I could only shake my head. "She came not because she cares about me, but to clear her own conscience. She didn't come to help me; she came to hurt me."

I hated myself. I sounded so downright whiney and needy.

"Joe, Becky obviously made a mistake. For whatever reason, now she knows that, but it's too late to do anything about it. She married somebody else. That business about you not being good enough in bed, that's just a smoke screen. She was trying to blame you for the bad choice she made so that it won't seem so bad, so that she can live with herself…"

She was saying some more stuff, but it sounded like so much psychobabble, so I didn't listen. It wasn't Rickie's fault, though. I had told her about Becky saying I wasn't good enough, but that wasn't the real issue. I hadn't told her about the reason for Becky's visit this time, so she just assumed all this was about Becky and me. It was really about me and my father, whoever the hell that was.

I thanked her for her insights and said she had made me feel a lot better. That was true, but it wasn't anything she had said, it was just because she was there.

I think she sensed that there was something else but that I had already scrambled out of bounds this time. She said she had to get back to town.

She left. She looked so good, walking to her Prius, so young, so pretty, so real. But she was walking away from me, just like everything else in my life that was any good.

Then I remembered that she still had my Beretta. My stump began to hurt. Maybe Judas and I were both just lonely.

CHAPTER 28

Victoria

Victoria hated plastic shower caps. She was wearing one, anyway. It would do until she got down to the lab and could get one of those blue paper caps everybody wore. Then she could fit in enough. Maybe.

Maybe that shower cap was some sort of hair growth thing. She took it off and looked in the mirror. She ran her hand over her head. Yes, for sure, sprouts were coming up where they hadn't been before. Maybe those transplants were going to work after all. Maybe she wouldn't shave her head this time, see what happened. Dr. Allison had told her he was going to make her a blonde because he thought she should have more fun. He was just crazy enough to do it, too.

She would have to find boots on her own. Maybe shoes would have to do. Nurse's shoes would work in the hospital, but not after.

She didn't much like the idea of stealing shoes from the nurses' locker room. The nurses had been great to her. That was how she knew as much about the damned place as she did, asking the nurses, especially the student nurses doing their clinicals. They were glad to take a break and talk to "the strange one." She knew they called her that. She didn't mind. It was true. Besides, they told her what she needed to know, what the place was like, the way it was laid out, what she had to do to get the hell out. Of course, they didn't know they were telling her that.

She did not like the idea of getting Gerri into trouble. Gerri was a student nurse. She was a nice girl, but fat, the kind who would end up being a good nurse when all she wanted was a good man. Fat girls didn't get good men, though, they just dreamed about it. Victoria had shamelessly worked Gerri's romance lever.

It was just the most romantic thing poor Gerri had ever heard, the burned-over black Medal of Honor winner in love with the beautiful blond patrician, the youngest general the army had ever had, who loved her back because he was blind and could not see her mottled skin, only her pure soul. Some of it was even true. At least, Victoria hoped that some of it was true.

Besides, she was just repeating stuff Joe Kirk had said, mostly, so if anyone was lying, it was Joe.

He was the strange one. On the surface, the all-American boy, natural leader, the one everyone else looked to for decisions. He didn't see it that way, but everyone else did. Underneath, though, she knew there were agonies in his soul. They were all soldiers, so they were all full of violence. She understood that all too well. But she, Lonnie, and Zan were the type to go off before their fuses were even lit. Joe had a long fuse, and it scared her to think what would happen if the fuse ever burned down to the bomb in his soul.

She didn't like to think about anything that burned, though, so she went back to running through her plan, what there was of it. Too much depended on luck, but she had no choice. She had to get out of the VA, and the first step was to get out of her room.

Then, before she got *out* of the VA, she had to get *into* the VA. She had to find out what the hell was going on here that made everybody so scared, because she was sure that if she didn't, she and the rest of the vets on the magic school bus were going to take the fall.

The thought of being in a cell in a prison was too much. There was no way she would take that. If she could find out what was going on, so they wouldn't take the blame, she would do it. If she couldn't, she would run. She wouldn't even take Lonnie. He would slow her down. She was a piece of shit for even thinking like that, but she had to be free shit. She would never make it as prison shit.

The uniforms who sat in the hallway were the hard types, which didn't make much sense in a VA hospital. Hard, but they had gotten relaxed. They spent their time chatting up the nurses. Still, though, whoever was out there was in position to see her door. She knew enough symptoms to fake gastroenteritis. They would be here soon, to take her down for the scope. Then Gerri would get her lost, if she didn't lose her nerve first. *Oh, Lord, please let Gerri be there.* If Gerri wasn't there, Victoria would have to improvise. Hell, she hated improvising. Every unit needed an efficient one, a planner, the one who was always prepared. That was the role she always played. Once she got out of the room, total chaos was a good possibility. She hated chaos.

Gerri would be there, though. The lure of living in a novel was too much for her. Victoria understood that. After all, she had been living in the stories of Barbara Occam-Roberts.

Barbara. Why hadn't Barbara come? Surely she had read about them in the newspaper, their arrest. It would have been big news in Delta County, where that poor dumb sheriff thought he had gotten Barbara pregnant a long time ago. Barbara had to get out of Sliver Lake once in a while, go to town, get some groceries, pick up a paper, get the news. She had to know.

She had thought there was a special bond between her and Barbara. Between Joe and Barbara, too. There seemed to be something there. Zan and Lonnie had perked up in Barbara's presence, too. It wasn't that far from Sliver Lake. Why hadn't Barbara come to see them?

No time to think about that now, though. Here was the student nurse with the wheelchair. The uniform would walk them down to the test area, but he would have to wait outside. She would have to pee. That was well established. She always had to pee. But instead of the restroom, Gerri would take her...

CHAPTER 29

Gerri

All the nurses kept an extra pair of shoes in their lockers. They changed on their lunch break. Wear the same shoes for a whole shift and your legs got tired. A different pair really helped. Usually they switched between nurse shoes and running shoes.

Gerri had started her clinicals with only a pair of run-down gym shoes. Florence Knightly had bought her a new pair of nurse's shoes. Florence was great that way. She was like a mother to all the young nurses. She kept telling Gerri that she would be a great nurse. Gerri liked that. She even thought it was possible—the first time she would ever do anything good. Gerri also knew that helping Victoria this way might put that great nursing career in serious jeopardy, but something better than nursing was at stake here.

Love. That was better than everything else put together. She knew she wasn't ever going to find love, outside of a paperback book, but she could be a part of it, in the same way nurses were always a part of things, by helping other people get what they need.

Anyway, she had started the day in her rundown gym shoes. Now she was in her nurse's shoes. She had scuffed them up a little, just a little, so they didn't look so new. It would be an insult to Florence to make them look too bad, but she had to look like the other nurses, the ones who had been around a while.

Everybody thought she was on her break. Nobody would

know that she was the covered-up nurse in full blue paper regalia—hair tucked into a cap, surgical mask, gown, the undercover nurse who made it possible for the Medal of Honor winner to fly to her blind boyfriend, and then...

It almost made her pee her pants just to think about it, or maybe that was fear.

There the cop was. Oh, shit, it was Vince. What was his last name? He was a friend of her father's, or at least that was what her father claimed when he wanted to sound big. Big whoop when your best friend was a jerk who hadn't been in town for even a month and all you did as friends was drink at the same time at *Lucy's Upstairs on the Square*. Well, it didn't matter. He couldn't recognize her in her undercover outfit. She would just breeze right by him.

Okay, past Vince. Through the door. No sweat.

There she was, in the wheelchair, Victoria, looking so fierce, like an Amazon warrior from the moon, or maybe Africa. Well, she didn't look all that fierce in the wheelchair. Why they always insisted on wheelchairs when a person could walk perfectly okay—it was just a way to keep nurses busy when they were already too busy. But wait, Victoria was kind of bent over. Oh, yeah, she was acting like her belly hurt. That was the reason for the wheelchair. Great.

Oh, shit. Wanda! She must have brought Victoria down for the test. This was a lot worse than Vince, out there in the hallway. She and Wanda had been in a whole lot of classes together, even tutoring by Florence. Wanda would recognize her voice. She was looking this way. Out the other door.

"Gerri?"

Oh, shit, she had recognized her walk or something, even with her back turned. *Keep walking. Don't look back. Out the door. Oh, shit, got to go to the bathroom. But if I do, that Wanda, she'll probably know that's where I'd go. She'll come looking. Okay, hold it in, girl. This is too important.* What was it Florence always said? "What are you going to do when you're holding a vein in place for the doctor? You can't run out and pee then. You've got to learn to hold it."

Okay, just think of this as surgery. Oh, shit, what if she comes after me? That Wanda's a slack-off. She'll not report back that she's done with wheelchair duty until she has to. Wait a minute. She won't come after me. She'll go out the other door, on the side where Vince is, so he can look at her butt wiggle while she's walking down the hallway to come to this door. That girl is sick. That Vince is old enough to be her father. But that's my chance! When I hear her...Oh, shit, I hear her now.

Back through the door. She won't come in. Oh, Lord, don't let her come in. She'll go back and hustle her bustle past Vince again. Oh, Lord, make Wanda go hustle her bustle. Bustle is a strange name for a butt, but that's what Aunt Nola always said.

Okay. Great. No Wanda. Just like I planned. There's Victoria. Got to get to her before they actually stick a scope down her. Just go smooth, smooth as silk, get behind that damned chair, act like you know what you're doing, start pushing, out the door, into the hall, around the corner from where Vince is. Oh, Lord, make Vince watch Wanda's bustle. Turn the other way, down the hall, a little faster. Whoops. Too fast. Victoria's falling. No, she's not, she's running. Great. This worked to perfection.

"Hey, you, with the wheelchair. We're looking for a patient. That Roundtree woman. The one that looks like she was caught in a fire."

Oh, shit. Vince. But too many footsteps for just Vince.

"She's disappeared from the procedure room. These guys are MPs. They want to talk to her."

Oh, shit.

CHAPTER 30

Gerri looked down at the wheelchair, then up toward the end of the hall, where it branched off. No Victoria.
You go, girl! That's so out of date. Well, shit, I'm always out of date. Always out of dates, too. Very funny. Don't giggle. Shit, if I giggle, I'll lose it, go hysterical, pee in my pants like Aunt Nola always did when she laughed too hard. But that Victoria is really fast.

The steps caught up with Gerri.

"What are you doing with an empty wheelchair?"

Vince's voice, mean, showing off for the new cops with him.

Gerri looked up. The MPs weren't wearing uniforms, like in the movies. They looked like the FBI guys on the TV shows, or maybe the Mormons who came around with their pamphlets. Or was that the JWs who had the pamphlets? It was hard to—

One of the MPs grabbed her mask and pulled it down. He scratched her cheek. It hurt, but she was afraid to put her hand up to it.

"Why is that wheelchair empty?"

The MPs looked like Mutt and Jeff. Gerri didn't know who Mutt and Jeff were, but whenever she saw a tall man person and a short man person together, Aunt Nola said they looked like Mutt and Jeff. It was the tall one who scratched her. Really tall. It hurt her neck to look up at him. He must have been taller than Ronnie Romano, the basketball star at the high school, and he was six-six. He was the one demanding to know about the empty wheelchair, his voice like riding through burned-over brush in an ATV.

"Taking it back to where we keep them 'til we need them again."

It was the best she could come up with. Her voice squeaked and cracked. Vince laughed like a donkey, except in his case it would be like a jackass.

"Oh, it's only Gerri. The student nurses get the scut work, like pushing empty wheelchairs. She's harmless."

He brayed again, and Gerri felt her face go hot. He hadn't even noticed she wasn't where she was supposed to be, that she was dressed all wrong for just pushing empty wheelchairs around. She was glad he hadn't noticed, but she felt insulted, too. She wasn't even worth noticing. She was *harmless*? If she had not felt like she was going to faint, she would have kicked Vince in the shins, *Harmless? I'll show you harmless, you—*

Vince and the MPs were talking, but to one another, not to her. She didn't understand them; the blood was rushing through her ears like the roar of Trevor Trueblood's customized hog. Then they were gone, Vince and the short MP went back the way they had come. The other MP, the tall one who had scratched her, was striding down the hall in the direction Victoria had gone.

Gerri put her hand up to her face. The scratch hurt. It was deep, too. Blood was running down and dripping onto her paper gown. He had hurt her, and he had no reason to, and he could see that he had hurt her, but he hadn't apologized. He wasn't the kind of man to apologize for anything.

Gerri wished that it had been the short one who had gone in Victoria's direction.

CHAPTER 31

Victoria

Victoria ran like a girl. Couldn't help it, with these hips. Running like a girl didn't mean you couldn't run fast, though. She had run often enough from the bullies, boys and girls both, on the mean and dirty streets and alleys of Chicago's south side. She had run in Iraq, too, but that was different. This kind of running, on smooth floors, with no pack or belt or weapon to weigh you down, this was simple, even going up the stairs. According to Gerri, only doctors and nurses used the stairs, and then for only a floor, maybe two if they were really in a hurry. If she didn't meet any of them, it was clear sailing.

Hell, that sounded like Sarge. Everything was always *clear sailing* to him. There had been no clear sailing for Sarge at the end. There was no clear sailing for her now, either. She had not been out of that cell of a room until now. She didn't know her way around the building, except for what she had learned from the nurses. If she got outside, there were open grounds all around the hospital. The MPs and the VA cops could chase her down easily. There was a little mall across the four lane street in front of the hospital, but it was too small to get lost in. She didn't know the town. There were so many hills and rivers that there were dead ends all over the place.

But she knew what she had to do before she could try to escape, anyway, and she knew where she had to do it.

Judson had been the new doctor, so he had the oldest and smallest office, at the end of the corridor, right off the stairwell.

She was breathing hard from the quick run up the stairs. She stopped, took a breath, pulled the cap down over her face like a mask. Hell, no, that wouldn't work. Her head was even more identifiable than her face. She put the cap back on, cracked the door, peeked out. A pair of nurses way down the corridor. A woman with a little girl coming toward her, but the woman was giving animated instructions on how to behave once they got into the room of the veteran they were visiting, so she wasn't looking up. A veteran in a wheelchair, just sitting there, but he was facing the other direction.

The nurses went into their station. The little girl and the woman went into a patient room. The wheelchair veteran was still facing the other way. Victoria dug into her pocket for the key Gerri had lifted off Florence Kneightly's ring while they were in the nurses' locker room. There was no yellow tape over the door anymore, but everyone knew it was off-limits. Quickly Victoria stepped around the corner, pushed the key into the lock, turned it the wrong way, turned it back, felt the knob twist turn in her hand, pushed it open, scuttled in like a mouse, pushed the button in the middle of the knob to relock the door, finally took a breath.

This was where the answer was, if there was an answer at all.

Something Pastor Rickie had said, when they were still cuffed together, had started the wheels in Victoria's brain spinning as soon as they had been un-cuffed and she was alone in her cell of a room.

There was some connection between that last patrol she was on and this VA hospital in Iron Mountain. It didn't make any sense. What could the Iraq desert with its heat and sand, and Michigan's Upper Peninsula, with its cold and snow, have in common? Then it finally clicked. Oscar G. Johnson.

Rickie had been trying to calm her as they drove up to the VA. "Here we are. You're safe now. See the sign? Oscar G. Johnson. Good people, the VA. Old Oscar G…"

That was who Sarge said they were working for, Old Oscar G. Johnson, the one who was giving the orders, he'd said. Johnson was a common enough name. Victoria knew a thousand Johnsons, but saying it like that, all the way through, the way a mother said a full name when a kid was in trouble, *Oscar G. Johnson, you get your ass in here.* It was the name of this VA Hospital, Oscar G. Johnson. *Old Oscar G.* That was what Pastor Rickie had called it, just like Sarge.

Pastor Rickie had been right about the people at Old Oscar G. They were good. But they were scared, and nobody would talk about why. Except Gerri. She liked to talk about it, but she didn't know anything. Except that nobody liked the new administrator, Ira Gasaway, and his right-hand nurse, Twyla Simmons. Everybody just called her Simmons. Gerri actually had to look her up in a directory to find out that her first name was Twyla.

Gerri said that Florence Kneightly, who had been Dr. Judson's nurse, knew something, but she wouldn't say anything because she was so scared. It was Florence who knew what Dr. Judson had learned. No, that wasn't quite right. Florence knew that Dr. Judson had learned *something*, but she didn't know what it was. Apparently, Ira Gasaway had reassigned Florence and made Dr. Judson take Simmons as his nurse so she could keep an eye on him.

It had to be here somewhere. A file, that would be it. And nobody had found it yet. It wouldn't be obvious, or it would have been found and taken away, and everybody would be relaxed. There was a bomb here in the Old Oscar G, a paper bomb, waiting to go off.

Victoria had had a lot of time to think about it, sitting up there in her cell of a room. She had gone back over every second of when she had been alone with Dr. Judson. The others thought she had gone to the restroom, but she wanted to pump Dr. Judson for what he might know about what happened to Dr. Allison, her skin doctor in Chicago. There wasn't much to the conversation. Judson was new. He had never heard of Dr. Allison. Then she had mentioned Walter the Penniless.

She hadn't actually *mentioned* him. She had just used his name in vain. That was the way Sarge did it. "Oops. I took his name in vain." Like Walter the Penniless was God, or something. More and more, he had just used the name. "Walter the Penniless won't like that. Walter the Penniless gonna smile at that. Walter the Penniless don't get around much anymore."

Victoria assumed it must be somebody from Sarge's old home town, down in Arkansas, some guy everybody quoted all the time. Except he talked about Walter in the future a lot. "Walter the Penniless gonna visit Batesville, you bet, gonna do some good. Won't need Wal-Mart in Batesville once Walter the Penniless come to town."

She had said it that way to Dr. Judson, even using her Sarge voice, just because it seemed like the thing to do. "Walter the Penniless ain't gonna rain no pennies from heaven about that."

Judson had gone white. "Who *are* you?" he had gasped.

Well, he knew who she was. That wasn't the point. He looked at her like she was from outer space or something. Most people did, but he had seen her the whole time she, Joe, Lonnie, and Zan had been there. He had just accepted her odd appearance the way VA doctors did. They were used to looks like hers. But after she mentioned Walter the Penniless, he looked like he was going to shit in his drawers, or like he already had.

Then that nurse they called Simmons came in, and that was the end of any chance to get anything from the VA.

That encounter with Judson, though, the way he had reacted, that took her back to that morning of their last patrol, although they didn't know it would be the last. Sarge talked about Old Oscar G and Walter the Penniless together.

"Got a mission from Old Oscar G. Johnson. Walter the Penniless gonna rain pennies from heaven on us, oh my God, yes."

What the hell did it mean?

They let Pastor Rickie in to visit her once.

"I'm sorry I haven't been here before, Victoria, but I've had trouble getting in. I suspect they'll keep me out in the future. Everybody here is really walking on eggshells, like they're afraid they'll get into trouble for something, but they don't know what it is. If I don't come back to visit, I don't want you to think it's because I'm ignoring you."

Victoria had nothing to lose, and preachers had gone to school a lot and learned lots of useless stuff, so she just asked her, "Pastor Rickie, have you ever heard of Walter the Penniless?"

The pastor's eyes got big. "Victoria, what in the world? Oh, that brings back bad memories. That was my worst subject. Dr.

Schlarman was *so* boring. I almost left seminary over church history."

The memories must not have been too bad because she was laughing. Victoria waited.

"Oh, my God, let me see. I think the only reason I remember it is because after that lecture some of us students got to talking about the Crusades and how they were a reason for Islamic terrorists now…"

Islamic terrorists? Now Victoria was getting some place.

"…anyway, Walter the Penniless led a bunch of people, I mean, a big bunch, like forty thousand, to the Holy Land. It was the First Crusade. Peter the Hermit started it, or maybe that was somebody else and Peter just got the credit, or the discredit, I guess. Anyway, Peter the Hermit led another big bunch, and they all got marooned in Constantinople, and other big bunches with other leaders got starved out or sold into slavery or something, so Peter the Hermit and Walter the Penniless joined their bands together…"

She kept talking, and Victoria kept listening then, but Victoria wasn't listening anymore to the tape in her memory bank now. What had Judson said just before Simmons came in and ushered her out?

"Kirk's a penny from heaven, but not from Walter the Penniless. I hope I get to spend it."

Kirk? What did Joe Kirk have to do with this? Maybe Dr. Judson had filed something in a folder on Joe Kirk. That would make sense. Joe wasn't an ongoing patient. Nobody would look in a file with his name.

Quickly she riffled through the two drawers of file folders in Judson's desk. Nothing under K. Nothing under J. What about P for Penniless? Nothing. W for Walter? Nothing.

Wait a minute. Judson had said something else, real quiet, as Simmons was coming through the door.

"I've got my own crusade to look to."

Crusade! Like Pastor Rickie talked about. Look under C for Crusade. Hell, nothing there. Wait a minute. The doctor had said that thing about Kirk being a penny from heaven. Look under P for penny. No, already looked under P for Penniless and nothing there. H for heaven. Nothing. S for songs. Nothing.

Hell. She had been barking up the wrong tree all along. Whoever murdered Dr. Judson would have gone through all of his files and taken anything they didn't understand. There was nothing there, not now. She slumped into the worn swivel chair behind the desk.

Then her eyes fell on the statue. Just a cheap little thing, four or five inches high, in among some pictures and bobble-head baseball players on top of the two-drawer file cabinet. Her mother had had one just like it. A little girl holding an umbrella. Victoria knew what song that music box played: Pennies from Heaven.

CHAPTER 32

Joe

It was surprisingly easy for the three of us to do nothing. Zan had always been able to go long stretches without saying a word, but now he was quiet, even for him. Lonnie liked to talk if women were around, but without Victoria, he was moping like a toad.

We'd had one of our usual skillet breakfasts, cans of hash, with bread straight out of the wrapper to push it down. White was cheaper but Lonnie had insisted on whole-grain, and I had to admit it made the hash better.

Lonnie had wandered off to the lakeside sand, challenging the wind. Zan was lying on his back, up on top of the bus like Snoopy on his doghouse. I was trying to get up the gumption to take the skillet and plates down to the lake to wash them in the cold water.

It kept swirling around in my brain like the wind off the water, the crazy idea that my answer was at Sliver Lake, with Barbara, the answer to who I was.

I knew better. I was pretty sure my answer was actually back in Indiana, with my two non-fathers, but I was afraid if I went down there, down in what they call the *pocket* of Indiana, where the Wabash and Ohio Rivers met, I would kill somebody. Besides, it was a hell of a lot easier to go fifty miles to Sliver Lake than a thousand miles to Princeton. And beyond that, I wanted to see Barbara.

There wasn't anything romantic about wanting to see Barbara. Sure, she was as cute as a button, but even if she hadn't been old enough to be my mother, she had been a Purdue cheerleader. That was a definite turnoff.

I had no idea then what Victoria was doing over at the VA. In fact, I had forgotten about her. "Sufficient for the day is the evil thereof." That was in the Bible somewhere. Grandma used to quote it. When I was in seminary, I could tell you chapter and verse on it, but that was in a different lifetime. I just knew it was true. I didn't need to be borrowing trouble by worrying about Victoria, or Lonnie, or Zan, or anybody else. I had my own worries.

What bothered me most was that it bothered me. I mean, hadn't I been through worse? And survived? What difference did it make who had donated the sperm to my mother's womb to bring me into existence? I had been my own man since the eighth grade. When Grandma died, that was the end of that life. Right now, in this life, I was being accused of murder. I had no illusions about this temporary lull in the proceedings. Once the sheriff and the VA cops got through with their in-fighting about who was in charge, one of them would take the easy route and we'd be back in jail. If they were really investigating, they would have a real suspect. And yet here I was, convulsing over my parentage. *Grow up, Joe Kirk, or Joe Prashwell, or whoever you are.*

"Growing up is hard to do." I began to sing that to "Breaking up is hard to do." I was trying to come up with some word besides "flu" to rhyme with "do" when the first snowflake hit my nose.

I looked at the top of the bus. A few flakes were floating down onto Zan, but he didn't seem to be aware of them. Lonnie, though, was working his way back toward me, helped along a little by the wind at his back.

"Joe?"

His voice was tentative but solid. He needed a sound to guide him.

"I'm just wondering if we leave Zan on top of the bus, if he'll get covered up with this snow."

I was trying to give him not only a homing location but as much information as possible about the whole situation without making it too obvious.

He walked toward me, steadily but with short steps. It seemed like the wind was getting colder as he approached, like he was a walking cold front.

"I'm not used to snow," he said. "Virginia and Iraq, you don't get much."

That was the first time he had mentioned anything about his background to me. I thought it was a good sign, for him. It was bad for me. I didn't want to be responsible for his mental health. Or anything else, for that matter.

Lonnie's head came up into a cocked position. Then I heard crunching on the gravel of the parking area.

"Mother Linden," Lonnie said.

He was right. It was Rickie's Prius.

"How do you do that, Lonnie?"

"Car sounds. They're all different. Heavier ones crunch more on gravel. Motors are different. If a fender or bumper is loose, there's a little vibration that makes it sound different. Put all that together, it's kind of like a finger print…"

His voice trailed off, as if he was a magician who had given away a trade secret. As far as I was concerned, he definitely was a magician. I was sure, though, that he would trade his magic for sight.

"Lonnie, how did you know it was Reverend Linden, when she came out here the first time? You hadn't heard her car before. She hadn't said anything, so I know you didn't recognize her voice."

"Perfume," he said.

"Perfume?"

"From the jail, when she took Victoria off."

"You were able to recognize perfume at the same time you were beating up on those Delta County deputies?"

"You aren't the only one she visited in jail," he said, his nose tilted in the air.

I felt a stirring in my belly, and lower, and was ashamed of the feeling in my belly, because that one was jealousy toward Lonnie.

Rickie parked her Prius, jumped out, and sort of trotted toward us. Now I felt jealousy toward her because she moved so easily. *Try that with a metal leg that doesn't work, preacher woman, and see how you like it*! Oh, man, I was in such a bad mood. I was delighted this woman was here, and yet inside I was acting like a jerk. I hoped I could keep it from showing.

She was wearing a dark blue toboggan cap over a matching padded jacket over black slacks and flat-heeled pumps. I wondered if she had a clerical collar with a clergy shirt under the jacket. I wondered some more about what was under the jacket.

She smiled a sort of sly smile as she pranced up to us.

Lonnie nodded, in his formal way. "Mother Linden."

"It's good to see you, Lonnie."

She gave him a big smile, which, of course, was wasted on a blind man, except I figured he could hear the flesh around her mouth and eyes go into crinkle mode.

"Pistol packin' mama," I said, trying to imitate his formal style, and immediately regretted it. It sounded like I was making fun of him, and Lonnie didn't know she was packing my Beretta, either. She curled the corners of her mouth so much that time I was *sure* he could hear it. Then she crinkled her nose, too, and looked up at the darkening sky.

"Looks like an early snowfall," she said.

"I thought it snowed all year long up here," I said, glad to be off the subject of mothers and guns.

"That's just a myth. It's snowed on July Fourth only once here."

"That would be more comforting if this weren't October," I said.

"I was listening to the radio on the way out," she said. "Only a light snow here. The rest of the UP calls us The Banana Belt."

She laughed. Lonnie smiled. I wanted to wrap a banana belt around Franklin Prashwell's neck and pull it really tight.

"It'll be heavier farther east, heaviest up around Marquette, and Munising, and the Keewenaw Peninsula, always is, Lake Superior effect."

"How light is light?" I said.

"Oh, six inches or so."

"Hell, even in Evanston, that's a real snow!"

"You should not curse in front of a priest, Joe," Lonnie intoned in his holy voice.

"Oh, can the shit, Lonnie!" I said.

For some reason, that made Lonnie and Rickie both laugh like hyenas.

"What the hell?" I muttered.

She put her hand on the top of my hand. Apparently, I was holding my hand out like a squirrel, which made me feel stupid; I hadn't even noticed it. Her hand was cold, but it burned like...something that's real hot.

Then I remembered that my father used to say that I looked stupid when I held my hand that way. I never even knew I was doing it. No, it wasn't my father who had said that; it was Norman Kirk. I didn't have a father anymore, since I would accept neither of them as my father. Maybe I would marry Rickie and change my name to Linden.

"Joe, what's the matter?" She was holding my hand now with both of hers. "We weren't laughing at you—"

"Yes, we were," said Lonnie. "You sounded so pretentious."

"M—me? You're the pretentious one, with all that *Mother* and *Don't cuss in front of a priest* a—and—" I was sputtering, and I couldn't stop it.

Rickie squeezed my hand real tight.

"Joe, what's wrong?"

"Dammit," I blubbered, not really crying, you understand. "I feel sorry for everybody who betrayed me. I want to be mad at them, all of them, and instead I feel sorry for them. That's not right. I should get to be mad. I'm still going to kill them, but that's not going to be very satisfying if I can't be mad at them, too."

I was shaking. Rickie put her arms around me and held on tight. Then Zan was there. I hadn't heard him get down off the bus.

"Snow getting worked up, Lonnie," he said. "We'd better get back inside. Leave the crazies out here."

Lonnie didn't say anything, just turned and followed the sounds of Zan's footsteps toward the bus.

"This isn't over, Lonnie," I yelled after him. "You're the pretentious one, and I'm going to make you admit it."

I tried to shake my fist at him. I figured he'd be able to hear it flailing around in the air behind him. But Rickie was holding me too tightly to get an arm out.

"Joe, Joe," she was murmuring, "it's okay. You can be mad if you want."

"You shouldn't hold me so close. I smell. We've not been around bath water for a long time."

She held my arms to my sides, stepped back a foot, looked up at me. "Oh, I understand now. You're upset because you think you smell. It's not about betrayal and pretentiousness after all. Those are just excuses to keep people from getting close to you, because you're embarrassed because you smell."

"Damned right," I said. "You're one hell of a smart woman. Most people wouldn't have figured that out so quickly."

"I'm smart enough to know if I let go, you'll wipe those tears off your face and then claim they were never there."

"You damn stupid people musta been raised by damn stupid wolves in the forest. Don't got sense enough to get in outa the damn stupid snow. Gonna be a big one, don't matter what the damn stupid radio says. They don't know damn stupid nothing. Worse than that damn stupid weather channel. Worse than the damn stupid newspaper…"

The voice was coming closer, from the parking area, but I hadn't heard any gravel crunches.

"Oscar the grouch," Rickie whispered.

Damn. The grounds keeper, or maintenance man, or whatever he was.

"What was your first clue?" I whispered

"The eighteenth time he said *damn stupid*," she whispered back.

It was fun to whisper with her, like we had a secret. It was a lot more fun than crying. I hadn't cried in…maybe forever. Now I was doing it all the time.

"You better get the hell outa here, preacher. I'm gonna close the gates. Don't want no damn stupid leaf peepers turning into the damn stupid park and getting stuck on the damn stupid back roads where we can't get them out."

He was almost up beside us now.

"You damn stupid campers better get out while the getting's good, too. You get marooned in here, I ain't gonna bring you no beer."

I thought about it, getting the bus out. There wasn't any

place for us to go, though. Besides, the sheriff had told us to stay put, and he was footing the bill for the camping spot. I figured Zan and Lonnie had been through worse, and I was pretty sure there were a few Leinies left. It didn't matter to me one way or another; I wasn't going to be here, anyway.

CHAPTER 33

Victoria

Victoria wanted to play the music box, to hear the tinkly little "Pennies From Heaven," to see the little girl twirl around with her umbrella. She was a little white girl with long bright yellow curls, but that didn't matter. It hadn't mattered to Nosmo, either. Victoria had taught her little brother to hold the statue where he could feel the vibrations without stopping the little white girl from turning. She would listen to the song, and he would feel it, and they would grin at each other.

Victoria had thought that if pennies dropped from heaven, enough of them, she would buy comic books with them. She was sure that Nosmo would buy candy with his unearned pennies. They grinned at each other and thought about things they could not have as the little white girl twirled and sang.

She looked around for a door. Maybe she could get inside a closet and listen to it without anyone hearing. *That's stupid, girl. You don't have time for that. The answer is with this little white girl. Got to be. Take the statue and get the hell out.* There wasn't a closet door, anyway.

She reached for the statue, in among the bobble-head baseball players and nesting dolls that looked like Einstein and the pictures of a little boy. In some of the pictures, he was being held by a beautiful young white woman with long black hair. In others he was held by Dr. Judson. Dr. Judson looked extremely satisfied and a little bit like he was off somewhere else.

Victoria wondered why the two parents weren't in the pictures together with the boy. Oh, these were homemade. They had taken turns with the camera. They had not wanted to share this moment with anyone, not even someone else to take the pictures. Now the woman and the little boy would always be in pictures alone. This damned war was leaving people stranded in photos all alone, even when they had never gotten closer to Iraq than their TV sets.

The statue was just a little lopsided. She hadn't noticed that until she had gotten up close, because one of the pictures of the little boy, the one with Dr. Judson, was too close in front of it. Carefully, she took hold of the top of the photo. She grasped only the cheap goldish dime-store frame so that she wouldn't leave a smear from her mottled hand on the doctor's face. She pulled the photo down onto its front.

She picked up the statue and turned it sideways. She would not have been able to play the song even if she had found a closet. The winding-key had been replaced with another key. It was too big for the hole. It was meant to unlock something, not to wind up a little white girl so she could sing about pennies you had done nothing to earn.

That was when she heard the click. It was behind her. The door. Somebody had opened the door.

CHAPTER 34

Joe

"It really sounds like you'd better get going, Rickie," I said.

"Are you trying to get rid of me? Oscar doesn't know what he's talking about. He always expects more snow than we get."

"But he's going to close the gate."

"Are you afraid of being snowed in with me?"

She grinned up at me. Snowflakes covered her bangs under her dark blue toboggan cap. She was the most beautiful woman I had ever seen, and she wanted to be snowbound with me. I had to get rid of her.

"I'm afraid of you being snowed in with Zan and Lonnie," I said. "They wouldn't be able to keep their hands off of you."

I knew that wasn't true. They would be perfect gentlemen. It was me I was worried about.

"Well, that would be bad, since they might get their hands in the wrong place and wonder what I'm doing with your gun."

My God, she still had my Beretta. I had forgotten all about it. Guns, the only love of my life that had not betrayed me, and I had forgotten about the only one I had left. My life was coming apart in ways I had no idea how to deal with.

"I guess I'll just have to go to the VA to see Victoria without you. On the other hand, we could go see her together. That's why I came out here in the first place, to see if you wanted to go with me. If you couldn't walk back in from Oscar's closed gate, I guess you'd have to stay with me."

"Oh, yeah, that would be great, the preacher keeping a

scruffy man in the parsonage. Snowbound or not, I don't think your congregation would approve of that."

"It's a rectory, not a parsonage. Parsonages are Methodist. Besides, we don't have one. Church is too small to have a resident pastor, but nobody would hire me fulltime. I have an apartment."

I couldn't believe this. *No mistaking an invitation like that.* That was one of the few things Zan said, when we were roommates, that didn't have to do with football. If a girl even walked through the same county, he was sure she wanted him. "No mistaking an invitation like that," he would say, as she went by a hundred yards away without even knowing he was there.

But here was this beautiful snow-flaked woman inviting me to her apartment. She was obviously lonely as hell, or she wouldn't be inviting a one-legged murder suspect into her life, except I suspected hell wasn't lonely but the place where you had to hang out with all the people who annoyed you. Anyway, I had to say *no*.

"Unfortunately, the sheriff gave all of us, especially me, explicit instructions to stay away from the VA. Since there are folks there who think we killed Dr. Judson, he thought they would be upset."

That wasn't the reason, of course. I was planning to pay the VA a visit in my own way. It was a good excuse, though, to make my lies to her a little more truthful. Her eyes went to a deeper shade of brown.

"Oh, yes, he's right. I hadn't thought of that. I guess—"

I took her by the shoulders.

"You've got to get going. Oscar's not the type to wait. Before you do, though, one thing I need—"

"Yes?"

I was going to ask her for the gun. Really. Instead I leaned in and kissed her.

I had forgotten what a kiss was like. Soft lips. A taste of honey. Or anything else I wanted to imagine she tasted like. The hair at the back of her neck in my fingers as I held her head in place. Best of all, she wasn't Becky Garlits. It was too much. I pulled back. I didn't want to cry again.

She reached up, trailed her fingers down my cheek, then turned to go.

Damn. Asking her for my gun now would be an insult.

"Uh, Rickie—I need my gun."

She turned around and stared hard at me.

"You know—bears and stuff around here. Need some protection."

She walked up close, reached into her jacket pocket, pulled the cold Beretta out, pushed it into my hand, turned, and walked to her car. I watched her go. She got in, turned on the motor, backed up, and did a slow turn. She didn't wave.

Naturally she thought I had kissed her just to get the gun. Now she was mad. That's the way women were. But now I had the gun. I didn't need her. The gun was all I needed. Except for transportation.

The snow was coming harder. I made footprints as I walked over to where I could stand behind a tree and watch Oscar without him seeing me. As soon as Rickie was out the gate, he jumped into his pickup truck, drove down to it, looped the chain around it, used his key to open the padlock, put it through the chain and snapped it shut. Then he was gone.

I had hoped what with all the snow he would leave the truck and take the snowmobile parked beside it in the maintenance garage. I'd driven lots of pickups, but never a snowmobile. I shrugged; first time for everything.

People did stuff they thought was rational, but it wasn't. Somebody once said that "Man may not be a rational animal, but he's definitely a rationalizing animal." We did stuff just because we wanted to, and then we tried to claim later that it was a decision we had thought out. I wanted to talk to Barbara.

The sky just started dumping snow, huge loads of it. By the time I got on the snow machine and got it going, the snow was deep enough for runners. I headed the damned thing toward Sliver Lake.

It wasn't as bad as I thought it would be. It was worse. I didn't have a map. The snowmobile didn't have a compass. I couldn't use the roads because of the snowplows and the police. There were snowmobile paths all over the place, but they would often lead to a river where there was no bridge, and I would have to backtrack and look for some way through the woods. The snow got heavier. The wind picked up. The snow machine was old and crotchety and loud. The roar hurt my ears. I just had a sweatshirt hood to keep the snow off my head and only a too-small and cracked windshield to keep it off my face. I began to freeze. My left leg got so cold it felt as metallic as the right one. I would have sworn it was January instead of October, except some of the leaves the snow was quickly covering were still red and gold. For the first time ever, I envied the guys I knew who were still in Iraq.

The cold froze my brain, which was good. It kept me from thinking about who I was, where I had been, where I was going, and what the hell it all meant.

It was almost dark by the time I got to the approach to Sliver Lake. I couldn't find a snowmobile path, but the light was so dim, and there was so little traffic on the road that I chanced it on the highway. No problem; I didn't meet anybody. The rustic wooden sign that proclaimed this was the way to Sliver Lake was on the ground, in two pieces. I didn't think that was a good sign.

Barbara wasn't there. Everything was closed up tight. There were no tracks in the snow. Her car wasn't there. Everything was dark.

I had to get inside though, before I really froze solid. I needed to hide the snowmobile, but I didn't want to walk back from the barn. I knew my stump had gotten so cold it had shrunk so much that the prosthesis might actually come off. So I parked the snowmobile behind Barbara's hotel of a house. Actually it wasn't all the way behind. The damned thing ran out of gas. Just spluttered and stopped. I hadn't even thought about fuel when I started.

That worried me. In football and in the army both, my reputation was as the guy who always looked ahead so that he never got caught unawares. "You always see what's beyond what's beyond what's beyond, Kirk," the major had said. Now I wasn't even seeing beyond one tank of gas.

No sign of Barbara. I tried to pick the lock, but my fingers were too cold.

Finally I put my fist through one of the small panes in the

back door, reached in, got hold of the dead bolt and the knob, and managed to let myself in.

It was probably only fifty degrees inside, but it felt good to be out of the wind and into silence, away from the snowmobile noise I had endured all day. I flipped the light switch and got the overhead fluorescents. I knew I needed to warm up fast, so I went to the old-fashioned wood cook stove Barbara had kept from the hotel's old days and got a fire going. I just stood there for a while, getting as close to the heat as I could. Finally I felt like I would live. I found some old rags and stuffed the hole I had made in the glass of the back door.

I didn't like the fluorescent lights. Too cold and harsh. I wanted the place to feel like it had when I was there with Barbara and Zan and Lonnie and Victoria, when we had laughed so hard together. I turned on the lamp on the kitchen table and turned the overheads off. I found the thermostat and turned it up.

I looked around. No sign of recent activity. The place looked like it was closed up for the winter. Damn. I had frozen my ass off to come see Barbara and she was gone. Well, like any other maneuver that went wrong, the first goal was to survive.

There was some stuff in the freezer part of the fridge, but it would take a month to get it to the eating stage. I found some cans and jars and did one of my skillet meals. It tasted really good. I had gotten only about three bites in, though, when I heard the back door open.

CHAPTER 35

Victoria

Victoria froze at the sound of the door click. She was not willing to turn and face the intruder. She knew she would have to do something drastic. There was no chance that she would go to a cell, anywhere. She hoped it wasn't a nurse.

"Ah, the hero returns to the scene of the crime."

A man. A cultured voice. Not pleasant, but not mean, either. Not gloating, just stating her presence as if it was a fact he had been waiting to verify. It was not a voice she recognized.

Victoria waited. It didn't sound like there was anyone with him. He would have to make the first move. Then she would react.

It was like when Joe and Zan talked football in the bus. "Take what the defense gives you," Joe said. "Don't give the offense anything," Zan said. She didn't know much about football, but she could tell they had spent their careers on opposite sides of the ball. She wasn't sure if she was on offense or defense, but she knew all she could do was react.

She waited for him to move. He didn't.

"I knew I just had to be patient. Someone would come and show me the way. I suspected it might be you."

"You know this isn't the scene of any crime I committed," Victoria said. "I'm no doctor murderer."

"Oh, I'm not talking about your crimes, Sergeant Roundtree. They are many, I am sure. This was where Dr. Judson's crime was committed."

Victoria's brain began to race. What crime had the doctor committed? Was that why he was murdered? Revenge for something?

"It would be easier for you to explain things to me if you turned around. Then we can talk face to face, as it were."

She had nothing to explain, because she didn't understand anything, but she would have to turn around sooner or later. Slowly, pivoting like the little girl with the umbrella, she did so.

The man's face went whiter than it already was. He knew who she was, so he should have known about the inferno, but obviously he was not prepared for what he saw. *Too bad for you, jerk.*

"I apologize for staring, Sergeant. I did not realize…"

His cultured voice trailed off. He was an ordinary-looking white guy, about fifty, pale, long face, average height. In a hospital gown. His right hand was inside the gown.

"Ah, now it is your turn to look confused. But I said, did I not, that I just had to be patient? To be completely accurate, I should have said, to be *a* patient. Yes, I am the poor soul in the wheelchair in the hall, the patient being patient, waiting for the one who knows…"

Victoria knew her time was running out. Those MPs would be up here soon. They knew she had to be some place in the hospital. If this guy was with them, all he had to do was call. But if he was playing patient in the hall, maybe he really *was* a patient. No, he didn't belong here. He didn't even know they didn't call them patients in a VA hospital. They were always veterans. So who the hell was he?

One thing you learned in Iraq was that even the guys who looked like they were on the same side and claimed to be on the same side usually weren't.

"I don't know shit," she said.

"Oh, you are far too modest. What is that in your hand?"

She had forgotten about the music box. She looked at it as if she was seeing it for the first time, holding it up close to her face with both hands, palming the replacement key.

"I think it's a music box," she said. "My grandma had one like it."

"Ah, nostalgia. How wonderful good memories are. But I suspect you know something about that music box I don't. After all, I have been through this office with a finer-toothed comb than you had time for and did not find what I needed. Yet here you are, in for just a minute, and you have what you wanted. We all know you are the lone survivor who knows all about it. I am your only friend now. I can, of course, provide the necessary evidence to convict you of Dr. Judson's murder, poor stupid man. But I shall not. You have served your country admirably. I alone can get you out of here. Where you go then I do not care. Right now, though, hand me the box."

He started toward her. The hand began to come out of his robe. She could see the butt of a gun in it. What the hell? He wasn't going to get her out of here. At the best, he would turn her over to the MPs and let her take the rap for the murder and rot in a cell in Leavenworth. More likely, he would kill her and take the key. She couldn't afford to take any chances. So she did.

"Sure, you can have it," she said.

The guy was left-handed. At least that was the one with the gun. That meant he would duck left.

She hurled the little white girl at him. Not at his head. Even if it hit his head, it wouldn't knock him out. Just had to distract him, keep that gun off line. She threw it a little lower than his face, a little to his left, his ducking side, make sure he had to take evasive action, give her time to move.

She was already moving when he ducked. Good God, it was true, what Reverend Wright said, that God takes care of little kids and idiots. She hadn't believed it any time he said it, too much evidence God didn't give a damn about little kids, except maybe the white ones in the suburbs. But now she believed the part about the idiots, because she was one, and God was taking care of her, making that guy duck his head right down where her throw went, duck his eye right into the path of the little girl's umbrella.

He let out a cry of anguish more than pain, like a man who had just found his wife in bed with his boss. Victoria was to him in two strides, the second one ending high in his groin, grabbing his pistol hand as he buckled, pushing the gun to the side, holding his hand tight so he could not pull the trigger. She was sure he couldn't get the gun back on line to shoot her, but she didn't want it going off and alerting anyone to what was going on in this little office at the end of the hall. She brought her knee up. His head snapped back. She heard the crack. He slumped to the floor. She took the gun out of his hand. Whoever this guy was, he wasn't military, or a cop. Or else she was a hell of a lot more efficient as a killer than she realized. It had worked just like she had been taught. Except now she had to pee really bad. She could hear Zan's voice saying "Victoria always has to pee."

Well, piss on him, and the bus he rode in on.

CHAPTER 36

Okay, now she really was a murderer. She hadn't killed Judson, but she had killed someone in his office. It was self-defense. At least it probably was. He had said he wasn't going to kill her, but who could trust a man coming at you with a gun? He would have killed to get that key.

The key! She looked at her closed fist then slowly opened it. Still there. Amazing. She had killed a man without losing her grip on the thing she had come for. She felt as though she should be surprised at herself, but she wasn't.

It didn't look like any key she had seen before. Its stem was a barrel, like the one for the music box, but it was too long for the box. That was why the box hadn't set level on the top of the file cabinet. The barrel was oval instead of round, and the top was in the shape of a trapezoid. Shit! This had to be the key to why Judson was murdered, but what did it fit? She couldn't just take it to Sheriff Avanti and say, "Here's the answer to why the doc was killed. You can let us go now."

She heard sounds, heavy footsteps coming down the hallway. She jumped over the body of the wheelchair guy and thumbed the deadbolt over. The little click sounded like a thunderbolt. The footsteps kept coming, thudding, marching, a thundering herd. She grabbed the body on the floor and began to drag it into the corner behind the door. Damn. The guy was heavier than he looked. Dead weight, of course, always heavier than live, but still, life and death were upside down if it was easier to kill a man than to drag him.

She heard voices now, men's, but a woman's too.

"What the fuck, Kneightly? You know empty wheelchairs

aren't supposed to be sitting around in the hallways."

Victoria recognized the voice of Vince, the VA cop Gerri didn't like.

"Maybe if you spent more time doing your real job instead of worrying about the nurses, you'd be able to do something as simple as keep track of a prisoner."

She did not recognize that voice. It was low and hard and menacing. *Must be one of the MPs.*

"It's hardly worth coming down here. The door to Dr. Judson's office is always locked now. Mr. Gasaway's orders."

She had never heard Florence use a whiny voice before. It didn't sound very convincing. Men, though, could hardly be expected to know the difference between an act and the real thing when it came to whining. They never did about anything else.

"What does a goddam hospital administrator know about security?"

That was the MP voice again.

"That's why you're along, Florence Kneighlygale. You were his nurse. You're the one with the keys."

Vince's voice. *What a jerk.*

"Well, I *was* his nurse, until Simmons—"

"Oh, can it. Just open the damned door!"

The MP's voice.

Victoria heard a key in the lock. Nothing happened. She heard it again. And again.

"What the fuck, Kneightly? Get a key into that lock and get it open."

Vince's voice again, then Florence's. "Simmons changed the locks. I don't have a key that works."

"Why in the fuck didn't you say so?"

"I was trying to say, when I was so rudely interrupted, that I was Dr. Judson's nurse until Simmons took over and changed the locks." She sounded very prim and proper this time. "But I went ahead and tried my keys, anyway, because you asked so nicely."

"Dammit, I'm sick of this shit between you two. Vince, go get the right key. This has got to be where she is. We've searched everyplace else."

"I'm not sure," Florence said. "That one door, down in the basement, toward the back. She might have gone to the maintenance garage."

"There's an alarm on that door, like all the others. It would have sounded in our office if anybody went out it," Vince said.

"Well, actually not," Florence Kneightly said. "People go in and out of it all the time. They like to smoke in the maintenance garage."

"Then what the hell is that smoking shed out front for?" the MP snarled.

"Oh, that's where they are supposed to go," Florence said. "But some of the veterans keep special…uh, medicinal beverages…in the maintenance shed, so they—"

"It still should have sounded an alarm in our office." Vince was sounding whiny himself now.

"Some of these veterans are quite clever," Florence said. "A couple were electronics technicians in the navy. I don't think they had much trouble disarming the door. Or disabling it. Or whatever it's called."

"By God, Kneightly, you're going to get fired for this," Vince whined.

"Simmons said it was okay. Better to have them doing it out there—"

"Dammit, Vince, I told you to go get a key! I'm going to look in this fucking office! Schotz, you go check out that back door the nurse is talking about."

Victoria heard foot falls, but only one set. Either Vince still wasn't going for the key or the other MP wasn't heading for that door Florence had talked about.

"I don't think it will do much good, to look in here," Florence said. Her voice sounded very close now. "Nobody's been in here to disturb anything. See. Everything is just like it always was."

"Get out of the way. Let me see in there."

Victoria pushed herself back farther into the corner. She couldn't see the door, but they were obviously looking through the long narrow rectangle of glass in the door.

"It looks like there's a photo on its face, there on that metal cabinet."

The MP's voice sounded so close Victoria felt like she could reach out and touch his tongue.

It was replaced by Florence Kneightly's. "Oh, that's a photo of him with his son. He's just so little." She began to cry. "When Dr. Judson was killed, I just couldn't stand to see them together, knowing they would never be together again, so I turned the photo down. I know I shouldn't, but—"

More sobs. They went lower, toward the floor of the hallway. It sounded like Florence was sliding down the door, weeping mightily. *Damn; that woman is good! She's blocking the door now. I don't know why she is working so hard to keep them out. She must have seen something in here the MP didn't. But why is she protecting me? She could get into a lot of trouble. Maybe—*

Victoria didn't get to finish her thought. Footsteps running. Damn. Vince was back with the key.

"Yeah, that back door opens without an alarm, and there are footprints in the snow going out to that maintenance shed. That's a damn big building to be called a shed."

Not Vince's voice. It had to be the other MP, the one called Schotz. But snow? What snow?

She looked up and out the window. Snow, for sure, great big flakes, coming hard and fast.

More running. Then nothing. Then more running.

"What the hell, Kneightly? What are you doing on the floor? Where are those—"

"She went out the back, Vince. That Schotz saw her. They're after her. They said for you to come, too."

"Goddamm."

Steps running. Then nothing. Well, Florence Kneightly was still out there, and there was no way Victoria was going to hurt her, but she had to get out of here. She went quickly to the door, looked through the narrow rectangle of glass. Nothing. She clicked the locks open and pushed the door open a crack. Still nothing. A little farther. Nothing.

She pushed her head out into the hall. Only a nurse, in a cap, far down the hall, walking a little funny. Victoria got only a glimpse of her before she turned into a doorway.

Victoria looked down. An empty pair of nursing shoes were

sitting outside Dr. Judson's office. A blue surgical cap and a matching mask were stuffed inside of them, with a pair of white gloves.

CHAPTER 37

Joe

I hadn't bothered to put the Beretta into my leg. I pulled it out of my jacket pocket and held it under the table with my right hand, pointed at the back door, while I continued to eat with my left hand.

I remembered reading some book about Viet Nam. It said that the soldiers ate the peaches from their meal packs first. If they got killed in the middle of the meal, they didn't want to miss the best part. That was sort of how I felt. I was hungry. I didn't much care who was at the door; I was going to keep on eating. It wasn't nearly as good as what Barbara Occam-Roberts had cooked for us, but I was in her kitchen, and that was sort of like eating the peaches.

I didn't hear anyone cross from the back door of the alcove to the kitchen doorway, but a dark face appeared in there. It was dark partly because it was in shadows, partly because it was dark to begin with. I knew that at the back of the dark face was a long black braid.

"How's Shits-in-the-Outhouse?" I asked.

"It is *Sleeps*-in-the-Outhouse," she said. "Everybody *shits* in the outhouse. Barbara Occam-Roberts calls him that because he is an old boyfriend, and she is ashamed that she had a Native American boyfriend."

"I guess it doesn't work the other way around," I said.

I kept shoveling food in. She tried to outwait me. That was a trait of Indians, I thought, that sort of patience, but she was no match for me. I learned first from Zan Zander, and then in Iraqistan, how to wait forever, or at least until all the food was gone. She gave in.

"What do you mean?"

"You're not ashamed to have a white boyfriend, Melva. Doesn't that get you problems with the braves on the rez? Or maybe you're ashamed but your lust is too powerful?"

"Big talk for a man on the run and out of gas."

So she was trying to pull that Indian stuff on me, that mysterious *I-know-all-about-you-because-I've-got-some-native-spiritual-thing-going* crap. The tribesmen in the 'Stan tried that, too. It wasn't very effective, though, because I didn't know what they were saying. I knew what Melva Althaus was saying.

There was something else in her face, though, as she said it. Ah, ha! A standoff. She thought I was pulling that mysterious *I-know-all-about-you-because-I've-got-a-leg-off-spiritual-thing* crap. Mine had a chance to work, though, because she understood my language. Of course, I only knew about her and Sheriff Del Shrader because Barbara had said something about it. "Besides, I thought Del Shrader was Barbara's boyfriend, back in the day. He's not Indian."

"She was a slut," Melva said. "Everybody was her boyfriend."

"Do I detect a slight hint of jealousy?"

I didn't know if I were more interested in defending Barbara's reputation or taunting Melva. Something about that braid bothered me, and I couldn't even see it.

"She's not here," Melva said.

Oh, great. Back to the mysterious talk again. Make me guess what she's talking about.

"Cut the *It's-an-Injun-thing* crap, Melva. I'm not the blind one. I can see that she's not here. Lonnie's the blind one, and even he would see that she's not here."

"So why are *you* here?"

I didn't exactly have an answer for that, at least not one I wanted her to hear. "How did you know I was here?"

I could talk the mystery chatter as well as she could, although I had to admit this was getting boring.

"I followed the ones who are following you," she said.

I tightened my grip on the Beretta.

"What the hell are you talking about?"

This suddenly got less boring.

"The big men, in the black SUV. Four of them. They picked you up when you crossed 41. They lost you when you found the snowmobile trail again."

It bothered me that I had a tail and didn't even know it. Of course, by the time I was crossing Highway 41, I was so frozen I wouldn't have noticed if a goosed moose had jumped onto the snowmobile with me. I was used to looking for bad guys in the sand of the al-Faw Peninsula, not in the snow of the Upper Peninsula.

Who was following me, and where did they come from? Obviously not cops. They didn't travel that way or in those numbers. Couldn't be the guys we beat up at Moe's Smoked Fish Fudge Convenience Store at Sagola. Only three of them. Unless they had called in reinforcements. But how much reinforcement could one guy be? Plenty, if it was the right guy. Whoever they were, this was not good.

Or maybe she was just wrong, or pulling my chain. It always paid to be paranoid about what women told you. I learned that from Becky Garlits. "How do you know all this? How do you know they were following me?"

"It's an Injun thing."

Everybody wanted to be a comedian.

"They out there now?"

"Not yet.

"Maybe we should put the light out."

It was a suggestion. She was closer to the lamp, and I didn't want to get up. I was through eating, even though I didn't feel full. I could eat in the dark if I had to, though. I'd done it plenty. She didn't take the suggestion, though. Maybe she just wanted to be able to see my handsome face.

"I'll know when they're out there."

"Another Injun thing?"

"Yes."

"Any idea who they are, or why they're following me?"

"You attract trouble."

Couldn't argue with that.

"Maybe I should put the snowmobile where they can't see it."

"It's out of gas. It makes too much noise."

"We could push it."

"What do you mean *we*, white man?"

I had to laugh. It was an old joke but still one of the best. My laughter didn't thaw Melva Althaus any.

"They'll see its tracks anyway. The snow has stopped."

Great. I finally get inside, and the snow stops. "You must be the accountant for the rez, the way you line up reasons. Double entry."

"Barbara lied to Del. You're not his son."

Apparently, she didn't want to talk about accounting.

"Barbara didn't tell the sheriff that I'm his son. She just said that he got her pregnant."

"It bothers him—"

I waited.

"—thinking he has a son that he doesn't know," she finally added.

"But it doesn't bother him that he got a girl pregnant? Just that he's got an unknown son? Or that it bothers his Indian girlfriend now?"

I thought I was giving her plenty of chances to jump in. She didn't take any of them.

"I'm a Native American, not an Indian. Indians are named Patel."

Her voice didn't change, but it almost sounded like she was trying to make jokes. That might be good. If you were joking, you might be a friendly. Maybe I could get some useful information from her. But I couldn't resist the bait.

"You certainly like to change subjects. Must be an Injun thing. And Patel sounds more Native American than Althaus. That's pure Nazi."

I didn't know why either one of us was bothering with this sparring match. Except that each of us wanted something from the other, and neither of us knew how to ask for it.

"We'd better turn the light out now," she said.

I instinctively ducked.

"They out there?"

"No, but it shouldn't be long."

"If you wouldn't mind," I said, nodding toward the lamp.

My leg was still bothering me. I still didn't want to get up. Besides, I wanted to know where she was. For all I knew, she was setting me up for another Indian attack.

Once the light was out, though, she disappeared into the blackness.

"Shouldn't you be leaving before they get here?" I asked.

I didn't care if she stayed. I figured what happened to her was her problem. I wanted to get an answer, though, to hear where she was. It came from no more than three feet away. The woman moved like an Indian.

"What makes you think I have a white boyfriend?"

"It's a one-legged thing."

"You have brought a lot of trouble with you. For everybody."

"I didn't ask for it."

I didn't like sounding defensive, and I knew that I did, so I resented her for pointing out the obvious.

"Why don't you just leave, and take the trouble with you?"

"Too late. Once trouble is out of the tube, you can't put it back in. Besides, it's your boyfriend who's making me stay."

That was neither true nor fair. It was Sam Avanti who was keeping us in the UP. But Del Shrader had turned us over to Sheriff Avanti. I figured, via the chain of possession, one sheriff was as guilty as another.

"Barbara Occam-Roberts caused trouble. She left. You should, too."

I felt real lonely right then. I was in Barbara's kitchen, where there should be light and laughter. Instead, I was there with a woman I didn't like, in the darkness, feeling sour. I didn't think the sour taste was from what I had eaten.

"Did Barbara's leaving solve the problems? Does Del Shrader feel better because she's gone? Does he know more about his son because she's gone?"

I was talking like there really was a son when I knew there wasn't. Or did I? When Barbara told us she was just putting Del Shrader on, that she hadn't really gotten pregnant by him, that they didn't really have a son, was she saying that just because she was embarrassed that she had revealed too much to a bunch of strangers? I knew for a sorry fact that women didn't always tell the truth about their bastard sons.

"Why did you come here?"

Her voice was almost tender in the darkness.

"Look, Melva, I'm sorry I've brought trouble. Me and my friends, we're just traveling around, trying to get by—"

"I mean, why did you come *back*? Here. By yourself? What did you think you would find here?"

"I wanted to find out why my mother lied to me about who my father is."

That was just mean. She was bound now to think Barbara was my mother. But it was the truth. I really did come to talk about the lies that were tearing my identity into shreds and flushing it down the toilet. I had hoped Barbara could give me some insight. Maybe Melva—

Hell, no, that was a bad idea.

The silence grew uneasy. I decided to explain what I had said, about coming here to find out about my father. After all, Melva hadn't done anything to me. In fact, she had come to warn me that there was someone on my trail. Unless she was lying about that just to try to soften me up so I'd tell her what I knew about Del Shrader's supposed son.

"They're here," Melva said, so softly it was almost a whisper.

"Time for you to get out then. This isn't your fight. I don't think it's mine, either, but those guys don't know it."

Okay, so I did care what happened to her. It was some kind of genetic failing, having to care about people. I just didn't know where my genes came from.

"Too late for anyone to leave," she said. "We're surrounded."

"I didn't hear their truck," I said.

"They had to walk in. I sabotaged the road. Their truck is mired down."

That wasn't going to put them into a good mood.

I heard a creak on the board sidewalk in front, then the sound of someone trying a doorknob. Then nothing. Well, they wouldn't come through the front anyway. That was a diversion.

The snowmobile was out back. They knew it was mine because they had seen me on it. They would find the rag stuffed in the pane where I had broken the glass.

I didn't know who they were, and I didn't care. All I knew was that they weren't friendlies. And also that I wanted to shoot somebody.

I started to get up to move over into the sightline for the back door. Melva put a hand on my arm and pushed me back down. Okay, good thinking. Better to stay still and stay quiet. They were already in. There was a rustling sound over by that door. These guys were good. They had gotten the back door open and gotten in and I hadn't even heard them. I didn't entirely like Melva, but I was glad she was there.

"Well, Joe, it looks like we meet again."

The voice was male, pleasant, conversational, from the back doorway. I trained the Beretta on it. Melva closed her hand over mine and slowly moved my hand to our left, stopped, moved it a little farther. Okay, one of them had gotten over there. The speaker was a diversion. He probably had full body armor on, so even if I shot him, no problem, and the one who had sidled, probably crawled, over toward the front door could follow the flash and sound of the Beretta, but I was ready for him, and—but what the hell? If they all had full armor on—

"It's all right to talk, Joe. We're not here to hurt you. Just the opposite. We know you didn't kill Dr. Judson. That matter has been taken care of. We've already taken your friends into protective custody. We're here to take you to them. Sergeant Roundtree was part of a sensitive mission. She has to be given a new identity and put into witness protection. It's a matter of national security. As soon as we've determined that she hasn't told the rest of you about it, you'll be free to go, with appreciation for your service to your country and an appropriate bonus."

A little low chuckle.

"Well, not really an appropriate bonus. A really large bonus, to compensate you for your trouble."

As he talked, Melva ran her finger up my arm, slowly, from the wrist toward the elbow, about half-way, then stopped. It was quite sensuous, but I figured this wasn't exactly a moment for romance. She was trying to tell me something.

Then I got it. The guy had been moving toward us as he talked. But he was making his voice ever so slightly quieter with each step, so that it sounded like he was right where he started. Melva's finger had been keeping pace with him on my forearm. It was a damned good trick, but Melva Althaus was some sort of shaman. She knew all the tricks.

Melva suddenly squeezed my arm hard. I sensed more than saw the figure rise up over the counter to our left. Well, hell, they had known where we were all along. That was why the talker was able to come toward us. I squeezed the trigger before the guy behind the counter was all the way up, squeezed it again as I pulled it down and dove for the floor. I hadn't shot the Beretta, or anything else, in quite a while, but my fingers were thawed, and that eye-hand coordination that I'd had from the moment I'd first picked up a gun and a football hadn't left me. I figured the first shot was between the guy's eyes and the second one in his Adam's apple.

I didn't feel Melva on top of me. I hoped that she had gone to the floor on the other side, because an automatic rifle was pouring about a million rounds into where we had been sitting. I guessed that meant they didn't intend to give me that big bonus in appreciation of all my service after all. I recognized the sound of the automatic. It was an Uzi. I didn't know any authorized US military unit who used them.

It was no problem to line up on the Uzi. I wanted to empty the Beretta, to be sure I got him some place where he wasn't armored, but I knew I had to save something for the other two guys. His voice had sounded normal, which meant his mouth hadn't been covered. I aimed for it, even though I couldn't see it. The Uzi went quiet and I heard something heavy hit the floor.

Melva materialized beside me, whispering in my ear. Actually, she was probably shouting, but my ears were in the middle of trying to shut down from all the shooting noise, so it sounded like whispering.

"Front door."

"There's somebody out there?"

"He's dead."

Wow. I knew I was good, but that guy was dead and I hadn't even shot at him.

We went crawling to the front door. I reached up and wrenched it open. Sure enough, a body was lying there. I saw another one, though, off the right, standing up. Damn and hell.

"Don't shoot him. It's Razer."

Who the hell?

"What about the other one, Razer?"

"Got away. Into the woods behind. You want us to track him?"

Oh, Razer Kabawgam, the young Indian who had been here before with his Broken Arrow gang. These guys were a lot more lethal than I had been led to believe back when they were just trying to run Barbara off. Quieter, too.

"No. Too dangerous," Melva said. "Besides, one of them has to take these bodies away."

She was right. They would have to come back to get their dead. They wouldn't want the local law to be poking around and tracing them. That wouldn't be very good for me, either.

She turned to the young Indian.

"Did you gas up the snowmobile?"

"Geronimo is doing it now."

Either they had a direct line to get help from the happy hunting ground, or they had some neat nicknames in the Broken Arrows.

"Did you tell him to put the extra can on the machine?"

"Yeah."

He didn't sound real happy about it. He was willing to kill somebody to help me, but gas was damned expensive. *Well, boy, you owe me, because I've killed a lot of people to keep that gas price as low as it is.*

I thought that, but instead I said, "Shouldn't Sheriff Shrader be brought in to—"

She put that finger onto my lips. She almost got into a nostril in the process. "For a man who is as dangerous as you are, you are incredibly stupid," she said.

Then she was gone, and Razer, too.

"Well, stupid and dangerous go together," I yelled into the darkness where she had disappeared.

I stood there, feeling all the energy drain out of me. The thought of getting back onto that snowmobile was like the thought of getting onto the back of a mule in the Af-Pak mountains again.

I didn't want to go back into Barbara's house. It was a killing field now. I didn't want to remember it that way. Too many of my memories were killing fields.

So I clomped around the building to the snowmobile and hoped that Melva would come back and close the place up once the bodies were gone. Through the window, I saw Melva at the telephone. I thought about shooting her to be sure she didn't run up Barbara's long distance bill. Once you start shooting people, it's easy to think that one more will solve all your problems. I was too tired and cold to care, though.

As I got onto the infernal snowmobile, I said a little prayer of thanks that I had gotten my genes from Franklin Prashwell. My father didn't have the sort of eye-hand coordination with which I was blessed. I figured I had inherited that from the preacher who had knocked up my mother while her husband was off defending his country. That genetic skill had served me well. It had also made me a killer. As soon as I got a chance, I would use that eye-hand coordination to shoot the man from whom I got it.

CHAPTER 38

Victoria

Victoria slipped out of her nonskid hospital slippers and into the white nurse shoes. They were a little too snug. But so what? She could run in them, and run was what she had to do. She didn't bother to tie them. Wait a minute. She couldn't go out the door at the end of the corridor. All the doors sounded an alarm in the police office when they were opened. Except the front doors. The police office was right inside the front doors. No need for an alarm for them. The cops could just watch who came and went.

She put on the blue paper surgical cap and pulled it down as far as it would go. She put the mask on and pulled it high. She slipped the gloves on. They were translucent, but she didn't think anyone could see through the latex well enough to notice her strange coloring.

She walked briskly down the hall, like she was just a little bit late for wherever she was going. She made it to the main junction, turned left, walked by the police office without looking inside. With any luck all the cops would be out at the maintenance building, looking for her there. If not, she would deal with whoever tried to stop her.

She was out the door and into the snow. She was almost blown back inside by a gust of wind. Okay, that could help. It was a long sprint to the mall across the street, but she might be able to blend in there, steal a car or something. *Hell, a nurse in surgical scrubs isn't going to blend in at a mall.*

Off to the right, she could see cars and trucks moving on

what looked like a highway. The big hospital parking lot was between her and the highway. That and a KFC. If she went that way, she could keep low, between parked cars, stay out of sight for longer than if she went across to the mall.

She angled toward the KFC through the parking lot. The snow was getting heavier, and the wind was getting stronger. As she cleared the parking lot, she started sprinting for the KFC. It was slow going. The nurse shoes had smooth soles that slipped in the snow. There was a high wire fence at the edge of the VA property. They must have been afraid some extra crispy would get loose and assault the vets. She had to angle clear out to the street to get around the fence.

She finally made it to the KFC and ran behind the two cars in the drive-thru. She dashed into a little wooden structure out back. It was just a fence, with garbage cans inside, but she was hidden, unless more cars came into the drive-through lane.

She peeked through the slats. A long lumber truck was sliding to a stop at the red light on the highway. She took a breath and dashed out from behind the fence, across the KFC blacktop that was now a whitetop, scrambled up a little hill, almost slid back down, got there just as the light turned green, came up right at the back of the truck, ran in front of the car that was stopped behind the truck, saw two rather astonished-looking old ladies through its windshield, grabbed hold of the rear end of the truck at the only place she could, the one spot where logs didn't stick out a little way beyond the end of the bed, hoisted herself up, worked her way in between the logs, could make it only about three feet, said a prayer that the gods of lumber trucks had piled those logs on in such a way the load couldn't shift, and realized, as the truck picked up speed, that as soon as the heat from her mad dash wore off, she was going to be very cold.

She needed to get off the truck once it was clear of the VA. She had to get somewhere warm. She also had to have a place to hide that nobody knew about.

The snow had driven pedestrians inside, so she hadn't met anyone on foot. Those women in the car behind the truck, though—when she jumped on—as soon as they got the word that a prisoner was missing from the VA, they would report what they saw. Maybe they were on a cell phone calling the cops right then.

The problem was that she couldn't see where the truck was going. They were picking up speed, too. The truck had slowed down for some traffic lights, but had hit them all on green. That would have been her best chance to jump off, but they were in the midst of downtown business buildings. She would probably have jumped off right in front of the city police station. There were cars coming up behind, too. If she jumped and slipped, she'd get run over. She clung to her precarious perch.

The truck finally slowed. She felt the weight shift and knew they were turning right. Maybe it was her last chance to jump. They had to be at the edge of town by then. No cars immediately behind now. But damn, there were business buildings on the corners. Someone was bound to see her. She was going to have to wait it out.

The truck made the turn and began to pick up speed again. They were definitely out of town. There was an occasional house set back down a narrow lane, and nothing else but tall evergreen trees covered in snow and forlorn-looking birches. The last gold leaves of the birch trees were barely peeking through the white flocking.

The truck kept slowing, though, because the snow was coming harder and faster. Soon they weren't moving much faster than they had in town. Victoria had trouble seeing beyond the first line of trees, and even that line was blurry with blowing snow. She was beginning to shiver. She knew she couldn't go on much longer like that.

Then she saw it. A one-story log building with a high false front and a porch. The porch had four by four posts and a loafer's bench, just like in a cowboy movie. A big sign above the porch announced bait and taxidermy. Three or four SUVs and pickups were parked in front. Best of all, she could see exhaust flowing out the tailpipe of a dark blue pickup. Or maybe it was black. Hard to tell in the snow.

The log truck was well past the taxidermy shop by the time she was able to take it all in, so she knew she had no time to consider. She just slid to the back, lowered herself off the end of the truck, and let go. She hit, ducked, and rolled onto the shoulder of the road. Sarge would have been proud of her.

She did a quick run-through of her legs and arms. No breaks. A few scrapes, some blood. She'd had worse, a hell of a lot worse.

The taxidermy shop looked a long way off back there now. She was cold. Her joints and muscles were stiff. Her legs didn't want to run. She knew, though, that she had no choice. She knew that idling pickup in front of the shop was her ticket out, at least for the moment. She had to get to it before its owner came back. If there was somebody in it, waiting for the driver—well, she'd deal with that when she got there.

Getting there took several days. That's how it felt. But her body began to warm up with the jogging, so her muscles began to loosen up, too. She went a little faster with each step. It took a long time, but she was almost into a full run when she got to the pickup.

She wrenched the driver side door open. Damn! There was a big black dog in there. Looked as big as a bear. The dog didn't growl, but it bared its teeth and came at her like a horizontal lightning bolt. She twirled toward the truck's bed. She felt the dog's hot breath as it flew past her. It hit the snow and skidded. Suddenly all the cold was fleeing from her body, pushed out by a churning river of adrenaline. She was into the cab before the dog could stop its skid. The dog turned. Its huge paws churned up snow and gravel as it tried to get traction. Victoria slammed the door shut and rammed the gearshift into reverse.

Now it was her turn to skid, but she didn't care. She didn't skid, though. She made a quick slide in reverse then twisted the steering wheel toward the almost invisible road, pushed the shifter into drive, and the gas pedal to the floor. The truck didn't hesitate. It just lunged for the road like some sure-footed prehistoric monster.

Damn! Some guy was running out of the shop. Probably the truck's owner. Too bad. Shit, he was jumping right in front of her. No damned pickup was worth getting killed for. She twisted the wheel to the right, slid sideways. His face flashed by out her window, a mask of horror as he looked at her. *Haven't you ever seen somebody from hell before, buster? Well, too bad for you.*

She gunned the pickup on. It began to fishtail when it left the gravel and hit the snow-covered pavement. Victoria desperately tried to remember which way she was supposed to turn the wheel in a skid. Or maybe you weren't supposed to turn it at all. She knew she had to get her foot off the gas pedal, though. It took all her strength of will to pull her foot up; her desire was to get that truck going as fast as possible as quickly as possible. But she got her foot up, and the truck slowed. Finally it straightened out. She pushed down gently on the gas pedal and let out her breath in a long sigh. It was the longest sigh she could ever remember. No surprise there. That had been the longest she had ever gone without breathing.

She heard a kind of gurgling, giggling noise. Hell, that wasn't part of her sigh. She looked into the rearview mirror. It was angled down toward the extended part of the cab, behind her seat.

Apparently, the baby in the car seat liked it when the truck twirled and skidded, because it was smiling.

CHAPTER 39

Florence

Florence Kneightly wasn't sure why she was taking such chances for someone she hardly knew. But Victoria was a vet. Florence was there to take care of vets, not cops or administrators.

They had no *patients* in the VA hospital, only *veterans*. The nurses were supposed to refer to them that way, as *veterans*, not patients, but when supervisors weren't around, they shortened it to *vets*.

Victoria wasn't just a vet, though. She was OIF, Operation Iraqi Freedom. Florence's son, Kenneth, was OIF, too. If he got into as much trouble as Victoria, she hoped someone would help him out.

Besides, she was sure Victoria had not murdered Dr. Judson. She wasn't sure who did, but it wasn't those poor souls on that old school bus.

She glanced back out into the hallway. No one in sight. She hurried back down toward the end, where Dr. Judson's office was. The shoes and scrubs she had left outside the door were gone. She didn't know where Victoria had gone with them, but Florence had done the best she could for her, even lying about laying that picture down.

She peered in through the slender rectangle of glass in the office door. Yes, the top of that file cabinet was definitely different. But what was it, besides that photo being on its face? She had not gotten a good look at it before, when the MPs and VA cops had been berating her about getting a key.

She was sure that Victoria had been in there while they were out in the hallway. Why had she been so sure? Well, they had looked every place else. This was the logical place where Victoria would have gone. In their talks, Victoria had told her that she intended to find out who had really killed Dr. Judson. But mostly, it was the top of that file cabinet. There was something—

Without really thinking about it, she reached down and grasped the doorknob. It turned in her hand. What the—

Well, of course. Victoria had not bothered with locking it when she fled. Gingerly, with a quick look down the hallway to be sure no one was watching, she turned the knob. Quickly she stepped in, her eyes still on the top of the file cabinet. She closed the door behind her and advanced quietly to the file cabinet. She wanted to set the photo of Dr. Judson and his son back up. It seemed wrong to have it on its face that way. Dr. Judson had adored his little Kirk. She knew she couldn't right the picture, though. The MPs were bound to notice it, and they would be back soon. Which meant she had to get out of there.

She turned to leave. That was when she saw the body on the floor.

Good God! It was one of their veterans. What in the world had that girl done? One of their veterans must have come down the hallway and seen her in Dr. Judson's office and walked in on her and—

What was she thinking? She didn't have to kill him! Well, maybe to her way of thinking, to keep him from alerting the VA cops or the MPs. But, good God, this was too much, and after all the risks she and Gerri had taken for her.

There was no question the man was dead. His head was at an impossible angle to his body. Still, she had to check. She knelt down beside him, took his wrist to feel for a pulse.

She held his hand with her right hand as she felt for a pulse with her left. His hand was so smooth. She looked at the nails. They were perfect. Florence had had only one professional manicure in her life, when Kenneth had given her a gift certificate while he broke the news to her that he was going to join the army. She recognized it easily enough, though. Why would one of their veterans have a professional manicure?

She looked at his face. The new man. He'd been there only a day or two. Maybe longer. Hard to know. You hardly ever saw him around. He had some kind of PTSD. He stayed to himself. Didn't even seem to be interested in going to the doctors.

A good-looking man, in a nerdy way. A little past middle age. Just a little gray at the temples. A professional haircut, too. Not just professional, high-priced professional. Penny loafers without the pennies.

She dropped his hand. She was dropping everything. She wanted out of this mess. She had done everything she could for Victoria. Now it was time to protect herself. She jumped up, ran to the door, listened, peeked out, saw no one, and hurried back to the nurse's station. As far as she was concerned, there was no dead body in Dr. Judson's office.

CHAPTER 40

Joe

The trip back to Iron Mountain on the snowmobile was as bad as I thought it would be. I was cold when I got on the damned thing, and I just kept getting colder. I was facing into the wind most of the time. And I was sure my face was going to look like Victoria's by the time I got back to Rickie—

What the hell? I meant by the time I got back to Zan, Lonnie, and the bus.

I spent a little time wondering who those guys were, the ones I killed at Sliver Lake. I wasn't sorry they were dead. They were hired killers. The world would be better off without them. Still, I thought I had left the killing life behind. I had enough to do just learning to live on my last leg.

That was the worst part of the trip, too—the last leg, on my last leg.

It took even longer going back than it had taken to get to Barbara's place, because it was dark, and I didn't know the territory. I kept backtracking and watching for signs that there might have been more killers in that bunch than the ones we did away with, and the one that got away. I didn't see anything, though.

It was full day by the time I got back to the county park at Iron Mountain. I didn't want Oscar the Grouch to know I had "borrowed" his snowmobile. He might think of it as stealing, and that would give Sheriff Sam Avanti another reason to get involved. So I had to leave it in a stand of woods way out at the edge of the park, where Oscar could think someone else had taken it. I zigged and zagged until I found a path that had been used both by cross-country skiers and deer. I figured I could mingle my footprints in the snow with theirs and no one would be the wiser. It was tough walking, though, and as cold as I already was, I began to wonder if I could make it back to the bus. I really thought about just lying down and going to sleep. That would solve all my problems. Except I still wanted to kill Reverend Franklin Prashwell. So much for leaving the killing life behind. So much for Freud, too, Goddamn his ego and the id he rode in on.

I finally made it to the bus, though. Maybe it was that desire to kill a certain fundy preacher that gave me the incentive to live. Or maybe it was something much more noble, like wanting to get into the pants of an Episcopalian priest.

There wasn't any heat in the bus, but there was a little combination office/convenience store/laundry building, which Zan had promptly broken into as soon as the caretaker was gone. He and Lonnie had slept in the bus but spent the rest of their time making baloney sandwiches and munching chips and just keeping warm in the store. They must have been really bored, because they had also done our laundry. Zan saw me arrive at the bus and came out long enough to yell at me to come over there to get something to eat and to get warmed up.

Either Lonnie had lost his super hearing or he didn't care, because the first clue that the sheriff had shown up was when I looked out the window and saw a high-wheel sixteen with a big star on its door. It was the kind of ride that wouldn't care if the gate was locked. It would just find a different way in. It pulled up beside the bus. Sam Avanti climbed down out of the driver's door.

"Sheriff's here," I said, for Lonnie's benefit.

To myself, I said a bunch of cuss words. Somehow somebody had already found out about those bodies in Sliver Lake and sent him out after me. I reached down and touched the Beretta through my pants leg to make sure it was warm enough. Then I took my hand away and went back to the baloney. No way I was going to shoot the sheriff. Or the deputy either, if he had one with him.

Lonnie and Zan were sitting in the only chairs at the only table. It was under the overhead gas heater. They seemed content just to sit there, although they looked like they were all tired out from eating the sad little cheese crackers they were chewing.

Sam Avanti pushed open the door on the bus and climbed in. It didn't take him long to figure we weren't there, or to figure where we might be. It was only about fifty yards to the store, but he got into the sixteen instead of walking it. I didn't blame him. The snow was drifted high, and the wind was still blowing. There was no new snow, though, and a ray or two of sun was lighting up the tops of the tall pines.

He drove over, climbed down, tried the knob on the front door. It was locked, because Zan had jimmied the back door, and we had come in that way. I was sitting on a stool in a corner by the front window, eating a baloney sandwich, which was pretty damned good, considering that I was hungrier than the average bear. The sheriff pounded on the door. Zan and Lonnie just sat there. My leg hurt. I didn't want to get off the stool. I finally got up, though, hobbled over to the door, and let him in, but I didn't let go of my sandwich.

"Cold in the bus," I said. "We've been staying over here, since everything is closed up anyway. We'll pay for everything," I said.

"Yeah, yeah," he said. "Where is she?"

Out of the corner of my eye, I saw Lonnie's ears perk up. There weren't many *shes* he could be asking about. So this wasn't about bodies at Sliver Lake after all. That was good. On the other hand, Victoria was on the loose. I didn't know why, but I knew it wasn't good.

"She's hiding back there in the laundry room," I said.

"Great. Where *is* she?"

Apparently my lying skills needed work.

"What happened to her? You had the responsibility for her, even after taking her to the VA—"

It was Lonnie's voice, a little quavery, and Sheriff Avanti didn't let him finish.

"The hell I've got responsibility for her or you or anybody else, you fuck-ups. It's the goddamned big-time VA cops that let her get away. They think they're so fucking hot, and they didn't even tell me or the smokies or anybody who could actually do some good at locating her that she was even gone. Aren't even admitting anything is wrong over there *now*. We wouldn't even know anything the fuck about her getting loose except I've got a nurse over there keeps me informed."

I was sort of surprised at the sheriff. He'd had plenty of opportunity to cuss like a sailor when we'd been in his jail, but he hadn't done it. Maybe he was just waiting for the right motivation. Real cussers, though, didn't need motivation.

"Look, Sheriff," I said, "if the VA cops let her get away, it's no skin off your nose. Why do you have to look for her? We're off the hook for anything in your jurisdiction. She can't get far in a snowstorm, anyway—"

I was going to say more, but Sam Avanti wasn't in a listening mood.

"She kidnapped a *baby* goddammit. Needless to say, the mother is hysterical and blaming the father and they're friends of mine and I'm getting tired of this shit. Now, where the *fuck* is she?"

This was getting into trickier territory than my half-frozen brain could negotiate. I needed time to think. I gave a shrug.

It made the baloney slip out from between the two slices of white bread. The baloney flopped onto the floor like— something floppy and inedible. I thought I was going to cry. I was really enjoying that baloney. I had just shot and killed a bunch of guys over at Sliver Lake and now I wanted to cry over dropped baloney. I knew I was going crazy. No, I was already crazy. Now I was just recognizing it. But if you recognize it, are you really crazy—

Lonnie's voice broke into my crazy thoughts. It was getting higher, and wavier, too.

"Kidnapped—a baby—she wouldn't."

Avanti sighed.

"You're half right. I don't think she intended to kidnap the baby. She stole a pickup truck, just to get away, I imagine, but the baby was in it."

Zan twisted around in his chair to face the sheriff. There was Cheetos powder on his lips.

"Sheriff, you'd better let us in on the secret," he said. "That maintenance guy locked us into this goddam nirvana you so graciously sent us to, and this goddam snowstorm came up, and the three of us have been sitting here with no heat and nothing to do and nothing to eat. We don't even have a goddam radio, so if you're looking to find somebody, well, hell, we're going to be about as much help as a pig in the third grade."

The sheriff and I looked at him the same way Lonnie *always* looked at him. I personally figured a pig was pretty smart if it got to third grade. I really admired Zan's lying skills, though. He had dropped that "the three of us" in there so subtly that I was sure the sheriff heard it without wondering about it. I had an alibi, two witnesses, and a snowstorm. Only a crazy man would have gone out in this storm, especially on a decrepit snowmobile he didn't really even know how to operate.

The sheriff sighed again. It was Zan who had asked for the explanation, but Avanti gave it to me.

"Your girl got away from the VA. Not exactly sure how. MPs were there, looking for her. A couple of hard cases. My source doesn't know why, and neither do I. Anyway, she got up north of town somehow. From one report we got, we think she must have hopped a log truck. Anyway, she stole a pickup from in front of a store. The guy had just run into the store for a minute, had his baby strapped in behind the seat, left the motor running to keep the baby warm. She jumped in just as he was coming back out. Almost ran him down. He got a good look at her. No mistaking who it was. Now she and the baby are gone, and—she wouldn't do anything, would she?"

I expected Lonnie to say something. He knew Victoria a lot better than I did. He didn't, though.

"Not to worry, Sheriff," I said finally. "Victoria wouldn't hurt a flea, let alone a baby."

I got a mental image of Victoria kicking the crap out of those Indians over at Barbara's place, and I knew for a fact that those guys were hard asses. I hoped I was telling the truth about her, but what would she do if her life and liberty were on the line? Surely she wouldn't hurt a baby on purpose, but if she had to leave it in order to—

The sheriff gave me a hard look, like he knew what I was thinking.

"If she shows up here, let me know. There's a phone in the office there. I'm just interested in the baby, not her. You're right. Those VA guys let her get away. They can find her. I won't turn her in to them. I *do* want that baby, though."

He started for the door, but when he got there, he paused and turned around, just like Columbo, that cop that Peter Falk played on TV, except Avanti had a parka instead of a trench coat. Lieutenant Columbo was one of Grandma's favorite TV characters, and I could almost hear her laughing at Avanti's ham-handed imitation.

"Seems you boys had a little fracas at Moe's Junction, up near Sagola, before you got arrested for Dr. Judson's murder. Nobody reported it, but word gets around. So I went up there and asked some questions. Didn't get very far." He looked at me, as if I was responsible for his inability to beat cooperation out of people. "Folks up there act scared," he added.

I didn't know what to say, so I didn't. I hoped Zan and Lonnie would keep their mouths shut, too.

"The folks over at VA, though, they seem interested in what you did up there. Seem to think if you could beat up a bunch of hunters, you'd be the type to murder a VA doctor who didn't give you what you wanted."

I still didn't say anything. I could sense Zan getting antsy, though.

"Even had a call from a US Senator about it. The Honorable William Dunawithe of North Dakota, head of all things military, or something like that. That's the way his secretary said it when she put the call through."

"Pretty impressive," I said. "Big senator like that interested in a bunch of homeless vets."

"Don't flatter yourself. He's not interested in you. He's interested in getting Dr. Judson's murder out of sight real fast. Now, *that* is interesting. You're just a quick means to getting that murder to go away. He knew more about that shootout at the Sagola corral than I did. Where would he hear about that? You boys been bragging?"

"Sheriff, who would we brag to who knows a U.S. Senator?"

"And why would we brag about beating the shit out of those pansies?" Zan put in. "Hell, I was ashamed it took me and Lonnie both. He should have been able to do it by himself, but he's just a pretty boy, more interested in making it with the ladies."

He gave Lonnie a sneer, but I don't think it bothered Lonnie.

"You're just jealous you can't make it with the ladies, because you're so ug—" Lonnie started.

"Shitfire!" the sheriff yelled. "You assholes act like you're in second grade. Why the fuck did Buffalo Bill Dunawithe know all about a bar fight in my county and I didn't know about it?"

"Gee, if I knew they had a bar—" Zan started, but I cut him off.

"Sheriff, you're right. There's something that smells, and it's not just that smoked fish fudge they sell up there at Moe's. My guess is those hunters weren't just hunters. They had the smell of mercenary on them."

"Contractors," Lonnie added, like a question he was pondering.

"I think if you could find out who those guys were, you might get some answers, Sam."

"Don't call me Sam," he said.

I guess we weren't friends yet.

CHAPTER 41

Victoria

Shit! Now she was in it deep. A baby! They would put out an Amber Alert, or whatever they called it in the UP.

Stealing a truck was one thing. The cops would look for it if they got the chance, but who cared? Black pickups were all over the place, and Michigan plates were only on the back. She just had to be sure no cops saw the back plate, and it was probably snow smashed by now anyway.

A baby was something else entirely. Snowstorm or not, every cop within a hundred miles would be out looking for her. Probably every nut with a gun, too, and that meant everybody in the whole damned state. Shit!

Her first instinct was just to take it back, but that was impossible. Everybody at the taxidermy shop would have a gun. She couldn't just drop off the baby and take off again with the pickup. They'd either shoot her or hold her for the cops. She preferred getting shot. There was no way she would let the cops put her in a cell.

The snow was coming harder and faster, blowing horizontally across in front of her, from west to east. She saw a road sign. It was plastered with snow, but she could barely make out a word that looked like Felch. Yeah, Felch. She had seen that sign before, after they beat the crap out of those hard cases at that convenience store.

Instinctively she turned. The big truck skidded a little, but she got it straightened up. She began to hum. "Straighten Up and Fly Right."

Where the hell did that come from? Oh, yeah, Sarge.

At least she now had the wind at her back, so she could see a little better. That was good. She had no idea where the sides of the road were, though. That was bad.

There was a fine mesh net of white from the tree line on either side of the road. There had to be ditches, but she couldn't tell where they were.

She heard a noise from behind her. She glanced in the rearview mirror. The baby was getting restless, fidgeting, waving its little fists around. Dressed in pink. Must be a girl. Up here, they would dress boy babies in camouflage.

If she could get it up into the front with her, she could tickle it or something to keep it occupied. Let it pull her finger. Yeah, that would be good. Poor kid would probably be traumatized for life if it saw what she looked like, though. But she had to leave it back there. It was strapped in. That was good, safe, especially since she didn't know about the ditches. Shit!

She couldn't just ride around with it. She had to do something with the Goddamned baby. No, that wasn't right. It was she who was damned by God, not the baby. The baby hadn't asked for this ride.

The baby began to cry. Shit! Probably doing that, too. Got to—

Sing! She had to sing. A lullaby, or something. "Jesus loves me this I know, for the Bible tells me so."

Where had that come from? Way back, of course. Church, Sunday school. It was just automatic, didn't mean anything. Jesus didn't love her. Might love the baby, though. What else? "Little ones to him belong, they are weak but he is strong."

She used the rearview mirror again. The baby was quieting down. "Yes, Jesus loves me. Yes, Jesus loves me. Yes, Jesus loves me, the Bible tells me so."

She sang it three times, the whole thing, staring hard through the windshield, through the whirling snow. She glanced up and into the rearview mirror again. The baby's eyes were open, but it wasn't crying or fidgeting anymore. Thank God.

God…Jesus. Dammit. She should have thought of it before. Rickie Linden. She would have to go back to Iron Mountain, give the baby to the minister. The cops would be busy with the storm. They might not notice another black pickup. It looked more white than black now, anyway, plastered with snow.

She slowed down even more, watching for a turn back south. There was a sign. She couldn't read it, but there had to be a road to go with it. She eased over into a turn that was almost motionless. The snow came horizontally again. Was it even harder? She tried to pick up speed.

Damn. She should have just gone back to the taxidermy place and faced the music. Now she and this baby were going to be stranded out here. And if she got to Iron Mountain, what if the cops did see her? Well, she would have to think about that then. But she knew she couldn't do anything to let harm come to the baby.

Her eyes filled with something. Shit, she couldn't see. Sand everywhere. A whiteout. Hell, that wasn't sand. It was snow. Why did she think it was sand?

She had to slow down, or she would crash, and she and the baby would both be done in. Damned pickup. Better she had just crawled off into the woods and died in the snow. That would show them.

Hell, show who? Nobody cared. Barbara? Why hadn't she come to see her? She had kicked the hell out of those Indians for Barbara, but Barbara didn't care. She had kicked the hell out of the Iraqis for her flag and her nation, but nobody cared about that, least of all the politicians who sent her over there. Joe and Zan had taken her in, but not by choice. They were just strangers she rode on a bus with. Lonnie? Did he care?

She couldn't think about him now. She had to get this baby to safety. Then she had to get herself to safety.

But the sand was just everywhere. She glanced back at the baby again. Its eyes were closing. What the hell? She was still singing. The song, the rhythmic rapping of the wipers, the warm cab—they were putting the baby to sleep.

She had to be careful or she would drop off, too. She had been too cold, and now she was getting too warm. Her adrenaline had run out. Her head was nodding. Goddamned sand everywhere. Her eyes—some sort of fluid—blood. She was on fire, crawling. There was the baby, sitting by the roadside. A car that was on fire, too. The crumpled body of a woman beside the baby. The rocket that had hit them must have gotten the car, too. Or there had been more—

Yes, lots of rockets. Rockets, or IEDs? She remembered that baby, just sitting there. And then it started to cry. And she felt the awful burning—

In the midst of the burning voices, one was Sarge. "That's not ragheads. That's Limpcocks."

What the hell? Why were Limpcocks there?

Limpcocks was what they called the security contractors. Their company name was L&C. The grunts figured out quickly what the L and the C stood for. L&C was security for all the non-military Americans in Iraq—the diplomats, the contractors. Algonquin Associates had all the contracts, but L&C provided their security. There wasn't any contractor activity way out on this edge of Baghdad, though, and there sure as hell weren't any diplomats. So why were there Limpcocks here?

She was on fire. The burning. But the voices

Now, with snow blowing in front of her like sand, she remembered the rest of it for the first time...

There was a thump and bang and the Humvee had turned over and skidded. It must have been hit by a missile of some sort. There was a big hole in the side, but a ragged sheet of metal had been folded in over Victoria. From around the edge she could see part of Wong. She heard Sarge screaming. It sounded like echoes of her own screams, and somehow she knew he was on fire, too.

There were other voices, yelling instead of screaming, at first faint, and then coming closer. There was machine gun fire, little bursts.

Then Sarge's voice again. "You goddam sumbitches."

A burst of fire and someone laughed. And Sarge stopped screaming.

"Shoot the woman," someone yelled in English.

A burst of fire hit the metal in front of her. Then there was a different gun firing, and a different voice.

"*Qaedas*. Get out of there. They're all done for, anyway."

"You got it?"

"I got it!"

"Then get going."

Victoria realized that she was slumped over the steering wheel of the pickup. They had stopped moving. The snow was still coming at them. She was still humming. The baby was still sleeping. Gradually she pushed down on the gas pedal. The truck began to move. The snow was thick on the road. Where in hell was she?

It was like waking up from a dream that seemed so real, still trying to figure out what to do about the lines you didn't know as you stood on the stage. Or where the final exam was. Or why the bridge had ended. You were awake, and you knew it was a dream, but you couldn't let it go. Except it wasn't a dream.

"I got it." Got what? What had they been talking about?

The squad had stopped at a little shop on the very last street, or what passed for a street out there. It didn't really look like a shop, but there was a sign. She had asked Wong what the sign said but he had just frowned and shaken his head.

Sarge had pointed at her and Wong and said, "You two, stay in the damned Hummer."

Then he had gone into the shop by himself. That was strange. Sarge always took Wong along to interpret. The others had climbed out of the Humvee and formed a casual and ragged perimeter of sorts.

"You think he's getting cold drinks?" she had asked Wong.

But again he just shook his head. "Vicky, you see that blue car back there?"

Wong was the only one who ever called her *Vicky*. He nodded in the direction from which they had come. It was a dusty and nondescript thing. She had to take Wong's word for it that it was blue. He was good with colors. It was not an American make. Probably European, maybe Korean. It sat low, which meant either a lot of passengers or heavy armor.

"I think they've been following us," Wong had said. "And I think there's a Hummer with them, but it stays way back—"

Just then Sarge came out of the shop, almost running, carrying a sort of satchel, except it looked metal. Victoria glanced back at the blue car. It was already on the move, coming toward them fast. Wong was right. A Hummer was pulling out from behind another building. It wasn't from behind the blue car, though. If it had been way back, it had looped around somehow and was coming from the other direction. It was accelerating, coming at them even faster than the blue car.

"Terry and the pirates," Sarge had yelled, his particular slang for terrorists.

The other guys in the squad began to react, but way too slowly. Then all hot hell broke loose…

What had Sarge been carrying? Was that what *Terry and the pirates* had been after? Why? And Sarge had said they weren't terrorists, after all, had yelled that they were Limpcocks. Why would Limpcocks attack them? They were supposed to be on the same side.

They had debriefed her, a bunch of them, when she was finally able to talk, before she was able, actually. They didn't seem to care about her pain. She couldn't remember who they said they were. Army Intelligence, probably, or CIA, or both. Finally they decided that she didn't know anything. They made her sign a statement. It said nothing about any metal satchel.

She hadn't told them everything, though. It was mostly because she was in pain and drugged up and couldn't remember. Or maybe it was because she knew the squad had been some place they shouldn't be, doing something they shouldn't do, and she wanted to protect the reputations of Sarge and Wong and the rest. They couldn't do it for themselves. She was all that was left. Maybe she just wanted to protect her career. She hadn't known then that it was already over. It was hard to remember now how important that army career had been to her.

It was hard to remember anything now, in this blowing sand—no, it was snow, blowing snow. She wasn't back in Iraq. She was in a Goddamned snow storm, with a baby.

She kept driving, because there wasn't anything else to do. She glanced down at the gas gauge. About half. That was enough. Within half a tank either she would get this baby to Rickie Linden or somebody would be shooting her and taking the baby back.

Then it was there, looming up like a desert mirage, except it was coming at her out of the snow, a low dark skyline, a bunch of buildings, a town of some sort, like a village in a Christmas snow globe that Santa just shook up. Was it Iron Mountain?

She couldn't be sure. There was a sign, but it was plastered over with snow. She had seen so little of the town before. She had no landmarks, no identifying points. About the only thing she would recognize for sure was the VA. And that taxidermy shop.

At least the town was big enough to have a plow, because there was one up ahead, an orange truck pushing a big blade, going way faster than she thought anything could move in this snow, so much more snow than she had ever seen in Chicago, clearing a path just for her, it seemed, since no other vehicles were on the street. She kept well back but moved along as fast as she dared in the wake of the plow.

What now? She could hardly stop and ask for help in locating Rickie's church. Could she just drive around until she found it? What if Rickie wasn't even there? In this snow, she would probably be sitting with a nice cup of coffee.

Victoria began to cry. It was too much. She didn't mind that Rickie could just sit there, in her kitchen, or maybe in her living room, in a comfortable chair, with an afghan that her grandma had knitted for her on the back, so she could pull it down around her if she got cold, staring out at the snow, seeing only its beauty and not its menace, not a care in the world, except to wonder if there was more coffee left in the pot. She was glad for Rickie, but she was so sad for herself. There was not a single good thing in her life, not even a simple cup of coffee. The only good thing she had was a sleeping little baby that she had accidentally stolen, and she was going to have to give that back.

She had to swerve to miss a car that was angled into the curb. Damn. She had to pay more attention. The car's back end stuck out like it had been abandoned. She maneuvered around it, slid sideways back into what she thought might be her own driving lane.

Then she saw a figure struggling along in the snow a block ahead. It was mostly just a dark parka with a hood, but there was something familiar about it. You didn't spend any time handcuffed to someone without having a feel for who they were even in a parka in a snowstorm. Damn; that had to be Rickie herself!

She could hear Sarge saying, "See, girl. It's better to be

lucky than good." Yeah, right, Sarge, look at how lucky you were.

She eased the pickup on along the street, looking every few seconds in the rearview mirror to check for plows or police cars.

Rickie was walking in the street because the sidewalks were impossible. At least the plows were trying to do something about the streets. The pickup was almost on her and she still hadn't turned around. Oh, yeah, wind, snow, big heavy hood. Hard for her to hear. Victoria didn't want to wake the baby, but she had to give the horn a quick toot. Rickie made a dive for the side of the road, fell to one knee, turned around, looked blankly at the black pickup that had come to a halt beside her. Victoria shoved the shift into park and slid across the seats, opened the door, made an urgent beckoning motion at the fallen preacher.

Rickie's eyes got so wide that the front of the parka hood went up an inch. Victoria kept beckoning at her as if she was urging her to round third base and dash for home. Rickie struggled for footing, got it, slow-motioned to the pickup. Victoria slid back into the driver's side, glanced into the rearview mirror, saw nothing but a sleeping baby, got the truck into gear, and the big tires digging into the snow before Rickie had the passenger door fully closed.

"Victoria, what the hell—"

Victoria made a shushing motion with her finger across her lips and jerked her head toward the spot behind the seats. Rickie twisted around to look. She spoke again, much more softly this time, but with a new urgency.

"Victoria, I repeat: What the hell?"

Victoria kept her eyes on the road. "I figured you'd be out walking around in the snow, need a lift home."

"I am *not* walking around for my health. There are a couple of old ladies I went to check on. My Prius got hung up and I had to walk home. The radio was totally wrong about how much snow we'd get. Now, please, what the hell?"

"You don't want to know. Deniability. But you need to take the baby to…I'm not sure where you take babies that are left in pickup trucks that people leave out for the grabbing—"

"My God, you stole the truck, too?"

"How else would I get a truck?"

"Hell, Victoria, that's serious. Up here, men think more highly of their trucks than their wives. But that's nothing compared to kidnapping. Kidnapping is a federal offense."

"I didn't know I was kidnapping."

"I know, but that's the way the sheriff will see it. But hold on a minute. Yes, I can return the baby. Sam Avanti won't give me much trouble. I won't be able to tell him anything, anyway. Just drop me off at the courthouse with the baby."

"Think, Rickie. The sheriff's in the back end of the court house. I can't go near a cop shop."

The priest twisted around again to look at the baby. "It's awfully cute. A little girl?"

"I think so."

"How in the—No, you're right. I shouldn't know anything more than I do right now. Take me to my apartment—No, wait. The church is closer. Take me there, and I'll call the sheriff. Is there a bottle or diaper bag or anything like that?"

"I don't know. Maybe beside her back there."

Rickie got up on her knees, poked her head back between the seats. "Yeah. A bag." She turned around and sat down again. "Keep going two more blocks. The church will be on the left. Take the street just past it. That will put us at the side door of the church."

Victoria followed the directions and pulled up beside the stone steep-roofed building. She checked her mirrors. No cop cars.

"Not very big," she said, looking at the church building.

"Not many Episcopalians up here," Rickie answered. She opened her door, pulled her seat forward, got into the rear compartment with the baby, unstrapped the car seat, got it into her arms as gently as she could, and backed out. "Hand me the bag, will you?"

Victoria got the bag, slid over, and handed it to Rickie.

"You know 'Jesus Loves Me'? She likes it if you sing that to her."

"Victoria, I may be High Church, but I *do* know 'Jesus Loves Me'!"

The baby started to stir. Rickie hooked the diaper bag over her shoulder.

"You're a hell of a good woman, Rickie."

Victoria's voice cracked a little as she said it. If the cops found her, she would make them shoot her before she would go to a cell. This might be the last woman she saw before she died.

The minister looked back at her. "*Vaya con Dios, Amiga,*" she said. "You're a hell of a good woman, too."

Rickie pushed the truck door shut and started wading through the heavy snow to the red church door.

CHAPTER 42

Joe

I couldn't figure this business with Senator Dunawithe trying to pin the fracas at that convenience store and Dr. Judson's murder both on us. I knew who Dunawithe was, of course. Everybody did. He was the head of the Senate Armed Services Committee, and some people thought he was more powerful in military matters than everybody in the Defense Department and the Pentagon put together. Sure, I knew who he was, but he didn't know who we were. Why would he be involved in something as minor as this?

I didn't mean that a murdered doctor was a minor thing. A dustup in a convenience store was minor, but not a murder. Any murder was totally major to the victim and the people who loved him or her. Even to the civilians in Iraqistan who were dismissed as *collateral damage*. They had people who loved them, and those people grieved. But that was the point. To an operator like Buffalo Bill Dunawithe, Dr. Judson was just *collateral damage*. Unless there was more to the connection between Judson and Dunawithe than Sam Avanti knew about.

Sheriff Avanti was more interested in finding the baby Victoria made off with, though, so he gave up playing Columbo and left for real, before I could get it sorted out well enough to ask him more. The door closed behind him, more with a whoosh than a bang.

I stood there, two limp pieces of white bread in my hand, looking at the boloney on the floor. I figured if I looked real close I could see Jesus's face in the boloney. That was the way people usually saw Jesus. I looked real hard, but it was Dr. Alan Judson's face that looked back at me. I looked at the bread. One slice was Dunawithe and one was me. Judson was the filler in this sandwich. If I could just get him back into place, the sandwich would make sense.

"Well, there's one thing clear. We'd better find Victoria and that baby before the sheriff does."

It was Zan's voice. He said it like it was just an obvious fact, not a total impossibility, and then he started licking cheese dust off his fingers again.

"Wait 'til I get this boloney cleaned up off the floor," I said.

I picked up the dropped slice of boloney and threw it out the door so that some animal could have a snack. The air that came in the door was still cold, but it didn't have that bitter feel to it. I looked across the deep snow at that battered school bus. Even though Zan and Lonnie were still sitting at the little table behind me, in my mind I could see them sitting in the bus. There in the bus I could see the wondrously shaped but terribly discolored Victoria sitting with them. That was our natural environment. That was our transportation to the war.

We were careening around life like bumper cars, or probably more like we were in a demolition derby. We were still feeling the whiplash from the last crash when the next one came. And each of us was in a Yugo with exploding gas tanks while everyone else in the derby was driving an eighteen-wheeler. If each one of us had only our own life to look out for, it would be a lot easier. But each of us felt the crash every time the big old Tanker of Life rammed into any one of us. Shit, I couldn't even think up a decent metaphor.

There was no reason why we should care about one another or feel like we had a responsibility for one another. Still, what Zan said about finding Victoria and the baby before anyone else did came naturally, even though we hardly knew her. Hell, none of us knew the others. Zan and I had been close once, but the war had made us strangers to each other. Except that we all belonged to one another now. Victoria had simply gotten on his bus one day, and brought all sorts of problems with her, but she was one of us now. She had a problem, so we all had that problem.

"You can pick your friends and you can pick your nose, but you can't wipe your friends on the sofa. You can't wipe your friends off."

It always surprised me when somebody said about some group of disparate characters who stuck together. "We're a family."

Hell, family members wiped one another off all the time. Sometimes even wiped them out. But you couldn't do that if you were a fighting squad. That was what we were, Zan and Lonnie and Victoria and me. We were all vets now, but we were still soldiers. We were a squad and, if one of us had a fight, we all had it. Zan didn't even like Victoria, but he knew what we had to do.

I knew, too. I was on my last leg. I had just killed three guys and lost my boloney. How much worse could my life get? Too bad. In a war, there wasn't time to grieve your losses. You just had to go on to the next fight.

I didn't believe any of that crap. I breathed deeply of the cold air, then shut the door.

"Okay," I said. "*How* do we find Victoria and the baby?"

"Well, shit, *you're* the brains," Zan said. "It's a cinch that preacher girl didn't come running out here to go gaga over you because you're good looking."

"It's rude to call Mother Linden a '*preacher girl*,'" Lonnie said, rather primly. "Still, maybe she has an artificial leg fetish."

He said something else, too, but I didn't hear it. The brain I was rumored to possess was booting up. I went to the telephone in the little office, found a phone book under it, looked up the Episcopal Church, dialed the number. The old brain was right on the money, even though it wasn't really that hard to figure where Victoria would run to. Who else did she know in Iron Mountain besides Rickie Linden? The phone on the other end rang five times and was finally answered by a crying baby.

CHAPTER 43

Florence

"Flo, goddam it, where the hell have you been?"

Florence Kneightly stared at Molly Quast. "Good golly, Miss Molly, I'm less than two minutes late in the middle of a snowstorm. I'll bet the rest of the staff isn't coming back at all."

Molly's frown told her that she was right about the rest of the staff, and that she did not like the *Good golly, Miss Molly* phrase any better than Florence Kneightly liked to be called Florence Kneightlygale. Which was why she had said it, of course.

Molly Quast added a sigh to her frown. "To Simmons, two minutes late is two minutes too many. She was here, on the dot, looking for you. I tried to cover for you, but…"

Right. Molly was a decent head ward nurse, but she wasn't the type to say anything to Ira Gasaway's right-hand hatchet nurse that would cover anything but her own ass, and it would take a lot of talking to cover that thing.

Damn. Florence was being bitchy with somebody who didn't deserve it, but the thought of Simmons looking for her—

"Anyway, she said for you to go right down to the administrator's office as soon as you got here. Like we can spare a nurse when we're short-handed anyway for…"

Molly was fishing, hoping she would tell her what it was about. Florence was sure she knew what it was all about, but she wasn't about to tell Molly Quast about it, or anyone else. A little knowledge was a dangerous thing, but so was too much.

She walked down the hallway to the administration offices with the tread of a Budweiser Belgian that had been drinking beer out of the wagon instead of pulling it. She looked at the new door of Ira Gasaway's office. It was some sort of hardwood, which in itself was expensive enough, but the big gold plaque in the middle, that proclaimed simply *IRA GASAWAY*, all capitals, no title, must have made the door as expensive as the new X-ray machine they needed and still didn't have. That door was the first thing Gasaway had replaced when he had come. The old door was blond wood and had a big glass panel in it. The new one was dark, solid, and impenetrable.

Florence had never been in the new administrator's office. She didn't know if she should knock. Surely there would be an outer office with a secretary—or with Simmons. She tried the knob. It turned. She pushed the door open just far enough to stick her head inside. A rather big room. No Simmons, thank God. Ira Gasaway himself was pacing back and forth on the plush carpet. It was new, too, a deep blue. He cupped a cell phone in his hand as he paced, looking as if he was debating with himself whether to make a call, or perhaps trying to remember a number. He looked up and saw Florence's nurse-capped head. He quickly stuck the phone into an inside pocket of his black suit, as though he was embarrassed to be seen with it. "Uh...Mrs. Knightley, is it?"

"Yes."

"Well, I'm sorry about the mix-up here. As you may have heard, a body was found in Dr. Judson's office. A man. We're not at liberty to give his name yet, but there is clear evidence that he is the person who killed Dr. Judson. A personal matter. A disgruntled former patient. Apparently, he returned to search Dr. Judson's records, to try to find evidence that Dr. Judson had treated him incorrectly..." He hadn't even invited her in, just spewed it all forth at her head. She decided that he had been rehearsing the speech as he paced and wanted to get it out before he forgot it. The words rolled on, like he had a teleprompter on the backs of his eyeballs. "...as it turns out, the other matter, the ones the MPs were here about, concerning the Roundtree woman, that has been cleared up. So she's been released. Her friends were already released by Sheriff Avanti. There's no suspicion now that they killed Dr. Judson, of course. I think she's rejoined her friends. I suspect they have gone away by now. Perhaps very far away."

He smiled as he said it, what her father had called a *shit-eating grin*. Florence didn't like the sound of *very far away*. Victoria was in deeper now than ever, and she could only hope it wasn't six feet deep.

"Now, of course, it is important that we keep all this to ourselves. Don't want to upset the rest of the staff."

"Or the patients," Florence put in.

"Oh, yes, the patients, of course. The patients always come first. Wouldn't want to upset them."

Damned fool. She had mentioned the patients just to bait him, sure that he had not even remembered that they had patients, and she was right. He didn't even know that in the VA they never referred to *patients* but only to *veterans*. Who *was* this shumck?

But he was pushing on. "…but especially important not to mention any of this to the staff, or to the local law officials, of course. They have been notified through official channels. It's important that regular VA people like you and me not interfere with official channels. I'm sure you understand…"

Florence was sure that she *did* understand, about why Ira Gasaway wanted her to keep quiet, but there was plenty she did *not* understand. Like whose body was really in Dr. Judson's office, and why they were calling the MPs off of Victoria. Then she looked at that shit-eating grin again and understood perfectly well. Ira Gasaway was lying through his teeth.

"Uh, why don't you take the rest of the day off, Mrs. Kneightly? All this snow. Won't be much to do here, just usual maintaining. Can't do surgeries and all that. Yes, you've had a hard time, with Dr. Judson's murder, and all the rest of this. You should get some time off. Go ahead home…"

She could have said *No,* that he was so dumb he didn't even know that they were *short*-handed because of the snowstorm, that Molly needed her, but she didn't. Molly Quast wasn't going to like this, but it came directly from Ira Gasaway himself, this order to take the rest of the day off, and besides, Florence had something to do.

CHAPTER 44

Rickie

The baby did not sleep very long. It started to fuss, then went into full crying mode. Rickie found a bottle in the diaper bag. About three-quarters full. Not warm enough. She grabbed the baby and the bottle and ran for the church kitchen. The baby must have liked the jostling. Its eyes got wide, and it stopped crying.

She stuck the bottle into the microwave. How long? Twenty seconds should do it. The thing started to hum. It was old. Were microwaves escaping? They would be bad for the baby. She turned so her body was between the baby and the microwave.

The baby started to cry again. Rickie got in two lines of "Jesus Loves Me" before the microwave dinged. She pulled the bottle out. *Got to test it, make sure it's not too hot. Don't you shake some out on your wrist?* The baby was in the way of her wrist. She laid it down on the counter. Could the baby roll off? No, the counter was big enough for five women to chop vegetables at a time. That had to be too big for a baby to roll off. It cried harder. She shook milk onto her wrist. Damn, too hot!

She ran to the sink, put the bottle under cold water. The baby kept crying. More drops on her wrist. She had gotten the damn stuff too cold. Well, better than too hot. She stuck the nipple into the baby's mouth. Oh, God, was she supposed to sterilize it first? The baby didn't care about sterilization. It gave a sigh that said, *Thank God the idiot finally got it right*! She sucked at the bottle like she was in the baby Olympics.

Rickie wanted to pick her up but couldn't figure out how to

do it and keep the bottle in her mouth at the same time, and she definitely wanted to keep that bottle in place! She leaned over the counter with her elbows on either side of the baby, just in case the counter wasn't big enough to contain a roll. The baby looked up at her with big serious blue eyes. Rickie didn't realize she had been breathing like she was under water. She finally exhaled and tried to match the baby's serious stare.

"I don't know your name, little one. What would I name a little baby? Not Richard, that's for sure. What shall I call you?"

There had been a time when Rickie Linden had longed for a baby of her own. She was fourteen and sure that she could do a better job of raising a child than her parents had done. *Had done* was the correct way to put it, because they sure as hell weren't doing it anymore. She had been raising herself for a long time.

She had fantasized about what she would name her baby. She had not fantasized about changing diapers, but she was pretty sure that would be the next step with this little…Emmie, that's what she would call her. She had not been able to decide between Emily or Emma when she had named her imaginary baby. Emmie got them both.

"Hello, little Emmie."

The baby burped and giggled and went back to sucking at the bottle.

Rickie giggled back at her. "Maybe you're a boy after all. They always laugh when they burp, even when they're as old as Joe Kirk. Guess I'll find out for sure when I change that diaper."

Now why was she thinking about Joe Kirk, and why was she telling Emmie about him? It wasn't like she was thinking of having a baby with Joe Kirk! He wasn't the fathering kind. He wasn't even the husbanding kind. But she spent a lot of time thinking about him.

She felt a draft, heard the back door slam. Damn. Who could that be? She started to grab the baby, to run some place to hide it, but whoever had come in was only two steps away, through the little alcove between the back door and the kitchen, where they kept the garbage cans.

She felt a hard lump developing in her throat. Robert Frost

said that each of his poems started with a lump in the throat. This lump wasn't the start of a poem. It was the start of grief. She was really going to have to give little Emmie back.

A form in a dark blue parka appeared in the doorway, the hood still up. At first she didn't recognize the form as an individual. In a parka, everyone looked the same, men and women alike. The form in the parka pulled a mitten off. The now bare hand reached up and pulled the hood back. A nurse's cap emerged. It had been tilted forward by the parka.

"Wow, Mother Linden. That was the easiest pregnancy in medical history. You never even showed, and your baby looks like it's twenty pounds."

Rickie had to smile. Florence Kneightly was an unlikely High-Church Episcopalian. She looked and talked more like a Pentecostal. Her family definitely did not fit into the social class of the rest of the congregation. But she was always ready to help, and she liked to share her earthy wisdom, and sometimes ribald humor, with her priest. It was a relief to see that it was the nurse in the parka instead of…well, almost anyone else. Except—forget him, dammit.

"I know this looks sort of strange, Florence, but the baby's parents asked me to look after it—"

Hell, what was she trying to do? The truth was going to come out. She didn't want to lie to Florence. She needed her as an ally. Besides, Florence knew all about—

"Let me start over. Someone stole a truck. She didn't know the baby was in it. When she did, she brought it to me, and—"

Florence didn't wait for her to finish.

"So Victoria stole a truck. Good for her. That damned lying Ira Gasaway. He said that Victoria was released. Well, never mind. I never believed that bastard anyway. I'm just glad she's okay. She *is* okay, isn't she?"

How had Florence put all this together? It didn't matter. Rickie was glad to have a friend, someone to share this burden. "I'm not really sure. She brought the baby to me, and then left again. I don't know where she is."

"What's her name?"

"Roundtree?"

"No, stupid. Forgive me. I mean, No, stupid *Mother Linden.* The *baby's* name."

"Oh. Emmie." It was out before she even thought about it.

"That's a pretty name."

"Thank you."

Florence gave her a strange look, one that caused her cap to do a little dance as her forehead wrinkled, but so what? They had to call the baby something, and Rickie really did give her that name, so why shouldn't she take the thanks for it?

"What are you going to do with Emmie?"

"Uh…what do you mean, Florence?"

"You need to call the sheriff and have him come get her. Those parents are bound to be worried. And the sooner she's found, the sooner the police will ease up on looking for Victoria, give her a chance to get someplace."

"Yeah, I guess you're right, but—" Rickie looked into Emmie's blue eyes. They were so clear, like a wishing pool. She could see anything there she wanted to see. She wanted to see herself in the arms of someone besides God.

"Besides, I need you to go with me to Dr. Judson's house."

"But I don't know Mrs. Judson. I know you were the doctor's nurse, but…I mean, grief work is best done by a person's own pastor. Doesn't she have a pastor of her own? I'm not very good—"

"This doesn't have anything to do with grief and Zoe Judson, although she's got plenty of it, I'm sure. But there's a key missing from Dr. Judson's office. It was hidden. He didn't know I knew about it. Nobody does. It appeared after he began to learn things he wouldn't tell me about. It was there after his murder. I looked all through his office, trying to figure out what it opened. Now it's gone. Whoever took it is going to figure out that it has to fit something at his house. I want to get there before they do."

"Florence, we shouldn't be messing in this at all. This is a matter for the sheriff."

The phone rang. The baby jumped and looked like she was going to cry. Rickie wiggled the nipple of the bottle around in the baby's mouth, trying to get her to focus on it.

The phone was on the wall right beside where Florence

Kneightly stood. She picked it up. "Episcopal Church." She listened for a moment. "Speak of the devil. No, not you sheriff. I mean Mother Linden. I was just thinking about her, because I came here to see her, but she's not here."

She listened again. An empty sound came from the bottle. The baby's face began to wrinkle up. Rickie grabbed her up in her arms and headed for the far corner of the basement, away from the telephone. "No, I'm in the kitchen, but I know she's not in the office. Have you tried her house?"

Florence covered the mouthpiece as she listened, being sure no sounds got into it from the baby, or from the supposedly absent priest, either. "No, they sent me home. I just thought I'd stop by to see Mother Linden about what I'm supposed to do for the service Sunday morning. It was on the way. But since she's not here, I'm going home to stay there…yeah, I'll tell her if I see her, but I don't know when that will be…okay, you, too. Take care."

She hung up and turned to Rickie. The basement wasn't very big. She didn't have to raise her voice much. "He didn't say so, exactly, but I think he thought Victoria might contact you. Frankly, I'm not sure I convinced him you're not here. We'd better get going."

"But Emmie…you said we needed to take her to the sheriff anyway. Why…"

"Something the sheriff said, and something he didn't say. I think we're running out of time. We need to get to Dr. Judson's house pronto. Bring the baby. Zoe is a pediatric nurse. The baby will distract her while I try to figure out something about that key."

Rickie was confused. This sounded dangerous. "But if time is running out—whatever that means—shouldn't we have the sheriff in on it?"

"Yeah, once I get it figured out. But Sam Avanti has the hands of ham. He'll mess it up. Besides, I liked Dr. Judson. He didn't deserve this, and that little baby of his definitely doesn't deserve it. If anybody is going to make this right, it's going to be *me*!"

Florence quickly gathered up all the baby equipment and put it into the diaper kit. Rickie put on her parka and stuffed Emmie into her bunting. Emmie didn't like it. Her face began to turn red. Florence led the way toward the back door. Rickie didn't like the direction this was going, but she picked the baby up and followed.

Just as she got to the back door, the phone on the wall rang again. Without thinking, with the habit of a pastor who is always on call, she picked it up. The baby exploded into a furious bawl. Rickie's face went as white as the baby's was red. "Oh, God," she muttered.

A hand came back around the doorway and grabbed the phone.

"Wrong number," Florence said, with an accent somewhere between Hispanic and French Canadian.

"Wait. I recognized that. *Oh, God.*"

Rickie felt her heart miss a beat. It was Joe Kirk's voice. She grabbed the phone out of Florence Kneightly's hand.

CHAPTER 45

The Hermits

Don Thackwell sat at the head of the table, as he always did. He was, after all, the chief Hermit as well as the CEO of Algonquin Associates. A former Congressman and a former Secretary of Defense, he was used to the head of the table. He was also used to knowing anything he wanted to know, and he was not happy.

"You mean she's been in the Iron Mountain VA this whole time and nobody told us?"

"What do you mean by *this whole time*? It's just been a couple of days," said Case Rome, III.

Rome was a political operative who had run some of the nastiest and most successful campaigns in history. He didn't have enough money to be a Hermit, or enough power, so he got the scut work, like keeping track of things, because he knew how to get things done. Thackwell eyed him. Rome was the most likely to be loyal, since he didn't have enough money or influence to strike out on his own, but Thackwell didn't trust him. He respected Rome as a brick layer, but not as a brick maker, and sooner or later, the layers would bite the hand that fed them.

"Well, have them take the bitch out!" Henry Janesway snarled. "We can't have this whole thing coming undone just because some piece of—"

Henry Janesway was the owner of Original Intent Communications. Thackwell frowned inside but knew how to keep his face bland. Janesway apparently thought that the original intent of the founding fathers was that he personally should control all the media in the world. He was an irascible old bastard, and he didn't need the money from their "Crusade," but wherever there was power, Janesway wanted some of it, and preferably all of it, and Thackwell knew how to use people who were in it for the power.

"No way we can do her in now," Case Rome broke in. "Think about it. That place already has too much publicity because we took that doctor out. I advised against that."

Case Rome III was used to having his advice taken. He knew he was smarter than anyone else in the room, and he resented being treated like an errand boy.

"Hey, we've got our own guys in there as security. Nobody would even hear about it." The speaker was Colonel Frederick "Fritz the Blitz" Demint, Retired. He got his nickname during the Gulf War. It hadn't done him any good in military politics, though. He had retired in disgust and a certain amount of disgrace for his relationships with "inferior" female officers. Fritz the Blitz was the "independent" military consultant on Janesway's OIC News Channel.

"There are those others, the ones she travels around with. They'd go looking for her, wouldn't they?" said Quincy Fortner.

Fortner had a PhD from Texas A&M and insisted on being called "Dr. Fortner." He was the founder and head of the Desoto Institute for Religion and Freedom. Thackwell didn't know if Fortner really believed all the crap he put forth as political philosophy, but he had gotten on the Algonquin board because they needed philosophical cover. They could hardly operate under their real motto, which was "All for one, and we're the one."

"How many are there? Four?" asked Edward Ensley

Ensley was a former senator who had often been on the short list for VP and never made it. He had scores to settle with everybody, especially those in his own party who had passed him over. Thackwell didn't trust people with axes to grind, because in the grinding they could easily slip and cut the wrong way, but he needed Ensley's contacts.

"That's right," Case Rome said. "Four, counting her."

"They'll all have to go," said Ensley.

"We can't just disappear all four," said Colonel Demint. "This isn't Guatemala."

He had a faraway look in his eyes, a look of nostalgia for the good old times and the good old places, when you could disappear as many people as you wanted and nobody cared.

Thackwell sighed, but not so the others could hear him. The Hermits were a democracy, of sorts, but some were more equal than others. He had put the Hermits together, and he had named them. The rest of the board of Algonquin Associates didn't even know they existed as a separate group. The only reason he put up with the charade that they had any say in this current Crusade was because he needed them—no, he didn't need anyone, but he could use them, just like he used the senior senator from his home state. Also, if anything went wrong, he wanted someone else to paste the blame on.

"We should have never sent those stupid Shoguns to kill that doctor," Quincy Fortner said.

Fritz the Blitz sneered at him. Fortner was always the pussy. PhD really did mean "Piled higher and deeper."

"It was absolutely necessary. You know he had learned about—all of it."

"Whatever, it's done," said Thackwell. "The point is, there are people in that hospital who know the Roundtree woman is there. Hell, the goddamned sheriff even knows. We have to get her out of there on the quiet. Aren't our MPs already on their way? Let them take her. Once she's out of there, something can happen to her—"

"But the MPs—" Dr. Fortner started.

"We've got control of that," Colonel Demint said. "The team that's looking for her belongs to us. Sort of. We can't have them do anything to her, but they can pick her up and deliver her. Then the Shoguns can take care of it. She's depressed. She ran away. Nobody ever heard from her again. Poor bitch. Maybe she'll get a medal."

"Yeah, that would be nice. A medal. Maybe Dunawithe can get her a biggie, like the Congressional Medal of Honor. That would be a hoot," said Ensley.

Dunawithe was the forty-year U.S. Senator from North Dakota and the Algonquin Associates point man in Washington.

"Don't push it," Thackwell said. "Dunawithe is just crazy enough to try it and get us unwanted attention again."

"I wish we didn't need that crazy bastard," Edward Ensley muttered. "You'd think he was from California, or Utah, the way he tries to throw his weight around. Hell, why do we even need Dunawithe? We've got—"

"Don't say that name!"

"I thought you had this place swept for bugs twice a day."

"I do, and there's never anything, because this place doesn't even exist, but you know the damn rules. We do *not* say his name. Besides, he isn't going to be there forever," Thackwell said. "But the senior senator from North Dakota is. The people in North Dakota get more freebies from Washington for less input even than Alaska. It's the ultimate welfare state. They'll keep voting their chief social worker into office. And even though he's crazy, Wild Bill Dunawithe knows he's nothing without us."

"I thought they called him *Buffalo* Bill."

"Hell, *Buffalo, Wild*, who cares?"

"Dr. Judson should never even have been there," murmured Fortner.

"How could anybody know? He was a wild card. He had already been hired before we chose Iron Mountain. We had to go someplace. Danville wasn't working out. Who could have known there was a doc coming on staff at the Old Oscar G who was an accountant before he went to med school?"

"Somebody should have known Byrnes would try something. Too much is never enough for a little crappie like him who wants to swim with the sharks. All that crap with calling himself Walter the Penniless. That was a giveaway. Somebody should have seen it," Janesway growled.

He glared at Thackwell. Thackwell knew quite well without the glare just who the "somebody" was that Janesway was accusing. When this thing was done, Thackwell was going to have the FCC cut Janesway off at the knees.

"Walter Byrnes is dead," Thackwell said. "It must have been the Roundtree woman, but nobody knows for sure, and nobody cares. His greed did him in. And his arrogance. He thought he was so smart he could outflank us, and after all we did for him. He wasn't even smart enough to outwit a burnt-up burned-out Negro vet. We don't need him anymore. It's time to cash in all the chips."

"The very fact that she killed Walter, though, that means she knows something—"Rome started.

"And somebody does know," Fortner broke in. "Ira Gasaway knows, and that probably means the Simmons woman knows, and whoever he got to remove the body, and—"

"We should never have trusted that little bastard, Gasaway. Why did we send him to run the operation through that Oscar whatever place, anyway? There had to be—" Janesway started.

"No, there wasn't," Thackwell said. "He was the best we had for that particular job. We had to use somebody who was already in the system. He had the right credentials, and just the right combination of stupidity and greed. And Iron Mountain is totally out of sight."

"*Was*, you mean. Until they hired Judson, and he poked around, and then those stupid half-ass vets stumbled into the shit pile," Rome said.

"Gasaway is small time," Ensley said. "All that business with ordering way too many supplies just so he could get a cut. It's a drop in the bucket at best, but it got Judson's attention. If he had just sent Kahlidi's records through Oscar G's, Judson probably would have never noticed."

"I don't like this business with changing our name from Algonquin Associates to QZX. It makes us look like a quickie oil change franchise," Janesway said.

"Or a fraternity," Rome said.

"Worse yet, it makes us look like Blackwater changing its name to—"

"Those dumbasses," Ensley muttered. "Give everybody a bad name."

"Don't we all deserve a bad name?" Fortner muttered.

"The point is, they call attention to us all—"

Thackwell gritted his teeth. This was worse than the university trustee meetings. At least those idiots could stick to the point.

"This is *not* a QZX board meeting, gentlemen," he said.

"We argued that out there. We haven't even announced it yet, because we have this other little thing to take care of first."

"Yeah, a *little* thing that could send us all to the damned guillotine," Fortner said.

"The gravy train is coming into the terminal, gentlemen. It's not a round house. The new administration will be cutting us off soon. We've got enough contacts in the military that we can keep on making billions on overruns and the like, but there is this one last big chance."

"At least we don't have to worry about 'Greedy Kahlidi' anymore," said Colonel Demint.

Thackwell frowned a warning at him, but it was too late.

"What do you mean?" said Fortner.

"Uh…he had an unfortunate accident. That happens in war, you know."

"This is getting way out of hand," said Fortner.

"It wasn't us," Thackwell said. "We weren't even in Iraq, at least personally. It was L&C."

"Limpcocks," Janesway grumbled, in what passed for a laugh.

"Why do we need sub-contractors anyway?" muttered Ensley.

"Deniability, you know that," Thackwell said. "We just provide services. L&C does the dirty stuff. We've got cutouts between us and them."

"Yeah, and since they figured out what we were doing, now they want the lion's share."

"Not the lion's share, because they have no idea just how big this is. They know too much and want too much, though, but there's not much we can do about it. We've already paid it, to get the records they lifted off Roundtree's squad and Kahlidi. Now we've got to get it back."

"But how can we do it without Kahlidi?" Fortner asked.

"We got everything we needed from him, everything he had. He's old news. That whole damned country, and all its oil, will be ours, if we just keep our cool. If Kahlidi had kept his cool, instead of going all nationalistic on us, he'd still be around to reap the dividends, too."

"Yeah, we got everything Kahlidi had, and then Dr. Judson

got it all, too," Rome said. "And for all we know, the Roundtree woman has it all, too."

"Dr. Judson didn't get the records from Kahlidi or L&C. He figured it out through what was going through the Oscar G. Johnson VA up there in Iron Mountain. The Roundtree woman knows nothing about Dr. Judson. It would have been nice to kill two birds with one stone, get rid of her by pinning Judson's murder on them, but now we've got to be more direct."

"She's got to go," Janesway growled. "And she might have told those others. They've all got to go."

Colonel Demint started to protest again, but Thackwell held up his hand. He was tired of acting like the opinions of others mattered.

"Our friend is right," he said. "We can't take chances. We'll send somebody else, and what's left of the Shoguns."

"Hell, Don," Ensley said, "they fucked up the last time so bad, and then when Fritz sent them out again, that Joe Kirk guy was…what's their motto?…an army of one. At least from what MacArthur said."

"Another reason to do 'em all," Janesway muttered. "They're killing our people."

"You don't even like our people," Rome said.

Thackwell held up his hand again. "Enough. We'll send Garcia with them this time. After the Shoguns have taken care of those school bus vets, he'll take care of them."

"Vlad the Impaler?" Rome asked.

"I don't want him exposed," Colonel Demint said. "How many Mexican niggers are there in the UP? He'll stick out. Too easy to identify. Besides, we've got our own VA cops there. Why not use them?"

"We can't afford to have more people in on this, especially people who might talk or who might be missed if…well, if it was necessary for them to disappear. The VA cops have families, regular lives. We picked the Shoguns because they're expendable."

"The VA cops have already been looking for her," said Rome

"I've told Gasaway to call them off, to tell them she's been cleared. They're being transferred out of Iron Mountain right now. The worst they can do is tell how incompetent Gasaway is."

"I still don't like exposing Vlad," said Demint.

"There are Indians up there. He could blend in."

"Yeah, get him some feathers and war paint. Nobody would ever notice he's a Mexican nigger."

"How come Mex women give their kids Russky names, anyway? Vladimir Garcia. That doesn't make any sense," Janesway said.

"What does make sense about Garcia is that he'll leave no traces. Those vets will disappear and we'll take the first step to owning the world."

CHAPTER 46

Barbara

Barbara Occam-Roberts was cursing in the same rhythms she had used as a cheerleader years ago. *Our team's great, we're a hit, why am I driving through a bunch of shit?* It was white shit, snow. Why in the hell didn't I just call that Sheriff Avanti, instead of thinking I should do this myself?

After the time at Sliver Lake, with Victoria and Joe and Lonnie and Zan, and the fracas with Melva and the other "natives," and the confrontation—if you could call it that—with Del Shrader, telling him he had gotten her pregnant, she just couldn't stay there, concentrate on some historical romance, or even the great American novel. She wasn't afraid. But the place she had always gone to clear her mind was now where her mind was fullest. She just threw her stuff into her car and went back to Indianapolis.

She didn't play the radio on her way home, didn't watch the TV once she got there, didn't read the newspapers. She didn't even know that the vets had been arrested for a murder.

Then that call from Melva, though, about Joe Kirk coming back to Sliver Lake, and—

Why in hell couldn't Melva just leave her alone? Somehow the two women were connected through that man that one loved and one loathed, and they couldn't ignore each other. So Melva had called her, and then Barbara had started researching.

Research wasn't hard. She always did it for her romance novels. And the Internet made so much possible, if you just knew how to use the search engines.

The more she learned about Dr. Judson's murder...

Could one of the vets have done it? She was sure they hadn't done it together. She ran each one through her mind individually. They were all violent. She had seen that with her own eyes. But they were not murderers. So why were the cops focusing on them? Certainly not because of the evidence.

Her research on the evidence took her in a whole different direction. Somebody was pointing at Victoria and the others, trying to get the cops to look only at them. But they hadn't done it. That wasn't just her feeling. It was the research now, too. The vets were just in the wrong place at the wrong time. Funny, that a VA hospital should be the wrong place for a vet, but it was. It had been the wrong place for Alan Judson, too.

So who had murdered Judson? And why? Who was pointing at the vets? The research began to come together. So now she was in the snow. It had not been so bad in Indianapolis. By the time she reached Lafayette she couldn't even see the town. She stopped for gas. They told her it would be worse the closer she got to Chicago. She got back in and kept driving.

It wasn't just what Melva had told her about Joe Kirk being at Sliver Lake and the dead bodies Melva and Joe had left. Melva was her usual mysterious self about who and why. Barbara wanted to see for herself, but that wasn't why she was driving through the snow that was driving back at her.

She felt that she owed that quartet of vets somehow. Especially Victoria. She had voted for Bush, and the guy had lied to get them into an unnecessary war. People like Victoria had paid an awful price for that. There was something more, though.

It was snowing just as hard through Chicago, but the roads were more passable, except for the idiots who seemed to think that you were supposed to drive *more* carelessly than usual when conditions were at their worst. She was about to die after she got through Milwaukee, but she found a Starbucks in Grafton that saved her life. That was when "Melody of Love" started playing in her purse, a mournful saxophone to accompany the snow and her bleary eyes. The ID said it was a 906, the UP, but she didn't recognize the rest of the number.

"Hello?"

"Barbara?"

A tentative voice, but melodious.

"Victoria?"

"Yeah. It's me. Am I bothering you? Is this an okay time to talk? I—"

"Victoria, where the hell are you? Google says you're in jail."

"No. Not exactly. Not anymore. I'm in some trouble, though."

"Yeah, I figured that out from reading online. Hey, how did you know my number, anyway?'

"I saw it on the wall in your kitchen, when we were there. I sort of remember numbers. My little brother is deaf, so I know sign language. I guess numbers and sign language are sort of related…" Her voice trailed off into the snow swirling around Barbara's Fusion.

"Forget that," Barbara said. "I know you're in trouble, about Dr. Judson, but I've been researching that, and I think I have come up with some stuff to help you get off."

"Yeah, I guess that's still part of it," Victoria's wistful voice said. "They put me in jail at the VA hospital in Iron Mountain, and then I escaped, but I stole a pickup, and there was a baby in it—"

"Good God, you kidnapped a baby?"

"I didn't mean to. I didn't know the baby was in the truck. I gave the baby to a preacher I know here. She'll take it back. But I'm still in the truck. That's where I'm calling from. There's a phone in the truck—"

"Whoops. They can trace that phone, Victoria, figure out where you are. You'd better get off the phone and get out of sight."

"I don't have any place to go."

"Do you have any idea at all where you are now?"

"I've just been driving around in the country—Wait a minute. There's a sign. There's snow on it—Oh, it's not a road sign. It says something about a B and B."

"That's even better, Victoria. I've got a GPS thingy here in my car. What B and B is it?"

"Well…the snow. Wait, I can see. It says The Loft—no, The Croft."

"Okay, wait a minute. Damn, can't work this thing. Oh, hell, doesn't matter, can't see the road anyway."

"Oh, yeah, I guess it's snowing at Sliver Lake, too."

"I'm not at Sliver Lake, Victoria. I went back to Indianapolis. That's why I didn't know about you being in jail until—someone—told me. Wait a minute, I've got the coordinates up. Hot damn! You're not far from Bear Hollow Wallow. I know a guy there. Nature photographer. We did a couple of books together. He might not be there. He travels a lot. Tell him I sent you. He's a vet, so tell him you're one, too, and tell him I'll come get you. If he's not there, you can get out of sight in his barn. Turn around and go—"

"But, if you're in Indianapolis, Barbara, how will you come—"

"I'm already on my way, Victoria. I'm almost to Crivitz. That's in Wisconsin, maybe 50 miles from Iron Mountain. Get off the phone and stay off until I get there."

It sounded good to Victoria. She thought maybe she should have told Barbara about the man she killed at the VA, though.

CHAPTER 47

Joe

"I'm assuming you haven't given birth since I saw you last," I said.

"Oh, thank God it's you. I was afraid it would be...somebody else."

So she recognized my voice. That was nice. Unless she thought I was her bishop or the sheriff or her boyfriend, and the *somebody else* she was afraid might call was actually me. "Somebody else like the po-leese?" I said.

"Exactly. I'm going to have to call the sheriff, anyway. I've run out of diapers and songs, and I think the baby doesn't like me anymore. It *is* a *she*, by the way, and her name is Emmie." Her voice kept going up and down in volume, like she was looking at somebody else while she was talking and moving her mouth away from the receiver. "Oh, you don't know any of this. Do you? It's kind of complicated, but I was given this baby to take care of—"

"No, I do know," I broke in. "The sheriff was here, looking for Victoria."

"Oh, well, okay. Uh, Joe, wait a minute."

There was a shuffling noise, and the baby cries got farther away. I was pretty sure Rickie was playing quarterback and had just handed the baby off to her running back.

"Uh, Joe, I can't talk very long. I've got to get Emmie to the sheriff. I'm sure her parents are frantic."

"Can you hold off a little, Rickie? I'd like to give Victoria some time. I don't know for what, because I don't know where she is…"

I let it hang, hoping Rickie knew where Victoria was, hoping she would tell me. She didn't.

"Look, Rickie, I've got an idea, about why Dr. Judson got murdered, or at least how to find out."

"Oh, that's good."

It sounded like something a girl would say when she knew you were going to ask her for a date and she was thinking up an excuse.

"But I need some time, you know, before anyone finds Victoria."

"Yeah, well, good luck."

I don't know what I was expecting. Obviously Victoria had taken the baby to Rickie. Now either Rickie really didn't know where she was, or she wasn't willing to tell. I guessed I was also hoping for some sign from Rickie that she wanted me to come see her, too.

"So I guess you'd better take the baby back, and I'd better get on with figuring things out."

"Yeah, right. TTYL."

She hung up the phone. What the hell did TTYL mean? Was it some sort of code message she was giving me, so the person with her wouldn't know what she was saying? I sure as hell didn't know. It made me realize how out-of-touch I was.

CHAPTER 48

I opened up the phone book, riffed to the *J*s. I didn't know what I was going to tell her, and when she answered, I just blurted out the truth. "Mrs. Judson?"

"Yes."

"My name is Joe Kirk. They say I killed your husband. I didn't. I'm sorry to bring this up even, but I just wanted you to know that I liked your husband. He was about the only VA doctor who has leveled with me."

I waited. I could hear her breathing.

"Our son's name is Kirk," she said.

"It's a good name," I said. "I'm sorry mine has to be associated with your husband's death."

I wasn't sure at all that I believed Kirk was a good name. It wasn't really mine. But with Dr. Judson's boy, it was just his first name, so maybe the kid wouldn't be tainted.

I waited. So did she. Finally, she said, "Do you know who killed my husband, Mr. Kirk?"

"No," I said, "But you do."

There was that breathing again.

"What is this to you, Mr. Kirk?"

"I'm a soldier, Mrs. Judson. We don't leave anybody on the battlefield. One way or another, we bring them home. I'm not willing to leave your husband out there."

"My husband was never in the military," she said. "He just went to doctoring for the VA after Kirk was born so he could have more time at home."

"He was one of us, Mrs. Judson, because he cared about us. He tried to take care of us. It got him killed. I can't let that go."

"Are you going to kill someone, Mr. Kirk?"

It was my turn to breathe.

"I'm a soldier, Mrs. Judson. A vet now, but still a soldier. I've killed a lot of men, and I regret every one of them. I wish they hadn't done what they did that made me kill them. I hope whoever killed your husband can be brought to justice without making me kill them. But if they force the issue, yes, I'll kill someone."

"Good," she said, "because nobody else seems to care who *really* killed him. Something was wrong before you showed up, Mr. Kirk. Alan wouldn't tell me what it was, but something was bothering him. You're right about me, about knowing who killed Alan. It was Ira Gasaway, the administrator at the hospital. Oh, not him personally, of course. But he brought someone in to do it. And it wasn't you or your friends. I know people at the hospital. Flo—they have told me about you, especially that poor burned woman. You're not killers. You're just vets."

She had no way of knowing that whatever had been bothering her husband, it went a lot higher than Ira Gasaway, I was sure of that.

"Did your husband say anything—"

She didn't bother to let me finish.

"Never a word. I know he wanted to be sure I was ignorant in order to protect me. I've thought about this a lot, Mr. Kirk. I've even written down almost every conversation we had in those last days, looking for…something. It wasn't hard to do. There weren't many conversations then. He withdrew into himself. He spent all his time on his collection of music boxes and antique record systems."

That sounded strange. Why would he do that? "Do you still have them?"

"Oh, yes, a whole basement full of them. He always liked music boxes, and he had several. He had always had an old record player that had belonged to his grandmother, but he never showed any interest in it. It just sat down there in the basement. Then, all of a sudden, he was buying all sorts of old record players, going to antique stores, ordering things on the Internet, like he had to have a big collection all at once. He didn't use them, just collected them. Bought more music boxes, too. Now our basement looks like an antique store." She sighed the sigh that every wife sighs about her husband's hobbies, but this wasn't a hobby.

I was pretty sure I knew what Alan Judson was doing.

"Mrs. Judson, may I come look at that collection of your husband's?"

There was a little intake of breath, and I knew she had figured it out, too, right then, something she knew but didn't know she knew, just because I wanted to see his old record players.

"Yes, good. Oh, wait. Could you stop by a store on your way to get some diapers? I'll pay you, of course, but I've not kept up with things since Alan—and I got caught in this snowstorm by surprise. And I'm afraid to take the baby out when it's so bad."

I looked around me in the backroom of the campground store and café. Sure enough, diapers. "No problem," I said.

She gave me directions. I hung up. I took a package of diapers off the shelf. I reached into the inside pocket of my vest where I had put the envelope with Dr. Judson's twenty dollar bill, the envelope with the picture of the little music box girl, and I put it on the shelf in place of the diapers.

By this time, Zan had come in. He looked at the diapers.

"Having some old age problems, are we?" he asked.

"Damn, now you spoiled your birthday present," I said. No more time for banter. "Think we can get the bus out?" I asked him.

"No way," he said.

"Okay," I said, "it's back to the snowmobile from hell. There's not room for three, but we can strap Lonnie on the front as a windbreak."

I only said it to be funny, but it was almost what we had to do. Except Lonnie was even worse off than Zan for winter clothes, so Zan had to go on first. I had to be where I could drive the damned thing, which meant the middle, mostly unable to see around Zan, and Lonnie hung on behind me somehow. I had to take my damn leg off and let Zan hold it. We put the diapers into an old rucksack Zan had in the bus and strapped it onto Lonnie's back.

Mrs. Judson had told me not to get Bear Wallow Road confused with Bear Wallow Hollow, and that it wasn't easy to find. And she was right. It wasn't that far out of town, and we were already on the right side, away from the river, and I thought we got started in the right direction from our campground. All the signs were plastered with snow, though. Since he was in front, Zan was supposed to be looking for the landmarks she had given us, the sign for a wedding planner and a totem pole with bear faces, but they were covered up, too, and his eyes were pretty well frozen shut anyway. We were cold and miserable and Lonnie was shouting into my ear that we should have put him in front since he would be able to see the landmarks better than Zan was. I was glad the snowmobile was so loud, so that Zan couldn't hear him. We wasted a lot of time and gas backtracking until we found the totem pole.

We made the turn onto Bear Wallow Road and took some more time looking for the lane to the Judson house. I was going real slowly, to cut down on the cold, to make it easier for us to see the signs, and to conserve gas, because I was sure we were down to fumes. It was driving me nuts, not just because I was freezing and my leg was throbbing and I'd lost my baloney, but because I had that prickling on the back of my neck that said our time was running out.

We finally found the birdhouse with a *J* on it that marked the Judson's lane. We had barely turned into it when Zan made a chopping motion at me, telling me to cut the engine. It wasn't necessary. That was the moment the thing sputtered and died on its own. No warning, just one sput. The silence was all the louder because it was so sudden. The wind was still making a moaning sound in the pine tops, but that seemed to add to the silence instead of breaking it. It was a strange silence, with my ears numb from cold and snowmobile noise.

Zan pointed ahead. Another snowmobile, a newer one than our dinosaur, was pulled up at the corner of Judson's house.

"In this country, even doctors have snowmobiles is my guess," I said.

My voice sounded too loud. It probably was. I was talking up because my ears were still reeling from the snowmobile.

"Doesn't belong here," Zan said. "It just arrived. Look, it's not covered with snow yet."

His voice sounded way too loud, too.

"There aren't tracks, though," I pointed out, trying to keep my voice down.

"Must have come in a different way," Zan said. "Up here in the north woods, they've got snowmobile paths all over the place. They don't rely on roads."

I couldn't see any paths through the thick birches, but that didn't mean there wasn't something behind the house out of sight. I was sure the snow machine didn't belong to Zoe Judson. Maybe it was just a neighbor checking on her, but I didn't like the idea of somebody beating us to the spot. "You think they can see us from the house?" I asked.

"No. Not unless they lean out the window on that corner."

"What the hell is going on?" said Lonnie.

I could barely understand him because of his chattering teeth.

"Somebody else is here," I said. "Let's get this thing out of sight. Give me my leg, Zan."

He was too cold to make a joke so he just handed it over. I had trouble getting it on as my fingers were like dead fish. I finally got it seated and began to push at the snowmobile. I hadn't gotten Judas on right, though. I slipped and fell on my face. Zan didn't bother with helping me up, just took Lonnie's hands, put them on the back of the machine, and said "Push."

The two of them together got it into some brush that was probably sorry now it hadn't taken off with the rest of the autumn foliage. By that time, I'd gotten onto two legs, but I wasn't confident about it.

I took Lonnie's hand and put it onto my arm so he could hang on. Then I took off up the blind side of the lane, where anyone in the house would have trouble seeing us. I slipped, slid, and cussed. Lonnie and Zan did the same.

We were about halfway along the lane when Zan grabbed me and pushed me into the ditch. It was fairly deep and narrow, as if it had been washed out with by spring rains and not worked on since. Lonnie tumbled in on top of me.

Lonnie's ears must have still been messed up from the snow machine noise because it was Zan who said, "Shut up. Car coming."

CHAPTER 49

Lonnie put a hand on my arm. "A Jeep Compass," he said.

Apparently he had gotten his ears back.

I didn't like this at all. If I could figure out where Dr. Judson had stashed his evidence, the people who murdered him could, too. I was still bothered by that snowmobile, too. Who had ridden in on it, and where were they now?

I glanced through the tree line, didn't see anything, but I didn't have time to do it well. I didn't bother waiting for Zan and Lonnie or giving any of those stupid orders, like "Follow me." I got the Beretta out of my leg and hoped it wasn't clogged with snow. I was already in the ditch. Instead of trying to claw my way back up to the lane, I just started lurching up the ditch-way toward the house. I hoped Zan was following and I hoped Lonnie wasn't. I had gotten a lot of respect for Lonnie, but in a snowy ditch or a strange house, he was going to be more of a liability than an asset.

Lonnie was wrong. It wasn't a Jeep, just a snow-blasted sedan of some sort. What good was Lonnie going to be if he had lost his ESP, or whatever it was?

It made slow progress up the lane, so I was almost to the house when it got abreast of me. Too late, I realized I should have jumped out in front of it before it got to the house. Whoever was in the car could get out on the house side and use the car as a shield, get a go at the house and Zoe Judson and her baby, while we couldn't do anything about it. My brain was frozen. I wasn't making good decisions. This was the opposite of Iraq, but it was still the same. There, when my brain got fried by the heat, I made bad decisions. Now my brain was freezing from the cold. Same result, just from different ends of the thermometer.

The car pulled abreast of me. The driver was shrouded in the hood of a parka. The car started to skid. The back tires started to slide toward me. I felt a hand pulling me back and assumed it was Zan. The pull made me slip and I went to my good knee.

"Dammit, Zan—"

Then I realized it wasn't Zan. He was nowhere in sight.

It was Lonnie. "I heard the tires coming this way sideways," he mumbled.

The car slid for a few feet. When it stopped, the driver killed the motor, leaving it half across the lane. The door opened, and Barbara Occam-Roberts got out.

There was a strange noise from the porch. We all looked up. There stood Victoria, with one of those funny little blue hospital surgical caps on her head. She had her mottled hands up to the sides of her mouth, like she was to make a megaphone. No words were coming out, though, just little whimpering sounds.

Barbara ignored the ditch dwellers and started toward the porch, a slight smile on her lips. I managed to get on my feet and braced well enough that I could get Lonnie up, too.

"What's going on?" he whispered.

"It's Barbara," I said.

"But she doesn't drive a Jeep," he said.

"It's not a Jeep. And what the hell is Barbara doing here?"

"She's a writer," said Lonnie. "Probably writing a book about us. That would include Dr. Judson."

Maybe he was just trying to cover up his mistake on vehicle identification, but he seemed to think it was the most natural thing in the world, someone writing a book about us. Lonnie was from that class that thinks the general public finds them endlessly fascinating. I hoped the title *Bus of Fools* was already taken. Maybe Lonnie was right. I could believe Barbara was writing a book about us, even though I couldn't believe anyone would read it. I didn't like the timing, though.

"Victoria's here, too," I said. "Up on the porch."

"Victoria? But how did she—"

"I don't know, but let's get in where there's some heat.

Maybe if we thaw out, we can put our heads together and figure out what the hell is going on."

I could tell Lonnie liked the idea of putting heads together, at least his with Victoria's. He didn't act like he cared much about figuring anything else out.

Barbara and Victoria were through hugging by the time we got to the porch. Victoria acknowledged me and seemed happy enough to see Lonnie, but not as much as I expected. She gave him a sisterly hug that broke off sooner than Lonnie wanted.

I didn't have to deal with that, though, because the most beautiful woman I had ever seen stepped onto the porch. Long black hair. A figure even Victoria would envy, in a black sweater and tight jeans. Deep dark eyes that I was sure were usually curious and joyful but were now dull and tired, but not resigned. I understood why Alan Judson had talked about his family being a gift.

"I'm Zoe Judson," she said.

Her voice was as smooth and tangy as the jam Grandma used to make for my pancakes.

A tall man in a buffalo plaid Filson vest, just like Lonnie's, stepped out onto the porch. Barbara grabbed him and hugged him, then turned to us.

"This is Ned Provo," she said, "a friend of mine. I sent Victoria to stay with him and lay low, but they must have decided—"

Lonnie winced a little at the word *lay*, and I was afraid I understood why Victoria wasn't as happy to see him as she should have been.

Zoe saved the moment, though. She wrapped her arms around herself, which pushed the front of her sweater out in disturbing ways.

"Oh, it's too cold. Let's go in."

We bunched through the door after her, the way little kids play soccer.

My stump was hurting and I wanted to sit down, but everybody started asking questions. Voices were coming at me like bullets in Iraqistan. Lonnie and Barbara and Victoria talking at once, Victoria telling about escaping from the VA and Barbara telling about how she had been researching and Victoria calling her. There was something about Barbara sending Victoria to somebody's house...Oh, yeah, the photographer guy. If Victoria said how she knew where Judson lived, I didn't get it.

I wasn't sure I was getting even half of it, especially since I was bothered by Zoe's presence. I wasn't really lusting after her, but she was definitely distracting. Well, yes, I was lusting for her, and it made me sad that she was so bereft and I was so immature.

There were a whole lot of things I didn't understand. When and how had Barbara and Victoria talked? This was getting more confusing by the minute. I tuned in a little better when Victoria paused for breath and Barbara got to talk on her own.

"Somebody—" She paused, apparently trying to figure out how to explain how she got back into this strange game. "I went back to Indianapolis, so I didn't know about you getting arrested and everything. Then—somebody—called, and told me about it. I just got to thinking about everybody trying to pin Dr. Judson's murder on you vets. I wondered why. I researched Dr. Judson's murder—and learned a lot—but I needed to know more. I got a map off Google Earth, and I've got a GPS on my husband's car. So here I am."

"Oh, that's why I thought it was a Jeep," Lonnie said, almost to himself.

I had no idea why a GPS would mess up his "cardar," but I didn't have time to think about it. I thought back to Sliver Lake, the second time, when I killed those uglies, and Melva cleaning up afterward. She was making a call on Barbara's kitchen phone while I was leaving. I was pretty sure I knew why Barbara had gotten to thinking about it.

I was distracted by Zoe and my own sadness. Lonnie was distracted by Victoria, and so was Ned Provo. Barbara was distracted by a writer's need to tell about her research, and Mrs. Judson was distracted by listening for her baby. So none of us heard the pickup coming up the lane until it slid into the back of Barbara's car with a crumping sound.

Barbara got to the door first.

"Shit. Somebody rammed my husband's Fusion," she said.

"Oh, a Fusion," Lonnie said.

"Probably couldn't stop, snow and all," Provo observed, his voice all laconic.

I reached down to be sure the bottom part of my pants was still unzipped enough from the top part so that I could reach inside to get the Beretta. I didn't think it was uglies, though. They wouldn't drive right up the lane.

We all crowded in behind Barbara at the door. It definitely wasn't uglies. It was Rickie Linden, holding a squirming bundle in her arms. A tall woman in a nurse's cap got out from behind the wheel of an old pickup.

"Sorry," she called toward the porch. "Gunned it too fast trying to get up the hill and it just took off on its own. Doesn't look too bad, though."

Barbara looked like she didn't agree with the nurse's cap woman's assessment, but she didn't say anything.

I must have pushed everybody else out of the way, because I was suddenly down at the bottom of the porch steps as Rickie walked toward me, her face rosy in its parka hood frame. In the looks department, she couldn't hold a candle to a woman like Zoe Judson, but she looked beautiful to me, and I had totally forgotten about the doctor's widow.

I wasn't really interested in the bundle in her arms, but I didn't figure I should comment on how pretty Rickie looked in front of everybody else, so I said, "So this is the famous Emmie—"

Rickie's rosy color became full red, and the nurse's cap woman broke in. "And so this is the famous Joe Kirk, who makes otherwise intelligent women curl their toes," she said.

She took Rickie by the arm with a little jerk, as if she didn't approve of big jerks, and marched her into the house. I followed like a bad dog, and we all went back inside. Zoe took the baby out of Rickie's arms so that she could slip her parka off.

We all stood around awkwardly in the front room. It was big, with a high ceiling and skylights. They actually made the room gloomy, since their snow cover grayed the light in the room. Mrs. Judson handed Emmie back to Rickie. That reminded me...

"Uh, we brought the diapers," I said to Mrs. Judson.

"Oh, thank you."

She sounded like I had just brought her the stars and the moon. I took a closer look at her. She was still beautiful, but there was a lot of murky around her eyes. She was holding on by holding hard.

I motioned for Lonnie to give me his rucksack then felt like a fool. I stepped over to him to take it off him. Had to get around Victoria to do it. She was just standing there, right beside him, looking up, as if he was a birthday present she didn't necessarily want. I wrestled the pack off of him, got the diapers out, started to take them to Zoe. When she saw me limping, she literally ran to me and took them like they were a crown on a pillow.

"Thank you again," she said. "Kirk is asleep right now, but when he wakes up—"

"I think we need one right now," the nurse said. "For little Emmie here."

She pointed at the bundle in Rickie Linden's arms. The bundle was squirming and making sounds like a chipmunk.

"Oh, yes, of course," Zoe said, as if she had just been reminded that she was a bad hostess.

That reminded Rickie of her own hosting duties. She nodded at the nurse. "This is Florence Kneightly," she said. "She's a member of my church."

She sounded quite proud of that. I wondered if my real father, Franklin Prashwell, was ever proud of any of his members, or if he just used them, the way he had used my mother. No, wait. Prashwell wasn't my real father. He was just a motherfucker. I felt my face going red and hoped nobody noticed it.

Zoe ripped the package open and handed a diaper to Florence. "I hope it's the right size. Of course, if you know how, you can make any diaper fit."

Florence took the diaper. She made sure she touched Zoe's hand as she did it.

"We know how, don't we, Zoe?" she said softly.

Zoe just nodded as her eyes turned liquid.

Florence dropped to her knees on the spot and spread the diaper out, then reached up to take the baby from Rickie.

"May—may I do it, Florence?" Rickie said.

"You know how?"

"I—I'd like to try."

"Get down here then."

Rickie handed the baby to Florence, dropped down beside her, took the baby back.

"Once we get her changed, Mother Linden, we'd better call Sam Avanti to come get this baby," Florence said.

"We didn't have time to take Emmie some place, to get her back to—I feel really bad about that. I know her parents must be worried."

Rickie got all that out in a rush. She turned to Zoe again.

"Maybe we could call her parents instead of the sheriff." Rickie glanced at me. It was clear that she figured I'd be better off without Sheriff Sam Avanti being on the scene.

"We don't know who they are, remember?" Florence said. "That's why we were going to call the sheriff and let him handle it." She turned toward the rest of us. "I'm sorry. I'm the one who insisted we had to come out here first. But it seemed important. I thought I had figured out something no one else knew, but it looks like everybody else…" Her voice trailed off.

"I'm sorry. I don't think that will be possible," Zoe said, "to call the sheriff or anybody else. Our phone is out. Happens every time there's a big snow."

"No problem," Florence said. "I've got my own."

She produced a flip phone from her pocket and displayed it, as if we were a bunch of rustics who had never seen one before.

"Do you need me to look up—" Zoe started. "Oh, but it would be 911, wouldn't it?"

Florence waved her phone in a gesture of dismissal. "No. No 911. I want to get Sam directly. But I've got his personal number. It's one of those easy ones to remember."

She started punching in numbers.

I wasn't eager to witness the diaper changing, and I was anxious to get at what I had come for.

"May I see your husband's antique collection, Mrs. Judson?"

"Oh, yes, it's in the basement."

She started for an open stairwell at the side of the room. There was a toddler gate across it.

"Damn," Florence said. "Begging your pardon, Mother Linden. No service on the cell phone."

"Oh, I forgot. That happens a lot out here, too, I'm afraid," Zoe said.

"Look. I got it done, and I don't think it will leak." Rickie's voice. She sounded very proud of herself. "But what should I do with—"

"Here. I'll take care of it. I have those diaper genie things all over the house."

Zoe headed for Rickie and the baby, grabbed the diaper, took it to the corner, and dropped it into some sort of contraption that looked like R2D2.

"Wait a minute. Did you say *antique collection*, Joe? What kind of antiques?"

It was Victoria. She started toward me, guiding Lonnie around an ottoman with one hand while she dug into a pocket with her other hand.

"Music boxes and record players," Zoe said. "As I told Mr. Kirk—"

Victoria pulled her hand out of her pocket and held up a funny-looking barrel key. "Would this key fit a music box in that collection?" she asked.

CHAPTER 50

Victoria was obviously very proud of herself.
"What the hell?" Florence barked out. "So that's why it wouldn't fit the one in Dr. Judson's office. Too big for a music box, unless it's a real big one. So you're the one who made off with that."

She sounded as proud of Victoria as Rickie did over the diaper.

There were a lot of things I didn't understand. When and how did Victoria call Barbara? What had Barbara learned in her research? Just how was the Kneightly woman involved, and could she be trusted? Well, yeah, Rickie trusted her, but—

Barbara said something, like a question. The nurse was answering. I turned around, saw Rickie, thought about how she would look under a waterfall, had to work hard to get back to where I could concentrate on what Florence was saying.

"…I knew Victoria had been in Dr. Judson's office," she said.

She gave Victoria a look I couldn't figure out. Victoria turned away. The nurse missed just a beat and then went on. "I had noticed that music box before, how it didn't sit right. I knew that wasn't the key that went with it. Then I went in after Victoria had been in there. The key was gone. I tried to look at the office through Victoria's eyes, and when I did—well, I think I saw the same thing she did…"

She trailed off and gave that palms-up *your-turn* motion to Victoria. She looked a little bit surprised, but also was glad to have the chance to say what she knew.

"I figured out the key, sort of," Victoria said. "I hid in Dr.

Judson's office while I was trying to escape the VA. I knew we hadn't killed Dr. Judson, so I figured he must know something that got him killed by people who wanted to keep him quiet. I think the MPs were after me, for the same reason, except I don't know shi—I mean, nothing. Something happened in Iraq, though, that...well, they *think* I know something because of it. Anyway, I saw the way the music box tilted, but the key didn't fit anything there in Dr. Judson's office. I'd never seen a key like this before." She held it up, as if she was seeing it for the first time. "So I was sure it had to fit something at Dr. Judson's house. Barbara told me to stay at Ned's house until she got here, but he said he knew where the Judsons live. I thought it was important to get here, and he sort of likes to get out on his snowmobile, so..."

She gave Ned Provo one of her Boston to Los Angeles smiles. I was glad Lonnie couldn't see it, but I'd gotten to know Lonnie well enough that I figured he could hear the corners of her mouth crinkle. So how long had Victoria and this Ned character had together? Was he attracted to her because she would be a good nature photography subject? Or just because of her figure?

Hell. None of that mattered. I didn't matter much, either. I had figured out the same thing as everybody else.

Judson was killed by persons unknown because of something he knew. They were trying to pin it on us to take attention away from the real murderers. That key in Victoria's hand would probably take us right to the bottom line.

I was too impatient to wait until the ducks were all in a row. I went for the bottom line. I wanted to make that key work.

"The key fits something in Dr. Judson's collection of antique record players," I said. "He didn't start collecting until after he started at the VA. He needed to hide something. He figured in the middle of a big bunch of stuff that just looked like a hobby would throw people off."

Everybody looked at Zoe Judson for confirmation. She nodded. "Yes, I think it might fit something," Zoe said. "We'd better go downstairs. That's where Alan kept his record players. He usually called them hi-fis."

She gave a wan little smile at the recollection. I didn't want to see it, so I turned, unhooked the baby gate, and started down the stairs.

It had been a long time since I had been on a real staircase. It was harder than I remembered. I had never been good for more than two or three steps with Judas. There was an art to a whole flight. I gave a glance over my shoulder. Dammit. Everybody else had held back, being polite, letting Zoe come first, after me, and she could see how poorly I was dealing with the leg. That shouldn't have embarrassed me. She was a nurse. She had seen worse. But I felt my face go red, and I was sad that I was so vain.

Voices followed me down the stairs. I heard Zoe talking about how cute Rickie's baby was and asking if it needed something to eat. Victoria and Florence were talking about how each one got suspicious about the music box when they were in Judson's office and saw the key didn't fit the music box but they couldn't find anything in the office it did fit. Each had figured out that it must fit something in his house. The antique collection would be the perfect cover.

I was miffed because I, too, had decided, without even knowing about a key, that the answer had to be in Judson's house, and now they were taking all the credit. But I had the key to the mystery now, dammit, and I knew exactly what it would fit!

I limped on down, into a family room so big it must have stretched under the whole house. The front of the house was built into a hill, so it looked like it was only one story. In back, though, the basement had a full wall of windows. There was a big glass walkout door in the middle of the windows wall. Usually all that glass would let in a lot of light, but now all you could see was darkly blowing snow. On the other three sides, it was just as Zoe had said—lined with old stereos and tables covered with music boxes.

Victoria still had the key, but I knew what it would fit. Grandma had a key like that. It was for a really old wax cylinder record player. It had belonged to *her* mother, even. I loved to listen to it. Other people told her not to let me play it, that she needed to preserve those old cylinders and the stylus, that the older it got the more people would pay for it. "The most value I can possibly get out of it," she told people, "is seeing my grandson enjoy it."

For a guy who had been collecting for a short time, Judson had really filled up the room with record players and hi-fi sets and tables and music boxes. Some of the things were almost new. You could play current CDs on them easily. Some, though, clearly went back to the early part of the last century. They weren't arranged chronologically, or in any other order that I could understand. It didn't take me long, though, to find what I was looking for, an Edison wax cylinder record player, in a big floor-standing wooden cabinet, almost identical to my grandmother's.

I looked over my shoulder. Victoria was coming toward me with the key. She offered it to me, but I waved her toward the cabinet.

"Your find, your show," I said.

She seemed pleased. She stepped up to the cabinet, pushed the key into the lock, and turned it. Nothing happened, no click, no nothing. Victoria got a frown on her face.

"It fits, but..."

I stepped over and took the top and pushed it up. I looked underneath the lid. The key was in a hole. There was no lock mechanism inside.

"But why hide a key to something that doesn't even have a lock?" she said. "There must be something else."

She began to look around the room for something else the key might fit, but I thought I knew the answer to her question.

I got down on my knees to look in the compartment where the cylinders were stored.

"Oh, I hear Kirk crying," Zoe said. "I'd better go get him."

I heard the baby, too, coming over a speaker in the ceiling. They must have had one of those baby monitor systems.

Victoria squinted her eyes hard. "Kirk? That's your son's name?"

"Yes," Zoe said, squinting back at Victoria.

"Oh. When I talked with Dr. Judson, back before...well, you know. He said that Kirk was a penny from heaven, but since we'd just been there, I thought he was talking about Joe Kirk. It didn't make a lot of sense—no offense Joe—but you're more like the bad penny that always turns up instead of a penny from heaven."

"He said that? That Kirk was a penny from heaven? That was Alan's favorite song. Went around humming it all the time. He—" Zoe teared up and hurried up the stairs.

"Damn," Victoria muttered. "I shouldn't have said that."

"I'm the one who should be crying, after what you said about me," I said as I rummaged through the cylinders.

She gave me a little kick and got a metallic sound. I hoped it hurt her toe.

I didn't know what I was looking for, but I found it. At the back of the drawer were some CDs.

One was *Pennies from Heaven* on an Avanti Records, Ltd. label. I thought that was interesting, since the sheriff's name was Avanti.

Another had a label that was also Avanti Records. I looked at it real closely. I had the impression that the Avanti label was off a copy machine. The title was *The Oscar G. Meyer Weiner Song and Other Jingles for Kids.*

"Is there a *G* in Oscar Meyer, like the wieners?" I asked.

Everybody looked at me like I was crazy.

"I don't think so," Rickie said.

But Florence was catching on.

"There is in Oscar Johnson," she said.

"Oh," Victoria said, with a sharp intake of breath. "The VA."

Barbara began to nod.

I turned the CD over in my hands. There was a table of contents on the back, just like a regular CD cover, but I could tell the cover wasn't commercially produced, despite the Avanti Records logo.

"Zoe is taking an awfully long time getting Kirk changed," Florence said. "What size were those diapers you brought?"

She said it to me, in an accusing voice. Hell, she should know. She had used one. All I could do was shrug. She nodded, as if it was what she expected.

I looked up to the speaker at the ceiling. I didn't know why people did that, looked at a sound source, as though that would help them hear better.

I couldn't see or hear any sound from the baby monitor.

"I'm going to go check on them," Florence said.

She started up the stairs. She had gotten to the third riser when she began backing down. Zoe and her baby were coming down the stairs above her. The problem was, they weren't alone.

CHAPTER 51

A guy in a black ski mask was pushing Zoe ahead of him, a big fistful of the neck of her black sweater in his hand. Another guy in an identical ski mask was carrying a baby in one arm and a short-barreled rifle in the other. He wasn't being careless with the baby, but he wasn't really paying attention to it, either. He was scanning the room, the SBR following along with his eyes.

When they got down into the room and fanned out at the bottom of the stairs, I saw that there were three of them, all carrying Arsenal SBRs. They were dressed alike in black snowmobile suits, black ski masks pulled over their heads. The only things that showed were their eyes.

Three pairs of eyes, one that looked crazy, one that looked hard, and one that looked mean. It was the crazy ones that bothered me. If you were a hard and mean man yourself, you could deal with other hard and mean men. But with a crazy-eyed man, you never knew what was going to happen.

It was the hard-eyed one who was holding little Kirk Judson. I decided that maybe I was more worried about him, because Zoe's eyes matched the crazy eyes of the guy groping her sweatshirt, and the only thing more unpredictable than a crazy-eyed man with a semi-automatic assault rifle was a crazy-eyed grief-stricken mother whose baby was in danger. If she went for her baby, Hard Eyes wouldn't hesitate to use his weapon.

"Well, well, well," said the one with Zoe in his grasp, his voice muffled by the ski mask. "Looks like a reunion of all the trouble-makers."

"Shut up," Hard Eyes said. "Over by the door," he said to Mean Eyes.

The third man moved to the door in a soldier's way, never taking his mean eyes off us, holding his SBR steady and ready.

"We're here for one thing. Hand it over and we'll be on our way. Nobody gets hurt."

I paid attention to the dog that didn't bark at midnight, what he *didn't* say. He didn't tell us just *what* to hand over, because he didn't know. The uglies had figured out what the rest of us did: whatever information Judson had was in his home, not his office. They didn't know exactly what they were looking for. They had been coming on their own to search Judson's house. Finding us all there was just a coincidence.

But Crazy Eyes's statement about a reunion told me something else. These were the same mercs we had encountered before, at that convenience store up in Sagola. I wasn't the only one who got that message.

"I know you," Lonnie yelled, loud enough that both babies started crying. "I kicked your ass up at Sagola and I can do it again."

He started rushing at the guy, the way a blind man rushes, his arms up close to the sides of his head, protecting his face in case he runs into something.

He had it wrong, though. I had a pretty good ear myself. Only two of them had been at Sagola. Hard Eyes was new. He looked surprised by Lonnie's rush, but he was disciplined. He held his AK steady but didn't use it. He just stepped aside.

I was surprised Lonnie didn't sense the guy move, but maybe there was too much noise, with the babies crying. He rushed right past the guy, barely brushing him, and crashed into the hard glass of the sliding door. It was a loud crash, but mostly because he screeched a quite-uncharacteristic, girlish-pain cry, scratched his big University of Virginia ring on the glass, and pulled the ring down. He looked dazed, although I didn't think his head had really hit the glass.

He slid down the door and, as he did so, his hand grazed the lock mechanism. He scrabbled at it, trying to hold himself upright, but missed and slid on down into a heap in front of the glass.

The position of the lever on the door lock was different now, though, and I didn't think anyone else noticed it.

"You blind piece of shit," Crazy Eyes shouted. "We've got a score to settle with you, and I'm going to—"

He started toward Lonnie, but Hard Eyes' voice cut in like a diamond saw. "I told you to shut up."

"Fuck you," Crazy Eyes said. "The cat's out of the bag now, anyway. Can't leave any—"

Hard Eyes grabbed little Kirk Judson out of Mean Eyes's arms and tossed him aside like a used rag. Now I was sure he was the one to fear, because he did it with a purpose. He tossed the kid right into his mother's arms. Zoe didn't hesitate. She went to her knees as she made the catch, making a cradle of her lower body in case she didn't get a grip. Kirk was okay, but Hard Eyes had made a statement to all of us.

Including Crazy Eyes, who was holding his ground but not without a defensive stance.

"Nobody knows who we are," Hard Eyes hissed.

"But they saw our faces at—" Crazy Eyes started.

"We don't even have the same faces anymore," Hard Eyes said, a little too loud.

That was for me. He was saying they'd already had plastic surgery. I didn't buy it. He knew I wouldn't, but he was reminding me and Crazy Eyes both that they could get their looks altered anytime they wanted, so any descriptions we could give from the fracas at Sagola would be irrelevant.

Hard Eyes lowered his voice and bore in on Crazy Eyes. The babies were crying, and so was Zoe, so I couldn't get everything he said, and he knew it, which was why he felt free to say what he did.

"Too many," he hissed. "You know our orders. Evidence first. Then we've only got authority for the vets. That's all. We can't disappear a dozen people, you fool."

I knew Crazy Eyes and Hard Eyes were distracted by their argument. I thought this might be my chance. I glanced at my pants leg to be sure the half-way zipper was undone far enough. Then I looked at Mean Eyes. He was staring right at me, and so was his SBR. Damn.

Hard Eyes finished up and turned back to me as I sat on the floor.

"It looks like you have found what we need," he said. "Give it to me."

He stuck out his hand. I reached out the *Pennies From Heaven* CD to him. He took it, looked at it.

"Give me the other one."

I handed him the other CD. He stared hard at it. His eyes crinkled a little at the corners.

"How clever. Oscar *G*. Meyer. So he put it all on a CD—"

He didn't get to finish. The short burst of gunfire was louder in the basement room than anything I had heard, even in a cave in the 'Stan. The bullets tore through him as his hard eyes got big and then went dead.

"You shit pile," Crazy Eyes yelled. "I'm back in charge now, big fuckin' primo assassin. Just a pile of dog shit," he added, giving the man's ragged body a kick.

"What the fuck—" Mean Eyes started.

Crazy Eyes turned his SBR on him. "Don't you start," he said.

"But the Hermits—"

"Fuck the Hermits. This is battle regs. The officer on the scene has to make the rules, and I'm in command. We're leaving no witnesses, especially not this human dregs quartet from that place up—"

He stepped over the body of Hard Eyes and picked up the Oscar Meyer CD and stuck it into his pocket.

"Hey, wait a minute," Mean Eyes said. "Quartet—" He scanned the room. "Four. Up at that Sagola place, there was another one. That guy's not one of 'em," he said, pointing at Ned Provo.

That was when the glass door slid down to its other end with a whoosh and a bang and the abominable snowman came into the room like his tail was on fire.

I didn't know if Lonnie had gotten that door unlocked as an escape route, or if he realized that Zan had not come in with us. Either way, it had been a smart move.

Except for me. I knew I was going to die. I didn't much care. There was nothing worthwhile in my life. Except Rickie.

But that was a pipe dream. And I wouldn't get a chance to kill my father. That was too bad. And if Crazy Eyes killed me there would be no one to keep him from killing little Kirk and Emmie and—

Suddenly I wanted to live, but I knew it was too late.

Crazy Eyes swung his SBR at me. I was trying to get the Beretta out of my leg, but it wasn't going to happen, not in time. I heard the shots.

Then Crazy Eyes did a crazy dance as his weapon rose up into the air, chattering, drilling holes in the floor of the room above us.

I looked to the door. Zan had hold of Mean Eyes, wrestling with him. Mean Eyes had his finger on the trigger. The bullets from his own Arsenal had killed Crazy Eyes and were still firing wildly.

Florence had Rickie and Emmie on the floor and was covering them with her own body. Barbara was pushing Zoe and little Kirk through a door that I thought must belong to a laundry room. I couldn't see Ned Provo. I assumed he had the sense to hit the ground. Victoria was on her hands and knees, crawling toward Zan and Mean Eyes.

Lonnie, of course, was charging, right at them. Zan's hand slipped off the SBR. I wasn't surprised. He had been out in the cold so long, his fingers probably wouldn't even curl. But it meant that Mean Eyes now had complete control of the weapon, even though Zan still had an arm around his neck and was trying to pull him backward.

Mean Eyes got the weapon lowered toward Lonnie, but he wasn't fast enough. Zan gave a lurch back through the open door. I don't know if Lonnie was following sounds and knew where the weapon was or if he just went in low automatically. Anyway, he made an almost perfect waist-high tackle.

The three of them tumbled through the door and into the snow in a thrashing pile like you saw in the comic pages when Sarge was whumping on Beetle. Victoria got up, went running through the door, piled on, and wrenched the weapon out of Mean Eyes's hands while it was still spraying bullets toward the fallen snow. She came away with about half of Mean Eyes' finger in the trigger guard.

Zan was trying to wrench the guy's head off while Mean Eyes screamed about his finger.

"Don't kill him," I yelled. "We need him."

Victoria whacked him over the head with his own weapon and he went limp. I hobbled out the door and grabbed him by an arm and started dragging him. Victoria took his other arm. We got him inside and tied him up.

EPILOGUE

Zoe and Rickie got little Kirk and little Emmie calmed down. Barbara worked on Zan's frozen fingers, and Victoria worked on Lonnie.

"Hey, there are nurses here," Zan said. "I don't need some Purdue cheerleader."

"He's an idiot. He's no dear. But I've got to admit, I'm glad he was here," she chanted back at him, in perfect cheerleader fashion.

"What happened to you, anyway?" I asked him.

"Head felt bad. Too many people to go in the house. Decided to go off in the woods and freeze. I did it once before, Joe. I let you down. Back at that place where you shot those mercs. I should have helped you, but something happened to my brain. I froze. I felt so useless, Joe. I couldn't even help my best friend. They say it's a painless way to go, freezing. Then I saw those guys sneaking up. Decided I'd better save your ass first."

He said it all so matter-of-factly. Barbara began to cry as she pulled on his fingers. He looked away.

I did, too. I was embarrassed. I hadn't even noticed Zan didn't come in with us. Neither had anyone else. He had felt bad all this time about not being in on the action at Moe's Convenience Store in Sagola, and I didn't know it. He was the invisible man, and he had saved us.

This was a time for some depth, so I went for the lame joke tangent. "Good thing Lonnie got that door unlocked," I said, "or the last thing that would have gone through your mind was your ass."

"He just did it to impress the women," Zan groused.

Lonnie smiled.

Florence drove out toward the main road until she got her cell phone to work and called the sheriff. Sam Avanti came in force and sent Mean Eyes off with a four-man detail who had orders to take him to the jail and say nothing to anybody.

"No hospital for him. The world will be a better place if he doesn't have a trigger finger, anyway," he said. "I'll keep him in the local jail as long as I can, try to get him to talk. Once the feds get him, either an *accident* will happen to him or he'll get paid off. I'd sure as hell like to know what's going on."

He wasn't the only one.

He sent Emmie back to her parents with another deputy. Rickie cried as she watched them go. I wanted to run to her, to hold her, but Florence was doing that, so there was no room for me. Victoria made a motion like I should push Florence out of the way, but I was coming to my senses. What chance did a guy like me have with a woman like Rickie? I was crippled in too many ways.

Then Avanti put his own crime scene people to work. He didn't want any other cops, like the FBI, coming in and taking over. He wouldn't let me or Victoria or Zan or Lonnie say anything. He made Rickie tell the whole story of what happened, then asked Florence and Zoe if she had put everything in, and they agreed she had.

Ned Provo hadn't done a thing to deal with the rumble in the basement except wet his pants. He wanted to go home, and the sheriff let him go. Victoria let him go, too. I figured any competition Lonnie might have had was no longer even a possibility.

"Did you see that CD?" Florence said. "It took a bunch of bullets. It's hardly even fragments. Some of the fragments are inside that jerk who was holding it. Now we'll never know what Dr. Judson learned."

"I think maybe we will," I said. I turned to Zoe. "Your husband was a smart guy, Mrs. Judson, and a good father. Did he ever play that CD of kid songs for little Kirk?"

She looked puzzled. Even then, her skin was so perfect it had trouble wrinkling her brow.

"No. I didn't even know he had it."

"I think it was a red herring," I said. "I think in case anyone found those CDs, he wanted them to think that was the one with the information. That's why he put the *G* in Oscar Meyer, and why he made the cover look like a fake. He said his son was a 'penny from heaven.' I think the info is on the *Pennies From Heaven* CD, as a gift of honor to his son."

Victoria picked that CD up and Sheriff Avanti took it from her. "Hmm. Not a CD, a DVD. This should be good. I know you want to see this, but it's official..." He stuck it inside his jacket and walked off.

Then we sat there, and I wondered what would come next.

Maybe Barbara would finally write the great American novel. A Purdue cheerleader? Yeah, right.

Maybe Florence would become head nurse at the VA. An LPN? Yeah, right.

Maybe Rickie would talk me into getting married so she could have her own little Emmie. Me, a father? Yeah, right.

Maybe Zoe would get a new husband as good as Alan Judson. Yeah, right.

Maybe Sam Avanti would get a confession out of that merc, get the info off the DVD, and bring to justice whoever... Yeah, right.

Maybe I would go settle some old scores I hadn't even known were in the record books. Killing people always made me feel better. Or worse. I couldn't tell anymore.

പ്രവ

LONNIE

Victoria's hand had these splotches. I could feel them. Did I want Victoria because she was black and scarred, because she was even worse off than I was, because it would piss my father off so much to see me with her? I still hated him. But would killing him be worth it? Maybe Victoria and I could go to Virginia and then I would know. Was love really stronger than hate?

പ്രവ

VICTORIA

What did he see in me? He didn't see anything, that was the problem. If he could see me, would he be interested at all?

Would they leave me alone now, the people who had been trying to kill me, and the ghosts of Sarge and Wong? Or would I forever be on the run? If I was, would he come with me?

Would I ever have a better home than an old school bus?

సొబొ

ZAN

I thought maybe getting frozen out there cured my headache. Maybe it cured me completely. Maybe Barbara would hire me to look after Sliver Lake and I could be an Indian fighter, like in the movies. Yeah, right.

I had to get back on the bus, get out of here. But maybe one of these women would fry some bacon first…

About the Author

John Robert McFarland's stories, articles, poems, essays, comic strip gags, scripts, reviews, and columns have appeared in newspapers, magazines, radio shows, web sites, anthologies, encyclopedias, dictionaries, hardback, audio, paperback, Czech, and Japanese. He wrote for Garrison Keillor's *Prairie Home Companion* radio show and for Bob Thaves' *Frank & Ernest* comic strip, Scribners' *Dictionary of American History* and Scribners' *American Lives,* plus the famous *Frosty and the Babe* poem for the celebration at Hofstra University of the one-hundredth anniversary of the birth of Babe Ruth.

His first oncologist said he would be dead "in a year or two." That was twenty years ago. Instead of dying, he had in-body experiences. You can read about it in *NOW THAT I HAVE CANCER I AM WHOLE: Reflections on Life and Healing for Cancer Patients and Those Who Love Them* (AndrewsMcMeel & HarperAudio, plus Czech and Japanese editions). Paul K. Hamilton, MD, the founder of CanSurmount, called it "The best book by a cancer patient, for a cancer patient, ever."

McFarland plays third base and charges every grounder [bad arm]. He is equally adept at going left or into foul territory. He has earned several graduate degrees but is most proud of his honorary contract with the Cincinnati Reds.